THE TANGERINE TANGO EQUATION

➡ THE
= TANGERINE
TANGO ➡
= EQUATION

or

*How I Discovered Sex, Deception,
and a New Theory of Physics
in Three Short Months*

A N O V E L B Y

Barry Targan

THUNDER'S
MOUTH
PRESS
NEW YORK

Published by Thunder's Mouth Press

54 Greene Street, Suite 4S

New York, NY 10013

Grateful acknowledgement is made for permission to reprint the following
poems:

"Musee de Beaux Arts" by W.H. Auden. From W.H. Auden: Collected Poems,
by W.H. Auden, edited by Edward Mendelson. © 1976 by Edward Mendelson,
William Meredith and Monroe K. Spears, Executors of the Estate of W.H.
Auden. Reprinted by permission of Random House, Inc.

"When I Heard the Learn'd Astronomer" by Walt Whitman. From Leaves of
Grass, by Walt Whitman, Reader's Comprehensive Edition, edited by Harold
W. Blodgett and Sculley Bradley. © 1965 by New York University. Reprinted
by permission of New York University Press.

Library of Congress Cataloging-in-Publication data:

Targan, Barry, 1932–

    The tangerine tango equation : or how I discovered sex, deception,
    and a new theory of physics in three short months / by Barry Targan.

  – 1st ed. (Contemporary fiction series)

    ISBN 1-56025-009-7 : $19.95

    I. Title. II. Series.

PS3570.A59T3 1990

813'.54–dc20   90-26567

Text design by Loretta Li.

Manufactured in the United States of America.

FOR
REBECCA HART TARGAN

"Once upon a time," we say to start a tale, and never ask the meaning of those words. The meaning is the magic of the incantation itself. "Once upon a time." The magic dust that the sorcerer casts about, the power in the wand which sweeps the spell across us. The enchantment of as if.

This is the story of the boy—Nick—who became a man, a teller, a storyteller, the narrator of this tale. It is a story about the search to find a story, a quest, because I think that, at last, that is what all tales are. And it is a story about time itself. And what is timeless. It is about what was once upon a time, or in the yet more ancient formula, it is a fable that begins where all such fables begin—when time was.

→1→

=

"Do you know what you're going to tell Dean Roskov about what you've decided on?" my father asked as we neared Cobbton where the college lingered gently out from the town's north edge into the wide estates and farms.

"Well, I have to take freshman composition. That's required of everyone, no matter what. Then there's a senior seminar called Twentieth Century Philosophic Thought. I might try that. And there's a graduate seminar on recent developments in topology. And then an independent study."

"In what?"

"I don't know. Dean Roskov suggested some sort of study for me with a group of professors, a kind of catchall kind of thing, something that will define itself as we go along. But it sounds more like I'd end up being the subject."

"Yes," my mother said, "I think it's better you take formal courses, at least for the first semester." To be with others, she meant, but did not say. To be first, but among equals. Wasn't that the point of going off to college: to be in the world, and, finally, on the world's terms?

But my schooling had always created special problems. When I studied logarithms for instance, not only had I exhausted the subject in a few days, but in a few more days I had invented a logarithmic system that worked on a base of twelve instead of ten. That sort of thing. It had always been like that. From the very start, schools had not been sufficient for me, and then not even the tutors. None lasted more than three or four months before I had exhausted them. Besides, they cost extra money, and we were not well-off, though not pinched either. So I stayed home and read and that was good enough. I had not been pushed to go further and faster than I had paced myself, although even to me it was hard to imagine how anyone could go faster than that.

Now, entering college, I would encounter a structure — a linear educational model — for the first time. I would sniff the sea wind for what might be my direction at last, a career, an exquisite point of application, the area in which I would nail my name up there in the universe with the rest of them — Heisenberg or Fermi or Planck, say, or inventors like da Vinci and Marconi. Scientists like Pasteur. Newton. Einstein. Can you imagine what baggage that might have been for a kid to carry around? Yet for me it seemed light enough, reasonable enough. And science did seem the area into which I was gravitating, like a comet drawn into an irresistible relationship to mass. But it was not my choice. I had never made a choice. Maybe not about anything.

"Well," my father said, "whatever you do, whatever courses you take, just make sure it all interests you. That's all that matters. Everything else will fit in around it."

But what interested me if everything could interest me?

Long ago (when I was seven) I had stopped being interested in my mind's enormous power, or in the interest that others took in it. My celebrity, however much my parents had guarded me against it, had seeped into my life and stained it, but now even that was as ordinary for me as it must have been for Leonard Bernstein or Princess Caroline of Monaco or Don Mattingly or an ex-president. And I had stopped constructing challenges to myself, like seeing just what my limits might be, what was the hardest thing I could learn: a knowledge of Chinese necessary to the reading of the poetry of the twelfth century poet L'chu Chaing, or my attempt to memorize all the star charts of the Northern Hemisphere including stars even as small as the fifth magnitude.

What must it be like to be bored or even to find the learning of something to be undesirable? What must it be like to *not* want to know whatever there was to know about whatever was in front of you? I had read about college students being bored and apathetic and uninterested. But what must that feel like? I had no sense of what that must be like, only the concept. What must it be like to have a mind that did not dance?

In the summer just past I had sailed my boat, a twenty-four-foot sloop, up through Lake Champlain for a week alone. I was a fine sailor, and at sixteen I had good size and strength, on the edge of manhood. I had a trim, athletic grace, an agility that made me good at tennis or skiing. Or sailing alone. Good at any endeavor that did not require a team. I could be alone and not be lonely. My mind to me was a kingdom even if I was both the lord and the subject. Not that I had alternatives. Where was I to find teams? Friends? With whom was I to people my world? Or even more to the point, into what other kingdom could I enter, to what could I bow down and swear fealty?

I had sailed in August expecting spotty weather, thunderstorms late in the day, gusty mornings or humid calms, but the weather had gone better than that. I never once had to reef the mainsail or run quickly into a sheltering harbor or cove. There had been no lightning. Only balmy days of steady ten-knot winds and cool, good sleeping nights. The lake sluicing away on either side of my sharp keel. And in the nights bright moons spangling the water. So even this adventure, like my life to now, had been without discomfort or mishap or even much risk.

I anchored on my last night in the nook in the shore just behind Cole Island. Tomorrow I would sail around Bennet Point into Westport, where my father would meet me at the marina with the large trailer. We would haul the boat and drive home. It would take the better part of the day. I listened to the weather report from NOAA. A system would drift slowly to the east turning the morning wind more southerly. The large high pressure area that had increasingly dominated the week was beginning to break up. I examined my chart and calculated the angle the wind would take by dawn. Against this water depth and with this scope of anchor I rode at just fifty yards to the northwest of the island. I would be perfectly protected. At this I was very good, figuring out the variables. In less than ten minutes I had secured my boat and was swimming around it in the still, cold waters.

I settled back in the cockpit against the cushions and read. This was a problem when I sailed, bringing enough books. It was hard enough to find space on a small boat to store any supplies. But the sailing had been so good, so continuous, that I had not used up what I had brought.

The sun sloped down quickly now. Soon it would fall behind the blue hill that rose sharply out of the cove. I had eaten an early supper. Now I browsed through a novel by Carl Sagan. *Contact.* It was about the first contact between our planet and intelligence in the universe. A message had come from Vega. It told how to build a machine that would transport five earth people to the source of the message in space. Reading novels like this, novels written by real scientists like Sagan or Asimov or the great Fred Hoyle, I would compare the fictional physics to the facts. It delighted me how accurate the writers had made their information. As novels, they weren't particularly good. Just melodrama. They fed off the wonder of the facts themselves rather than what they created on their own. The characters were cardboard, but the plausibility these writers gave to time warps was exciting. I turned a page, and almost as quickly as that, I turned another one.

Wonder. The darkness had closed down. I looked up at the actual Vega, the major star in the constellation Lyra, the lyre. Ten thousand years ago it had been the North Star, the pivot around which the heaven above the earth turned. A process called precession had twisted our North Pole away from Vega, though in another twenty thousand years it would become the Lode Star once again, coming and going beyond imaginable time. Across the water I heard the sounds of revelry from the boats that had tied up directly to the island, a stern line to a tree, the bow tight to a short anchor. If the wind turned north, they would all be in trouble. But tonight the wind would not change. Six boats were all bound together so you could walk across them. French Canadian ones. I had sailed amongst them all week. Boats heavy with their vacation crews. Boats full of gaiety and verve and melody. They would not begin to eat until nine, and well past midnight there would be laughter and the crackle of people. They would swim in the coldest water. All the men wore bikinis. And the women too. All the women seemed to me to be firm and beautiful and a provocation. I spied on them with binoculars, but closer, magnified, they were not as glamorous as they were when sunbathing two hundred feet away nude on the forward deck. I

4

had stopped looking closely, leaving them, like the stars, far enough away to live on in my imagination.

Behind me, on the shore, at a summer camp, the distant sounds of teenaged boys shouting broke out of the darkness and the trees. At dusk the boys had banged and thunked their aluminum canoes along the shore oblivious to rocks and logs or the ragged shale that was their beach. Now they had been driven into their cabins by their keepers. The lights from their houses flickered and paled and went out under the silence. They were not much younger than I. The junior counselors would be as old.

Once I had gone to summer camp, a summer camp. If I could not go to school with other youngsters, surely I could go to summer camp where I would be on the same level ground as the others, my parents had reasoned. A good opportunity for me to meet my peers. I had eagerly agreed. But even summer camp had found me out, I do not know how. But it was always that way. Despite my family's efforts, we could not keep me altogether hidden. And after the excitement of the phenomenon would come the bullying resentment. If I had not made up my bed tightly enough or my footlocker was not properly arranged or I was late for my duty assignment in the kitchen, I would not be chastised or punished in the usual way, only denied the privilege of going into the village for candy or such or being excluded from visiting the sister camp across the lake. For Nicky Burden there was the additional lash, the deeper blow. I would be cudgeled with myself—burdened with myself, in fact.

Because of what I was, I was allowed no margin at all even for the most petty of failures. "Hey. Genius. You're so smart, Burden, how come you can't roll your socks *tight*?" the counselor would shout at me. And the others would laugh. It had become a constant taunt. And when I had been allowed to go with the others to the weekly visit across the lake, the girls would knot together and point at me and whisper and giggle.

It was not that people were purposely cruel to me, either the kids of summer camp or everywhere else in my life, though there was meanness and ill will enough. That I could understand. *Odi et amo.* The fate of all excellence. We need and worship our heroes, but we hate a man for being one. It was that I could not be Nicky Burden, that was my ache. When my parents had tried to enter me in the third grade—for the socializing experience (their constant concern), some of the other parents had objected strongly enough to force a ruling from the superintendent. A "brain" like that didn't belong in the third grade, one parent had said. A brain, as if it floated unembodied through the corridors. A brain. It would frighten the other children, make them feel inadequate, give them the wrong idea about school. The superintendent had ruled in my favor, but my parents had withdrawn me anyway. Already they knew from experience that we could not win this battle this way.

And maybe they were right, the others. Maybe my presence, however muted, would blast those who came however close to my light.

I managed my way through summer camp, but had never gone back to another one. Instead I kept to my boats, sailing with my parents in home waters, first small racers, then day sailers, and now *Yarps*, which I could sail alone.

Yarps. "Spray" backwards. *Spray*, the immortal boat of the immortal Joshua Slocum, the greatest sailor of them all, the first to go around the world alone, his life on the high seas easy in his knowledge and skill and courage, and full of wonder. It was one of the few books that I had willed myself not to remember so that I could take pleasure again and again in reading anew the book that Slocum had written.

Wonder. Awe. Risk. Courage. Were these my goals, a quest? Is that what my life would be about, a struggle against myself, a struggle to get outside of my own unlimited possibilities? I didn't even know what I meant, only that I knew from all I had read there was a condition denied me that was not denied to the rest of humanity—doubt, uncertainty, the soils out of which wonder came. The awe. Mystery. So *this* was the critical isolation in my life, not the small disputes with overly cautious parents or the occasional seige of the ferreting reporters, the PTA or the scientific testing or the special arrangements that nearly everything in my life seemed to require. Not any of that. It was that I could not doubt myself. What I did not know I would eventually know. It had always been that way. There was no reason for me to expect that that would change. I would always live in the light.

Of course I understood that I could fail at things—the inability to control my backhand or to directly solve some of the problems posed in the more arcane reaches of mathematics or physics or molecular biology. I could not speak most of the languages that I could perfectly read. I could miss my bus or forget my keys or lose library books. I could not trade for a mint-condition rookie year Pete Rose or Mickey Mantle card. I knew about the configurations that I would live in, that I, like Romeo or Juliet or Axle Heist or Michael Henchard or Pip would live in, a world of human expectations and limits and triumphs and tragedies. I would not escape the quotidian or mundane. I did not think that I was different from the life that all our literature—*all* our literature—told us we must share.

But I thought that I was different, not because of my power, but because of what that power would do to the shape of my life. I understood that I could fail in all the ways that others failed, but I could not imagine how I would ever not know all the circumstances.

Far into the night all the French Canadians were asleep as were the boys in their bunks. Here in the absolute ebb of the evening, when the air and the water are equal and calm, the thermal engine of the planet still, in a dark cove with no ambient light at all, the moon long set, the stars spike the sky so brightly that it is nearly impossible to make out the imagined shapes of the Great Bear or the Dragon or the Swan. The star light swallows them, swallows the ecliptic. Vega.

Ten miles southeast, forty regularly spaced beads of light hang in two rows just above and below the horizon. They hang in two curves, the lights and their reverse reflection. They are the lights on the bridge across the narrows of Crown Point between New York and Vermont. I know this because that is all they can be. They fit the chart. I have seen the bridge in daylight. But now the lights look not ten miles away but much closer, not ten miles but ten feet, as if they are candle lanterns made of paper hanging over a Japanese water garden. The lights flicker as if they are candles, but it is the last of the heat in the air that makes them undulate, glow and dim, just as it is the atmosphere of earth that varies and pulses the light of the stars.

I am stirred. Between what I know and what I see is a reality that I cannot name nor embrace, only desire. Wonder? Mystery? Surprisingly close, even in the cove of Cole Island, a loon shrieks out of the night. From an opposite shore it is answered by another loon. Or is it an echo? Only one loon calling to itself.

➤2➤
=

Mike Tremain was not in the room but had been there. Half the walls and half the ceiling were covered with poster-sized photographs of nearly naked young women in sexy attitudes and gestures – arms, legs, mounds, butts and breasts, hair blown wild in studio wind, mouths puckered on tongues sweet as candy, come-here-go-there eyes. The photography was superb. The color as accurate as flesh, the deepest shadows and brightest highlights still keeping precise detail. This was not simple soft pornographic sleaze. The finish of the work was too specific to have been run on a large offset press in a warehouse in Newark. This was custom lab work. The best.

"They were made in Switzerland," my mother said, examining the fine print on the lower right border. What else could she say?

"Think of it as wallpaper," my father said. To whom? His wife? His son?

"It won't be easy to study in here," she said.

"That's true. It would be like studying in heaven," Frank Burden said.

"Frank!"

We had gotten stuck. We had gone up to the room on the second floor of Jameson Hall, each with a box of something, and had walked into this phantasm of flesh and had gotten stuck. Should this be a problem? Or was it just what to expect in college? Wild oats? Young boars? My parents didn't know which way to go, or rather which way they were supposed to go. Here, in college now. "Do you think I've never seen a picture of tits before?" I said to help them out. A picture yes, I thought, but never the real thing. Or was that what they were thinking too? What I was always thinking? We finished unloading the car and they helped me fill in the spaces Mike Tremain had left for me. On the wall over my own desk I unfurled a large chart of the periodic table and taped it up. On my desk I propped a photograph of *Yarps* taken on a long cruise we had all gone on just the year before down into and across Long Island Sound. Then we left the clattering dorm and walked around the campus busy with parents and their students.

In the brightly lit day, scattered across the dappled campus under the century-old maples and oaks, were tables where students like salespeople at a happy bazaar offered membership in such organizations as the Newman Club and the Canterbury Club and Hillel, in the Cobbton Athletic Boosters, in the Black Students League and the Women's Coalition, in the Cobbers (a student service organization), in the Cobbton College Glee Club. There was a table where you could register if you were interested in joining a fraternity or sorority. Everywhere the tone was muted and congenial. No smoldering of angry rhetoric threatened to burst out into conflagration. No pugnacious banners or signs rattled in the soft, late-summer breeze. The students were all signing up.

"The seventies are over," my mother said, surveying the freshman class.

"That's good," my father replied. "It wasn't an easy time."

"It was exciting," she said.

"Yes it was. But what was it about? Was it about the issues? Was it about Mississippi and Chicago and Cambodia? About Kent State? About personal moral commitment? Or was it just about the excitement itself?"

"You make it sound like a long party," she said.

"For a lot of people it was. I knew guys who did nothing but think of ways of attacking the ROTC building. I knew guys who majored in protest marches. You know what I mean. Maybe it was the excitement itself, the *high*, that was taking us and not our nobility."

"You make it sound dishonest. There was a lot of information that got out, a lot of focus on issues. A lot of genuine caring." But what was she defending? My mother agreed with his assessment. There was a lot that was good, but a lot that was nothing, too. A lot of smoking grass and smoky political rhetoric and moralizing pomposity. But he hadn't been making an attack on their past, maybe just a course correction.

"I was there, remember?" he said.

"*We* were there," she said. Then she took his hand.

These were the times in my life that pleased me most, when my parents dissolved entirely into their own lives, when I was not either the subject or object of their concern. It delighted me to hear them batter at their past, pushing and poking it into their own changing shapes. I was not there when Dylan sang or the police rioted in Chicago or the National Guard shot the students at Kent State or when the bumbling agents broke into Watergate. Then they had been their own material. Since me, the three of us were more like one.

By four o'clock they were ready to leave. My parents gave me all over again the advice they had given me in the months and weeks leading up to this decision. I bore with them. They were only doing, after all, what parents were supposed to do, and should do. And I knew that they had no concern about my capacity to figure out this new world—how to do my laundry, not to go wild with my modest bank account, that sort of thing. But sooner or later it was always the same point that would jab at them: How would this new world figure *me* out?

"Look," I said, "I'm just another freshman, that's all. That's who I'll be."

"You're another freshman who's ready for postdoctoral work, so that's not the same thing," my father said.

"Just don't try to be older than you are," my mother said. But how old was I?

"Look around, Mom. Just look around. I'll bet some of these freshmen aren't much older than I am. And look at them. Some of them seem like they're twelve. I'm bigger than some. I'm even starting to shave. I look older than a lot of them. I'm not exactly a geek." But that was not the point. I was not like them. I knew that, they would know that. That was the adjustment I would have to make. That was always the adjustment. "Hey, Mom, the point of my coming here was to get involved, right? So it looks pretty stable. This is not exactly the college of hard knocks, the Bowery, the gutters of Istanbul, the streets of Calcutta."

"I'm not worried about you that way. We've got a lot of faith in you. You may be brilliant and all that, sweetie, but you're also mature," she said. I laughed at the failure of the sequence. "It's that I don't want you to be disappointed."

"Disappointed with what?" I said. "With life?"

"It doesn't work that way," my father said. "We don't mean disappointed with something, like a course or a professor—just . . . just disappointed," he struggled. "Disappointment in itself."

"I don't understand that," I said, though perhaps I did. "Anyway, all I'm saying is that I don't want you worrying about me here. Your worrying days are over. Sure I'll probably get written up in the college newspaper and some of the kids are going to make cracks, but here it's going to be a lot better than the third grade. For sure, for sure. Or Camp Gingacook. Wow. You're free, my parents, free. You've shipped the kid off to college and now you're free. I'm society's problem." I whooped and grabbed them both. You're off the hook. You've got nothing to worry about now."

In the car, just before they drove off, my mother said through the window, "I wish we could have met Mike Tremain. That wallpaper," she said, but laughingly.

"You will," I said, "I'm sure. You will."

And then they were gone and here I was on this playing field or maybe battleground without any idea which way to go or how to begin. Start at the start, then. Square one, at the beginning of this new time and space. I returned to my room in Jameson Hall and the cornucopia of bodies in which I would for some time live. Back to heaven where I would lie upon my back and contemplate navels.

In the hallway in front of my room, and pushing into it, a crowd of young men bellowed and hooted. When I tried to get through, I was blocked.

"The end of the line, guy."

But there was no line, only a heaving and a clump.

"I live here. This is my room." At last I managed through. In the room another dozen young men more or less revolved around a central figure.

"Don't touch, just point," the young man in the middle said. "Some I have, some I have to order. You get it in a week." Then he ducked down and pulled up a tube and the purchaser wriggled free and out. "Satisfaction guaranteed," he said to all their laughter. "Next."

At last they were gone.

"What?" he said, looking up from his book of orders, his notation of accounts, his pile of cash and checks. He looked around at the ceiling and walls. "I don't have much left. I can sell you whatever you see. Ten percent off. Demonstrators. Or you can wait a week. So?"

"I'm Nicky Burden. Your roommate."

"Nicky. Hey! Mike Tremain." He came over and shook hands. He might have been an older brother. He had the same lightly dark coloring, his hair straight and soft. His eyes, like mine, wide-set and brown. He was taller by maybe an inch, but maybe not as broad as I was, or would be. "When did you get in? Are you set? This is wild, huh? Some business. I knew this would work. I just knew it. Some things you just know, you know what I mean? Some chances you've got to take." He smacked his fist into his palm. There was a knock at the door.

"Later," Mike said to the student in the hall. "I'm really busy now. I'll post hours." Back in the room he printed out sales times and stuck it up outside. He flopped down by me on my bed, but even then he was all motion, a charge of energy. "We've got to have sales times or we'll get eaten up alive. When this gets around campus, we could go nuts. You'll want in on this. It's your room, too, right? We'll split hours and I'll give you 5 percent over all. At twenty bucks a poster, that's one buck for you. In the past hour and a half I sold thirty-five. In an hour and a half! I've got to get to a phone. I've got to call my source in the city. I've got twenty orders."

He went on, higher and higher. I listed and watched. Success. This was success. A specific success, not just being successful. My education had begun.

"How about supper? You got plans for supper?" Mike said.

"No. O.K."

"Let me straighten out the paper work and then we can float around a little, maybe get into the village, check it out. Make my call. What do you think? Get to know each other?"

"Good," I said. My heart was thunking in me. "There's a freshman convocation at 7:30. In the chapel."

"That's right. You're a freshman."

"Aren't you?"

"No. Yes. I went to college for a year. Then I dropped out for a year. Now I'm going to start over. I'm not even going to transfer anything. To tell the truth, there isn't much to transfer. I busted almost everything. Actually I've never lived on a campus. I lived at home. I went to Clark County Community College. . . . Yeah. I'll go. Let's see what the freshman class looks like." Then he bounced up. "But first the books."

He made piles. He produced other figures out of a notebook. He explained to me his costs per picture, his expenses, his profits, his dodge around the sales tax, his gross and net. The money he had to have up front. He wrote down numbers and drew arrows from one column to another.

"What are you trying to find out?" I asked.

"Everything," Mike said. "But right now, what I need to know is what kind of money I'll have to use to order. Before I call. You know, what can I count on? I mean, I have to cover myself. We're talking about real money here. Like maybe thousands. These people I deal with are real people. They don't kid around. Your credit is your name. You can't say, Hey, I'm just a college kid, give me a break. Me, I got nothing but what I make on the transaction. For awhile I've got to put all the capital right back into the posters, but I got to know what I can count on in, say, two weeks. I've got to hit this market quick and hard before others start to move in on it. Is this clear? If this is clear, explain it to me." He laughed and bent down to the numbers. He started to poke his calculator.

"Four hundred fifty posters," I said before Mike could add up anything. "You can order 450 posters and be safe."

"Maybe," Mike said, paying no attention. To him what he thought was my guess was as good or bad as any other estimate. But guessing was not what was allowed here, was not possible. Inventory problems had harder demands. He knocked away at the calculator, pushing totals around for five minutes. "Four hundred fifty," he said at last looking up. Then, "But that's what you said, wasn't it? 450?"

"Yes."

"So how did you know that? A wild guess, right?"

"No. I figured it out."

"You did?" Mike said. "No shit? How?"

How? . . . What could I say to that; till now the central question of my life? Only the truth. Any other explanation would have made as little sense.

"I don't know how. I can just figure things out. Quickly." I added. "It's like I just see the answer."

"See it?" Mike said.

"Yeah. It's, well, sort of like this." I held up the fingers of my left hand. "What do you see?"

"Five," Mike said.

"Right." Then I held up the fingers of my other hand and put my two hands together. "Now what do you see?"

"Ten."

"So that's exactly what it's like for me. You didn't count one to five or add five and count another five and add it. You just saw it. So I just see the answer. Only the numbers can be larger. A lot larger. And I see it faster."

"Jesus," Mike said, "that's great." But he had immediate work to do. He opened an envelope and drew out a list of the photo posters. "Oh shit." He grabbed his hair.

"What?" I asked.

"All the posters are listed in this," Mike said, pointing.

"French," I said.

"Yeah. Is that what it is? But the posters are in English. See. They've got titles. So how do I order the right posters? I've got twenty orders just *today*, just in a couple of hours. I've promised them in a week. I took deposits." He pointed to a poster. A young woman, maybe even a college student, had jumped up into the air and her body was coming down faster than her chest. Her hair, her arms, her breasts were all pointing up. Behind her the sky was psychedelic. "Falling Down a Rainbow," Mike said. "That's what it's called. I never checked; I thought the order form would be in English too. It never occured to me. These were made in Switzerland. Why are the order forms in French? Maybe I can order in English anyway. Maybe I can just describe the picture. But who am I talking to? A secretary? A clerk from Porter Rico? Shit? Nothing is easy in this fucking world."

15

"Here," I said, putting my finger on the order form, "*En Glissant sur l'Arc-en-ciel.*"

"You can read this?"

"Yes."

"What about this?" He pointed to a poster of a sleek black woman pulling herself in a feline stretch along a jungle vine thick as a man's arm. "Panther puss."

"*Le Chat de chat,*" I said. We did three more. The Crack of Dawn, Thunder in the Hills, Behind the Times. There was a knock on the door.

"No orders now," Mike shouted. "Check the hours."

"I'm Sam Pelton. I'm the RA. The resident advisor. Maybe you guys need a little advice."

"Sure. Come on in."

Inside the room Sam Pelton looked around. He was a graduate student, maybe twenty-three.

"You know what this reminds me of? The Sistine Chapel," he said. "Have you ever seen the Sistine Chapel? Do you know what I mean?"

"I've seen pictures of it," I said. "I look forward to going there someday. To Italy. To Europe."

"Me, I'm not too religious," Mike said.

"Yeah. The Sistine Chapel," Sam Pelton said.

"Like heaven," I said.

"Right," Sam Pelton smiled. "And Judgment Day, too. You should be so lucky. But the problem is this, guys. You can't run an operation like this out of your dorm room."

"What? Why not," Mike said. "What are we selling, dope? What's the problem?" He got up from the bed.

"It's a regulation. You can't sell anything without special permission. A permit, in fact."

"That sucks," Mike said. "What about capitalism? What about the free enterprise system?"

"That's the point," Sam Pelton said. "This is a tax-free, tax-supported, nonprofit institution. You can't use it as a base to compete with the people who pay the taxes that support the tax-free institutions. You can't compete with the merchants in town."

"Goods like this, I'll bet you, are not being sold in this town," Mike said. "Nothing even like it."

"Which is not the point. The point is the principle. The principle in law. Sorry. No sale, Get it? Sorry, but you guys are out of business."

"How about you point to one of these pictures and I take it off the wall and give it to you?" Mike said. "A gesture of welcome. We're glad to be living in your dorm. Go ahead, point."

The blood spun through my head until I could actually see it in back of my eyes, red, a red wave throbbing with my pulse.

"Do you know what I'm saying?" Mike Tremain said.

"Sure. You're offering me a bribe."

"You said it, not me," Mike said.

"Listen you guys." He forked his fingers and pointed at the two of us. "Oh already you are sweethearts. The first day and already you are sweethearts." He laughed and said I'll be watching you. He wagged a finger at us. He left our room quietly closing our door behind him.

The evening, my first evening, went well. We had gone to a nearby Pizza Hut and ended up at a table with two other guys from Jameson, the first floor. Already the news of Mike's business had flown through our dorm and was even now crossing the campus. I started to tell them about Pelton's edict, but Mike broke it away from me. No problem, he had said. No problem that he couldn't work around. We went to the freshman meeting where, for half an hour, we were introduced to President Turner, Provost Smith, Dean Roskov, and two or three others. They all might have sounded like valedictorians at their high school graduation, exhorting their comrades to advance into life full of confidence and high hopes. If only we did our best, tried our hardest, the world was there for us to take. "Right on," Mike muttered to me with a poke. After twenty minutes there was massive fidgiting, a dry, foot-scuffing, throat-clearing hiss like wind in a corn field in October. But I had never gone to a high school graduation. I, perhaps alone, listened attentively and with acceptance in my heart.

The presentation soon turned to more practical matters: how to register for courses in the next three days, where to take physicals if we were going to go out for a sport, how to secure a season ticket for the at-home football games, the services of the financial affairs office that would help you manage your money—that sort of thing. Just why my parents had decided upon Cobbton for me, a school that still accepted the notion of traditional structures, that still saw itself in loco parentis. A school that still had the freshman wear beanies, at least for the first two weeks. A school that still had weekly convocations.

We were out in an hour to mill around like small wind devils, little cyclonic bursts crossing and crisscrossing the campus. Already from the opened windows of the dorms the loud and storming music leaped into the night and bounced around between the buildings, silent through the summer until now. Shouts, screams, yips. Mike streamed through it all like a prince coming home. I listened. To me it was an inverted music of the spheres, a marvelous disharmony of human voices.

At last the dorm, by one o'clock, drew down, quiet enough at least to attempt to sleep, though all through the night there were sudden commotions, doors slammed, late arrivals just flown in from the middle of America. Gusts.

"I never asked you your major," Mike said. "If you've got one. Any ideas?"

"Nothing firm. I'm interested in a lot of things," I said, true so far.

"Math? French? You're good at that. What courses are you going to take?"

"I don't know. What do you suggest? Freshman comp. I'll take that."

"Sure. You've got to. I've got to take it, too. What else? You've got to get started on the general ed requirements—something from column A, something from column B, you know? History, social sciences, lab science. . . . "

"Physics," I said, "I'll take some physics. Quantum mechanics—whatever that is," I added.

We were both in bed, the lights out. The window was open, summer still chirping in the night.

"Hey Nick," Mike said, "let me ask you something. How old are you?"

"How old?"

"Yeah."

I held my breath. What would happen? Everything had gone so

18

well. Was this the way it was going to be, on the run even in my own room?

"What do you think?"

"You don't look too old," Mike said.

"Well, actually I'm sixteen. Sixteen and a third."

"Sixteen," Mike said, but nothing more, nothing committed by his voice. I waited. Mike was silent, then he asked, "Are you one of those super smart kids, Nick? A genius? Is that what you are?"

"Smart. Yeah, you could say that. Smart." Again I waited.

"That's good," Mike said. "In fact, that's terrific. It is better to be smart than dumb, Nick. Everytime."

"I'm not a genius," I said. "Just smart. That's all."

"So maybe you'll get smarter," Mike said, turning on his side. "You're sixteen and in college. You've got a good start. And we're going to need your brains. I'm working on a plan. I'm not going to lose this kind of money. Tomorrow I'll tell you. Sleep, smart guy."

"Mike?"

"Yeah?"

"Don't tell anyone I'm sixteen, O.K.?"

"No sweat."

I did not want to lie. I didn't think that I had ever lied before. Maybe because I had never had an opportunity or need to lie. And maybe even now I hadn't lied. Technically, I was not a genius. What I was, there was no name for, no category, according to Sorenson and Lyle, the team that had examined me extensively when I was ten. They had been kind enough with me, but it was the last time my parents allowed me to be examined or to be a part of any research project, though once a month since I was two years old, they had received such requests. Already Nicholas Burden was famous in the literature of developmental psychology.

I had discovered the letter accidentally. It was in a journal that my father kept. He had left it on the desk in the room in the house that we all used as a study, but which had become increasingly my room, my study, just as so much else in the house had become me, mine—my father's work, my mother's career. I saw the name and return address in the upper left corner and took the letter out of the envelope in the journal and read it. I had never been denied the reading of anything. My mother might threaten to swat me if

I didn't pick up my room, but I was allowed to read at will. I felt no compunction now.

Whatever else the letter said, it said this. Prodigy was narrow, a specialized skill or knowledge, such as that exhibited in chess prodigies, who might have quite ordinary intelligence in other intellectual areas. But genius was a general intelligence, able to apply that intelligence without subject limitation. Nicholas was of this latter category. But the letter went on. The study of genius in the past is necessarily all anecdotal. Present studies use sophisticated tests and massive statistical materials in order to examine all sorts of developmental subjects, including high intelligence. Nothing in the past or in the present has produced anything like Nicholas Burden. He is so far off the charts (his IQ score was limited only by the nature of the test) that he constitutes another category of intelligence altogether, one for which there is as yet no name. It is hard, Dr. Sorenson stated, to imagine what the limits of such intelligence are or can ever be. That is when he made the pitch for the special study he wanted to do. He was too subtle and even gentle a man to say that it was the Burdens' obligation to science and the world to "give" their son to him, but it was an implication left lingering. My parents had turned him down. I never saw any of these scientists again, never even had to answer any questions about myself or display myself. And I had stayed at home.

But now I was not home, and I had no reason to think that people like the Drs. Sorenson and Lyle were not out there waiting for me, maybe even the Drs. Sorenson and Lyle themselves. They *would* happen, I knew. *It* would happen. But let it happen slowly, not yet. Not now when I had, finally, a friend.

Mike breathed in the slow, solid rhythm of sleep. Soon I slept too.

→ 3 →
=

I called my parents the following evening as I had promised.

"So how's it going?" my mother said. My father was on the extension.

"Good," I said, "very good," and nothing more.

"That's it? That's all you're going to say?"

"What's there to say, Mom? Nothing's happened yet."

"*Some* things have happened, Nicky. Maybe nothing important to you, but something. A detail. A crumb. Nicky, we're dying to know. Anything. Sweetie, *please*."

"We all got drunk. A guy in the room next to me O.D.ed on crack. Right now I have a beautiful girl in bed waiting for me to get off the phone to my mother. Her boyfriend lives on the third floor. He rented her to me. How's that, Mom? You want some more details?"

"See," my father said to both of us, "I knew he'd like college."

"Wiseguys," my mother said.

What I hadn't told them was that I had gone for a sports physical. At breakfast in the commons, me and Mike and George and Lew discussed the day to come, the busyness of it – advisors to be found, library orientation, the introduction to clubs and organizations, and the sports physical. Both George and Lew were going out for baseball.

"Baseball? That's in the spring," Mike said.

"No. There's a fall season, too. For the varsity. Freshman get a chance to work out. Show their stuff," George said. "What about you?"

"Not me," Mike said. "It takes all your time. A sport. And for what? What do you get in the end? A big league contract?"

"Maybe," George said. "But the real reason is, it's, you know, fun."

"What about you, Nick?"

"Wrestling," I said, "or maybe track. Swimming." I had no idea I would say that, certainly I had had no intention of going out for a sport, and even no special ambition. But now I felt that I had made a promise. And why not, why should I not have just this sort of fun?

And that is why at eleven o'clock I found himself standing in my shorts in the college infirmary in line.

At the head of one line were two doctors, one elderly, portly and wheezy. He sat on a stool as he examined us. The other doctor was a woman with a clipped and efficient manner, maybe not even as old as my own mother. She stood, she did not sit down. As one doctor finished an examination, whoever was at the front of the line moved on, like in a bank. The doctor would listen to the heart and lungs with a stethoscope and take blood pressure and look in your ears and eyes with a flashlight and ask some questions and move your joints. Then he (or *she*) would have you pull down your shorts and would place a finger beside the scrotum and order you to turn your head and cough.

I hoped intensely that I would not draw the woman doctor, or that if I did, I would not suddenly have an erection before her, before them all. The word would spread across the campus in an hour. Anything that Nicky Burden did, especially if it was worthy of an attack, would blaze forth. "Genius Stands Out." It would be the feature story of the Cobbton College newspaper next week. Ah, if only I had a god to pray to, a divine power with whom to make a deal. I wanted to laugh at myself, at the spectacle, at the chances, such as this, that I would more and more have to take. But I also wanted too badly to run, to put my tail (or cock) between my legs and flee. Comedy, I knew and understood—from Aristophanes and Ben Jonson to burlesque and buffoons—was the realistic view, the detached perspective, the view from outer space, Puck looking down on the fools that mortals be. I had read it all, so I knew. I knew so much. But I did not *feel* what I knew. Instead of comfort in Quintillian or Bergson, more urgently I counted the bodies before me and the time each doctor took for an examination (with a variable of v) and I constructed a simple differential equation – time against position. It would work out. I would get the male doctor. Five to go. Four. I would be safe. Then the doctor dropped his flashlight. It bounced twice and rolled away only five feet. He got off his stool and retrieved it and then sat down again. It hadn't taken long. But long enough. The axis of x against the axis of y was skewed, the fragile rhythm shaken. I would be examined by the woman doctor. Reason, as I had always suspected, had nothing to do with life.

"So this is how it will work," Mike was explaining after supper. "People will come here to shop around. They will place orders. But no money changes hands. No merchandise. That happens here." He produced the map of the area that we had all been sent in the orientation package in the summer. Three miles from campus was the Cobbton Plaza, a shopping strip. "See, right here at the bus stop. You can't get lost. And there is even an overhead cover so nothing has to get wet if it rains or snows. The stuff comes in, we call the customer. We use the bus schedule. You don't even need a car. Isn't that beautiful? No wasted time. We know and the customer knows exactly where to be and when. You can even go and come on the same bus. Beautiful."

"But won't it take a lot of time? Going down to the plaza to fill an order?" I asked.

"We don't go for every order. We deliver a few each time, we stack them up. But what's important here, Nicky, is that we're setting up a distribution structure. It's like a little investment. We get our distribution structure in place and then we're ready."

"For what?"

"To distribute," Mike said. "What did you think?"

"What? Distribute what? Besides the posters?"

"Well, that's what we've got to find. We've got some satisfied customers already, and a lot more to come. We've got that base. And now we're going to have a very satisfactory distribution setup. And eventually some capital from the sales. Now we've got to find a product. Products."

The knock on the door. Sam Pelton.

"Well, guys, how goes it?" He came into the room and looked around.

"You got a search warrant?" Mike said. "You going to read us our Miranda rights?" But he was laughing as he said it, and Sam Pelton laughed, too.

"You get one phone call," he said. "Actually, there's two of you, so you get two phone calls. *Actually*, you can have as many phone calls as you want, but they have to be on the dorm phone. No private phones. Sorry guys."

"What?" I said. "What are you guys talking about?"

"Why not?" Mike said. "There are rules against that? This phone is important to us."

"There are, indeed, rules against that," Sam Pelton said. "Sorry."

"Why?"

"Why am I sorry? Because I always want to see people get what they want and need."

"Why is there this rule?" Mike said. "That's what I mean. There is a rule against this, a rule against that. Lots of rules. Anyway, most colleges allow private phones in the dorm rooms, so what is this with Cobbton?"

"There wouldn't be enough circuits. Cobbton isn't wired for it," Sam Pelton explained, calmly, patiently, and not without friendliness. "If everyone wanted a phone, our lines into the campus couldn't handle it."

"Does everyone want a phone?" Mike said.

"Probably not."

"So why make a rule before there's a problem?"

"You anticipate a problem. You move to head it off before it gets here."

"But life's a problem," Mike said. "According to you, why start living at all? Why get born?"

"It's not a good analogy," Sam Pelton said. "Do you know what an analogy is? That's not an apt one and, anyway, you can't argue from an analogy. After you take freshman composition, you'll know that. But you tell me, Mr. Tremain, why start living it? What is the good life, and how do we live it? What makes it worthwhile?"

"Pleasure, my man, pleasure," Mike pushed back.

"Pictures of pretty girls on the walls of the cave?" Sam Pelton said. "That's an allusion, Mike. Plato. Philosophy 101. An excellent course. I suggest you take it."

"The examined life," I blurted out. They both turned to me. "If the unexamined life is not worth living, then the examined life is more worth living." They waited. "The examining of life itself is what gives life its value. It's not what you find, it's that you look." This morning I had committed myself to the physical examination, and now this. What was I doing, all this talking out? "It's a tautology," I swallowed and croaked. "It's a tautology," I waved my hands over my head. "But it's all we've got. The tautology."

"See?" Mike said to Sam Pelton, as if I had answered him for both of us, as if I had settled the question of the phone. "The kid's a genius."

"Yes," Sam Pelton said, "I know." He looked at me, and I saw in his eyes that he did know who—*what*—I was. Was I, then, Sam Pelton's special assignment? Had special instructions been given: Look after this kid, keep an eye on him, don't let him get into trouble.

"Shit," Mike said after the RA had gone. "No phone. Now I've got to think about that." But for the time he turned away from such obstacles. "Let's go to the movie. They're showing a movie in Lecture Hall One. Free. *Blue Angel*. You ever hear of it? It's supposed to be a classic film. It's about a professor who goes gaga for this whore. I think. Something like that. You want to go?"

"I've never seen it," I said. "Sure."

➡4➡
=

Dean Roskov's office looked like the offices of the deans and professors that I had read about in Edwardian novels: the bookcases of muted, polished oak rising to the ceiling, wainscoating where there were no books, an ornately carved desk, even a full fireplace with a mantle, a painting of a dean of long ago above it. A sideboard with amber crystal decanters upon it and delicately stemmed glasses. A rug that nearly filled the floor, a rug that could have come from India first to a room in Oxford and thence to here. The room was dark with the soft penumbra of learning's history, weighted with musty deliberation. The only discordant note was the computer on the dean's desk.

The meeting had gone on for about thirty minutes. Introductions had been made. The dean I had met with twice before – last year and in the summer, when the plan for my coming to Cobbton had been proposed and then made certain. Now in the office I met Dr. John Lambert, a developmental psychologist with whom I would keep in contact, not as a part of any study, but only because the dean had convinced my parents that it would be a good idea to have some kind of monitoring going on, at least at first. In case there were special problems. Something Dr. Lambert could spot. Nothing formal. Still, I could feel the man examining me. Even through the friendly demeanor, I knew the pressure inside the man, his desire to observe me. The scientific mode. The reductive urge. Like Sorenson and Lyle and a hundred nameless research-

26

ers. I knew better than anyone the emanations that rayed out from others to surround me, that tried to reach into me, take me apart. To probe. To plumb. To find the magic.

Dr. Andre Schwartz, a biologist, would be my academic advisor, although all of them, those in the room, would continue to help me as they were helping me now, to design my Cobbton education, my personal curriculum. But Dr. Schwartz would be my contact, the man to see to help me around the usual boundaries of college life.

And then there was Dr. Thomas Culver. He had come to the meeting because he wanted to make a proposal directly to me about my immediate course of study, but more: maybe about my entire future.

And wasn't that why they were all here anyway? Wasn't the future the subject? Nicky Burden's future, but maybe to some not insignificant extent, the future of mankind as well? Not that anyone said that or anything as portentious as that at the meeting.

It was all cordial enough, friendly, and genuinely well intended. But some whisp of strain could not be entirely blown away. It was more difficult for them than for me. However far they had gone in their fields of study, whatever achievements they had managed, or even honors won, whatever they might look forward to, before me, this *child*, they must stand (sit) in a dutiful obedience because intellect was their master; the process and application of thought was the absolute rule of their own existence. And here was a messiah. Before me they acted like priests, *mere* priests, who had no recourse but to serve me, or rather what I represented. Envy, natural enough in this league, at this level, was doused with a volatile fume of resentment: that none of them would ever see as far as I would someday see. So even against their will, though not so much against their will, they would probe for the thing in itself, for the source of the enormous, unfathomable power, as if it were an amulet, something within me that was not me, something tangible that they could grasp, and grasping, hold and use.

But it was not corrosive or pernicious envy or resentment. I was, after all, mannerly and not arrogant. I was compliant. I was nicely easy with them, and not particularly sophisticated. And not guarded or defensive. An open and pleasant boy. Young man? There would be some pleasure for them to help me, to watch me grow into my possibilities. Perhaps, even as only a footnote to my career, they would hitch a ride into immortality.

They had all read the dossier Dean Roskov had prepared for them.

"I see you're a fairly accomplished sailor," Dr. Lambert said. "We're a little far from good water here at Cobbton. You'll probably miss September. Isn't that supposed to be the best month? For sailing?"

"Yes, the best month. Yes. I'll miss it, I think. I mean I know what I'll not be doing, what pleasure I'll not be having. But I'm looking forward to this new pleasure. College. Besides, I just had a terrific sail. On Lake Champlain." I told them about it. Were we having a conversation? Or was this an examination? It is always an examination, I reminded myself. I would always be examined, I would always be a specimen sui generis, and all the ways in which they (the ubiquitous and shifting *they*) saw me would be right, though incomplete.

I had no secrets. I could have no secrets.

I have no secrets.

It was the strongest physical sensation I had ever experienced. I had the thought: I have no secrets. And then there was a rush, like the top of my head was coming off. I had never had that idea before. The light glinted off the facets cut into the crystal of the decanter. The pattern in the rug moved for an instant. I *have no secrets*. But it was so obvious. And so true. In an instant. Nothing had changed in the room. Or in me. Only my life. And only now, for the first time did I know what I wanted. A secret. I thought I might giggle.

"Maybe you can take off on the weekend. Get back to the boat," Dr. Schwartz offered, bringing me back.

I wondered if they could see my elation. I wanted to leave right now and begin to make a secret, something that no one would ever know. Maybe not even myself. I had the sensation again, the rush. Only what could not be known by me could be the fulcrum of my life.

But how would I know if I had a secret? How would I know my wonder when it came? How would I keep it?

Maybe I would make a journal. Like my father. I had been urged to do so by some of my tutors (and examiners) but had always resisted. What I needed to know, or remember, I could summon up at will. And what was the point of a journal? Why do it? For reflection, for working out, or getting ready to work out, what you meant by what you thought. Emerson, but especially Thoreau, who used his journal as a friend, a wife, a son – they had used their journals like treasure chests. But a journal made you vulnerable, too. It left you open to any who might read it the way I would sometimes read my father's journal. But wasn't it vulnerability that made love possible? Sometimes I thought that my father wrote his journal for me to read, if not immediately then someday. Maybe that is what journals were truly for, a heritage, a memorial; for some, a way of getting the last word. But I had no impulse toward reflection, meditation. And certainly I did not want to leave a door through which I could be approached when I wasn't looking.

I remembered completely an entry from my father's journal that had struck me with particular force and agreement:

"I do NOT think of Nicky as two people – the wunderkind but also the little boy who is like any other kid who has to grow up into a man and into his life. If some person or something in the future will be profoundly different from other people, other things, then I believe that it is profoundly different from the start, so Nicky is different now, but he is not separate from himself. If he has a problem because of his great power, that will be the problem he will have to solve: how to be the one person he is and not the two – or separate – people the world will see him as being. As his parents, that is what we have to do – not teach him to be as smart as he can be, but teach him to be one person. It is the deepest irony of his life that he will have to be taught (will have to teach himself) that which is natural and automatic to others; it will be like teaching someone how to breathe."

"How would you like to work with me?" Dr. Culver said. "Come right in on a major project? Math, physics, chemistry, astronomy altogether. If we get it right, we win a Nobel Prize."

I looked up. Dr. Schwartz shifted in his seat and drummed a finger on his knee.

"Maybe that should be my entire curriculum," I said. "The Nobel Prize." I smiled.

"And freshman composition," Dean Roskov said, but to everyone, to all of them, to make a joke, to deflect whatever Culver might get started.

"Or phys ed," Lambert said. No joke. "State requirement," he offered.

"Fine. Just great," Schwartz said. "Freshman comp, phys ed, and the Nobel Prize. Well, young man, that should keep you busy for a semester. That should keep you out of trouble." He was unhappy. He clapped his hands as if to signal that the meeting was over, but it was not.

"Comp, Twentieth Century Philosophic Tradition, Guzman's Topology," the dean was jotting down what he was saying, "and maybe work with Culver." He made additional notes.

"For credit?" Schwartz asked. "So, for how much credit? How many credit hours toward graduation do you get for a Nobel Prize?" He could not let it go. But Lambert, too, was disconcerted. Such inflationary notions were not the best way to start a career in college, even for a genius, especially for this genius. He needed to find his own direction, not be tempted or bought by such rash pronouncements and blandishments. He was sixteen.

"We'll work it out," Culver said. "We'll see what he does, how it works out. What it's worth. He'll learn a lot even as he contributes. He won't be under any pressure. He'll do as much. It's a way for him to find his pace. Maybe his center."

"Still," Lambert started to say.

"Gentlemen," Dean Roskov said, standing up. They were starting to talk about me as if I wasn't there, like an object instead of a subject. Or Nick Burden. "Thank you. I'll keep in touch with you. Nick and I have a few other items to discuss." He was dismissing them. I wanted to say that they were needlessly overly concerned. I wanted to reach out and help them deal with me. But that was not my position to take. My mother had told me: don't be older than you are. It was not what these men thought they knew about me that I must honor but that they were men whose responsibility it was to believe in their responsibility. You must value people in the way they value themselves. I knew that. That was apparent in the addition and multiplication of so much of what I had read about the human experience. But because I had no special value yet for myself, no currency whose worth I had to protect, I could afford to see with clarity, to see with what amounted to an amoral lucidity.

Besides, this is why I was here at Cobbton. Precisely at Cobbton rather than at some other school. Cobbton was small enough for me to be found in and protected by the responsibility these fine men bore for me even as the college, because of happy accidents of wealthy local patrons and a fiercely proud alumni, was sufficient to my immediate needs. It was like a "pocket" university, able to attract and sustain major scholars like Thomas Culver, to support an important collection of art and art studies, to offer an expensive variety of innovative courses and some graduate programs, and dare to keep a teacher like William Appleton, whom I was shortly to meet. Cobbton College was like a good middleweight boxer: small enough to be agile and inventive, big enough to hit hard.

"Come to my lab if you want to know more," Culver said as he left the dean's office. Then they were all gone.

The two of us settled back.

"You've been here four days now," Dean Roskov said. "Any thoughts? Any problems?"

"I'm having a lot of fun," I said. "No problems. Nothing that everyone else isn't having. Of course so far there's not much to cause problems. I guess it gets rougher once classes start and the older students get back."

"Good," the dean said. "I don't think you're going to have any big problems. Least of all with classes. I think you're going to do fine." He looked down at his paper. "For freshman comp I'm assigning you to Mr. Appleton's class. It's a star section. Bill Appleton is a campus character. An academic zany, if you know what I mean, but a great teacher. I think." He smiled. Maybe it was a dean's job to tell the truth in order to run the show, but only as far as grinding off the edges. I clicked off his observation. Maybe I would have a journal after all. But not only about myself, my own thoughts. Instead, this is what I would put in the journal, these outward observations.

"How do you know he's great? Why do you only think so? I mean I'm not challenging you, I'm just curious."

"His students praise him extremely. Of course, he starts with the best students. The best students are usually most responsive to a good teacher, a lively teacher. And they're free from the pressure of grades. They're probably all destined to get As, so that's never an issue. Do you see what I mean?"

"Yes. I'll look forward to him."

"Why don't you drop in and meet him before classes start? I've told him a little about you already. You understand."

"Yes. I'll try to find him today. And Dr. Culver."

"Dr. Culver. Sure. See if you're interested."

"Sir, how do I register? My program won't run through the computer. I'll be stuck at the registrar's forever."

"Dr. Schwartz will take care of it. You'll be signed up for the three courses. Tell him if you do some work with Culver." He stretched back in his chair. Only now did I see it clearly, a high-backed chair in leather as dark red and as deeply polished as the back of a fine violin. The refracted light from the decanter made a circle of light next to the dean's head and illuminated the depth of the leather just as the light from the decanter had shone into me earlier. "Nick, please remember. I'm not making exceptions for you because you're exceptional, giving you privileges, that is. I just think it's honest for all concerned to recognize that some re-structuring is necessary sometimes.. It's reasonable. But some other structures are also reasonable and those you'll have to live with like anyone else."

"Of course."

"How's your roommate?"

"Mike Tremain? Terrific. We get along very well."

"And his business?"

So Sam Pelton *was* working for the dean, even if the dean was working for me, looking out for me. Running interference from the start. Fair enough. The dean was not an enemy, nor were the rules and regulations obstructions to my life, my very happy life. I, after all, Nicky Burden, would be the beneficiary, the heir to all of this—society, civilization itself. I did not have to confront, only learn. But I did not know what was important to learn here. For the moment response itself seemed to be enough. Or even everything. Mike Tremain was my friend.

"It's not Mike's business, sir. It's *our* business. I'm a partner." I cast my cloak around Mike Tremain. This was delightful. I would push it. The dean would like that. It would be a little cheeky. Normal. "If you'd like, sir, I can offer you some posters at a good discount. Nearly cost. But not on campus." And the dean did smile.

"Go on, Burden. Get out of here."

➡5➡
=

"Clutter and bang. Sophistry and intrusion. Like Orpheus going up instead of down into the underworld. Down or up in to the up-perworld. Orpheus. Do you know who is Orpheus?" The man was pacing around his office, or more like prancing. He raised his feet high as he moved, nimble and awkward in the same motion. He was very tall and windblown, although he did not seem to be the type who spent hours in the sun either climbing mountains or clawing in a garden. He was, I thought, bookish, a word, a description, I had caught out of my own reading. It was a term I loved. Bookish. It said so much, as if the bookish figure was like a character in a book, more exactly, like a character in Dickens. William Appleton. I guessed he was close to my father's age, forty-five.

"Orpheus was the son of Calliope and Apollo," I answered him. "He could play his lyre so beautifully that he could quiet wild animals and make the rivers stop. He married the nymph Eurydice, who was killed. When he went down to Hades. . . . "

"Enough. I forgot. You're the boy who knows everything. Sit. Sit," he waved to a chair piled deeply with papers, books, folders. "Push them aside. Dump them. Go on, go on. Onto the floor," he said at my hesitation. "That way I'll know where everything is, however inconvenient. Just don't kick about." I tipped the chair, clearing it, and then sat down.

"Not everything, sir."

"What?"

"I don't know everything."

"A manner of speaking, Nicholas. Hyperbole, though attenu-ated. Do you understand those words? Hyperbole? Attenuated? Yes, yes. But of course you would. You scored a perfect eight hun-dred on the SATs. Sixteen hundred altogether. It is true that you've read the dictionary? I assume it. But tell me, Nicholas, do you understand what I was saying to you as you came into my office? Clutter and bang? Sophistry and intrusion? Like Orpheus going up or down into the underworld?"

"No."

"Ha. So. Then you don't know everything."

"I don't know everything, but what you were saying, that's not the kind of thing one can know."

"No?" Appleton said. "Why not?"

"You can't 'know' what you said in the same sense of 'know' that you used when you asked if I 'know' about Orpheus. I can know about Orpheus, but I might not know what you mean. It's the difference between knowledge and insight," I explained.

"Exactly," Appleton said. "You're absolutely correct. Right. But see, you can be right about something that you can't know. Isn't that an anomaly?"

"I wasn't right about *knowing* the meaning of the statement you made. I was right *in* the statement I made. They're two entirely different statements. You're still confusing the two. Sir."

"Yes. You're right, Nicholas. Perfectly right. And please stop calling me sir."

"What should I call you."

"William. Or Bill if you prefer."

"William? I can't call you William. I can't do that."

"Why not?"

"I just can't. You're my teacher. Dr. Appleton."

"I don't have a Ph.D. I'm not a doctor."

"Mister, then. Mister Appleton."

"Ah, Nicholas," the man clasped his hands behind his back and walked to the window and looked out. "See, the peach tree is in bloom. Don't forget your Santayana. Do you know the story? One day while lecturing, Santayana looked out of the window and saw a peach tree in bloom. He stopped in the middle of his sentence and walked out of the room and out of the college. Out of teaching. Out

34

of talking. He went to Italy and retired into a monk's cell in a monastery, there to live out the remainder of his life in reflection and what must have been the marvelous solitude of his own mind." In the room I began to snort against my laughter, then I had to give into it. Appleton turned.

"This is September," I said. "Too late for blossoms."

"Excellent," William Appleton said. "We shall get along fine. Here." From out of the swirl on his desk, he extracted a mimeographed sheet of titles. Books, essays, poems, stories. "This is the reading list for the course. We meet Thursday afternoon. Three hours. Think you can take it?"

"The course or sitting in a class for three hours?"

"Are there problems?"

"I don't think so, but I've never taken a course. I didn't go to high school. You see. . . . "

"I saw, Nicholas. The dean has spoken to me about you. He has shown me your history. He also has shown me examples of your writing, your writing sample for admission. I was not impressed. I was singularly not impressed."

I had never in my life heard that, someone say that about me.

"But I was excited," Appleton went on. "Ah, what a block have we got here! What a challenge! To see if there is any spirit in the stone. Life in the bone. More than a drone. Or only a clone. Skelton, Nicholas. Read Skelton. Here." Quickly he scribbled Skelton's name and dates on a scrap of paper he swiped off a nearby book shelf. "Try this," he said, handing me the paper. "Good for what ails you. I hope. You may be a desperate case. If Skelton doesn't help, I don't know what will. And that's *Skel*-ton, Nicholas, not Skel-e-ton. Don't be a dolt, O.K.? John *Skel*-ton."

"You don't like the way I write, Mr. Appleton?"

"It's not what you think I mean. It's more that you don't write at all. You repeat the styles that you've read. You formulate. You make things clear."

"But isn't that the point? To write clearly."

"If you're writing the directions for opening a can of cat food, yes. If you're writing about what is already clear, or what should be clear, yes. But what about what isn't clear? How do you write about that? You're sixteen years old and you write like a college professor, god help you. You've got no *doubt* in your writing, Nicholas. Maybe there's no doubt in your soul."

"Yes!" I shouted, standing up. "Yes!"

"No!" Appleton shouted back. "No Doubt!"

"Yes," I said, "you're right. That's true. No clutter and bang."

"No sophistry and intrusion."

"No singing."

"No singing," Appleton encouraged me.

"No singing," I repeated, nearly humming the phrase.

"The beasts won't be tamed, the rivers halted, not with a style like yours."

"The women won't tear me to pieces."

"But you might lose your head," Appleton concluded.

"Where do I start?" I said.

"Write a poem."

"What kind of poem?"

"What's a poem?" Appleton said, and before I could answer, or ask, he said, "This is a riddle, Nicholas. Answer it carefully. Your life might depend upon it." He leaned forward, not only accepting his caricature but insisting upon it.

"A poem," I said looking at Appleton's chin as it bounced toward me. "A poem is . . . what . . . *the underworld sounds like in the upperworld.* Wait! I've *got it.*" I would take him at his casual word. I would try the wings of intimacy. Not Mr. Appleton. William. Bill. Billy! "Listen to this, Billy. Zeus destroyed the Titans for killing Dionysus. This is what the Orphic cult was based on. They believed that the human race was raised from the ashes of the Titans and that it was made up of them and of the Dionysian, the sacred and the profane, the eternally beautiful and the earthly, temporal, and profane. *Poetry! Get it?*"

"Nonsense," Appleton said. "But exactly so, too. Now go, go on. Out of here. I haven't all day for this. Go and write your poem. And for godsake, Nicholas, get it right for the first time in your life." He waved me out. "Oh, and one more thing. Never, don't you ever call me Billy again." He shook a boney finger at me. "Billy Billll-ly Billlllllll-ly," he howled. "Jesus."

▸6▸
=

Culver's lab was nothing like I had expected. There was no equipment, no apparatus, only a small flat elegant eighteenth century writing desk and a computer terminal. And on the walls were mounted large blackboards that ran in a continuous band around the four sides of the room splitting the walls into hard-edged areas of white and black and white. One wall of blackboards was scrawled on with the usual hieroglyphics of physics. I took them in at a glance. Culver watched my eyes as they read his configurations.

Thomas Culver was as white as his lab, but unlike the lab which was totally open, there was a dark streak through his features, nearly a matching image of the black and white of this room. I could not tell where the dark shadow came from in that shadowless place, but there it was, an oddity, an illusion, not that I then thought overly much about such things or about Thomas Culver, for I was as open as the lab, as bright and unwritten upon as the other three empty walls. But I did wonder why the lab was what it was, so large. And all that blackboard. Was he so prolific that he needed so much space? It seemed to me that the three unwritten upon blackboards had never been used, seemed pristine, pure almost as if they had been waiting for something to happen to them, something extraordinary, almost as if they had been waiting for me.

Culver seemed, like Appleton, to be no older than my father, though not as muscular. "The condition before the beginning of space and time is not conceivable," he said. "Certainly it is not measureable. Any sign of whatever it was or might have been was totally absorbed or changed or destroyed by the formation of the universe. Or maybe there wasn't anything at all. Basic physics, right? So here, too, is the basic positivist trap. You can't know what you can't measure. You can't even speculate about what you can't demonstrate experimentally or prove theoretically. You see the problem?"

"Clearly," I said. It was not, after all, either a difficult idea or a new one. If time began at the start of the universe, then you can't also have time existing before it began. If you can measure one, then you can't measure the other, so it can't exist. The same for space.

"So what are we supposed to say?" Culver asked me.

"Nothing," I said.

"Except that it's an absurdity to speculate about the other side of the beginning of time and space. But it is also an absurdity *not* to speculate about the void. We have a finite universe, but it's expanding. It's expanding into the void. One second there is no universe and in a second the universe has expanded into the void and what was once *not there* has now been added to the universe. Second after second, year after year, the known universe is expanding at nearly the speed of light into the unknown void. So what is the nature of the void? Now? And before the beginning of time and space?"

"Science is full of absurdities, Dr. Culver. Sometimes that's the only way to answer questions about the natural world. And besides, hasn't Hawking answered the question, sort of? His idea of a finite universe but one with no boundary, no edge?"

"No. Hawking is still accepting the idea of time beginning. His postulates only work in an expanding universe. And yes. You're right about the absurdities. So why not go for the greatest answer of all, the grandest of all absurdities? Do you want in?"

"But what would I do? What *could* I do? There's so much I don't know yet. There's so much physics I haven't gotten into. I may be, . . . " but I stopped. For the second time that day I was experiencing myself as I never had before. Never before had I ever referred to myself, or had cause to, as brilliant. As a genius. I had never needed to think in qualified terms about myself because I

38

had never had to do anything to demonstrate what I was to my-self. All I had done for sixteen years was wake up in the morning and take. Take and take and take. I tried to remember if anyone had ever asked me a question. Not the personal questions of reporters or researchers, but questions about my knowledge, what I could do with it.

"Listen, Nick. Don't confuse knowing physics with doing physics. You can understand—you or any reasonably bright person can un-derstand what physics is about in a long afternoon: subatomic par-ticles or quasars or what have you, the idea of them is easy enough. What makes them work, how do they work, that's the tough part. For that you've got to spend some time learning. Even so, what is, what is known, even that is not so hard to learn quickly. Most of us spend our time trying to figure out *where* we can go next, what we can look at. That's the hardest part. Do you understand?"

"Yes."

"What you can do now is start fresh. No strong commitment to a position or to a career. You can associate yourself with an un-fashionable idea and not be damaged by that."

"With absurdities? I can play with absurdities?"

"Exactly," Culver said. "I can because I'm established. I've got a solid reputation. My colleagues can think I've lost my marbles but they can't scorn me or reject the work out of hand because I've been too good in the past at the work we all share, the concepts we're willing to live with. And you can because it's too soon for you to count. You're not even in the ballgame yet. So you're a great opportunity. You're someone who will be able to do a lot of the work who is young enough, new enough, to be allowed to do it. You can do what you want. With your mind at your age, you can do whatever you want."

Which was the final point, after all, the beam bearing the main weight of Culver's argument, but of my own best argument as well, or so it then appeared to be. With my mind at my age, I can do anything I want.

"Here," Culver said taking a notebook out of a drawer in the table-desk. "You know something about superstring theory? The work being done at Princeton?"

"Something," I said. "It's very hard. Those guys are inventing a new kind of math. That guy Witten."

"Yes. O.K. This is pretty much all of it." He put the book into my hand. "Study it. It's pretty consistent. One page will get you to the next. But here," he thumbed to page fifty-eight, "are my interpolations. With this I can get down to seven dimensions. And here at the end of the book are some possible directions for applying this stuff. See what you think. Then we can talk in detail about where I'm going. O.K.? Don't even answer now. I'm throwing so much at you, this is so general. Take the book and look at it and think about how exciting this kind of challenge is. Think what it's going to be like when the pieces fall into place. You can learn a helluva lot in a hurry, but I really think you'll be able to make a real contribution. I'm telling you, Nick, this is a win/win situation. And I want to give you this." Out of the drawer he took a key and gave it to me. "This is a key to this room. It's always light. I designed it. Sunlight or daylight or flourescent, the light stays the same everywhere."

"Just like in the first second after the Big Bang," I said. "Everything *was* light."

"Yes," Culver said. "Yes. Yes."

"And the second before that, everything was absurd," I said.

"Right, Culver said. "And for fifteen billion years it's remained that way. But not now. Not for much longer. Come aboard, Nicky. Join up."

I looked around at the room as if now seeing it for the first time. It was true, the light was unvarying. It was like a blizzard must be that I had read arctic explorers would sometimes encounter where there was no up or down, where the snow in the air was as thick as that they tried to plod through, and if you fell you might try to burrow further in rather than try to stand up. Even the black of the boards seemed to be absorbed into the incident and reflected light that bounded through the room. But when I blinked the room did take on shape and proportion, dimension. It was like being inside one of those optical illusions that trick the eye between flatness and perspective. It was like one of the Escher graphics where there was no correct way to see, where only the illusion itself was real.

"Do you have any questions, Nicky?"

My eyes began to tear, my nose began to run.

"What's wrong?" Culver said. "Is something wrong?"

40

"The chalk dust," I said. "It must be the chalk dust. I'm allergic to it. I won't be able to work here."

"Wait," he said as quick as that. "Paper. Large paper pads. Huge paper pads. I'll have the room scoured and then I'll have these huge paper pads made up and mounted on the blackboards. No chalk. It's not a problem, Nick. It won't be a problem."

"But what about you? What will you use?"

"Crayons," he laughed, "whatever. It makes no difference."

He made it all seem as simple as that, and as I was to learn, that was often Thomas Culver's way, to make things simple, or at least to make the attaining of them seem to be a simple act, as simple as doing what you wanted to do, taking what was available.

⇥7⇥
=

I lay on my bed half-propped against the wall, my legs up like a desk. I had been reading in the book that Dr. Culver had given me, the summation of the superstring theory work being done by Witten and his colleagues (the string quartet they were called) down at Princeton. It wasn't a published book; instead, it was a bound sheath of xeroxed material. On one page there was a faintly scribbled date. Only a month ago. This, then, was the edge of what was known about this arcane subject: a universe in which there were eleven dimensions – length, width, depth, and time, and then the other seven, which were actually only mathematical configurations. But the math was like no other that had ever been. Its greatest difficulty was that it kept developing. The math changed, grew, with every equation, more like a plant than an abstract system. What it meant was that unlike Newton, say, who had invented differential equations in order to describe his universe, string theory invented a universe and then created a math to justify the description. I didn't like it. I thought it was wrong, but I couldn't say why. I didn't understand enough of it yet, it was that hard. But I would soon. And the physics. I would need a lot more of that than even I had. On the cover of the book was the paper I had been writing on. The poem for Appleton.

This is a day in the life of poem,
where a clip of words tatters at the edge of events

and nips the pieces into the dust that breaks the sun into light.
The little girl dancing in the school bus glow,
my mother blurring porridge at the stove.

Through porridge I had drawn a line. No, I thought. That's too archaic. There was a knock at the door.

"Come in."

The door opened but only a little light came in around the squared figure standing in the frame. It did not seem that he could move through the doorway without pushing it apart.

"Is Mike here? I'm looking for Mike. Mike Tremain."

I had never seen anyone so large. At least I had never been this close to anyone so large.

"Not here," I said.

"He said he would be here at three o'clock. I got to go soon. Practice."

"Football?" I said.

"Yeah."

"Maybe I can help you with something."

"I want to buy a car, you know, something cheap. To get around with, out to practice. I need to save some time. Getting around. It's a problem. Mike said he could help me out. You're Burden? I'm Albert McGuire."

"Yes." I got off the bed and waved Albert McGuire into the room. "That's me."

"Mike said you guys knew cars pretty good, that you could get me a good deal."

'Right," I said. "If that's what Mike said, you can bet on it."

"I don't know," McGuire said. "That guy. He's something else. One minute I think he knows everything, the next minute I don't know if he's bullshitting me or what." In the room he seemed larger still.

"Don't worry. Mike knows. He delivers."

"Thumper," McGuire said, "that's my nickname."

"Your friends call you Thumper?"

"You got it."

"So why don't you sit down, Thumper. Wait a bit. If Mike said he'd be here, you can count on it. O.K., Thumper? Is it O.K. to call you Thumper? Any friend of Mike's is a friend of mine, right?"

43

Albert Thumper McGuire didn't say anything, although he did sit down on Mike's bed. He opened a book he had been carrying, a black binder identical to the one that I still held containing the work on string theory. It was the kind of binder you see by the thousands in academe, the kind with a spring back that clamps down on the papers. No rings. In McGuire's book, on the xeroxed pages, were little squares and circles, some hollow, others filled. Lines and arrows ran hither and yon, some bumping into each other, some snaring others in half circles like pinchers. Xs and Os jumped about. On the bottom of the page was a code of numbers. It could have been a diagram of the collision of mesons and quarks as revealed in a cloud chamber in a high-energy subatomic particles lab, but it was not: it was the play book for the defensive linemen of the Cobbton College football team, the Cobbton Revolutionaries.

"I got to learn this perfectly," Thumper said. "And soon. I've got to know it by tomorrow, and I've got to know it perfectly by Monday. The first game is next Saturday. What a pisser. I've got the first week of classes and then the first game all in the same week." He looked up. He had been looking at the plays, but now he looked up at me, as if he were angry. "It's a helluva price to pay."

"I thought the freshmen played only during the week. You are a freshman, aren't you?" I looked up at the beanie on Thumper's head.

"Yeah, but I'm on the varsity. I'll be doing this for four years if I don't break a leg or something."

"You don't sound happy," I said.

"Yeah, says who? I'm doing what I want. No one's got a gun at my head. I like playing football, O.K.? It's just the rushing around. The games are O.K., it's just the pressure in between the games, you know? I need a fucking car just to exist, for christsake." He seemed to be getting worked up. I wanted to avoid that. "And it's good to get away sometimes, you know? I like to get away. Maybe go fishing. I love fishing. Otherwise I'm nothing but meat."

"Yeah," I said, "a bitch."

"What do you know?" Thumper said. He slumped back into his book. After five long, silent minutes, Mike finally arrived.

"You're late," Thumper said. "You said three. I got to go to prac-

44

tice. I got to take the practice bus out there. If I'm late for the bus, I got to take a cab. If I'm late for practice, I got to run around the fucking field three times after practice. You know what that's like?"

"You've got the time now, Thumper. No rush at all," Mike said.

"What do you mean?"

"You've got a car, O.K.? You're your own man."

"What do you mean?"

"Wheels. Wheels is what I mean. I got you your car. Outside."

"You mean now? Outside now?"

"That's right, Thumper. I promised you a car, I got you a car."

"*All right*," the big man said, standing up. He was quick, light and not ponderous. An athlete after all and not just enormous. "Let's go look. Let's go *drive*."

"One problem, Thumper. The car is eight hundred, not five hundred."

"Hey. *Hey.* Five hundred, I said. What is this shit, eight hundred? I don't have eight hundred. And I got to be careful. I can't borrow money around here. They watch you bad. The coach said, don't take nothing. So what is this eight hundred? So what is this, Tremain? What are you doing to me? Why are you killing me?"

I watched. I could see, but I could not match what I saw to what I could understand. Thumper McGuire was not a violent person. He was not threatening. The tone of his voice was going in the opposite direction from his words. He was disappointed, that was all, but he didn't know how to back up. All his life he must have been the biggest kid around, the star of the smallest football teams that kids play on when they are seven or eight. He had never learned how to back up. He was always expected to move forward. When you're that big, you never back up. He's just like me, I thought.

"What this is," Mike said, "is called doing you a favor."

"Favor? This is a fucking favor? Shit. I got to go." He moved toward the door. Mike blocked him. Thumper McGuire stiffened, his right shoulder dropped a fraction, his wonderful reflexes taking him into the shadow of a stance, the whisper of the idea of taking a hit, or hitting first, but he was under control. He was an athe
lete, trained and in top condition. As a freshman he was playing varsity football. He must have been very good. Good means knowing where to go next and exactly when.

"There isn't a five hundred dollar car in town that isn't an absolute junker. I've checked them all out. I've got friends. You go out and buy anything, you're buying crap. Right, Nicky?"

"Right."

"But crap is all I can afford. It's all I need."

"This car is unique. It was owned by a little old lady school teacher for fifteen years who never drove it above thirty-five miles an hour. And for the last five years she's been retired. It's only got fifty thousand miles on it. It's hardly broken in. The whitewalls aren't even dirty. She never used the ash tray."

Now Thumper was laughing.

"She never drove at night. The lights are new. She had the car washed once every two weeks."

"So why did she sell it, it's such a fucking good car?"

"She bought a Porsche. She met this thirty-year-old stud and that's all she wrote. She sold the house, bought a Porsche. They're in Atlantic City right now."

Thumper howled with laughter, but then he darkened.

"Fuck off, Tremain. I got to go. I'm really going to be late." He leaned Mike out of the way, gently.

"You haven't heard the rest. You haven't heard the deal. Listen to the deal. I'll drive you to practice if you don't like it. You won't be late either way."

The deal was simple enough. Albert McGuire gave Mike the five hundred up front and the car was his. Mike would cover the three hundred plus the basic interest, regular used car interest, 9 percent, with nothing going to taxes. Nothing to sign. Nothing to know. A handshake. Even the ownership papers would say five hundred. There would be no trail for the NCAA to sniff after.

"You'll trust me?" Thumper said.

"Yes. I'll trust you Albert, but if you don't pay up I'll break your leg." It was of course a joke, but Albert Thumper McGuire could not laugh at what was obvious. What was obvious to him just then was the sweet and easy friendship of Mike Tremain's act.

"The knee cap," Mike said, trying to make the giant smile. I followed. I had been thumbing through the play book.

"Then you wouldn't have to play football, Thumper," I said. "You can go fishing." But still the interior lineman was too moved. He put out his hand, the ritual of the warrior for whom ritual was, like the game he played, his life.

46

"Thanks, Mike. Thanks."

"So come here and sign some registration papers." In a few moments it was finished.

"I've got some time now. Let's go look at the car."

"Hey, Thumper," I said. "Can you tell me something?" I opened the play book. "These are the routes you run, right? But these angles? Are these the actual angles?"

"Yeah. Exactly. The angles and the number of steps. See here, these little cross marks? O.K. So this is me." He jabbed the paper. "And I go here." He traced the line. "I should hit the middle linebacker right here in four steps. Pow!"

"This is wrong," I said. "You've got the lines for the steps running parallel to each other, but they should be running perpendicular to the angle of attack. If you did it this way," I wrote on the page, "you get here in three and a half, maybe three steps. And here," I turned some pages, "where the cornerback comes across, you can . . . "

"What the fuck do you know?" Thumper said and took the book out of my hands.

But I held on to it until he wrenched it free. "No kidding. Listen to me. Let me explain it. It's a common mistake." I put down Witten's superstring theory and reached for the football playbook, but he pulled back.

"I don't have the time, Burden. I'm lucky if I have the time to learn this. This is what the coach says to learn. This is what I learn. This is also what everyone else is learning. If you get me through the line sooner, I'll be out there alone. I'll get killed."

"So show the coach what I'll show you. You'll be a hero. You'll be an all-American."

"I'll be a hero anyway. I'll be an all-American anyway. This way." He slapped the playbook. "But if I don't get to practice, I'll be dog meat. Now get out of my head, O.K.?"

But it had become important to me, a need to help someone like myself. Someone whose power was driving him into his ambition and not the other way. If I could not, at least not yet, determine a fate of my own, maybe I could determine that of another.

"Come on, Thumper. Let me help you."

"No," he said.

"It will only take a few minutes."

"*No*," he shouted, "*no*." But I thought that for a moment he wavered, and I thought that for a moment he sensed in me the odd community of two that he and I were. But "*no*" he shouted again, and then he was gone.

In front of the dorm Thumper took possession of his car, a 1973 yellow Plymouth Duster. With the immortal slant-six engine.

"That motor will still be going after you retire from the Jets, Thumper. That's the greatest motor ever designed. The true truth." Mike raised his right hand.

What did Thumper care? The car *did* look good. It was his for what he could afford. And he wouldn't be late for practice. Shave and a haircut, he honked the horn. Two bits. And he was gone.

"Was that right?" Mike asked him. "About the football plays? The angles?"

"Yes. Actually it's a common mistake. People are always drawing lines in one plane when they should be in two planes. Or they'll confuse one measuring ratio with another. For instance, if you have to mix fluids in ounces, say, 1 to 9, most people would mix one ounce to nine ounces. But that's wrong. In ounces the correct ratio is 7.29 to . . . ah . . . 65.61. Or if you want to figure time over distance, then. . . . "

"Forget it," Mike said. "Save it. Come on. We've got to see the football coach. You may have changed the game, Nicky Burden. You might just become an immortal. Come on. Maybe we can catch the bus." We raced to the main gym from which the bus left to cross the river to the stadium and practice fields, but it was gone. "Tomorrow," Mike said. "What's your schedule? I'm going to call the coach and make an appointment. Maybe you could write something out, or draw some pictures. Some plays."

"I don't know any plays," I said.

"Make them up. What is it, Xs and Os? Big deal. But you're sure about this?"

"Yes. I'm sure."

"Right. Of course. What a smart guy. Jesus." We went back into the dorm. Mike looked up the extension of the coach. Coach Warren Mecklenberger. He called the gym. The secretary was still there. He told her he was from the Cobbton College *Clarion*, the student newspaper. He was assigned to do a story on the coach. They've come and done a story on him already, she said.

Not on him, Mike said. On opening day. He's busy, she said. Very busy. So what should I do, Mike said, write about the coach being too busy? What am I asking for, thirty minutes? Twenty minutes, O.K.? I'll talk fast. I'll tell the coach what to say. She laughed. O.K., she said. To whom as I speaking?

"Nick Burden," Mike said. "And eleven o'clock will be fine." He hung up. I came alert.

"I've got my topology class at eleven. It's only the second meeting. I can't miss that. Jesus, Mike."

"This is too big to not move on it, Nick. You'll catch up in topology, but the season is only once. And it could lead to something. Where will topology get you?"

"You don't even know what topology is," I said.

"See," Mike said. "So how important can it be?"

"And how can you say I'm a reporter? I can't write a news story. I've never done a news story."

"But you don't have to. There is no story. All you need to do is get in to see him and then we tell him your idea. There is no news story. What you're going to tell him *is* the story. After twenty minutes he is going to kiss your ass, Nick. And at the end of the season, when Cobbton has gone undefeated and won the conference, he's going to tell the entire world about this, and then you are made, man. *Made! We're on our way!*"

"Where to, Mike?"

"That I haven't figured out yet."

But I didn't care. Didn't want to know. All I wanted to do was *go.*

We left the dorm and wandered over toward the touch football fields where the intramural sixes played, teams with three girls and three boys on them. These were the old teams, left from a year ago. New teams and leagues would be formed. This was a pickup game. They all had jerseys with numbers on them and block letters that said whatever they wanted: JED'S GIRL, HOOCHY-KOOCHY, MARONG! LEFT AND RIGHT was stitched across one girl's ample chest. There was much squealing and pushing, though nothing too rough. Just enough contact to make it, the contact, the subtext of the game. The contest was the efficient cause of the legitimate, open-air sexual grope. Aristotle would have understood. And I, who had never touched any other flesh at all, perceived the two levels of the game at once as well as the lofty Aristotelean view. Looking at life, I looked through it, at the crisp abstractions. The neutrinos no one has ever captured, seven mathematical dimensions of space, Aristotelean explanations, the xs and os.

But now I stopped for a moment to watch the life itself. The exuberance was compelling. Nothing abstract here. This was not the martial ordering of Thumper McGuire's game with its pincer movements and precise defenses, intelligence reports, logistical problems, its arcane strategies and tactics. Here was play in its purest form. And here I was on the sidelines observing.

One of the girls, the prettiest, was SARA LOGAN, but was that her own name or the name of a club, an organization? The Sara Logans? What was SARA LOGAN? Soon she was the only one I watched. She was very good. Unlike the other women, who ran with the typical spraddling gait of girls, she ran with her legs pumping up and down in a straight function. And she was the passer on the team. Her spiral was perfect everytime; her trajectory slightly, delicately arched; her aim exact. Sara Logan, Sara Logan.

Finally Mike dragged me away.

We ate supper, went to the library to study, cracked back to Jameson at eleven, caught some late-night news. By one o'clock we were in bed, the lights out, the sounds of the summer night washing over us, over Cobbton, over all that could be our world like a white noise.

"That was a fine thing you did today, Mike," I said. "Lending Thumper the money, the three hundred. I just wanted to say that. And protecting him. Not letting him buy the five hundred car."

"It was a five hundred car," Mike said.

"What?"

"It was a five hundred dollar car. That's what I bought it for," he said. I waited.

"So?" I finally said.

"So what?" Mike said.

"The other three hundred? What about that?"

The light went on. Mike had turned out of bed.

"What about that, Nicky? I'll tell you about that. That is called profit. That is called what we make for finding Thumper a car and taking the risk and getting it registered and setting up the insurance for him. And by the way, making sure the car isn't junk. Do you think Thumper could handle all that? And on his schedule? Between his classes and his practices? And it was a seven hundred dollar car. I got it down to five. So I figure our cut is really only a hundred."

"It's three hundred, Mike. Three hundred."

"Yeah, well I can't argue numbers with you, Nicky. But whatever it is, it was worth it to Thumper McGuire. He is a very happy dude right now. He has what he wants, and that includes the three hundred dollar debt. We gave him good terms. We gave him forever to pay. That's capital we could be using elsewhere."

"What 'we' are you talking about?"

"You. What other 'we' is there? You're my partner. I've given you a piece of all the action around here, haven't I? *Haven't* I?"

"Yes."

"So what's the complaint? Do you want me to have a meeting to consult on every deal that comes along? Do you want me to wait until every little detail is in place?"

"No," I said, still in bed. "But this isn't a little detail. This is a big moral detail."

"Thumper McGuire is on the biggest scholarship package you can get. Room, board, tuition, books, and some spending money for sweeping out the locker room once a week, or something like that. What kind of deal did you get? What kind of deal did I get? So don't worry about Thumper McGuire. When he makes it into the pros for a million dollars for his rookie year, see how much he remembers good old Mike, good old Nicky. So he needs a car now to get to practice on time so he can get into the pros. Three hundred? Shit! We didn't charge him enough. Anyway, did you ever hear of caveat emptor, Nicky? Let the buyer beware?"

"That's no longer true in law," I said. I almost said *Frederick* v. *Simington*, The Second Circuit Court of Appeals, 1973, a landmark decision. I almost started to talk about the Sophists and sophistry or about Kant's categorical imperative, but what were ideas to do against such harder truths as these except blunt their edge and break their shaft?

"Yeah, well even if it's not the law, it's still a good idea."

"So is morality a good idea, Mike."

"Yeah, well so is your asshole a good idea, Nicky, and that stinks too." He swung back into bed and turned out the light. "Go to sleep, Nicky. Save yourself. Tomorrow is our big day. We're going to sell the coach his future. Sleep. You'll need your strength."

And indeed I did not think about Thumper McGuire and the three hundred dollars that he owed the firm. In for a dollar, in for three hundred. Instead I found myself thinking not about tomorrow and my future or the future of Cobbton College's football team, but rather about the game of touch I had watched in the late afternoon. JED'S GIRL and HOOCHY-KOOCHY, and SARA LOGAN. And just before I slept, at the very edge of sleep, I thought about sequence. The string theory did not sufficiently account for sequence; it hardly even took sufficient notice of it. Yes! That was the chink in contemporary physics through which I would thrust. And then I thought about the little girl in my poem dancing in the reflection of the school bus in the bright morning, *as golden as glory*. And then I fell into the dark.

→8→
=

I awoke to the clutter and bang of life in the dorm, the morning existence. My second week in college was ending. Nothing much in my classes had firmly started–the first classes had been short and introductory, the handing out of syllabi, conference hours listed, a neat description of the professor's intent and method, yet something more had begun for me, and now I felt farther away from any old base than ever I had before. Maybe for the first time I was excited about the life outside of my head. Not that I had been excluded from such a life in my years at home, only that I had never had a chance to participate in anything. Though I had neighborhood and friendliness in Seffanville, and had taken my turn at the young and boisterous swing of boyhood (I had never been sheltered in that respect), I still had always been who I was: special, different.

Among the friends I had, I stayed with them in their world so narrowly and bounded that all I could do was take their limits as my own in the hours I spent with them, but I could not give my expansion to them, take them with me anywhere. I could be less than who I was, but with them I could never be as much as who I was. So we talked about girls and what we thought was sex and conquest and about their teachers (though not mine) and sports and music; the work we had to do, the chores at home, the proclaimed nuttiness of our parents. Movies, TV, (rarely) a book. And that was part of my life, too. But about the rest? They were still there, these friends, my after-their-schoolday friends, these weekend friends, still in high school with years to go before they might go on to college or to anything else.

But now I had a place, a niche. I was in a flow, no matter how much more quickly my movement in the stream would be. Here, at least, I was going along with everyone else into a learning that glided on into a job and a career. A life. I lay in my bed and listened to the scuffle and howl and thunk in the hallway, the water running in the shower, the sink, the commode, and imagined the dendritic pattern, the classroom that might lead, at last, to the ends of the earth. Or for me, to the edge of the universe. But it didn't matter, that difference. We were all in this together. Together. I had never felt so positive, so good about my life before. My mother had been right. I had come to college, maybe as first among equals, but as an equal, that is what was important. And my father, what did my father think?

Mike came into the room, already dressed.

"You better hustle, Nick. You've got a nine o'clock, right?" Mike checked the schedule that he had pasted to the back of our door. "And then there is a delivery. You'll just have time to get to the bus stop and back. Here are the tubes, six of them. Paid for. No hassle. Just give them to these guys, here's the list, and get back on the bus. I'll meet you at the gym."

"The gym?" I said.

"Yeah. Right. The gym. Coach Mecklenberger, remember? What the hell kind of reporter are you?"

"I forgot. Do you think we should really do this?"

"What's to lose?" Mike said. "But think of what's to gain. Eleven o'clock. I got to run."

I ate breakfast in the commons close to Jameson. In a small notebook I wrote out a pattern for my day, a list with hours and lines connecting one item to another: where I would go, what I needed, what other errands or connections intersected. What I might think about along the paths. I made a molecule of my day. Early in my life I saw this paradox about myself: though there was nothing I could not remember of what I wanted to remember, and in an instant, still I could not remember with certainty actual moments of decision; I always needed to make a list of what I was going to do. Why was that? Why did someone who could tell you the gross national product of Liberia in 1978 or name all the prime ministers of Great Britain from the elder William Pitt to the present, and describe the principle legislation they enacted, why did he who could chart great rhumb lines through the heavens from Andromeda to the cephids M41, not be able to go around his day without this crutch of paper? But I liked that about myself; it wasn't an oddity, one of those quirks associated with genius. Indeed, it was quite human, an organizational aid such as many needed and used. Still, I wondered about it.

"So you see," William Appleton said to us in our first class meeting, "or *do* you see, why the poet made these particular choices? Given all the options, why this instead of this, or that or that? Why? Where do the choices come from?" He waited a moment. "And don't slouch. Don't slouch down and avert your eyes, you *ostriches*! Do you really think I don't know you're there? That if you avoid eye contact then I won't call upon you? Do you really think I can be so stupidly fooled? Good grief. Martha Blimmer," he slapped at his desk. "Speak!"

But Martha Blimmer was silent. As were the rest.

"Is this English 115. The star section?" And still we were silent. "Do you mean that you can't even tell me that? You. Garrison. What do you think? Is this English 115, the star section?"

"Yes sir, it is."

"Excellent. Excellent. Now let us see what we can build from that. We take the lines," and he turned and scrawled them upon the black board.

> The crows settled onto the telephone wires.
> They looked like notes of music on a page,
> a passage the wind might play.

His writing was hardly readable. "Now what have we got here?" he said, turning back to us.

"Sanskrit?" someone said. Everyone laughed.

"Excellent. Excellent." Appleton clapped his hands. "Now we're getting somewhere." He returned to the board and smudged and twisted the words into a slightly better shape. "O.K. Now what we have here are some images, some direct description and some

55

shaped description. We have metaphor. Two metaphors, in fact. The crows look *like* notes of music. The wind might *play* the music. Now why these decisions? Try to imagine the poet making these choices. What do you think was going on in her head?"

At last we spoke, and now eagerly and with the assurance that only small knowledge and less experience allows, so that eventually assertion is confused with certainty. But it was a good discussion, and Appleton spiked us with the point he wanted to make. The power of metaphor, the magic of *as if*. Description is not enough. Metaphor allows for–demands–the pressure of invention. It is how we give shape to the ineffable.

"So that's what makes the poem *hot*, do you see? Even a bad or weak or limp metaphor will do some work. It is the making of the metaphor itself that matters. That is what the poet is struggling for, that heat. That is why she makes the choice. Now isn't that right, Mr. Burden? Or wrong? We haven't heard from you. What are you thinking? I assume you are thinking."

I was in fact thinking of two things. One of my thoughts I expressed.

"Maybe the metaphor chooses her," I said. "Maybe language is sending and the poet is receiving."

"Like messages from the gods? The muse from Helicon?"

"Something like that."

"Something like *what*, Mr. Burden? Like what? You can't leave a speculation like that hanging in the air."

"Individual metaphors change with the individual poets," I said. "But metaphor doesn't. We have different poems, but not different poetry. Poetry is a constant. So maybe that means that we are all wired in such a way that only certain stimuli will set us off." I was figuring it out as I went along. Ernst Cassier, Noam Chomsky, the past two decades of arguments for precognitive knowledge of language. I swept what I knew up into this easy compression. The more I thought about my idea, the better I liked it. I stopped for a moment. Three other possibilities for my idea came to me. "We don't think of all forms as poetry, do we? At some point we say this is a novel or this is a play or this is a magazine article, and that's never changed. Maybe we invent particular forms, but the point is that we *do* invent them, fully known and realized forms. So maybe it goes further still. If the overall condition reads *make a poem*, and that also means, or can mean, *make a sonnet*, then maybe that condition can also say *use metaphors*. So maybe then it's only a small step to make certain kinds of metaphors once certain other assumptions are in place. And so on and so on down to the smallest choices." Again I stopped. But before I could continue, Appleton said, "That's brilliantly provocative, Burden." Then to the class, "Well. What do you think? You." He pointed to a student urgently waving a hand.

"What's a helicon?" she asked.

Then I fell out of my seat, actually slid to the floor.

"*Whaaaa?*" Appleton said.

"Sorry, I said to them all. "I had an idea." They all waited for more of an explanation than that. "Maybe light doesn't move at a constant speed," I shouted. "There's an eight arrow of time." I ran out of class. I had to find Culver.

"Sure," I heard Appleton say as I left. "Why not?"

What superstring theory had done was bring the constant speed of light into doubt, but it didn't realize that it had done that. In fact, it hadn't done that yet, but the implications were there. Unless I had missed something big. Culver would know. Maybe. I started to run. But I could not find Culver that day, nor the next or the next.

But what was this? Now. Today. After topology and before Mecklenberger. Yes. Under one arm were the six tubes I had to deliver by bus. Instead of Culver, I had to do this. Shit. There it was. The blue bus. The campus bus driven by students, a private and free service to the strip mall and back. I checked my watch and my list. At the bus I boarded it. I had two ideas. The possible inconstancy of the speed of light and the idea that we responded to language rather than created it, or at least that our creation was a response to it, to the properties of language itself. But I had six tubes of posters to deliver, the one that had rapidly become our best seller. In small print on a tube I read *La Pomme du Mal au Pardis* – "The Evil Apple of Paradise." It was a simple enough picture. A beautiful naked woman on her knees leaning forward, her arms bracing her, held in her teeth an apple. Nothing else. The photograph was bathed in a soft swirl of filtered red. The bus lurched forward. I showed my ID and flopped into a seat. If imagination was the act that brought us closest to the god we were sup-

57

posed to mirror (as Coleridge argued), then metaphor was the link. Or was it?

Mike was waiting for me at the gym.

"How did it go?"

"They were there. People was there. I gave them the posters."

"Good. O.K. Are you ready?"

"No. What am I supposed to do."

"Just follow my lead. And when I get it set up, you explain about the angles and steps. Don't sweat it. Be cool."

The secretary brought us immediately into the coach. The office was not what I had expected. It could have been any other office on campus, except more luxuriously appointed. But except for three old football trophies, it had no special identity. Coach Mecklenberger, however, did look like a football player, twenty years later. Pouchy, but still hard and big. He was not friendly.

"You've got ten minutes."

"Coach, my name is Mike Tremain. This is my partner, Nick Burden, who has an idea that could change the game of football. He wants to explain it. Show him, Nick."

"What is this, a new way to do a story?" But what did he care? All he needed was to get through the ten minutes. Keep good relations with the press, even with this press. Any press.

"I'm not a reporter, sir," I said, unfolding my papers.

"What?"

"He's an idea man, coach," Mike said.

"A what?"

"See," I said, "the line of attack, you see how it makes an acute angle here?" And I rushed into my explanation, quickly translating the sines and cosines into inches and feet. It only took sixty seconds. It was simple enough.

"Think of the implications," Mike said. "On every play every lineman getting an extra step. Devastating."

I was finished. Coach Mecklenberger sat back into his leather office chair. He let sixty more full seconds tick by. Time out. Absorbing. Then he leaned forward and took my papers in his large, scarred paws and crumbled them up into a ball that disappeared, he crushed it so tightly.

"O.K." he said, calmly, even. "This was about four minutes altogether. You took a minute getting in here and I'll give you a minute to get out. Or maybe I should just pick you up and throw you out right now. *Move*."

I scrambled up, but Mike held on.

"You mean you're not impressed? You mean you're not going to use this great idea?"

The coach stood up. I was at the door. Mike stayed seated. "*Out!*"

"There's no way to get you to reconsider?" Then he took out a card: T&B Enterprises. He had written in Jameson 208 and the dorm phone number. "Here. I'll leave our card in case you change your mind." The coach started around the desk, I leaped through the door. Then Mike got up off the chair as would any business man. He waited for the coach, then he extended his hand. Shake. What could Coach Mecklenberger do? He put out his hand, still tightly clenched. He opened it and the tiny lump of paper fell to the rug. They shook. Properly. Then Mike left. He found me waiting outside of the office, close to the secretary, far enough away to feel safe.

"I thought he was going to kill us," I said. We walked toward the dorm.

"Nah. That's what he's used to. Listen Nicky, you can't let yourself be moved around by everybody, what they want. You'll spend your life doing what someone else wants. My philosophy is this. You draw a line and you follow it. And you've got to be prepared to take some hits. You understand? No one's going to get through life without taking some hits, so if that's the way it is, then you don't run everytime it looks like you're going to get it. You draw a line, you follow it."

"But what happens if the line runs you into a brick wall? Or a pit of fire? Or off a cliff? What about then?"

"Simple, Nicky. Simple. Before you go over the cliff, you draw another line.

At the circle that was the center of the campus, Mike turned toward Jameson, but I turned toward the science complex.

"I've got to go find one of my professors. I'll see you later."

"Wait," Mike said. "Maybe we could send your idea to some other football coach. I think the way to go is to write it up, like a small book or something like that and then get it copyrighted. Somebody out there will eventually . . . or maybe better would be to get some publisher actually to print it. Get an advance. What do you think?"

"I've got to go, Mike. I really do. You do what you want with it." He started off.

"Wait," Mike called me to a stop. "Here. I forgot." He came to me and gave me a small box of the business cards. T&B Enterprises. In the lower corners of the card was printed Michael Tremain and Nicoholas Burden, left and right.

"Pretty classy, huh?"

"Yes," I said. "Yes, it really is, Mike." It was. How important an ampersand could become in my life.

Then I turned away from this vital present to enter into dubious battle with time.

→ 9 →

=

"Say it again," Culver said, "slower." But I could not say it slower than I could think it, so I thought it down to something thinner than I was imagining. It wasn't that Culver couldn't understand; it was more the problem that you can't really talk about physics with words, only math. But that was part of physics's problem: it confused the math for a larger reality. Besides, I didn't have enough of the math I would need for this, not yet, and not enough of the physics. That math and physics hadn't been invented yet. That was also part of the problem. But maybe at this point that was my advantage.

"O.K. It goes like this. According to Einstein and Planck, a particle that moves at the speed of light has zero duration, so it can never be anywhere long enough to be measured. That's basic to Heisenberg's uncertainty principle, also to Schrodinger and Driac, right? O.K. So if a particle moves at the speed of light and time *must* move at the speed of light, then the particle could never catch time. But no increment of time could be so small that a Planck particle could not touch it. Don't you see? According to Einstein, you can't separate time and particles. But that's exactly what happens when you got to $10 (-43)$ from the beginning of the universe. You have an increment of time that is larger than a Planck particle. Which means that the Planck particle, some part of it, had to exist on the other side of the beginning of time because you can't have a piece of a particle. You either have a whole particle or you don't have any particle. And what also supports this is that after 10 (-43) seconds you don't get particles in the universe again for another five hundred thousand years. Only energy."

"And you think that's where the energy came from, from the particles that existed before time began?" Culver asked.

"Where else?" I smiled. "But that's only the start. Others must have noticed this. There's all that work that's been done on the tachyons, the particles that are supposed to be able to move faster than the speed of light. But nothing's been proved there, nothing at all. But what's different here, what I'm thinking is, I guess, is that no one questioned the speed of light because light is a constant speed *now*. It's taken for granted. But what about *then*? What about in the instant before 10 (-43)? You see, if the speed of light is a variable in a singularity and not a constant as all physics assumes, then all bets are off, aren't they? You could have a big bang and still have time and space preceding it, couldn't you? You could have a lot of things come out differently in the universe."

"It's ingenious," Culver smiled back, "but it's got a big problem. A *very* big problem."

"Yes. I know. The speed of light would have to be a variable and not a constant."

"Yes. And we can't have that now, can we." Culver looked away, not only from the impossibility but from the fear of it. That sort of speculation made him feel nervous and unhappy I could tell, as if physics could crack open and fall into itself, tumbling down into a deep black hole, taking him with it. Taking us all. He actually shuddered. "If we know anything, we know that can't be."

His timidity at this point surprised me. I thought that the idea of our working together was to question everything, challenge everything. I had hardly started and now he seemed to draw back.

"Why not?" I hadn't told him yet about the unexpressed implications not yet unearthed in superstring theory. So far I had nothing begetting nothing, a hunch based on a hunch. Still, what was science about if not the following out of hunches?

"No, Nick." I suppose he felt he had to be firm; he couldn't allow himself to be intimidated at every turn because of my intellectual power. My power without his experience could do damage to me as well as to physics. And especially to his own ideas about the other side of time. In the past two weeks I had read through his

62

major work. What he wanted in me was an ally, not a competitor. "That's not the right question for a scientist," he said. "That's too easy. That's a layman's question—'Why not?' A poet's question. Science *isn't* empirical. The physicist constructs a theory and then tries to prove it. Newton didn't explain the falling apple; he used the falling apple to demonstrate the theory. The theory came first. Einstein said that when he thought about the structure of the universe he would ask himself if he were God, how would he have designed it: simply and perfectly was his answer. The constant speed of light throughout the universe is a simple and perfect answer, a simple and perfect base to every question physics has answered so far."

"Unless the speed of light is not a constant. Unless what we have here is a metaphor," I said.

"A what?"

"A metaphor."

The whiteness of the cube in which we were sitting pulsed with natural brightness. The falling September light angled in through the high slits of windows near the ceiling that acted like a large defraction grating pressing the light into bright or yet brighter bands, more and more light, the opposite effect of a prism, which broke light into a rainbow.

And now—already—that the blackboards were almost entirely covered by the great white pads, the effect was even more intense. Culver had delivered the paper, but now he was tugging at me. A leash? Was it that he wanted to go with me (or have me go with him?) but at his pace, a proper pace? But though I thought about this, I dismissed it as quickly. I hardly knew the man. And who, after all, was I to make judgments about people, much less trust those judgments? Still, it seemed to me that in the room/lab, entirely white now, Culver had lost more definition, tone. He had become more white than ever.

"I'm losing you, Nick."

"The seven arrows of time. They're just metaphors, aren't they?"

"The expression is, yes. But what the arrows represent are real enough."

"That time has no direction? The time reversal invariance? You believe that? You believe that time can move either forward or backward?"

"It's not a matter of belief. It's a matter of proof."

"Yes. That's it." I stood up. Leaped up. "Proof is the trap. The metaphors are too small. We need another arrow of time. The seven arrows of time don't prove anything, it's just that they don't *disprove* anything, that's all. An eighth arrow." I placed the arrow in my bow and drew back the string. "Twang," I shouted. "Bullseye." I was going too far with the physics I had, but I couldn't resist it.

Culver watched the arrow's shaft quiver in the heart of physics, the feathers shake, ever so slightly, betokening winds, betokening storm. What had happened here, I could see him wonder. Was I mad, suddenly mad, the instabililty of genius? I think that is what he wanted to believe even if that would mean that his own excitement about working with me would be dashed. But I could also see how he felt the tug, the seductive urgency, the lick of salt on his lips. He took a pad of paper from the elegant, odd eighteenth century writing desk that he affected in his studio/laboratory and began to write down work for me to consult. But when he looked at what he had written, he could hardly read it, hardly discover his own hand. On another piece of paper he began again, working slowly and carefully. Priggogine, Canelli, Sopher. I paced around the wonderful room measuring it, perhaps at some level preparing to take it as my own.

"Here," Culver called to me and waved the paper. "You've got a lot to learn, a lot to study before you can get anywhere with your . . . ideas. You don't have the math yet for what you're talking about." I came to him. "You can't just speculate, Nick. Even if you're right, you've got to be right in the terms, the language, the tradition of the subject."

"Yes," I said, "sure." I smiled and took the paper. I glanced at it quickly and saw that I had already read much of the work of these men and women. "And thank you, sir." Did Dr. Culver understand me?

"We're going to have fun, Nick." He settled. I thought I could read his mind, his attitude. I *was* pleasant, after all. Polite. Exuberant. Culver settled further. Give me a little room to run, some space to fly in. Of course. Why should he have expected less of such a treasure as me?

"Here, Nick. I want to give you this." He handed me a small, antique key. "This will fit the drawer on the left. In the desk." He pointed. "Your own drawer."

"Thank you, Dr. Culver," I said, then, "Oh," looking suddenly beyond him. "Oh. Think of this." I ran to the wall. From a tray beneath one of the large pads of paper I took an ebony pencil and wrote. It was the first time I had used the paper. I stepped back. "What about that, Dr. Culver? What about *that*?" Then, "Bye," I waved and left through the door, which disappeared like a secret panel into the white blank wall. "I've got to get to supper." I imagined him trying to imagine what I was looking at, what I had sketched out on the paper. Or what physics meant to me.

But by the time I got back to the dorm, I had decided that all the work of physics could not be wrong; I would have to integrate it into my own field theories. Still, I had a problem with that sort of acceptance. Or maybe it was the idea of the simplicity and the perfection that was the problem.

If the universe was not finished forming itself, then why should the laws by which it measured its changes themselves be exempt from change?

Why could there not be perfect and simple *inconsistency*?

Opening the door to Jameson 388, the end of the statement I had written on Culver's wall appeared in my head. It was a tiny opening, a pinhole smaller than the point of a pin. With my hand on the door I stopped. A larger configuration began to occur to me. *If I were God, how would I imagine the universe God would imagine and create?* Einstein had his answer, why couldn't I have mine? A statement from superstring theory (page twenty-seven) began to sing and I sang with it, like the counterpoint in a madrigal. The newer music of these newer spheres. Oh this was terrific. Oh maybe this was where I was going to go. Maybe this was my future. Maybe this would be the future of the world that I would take with me. The future of the universe.

"Nicky," Mike said to me even before I was in the room, "sit down. I've got something very important to ask you. Very important. Are you ready? I want you to take this the right way. I want you to listen and then tell me. O.K.?"

"O.K."

"Are you paying attention?"

"Yes."

"Because the future may depend upon it."

"O.K., O.K. already."

"Have you ever been laid?"

If Delta [ay] was = Sigma [aA], and if [-aK] was *not* [-aY], then. . . .

"Nicky? Are you listening?"

"I was thinking of something else. The fifth dimension."

"Come on, Nicky, pay attention. They haven't made an album in years. The Fifth Dimension doesn't even exist any more. What's with you? Listen to me. This is important."

"No," I said.

"Yes," Mike said. "Yes it is. Very important. What could be more important?"

"I mean, no, I've never been laid. I'm a virgin."

"That makes you happy?" Mike said. "Do you want one of those little buttons to wear saying that? Do you like being a virgin?"

"No. Of course not. But it's not so easy. I mean I've not had a lot of chances to do anything about it."

"Right," Mike said, "exactly. And that's true of a lot of guys. Everybody talks a better game than they ever played. I'll bet two-thirds of these guys, three-quarters, I bet you they're cherry."

"So," I said. What Mike said sounded plausible. At least I wanted to believe that it was true, that I was, in this matter, not such an isolate after all.

"So how would you like to get laid?"

I put the universe aside and paid closer attention.

"Do you mean in the general sense – would I like sex? Sure. Or do you mean that you are offering me a specific, particular opportunity? I'd have to know more. Who is she? What's going on? It's kind of a problem now, isn't it, what with AIDS? I mean even with a condom you're taking a chance. Aren't you?"

I didn't know where I was. This was all ideas/attitudes I had picked up in the ambient air. I knew far more about the edges of ultimate space than about the immediate body of a girl or how one went about getting her to have sex with you. All I knew about sex, really, was the exactness of my own fantasies. Maybe that *was* what sex was, finally, only an antrophic projection.

"This is a survey I'm doing," Mike said. "Don't get too excited yet. But suppose I could produce for you a certified healthy attractive young female who was ready and willing to take you to bed?"

"Certified?" I said.

"Yeah. Doctor's statement. Hospital blood tests. The works. No AIDS. No herpes. No nothing."

"You could do this?" I asked.

"I think I could. I don't think it would be the toughest thing to do. I could get sellers I could explain things to. I could get buyers. Doctors would be easy. What do you think?"

"It's called pimp, isn't it, Mike?" I said.

"No, Nicky. A pimp is a son of a bitch who owns a stable of women who make money for him. He protects them. He beats them. He screws them. They have to find their own customers. It's a very sick thing. Here I'm an entrepreneur. I bring together the two parties, I take a percentage, only instead of selling a house, what's getting sold is ecstasy."

"But," I said.

"But?" Mike asked.

"That's still prostitution, isn't it? That's against the law. How would you do this? Where would you do this?" Then I jumped up from the bed on which I had been sitting. "Oh no. Not in here, Mike. I'm telling you. . . . "

Mike raised his hand to stop me.

"Of course not. Do you think I'm crazy?"

"Yes."

"A little," Mike laughed. "But what's the big deal? You think college boys don't go to whores? You think it's only guys in the navy on shore leave, something like that? Come on, Nicky Burden. I'm not into prostitution. I'm into health. That's what we're selling. Security. Insurance. That's the point here. The where and how, that's up to the private parties. Our percentage is for making sure she is safe. Or work it the other way too. Certify the males for interested young females. This could be a bonanza, Nicky. AIDS may be the best thing that ever happened to us."

"Mike, for Christsake!"

"Hey, Nicky, a little humor, that's all. But what do you think?"

"From a business point of view? Is that what you mean? It's probably a brilliant idea if you could make it work. You've sure got a demand—safe sex. And you've sure got a market. From a moral point of view, I guess I'd have to say it's still what it is, prostitution."

"And that's bad?" Mike said. "The oldest profession, and you call it bad?"

"It's not a profession," I said.

"So what is it then, a calling? Like being a priest?"

I burrowed into our closet to find a jacket to wear to supper. The September evenings were chilling down. Tomorrow was the first day of autumn. "The trouble with you, Nick, is that you've gotten stuck in ideas about life that aren't really about life." I pulled out of the closet quickly, without the jacket.

"That's strange," I said. "You saying that. That's just what I've been thinking about physics. It's getting stuck in ideas that aren't about the physical world."

"About physics I don't know anything, Nicky, but I can tell you this. All life is about is turning one thing into something else. You hammer nails to buy the food somebody grows so he can pay you for hammering nails. It's all a matter of turning one thing into something else that somebody wants. So what's so bad about that?"

"All life is is the exchanging of energies. Hydrogen turns into stars, the stars explode and turn into people," I said.

"That's it. Right. And without me, the process would stop. I am a mercant, Nicky. Without me, nothing happens. War is bad. People killing people and stealing things. People hitting people over the head. That's bad. But selling? Jesus, Nicky, selling is what is meant by civilization."

"Henry Ford and Andrew Carnegie and the Mellons and the Medici and the Sforzas."

"Sforzas?"

"Merchant princes. The patrons of Leonardo da Vinci."

"Right," Mike said. "Exactly. But don't forget the peddlers and the tinkers and the little shopkeepers, the bakers and the shoemakers. The tailors."

"Princes all," I said.

"Fucking A," Mike said. "Let's go to supper."

68

But there was a knock on the door.

"Come in," we both said together.

The SARA LOGAN girl entered the room.

"Hi," she said.

All over I became alerted, like a cat reacts to a footfall. But I was on the edge of fluster, too. I knew the hormonic formulae for what was going on in my body, the enzymes racing around, the synaptic patterns. But nothing else.

"Would you like to sit down?" Mike said. "My name is Mike Tremain. Listen, would you like a job? Would you like to work for us?"

"Mike."

"It's a joke," he explained to SARA LOGAN. "Between us."

What was happening? I had been quietly wishing the SARA LOGAN girl into my fantasies ever since I saw her throw the football, and now here she was in my room. Was this what Jung and Freud and even Einstein meant by synchronisity?

"My name is Sara Logan," she said.

"Sara Logan," I said. "What was printed on your jersey? That was your name?"

"My jersey?"

"Football," I tried to explain.

"Oh," she understood, maybe even more than I understood.

"This afternoon we were watching you for a little," Mike said. "You throw an excellent pass."

I struggled to comprehend.

"Thanks," she said, and turned to me. "I write feature articles for the college newspaper, the Cobbton *Clarion*, and I've come to interview you and work up a story. O.K.? It's for a series the paper is running through the semester. Freshmen to Keep an Eye On. Our first stories are on Thumper McGuire and you."

"Nicky? Why Nicky?" Mike said.

Sara Logan looked at me and saw at once that I had not told Mike about myself, which meant that I had told no one else either, as she had expected. Good. What a story this would make for her. A scoop. I thought I saw her eyes glitter at that. I would be hers alone.

"What?" Mike asked, but now to me.

"How did you find out?" I asked her.

"A reporter can't reveal her sources, Nick. You know that. But how about it? How about the story?"

"What?" Mike shouted, "what?"

"I don't know. I'd rather not. It wouldn't make my life any easier."

"Then let me explain to you why it would, O.K.?"

"Sure."

"This sort of thing is bound to get around. I'm not the only person to know. If it just gets out on its own, rumors get out of hand. And once they get going, all distorted and everything, you can never get them back. Do you follow? You'll end up sounding like a freak, and that's what will stick. Let me break the news and I'll make you look like what you are, a nice, normal guy," she looked up at the ceiling and at the wall, "with normal interests and ambitions. A nice normal guy who just happens to have the highest IQ ever measured."

"I knew it," Mike crowed. "I *knew* it. I knew you were too smart just to be smart." And without missing a beat, "She's right, Nicky. She is absolutely right. Do it her way. Do it. Do it."

Sara Logan bent to her many-pocketed bag, the paraphrenalia of her busy existence heavy and strewn about in it. Half of the bag held sketching pads and a box of pencils and cray-pas, elsewhere was a camera and a case with another lens in it, a flash unit, related equipment, notebooks, a scrunched paperback, half a large bag of M&Ms. But that was all I could see in a glance, for mostly I looked at her, at the flume of her hair, boldly full, the natural mix of reddish auburn brown that no tint could manufacture. Glowing. Clean with light. Brightness fell out of the air in the room into her, illuminating her, making the room dark. I fell in love with her hair. And then I fell in love with all the rest of her. Certainly in love with her now, and not like before when she had speared me with the sexy grace of her well-thrown football. I would give her my story. I would give her anything she wanted. And now—*now at last*—being who I was, what I was, being Nicky Burden, had finally brought me something that I truly wanted, the serious attention of a beautiful girl.

"O.K." I said, "fire away. I'm all yours."

I wondered about her, thinking about her even as we spoke about me, but I was good at that, thinking on numerous tracks at the same time. I was impressed at how hard she must have worked–and how quickly–to get all the information about me that she had. It seemed quite professional. In the past I had never given this interview; my parents had always prevented it. But I had heard from my parents how unprepared the interviewers, the media people, had been. All they had was distortion and my amazing brain power. In effect I would do their work for them: with a subject like me, what more did they have to do? But Sara was different, her curiosity about me was natural enough, but time and again her focus was on the me who was me. Simply me.

"What about you, Sara?" I asked. "What's your predisposition?" I was amazing myself, talking so much, to talking so well, I believed.

"I don't have a special skill or power, like you, like Thumper. I do lots of things. I'm a very active person. What I'd like, I think, is to be famous. Isn't that awful?"

"No," I said, though fame was what I feared, or the consequence of fame. Or thought I feared it. That was what, in a sense, my parents had taught me. But, "No," I insisted for her, "fame's O.K."

"Oh, it's not the fame being awful," she said, "it's wanting it. It's so shallow, so superficial." But she laughed it away. "Well, maybe I'll outgrow it."

And so we went on. She was well informed. She didn't just ask general questions; she knew specific things about me: the courses I was taking now, including the special relationship with Culver; why I had chosen Cobbton College (surely Harvard and Yale were easy options); some of my hobbies (chess, ham radio, baseball cards, astronomy, stamp collecting). And she knew about *Yarps*.

"How did you know about *Yarps*?"

"I told you. It's my job to know, to get as much information as possible. But I can't tell you sources. Don't ask me, O.K."

"O.K.," I said. O.K. to anything is what I was thinking.

We went on mining my background, but even early on I could see that she was trying to slant away from the obvious stupendous brain power angle. That might be the hook, but how far could she go with that? Who was I besides my IQ? What was the human "I" like?

"What about your future? Any firm ideas yet? Any hints?"

"His future?" Mike Tremain leaped in. All along through the interview, as he heard more and more about the fabulous Nicholas Burden, he had fluttered around the room like a bird caught in a storm, blown around in it by his excitement. Now he was beyond his containment. "Put your hand in the hat and pull something out. And then do it again. And again. Futures, not future. Why *a* future? Why put a limit on what he's got?" Mike told the world.

"It's not what he can do, it's what he wants to do," Sara Logan answered him.

"Sure, but why should he want to do one thing, or a little thing? Why any limits at all?"

"Because that's the way it goes, Mike. Life imposes limits. It makes you choose. Even if you're a genius. Anyway, it's not a debating point, it's a question." She turned back to me. "It's Nick's question, it's Nick's answer."

But maybe it wasn't my question or my answer. Certainly Mike wasn't so sure about that.

Nick. She called me Nick instead of Nicky. Nick. I liked that.

"Nick?" she said.

"What?"

"About your future? Any thoughts?"

"Don't answer that, Nicky," Mike said.

"Why not?"

"Why not? You want to know why not? I'll tell you why not?" and he paused. To think of what next to say? To dare to say it? Sara and I waited. "Because your future is to take the chances that the rest of us can't." It was a stunning thing to say.

"Wow!" Sara Logan said. Quickly she wrote it down.

"T-r-e-m-a-i-n. Michael Tremain," Mike said.

"I can't quote you," she said. "Nick would have to say that. Do you want to say that, Nick?" She rephrased it for me: "My future is to take the chances that others can't."

"I can't say that," I said.

"Why not?" Mike said. "It's true, isn't it."

"I just can't say that, something like that. I've only been here three weeks." I turned to Sara. "The truth is I want to play first base for the Mets." I smiled. She smiled back.

"You could do it," Mike proclaimed.

"No, Mike. I'm not left-handed."

"You could figure it out," Mike said.

72

She concluded the interview.

"And now my surprise for you," she announced. "I'm taking you to supper. How about the Corner Tavern? The best pizza in Cobbton. You, too, Mike."

"Really?" I said. Was this a date? Or just more of her business with me? But what did I care? I was hungry. I would be with her. She was buying. How smart did I have to be to figure some things out?

"Burden," someone in the hall shouted, "phone."

Thursday. Thursday night, seven o'clock. I had forgotten. That would be my mother. Checking up. That was all right. Checking up was a form of love. My father would talk to me, too. How often now when I thought of my father there would be a pang of affection that I could not account for easily, only that I had come to a deeper bonding with my father away from him that I had not had under my own roof, for all our affection and sharing.

My mother went through the perfunctory routine of questions, the rituals. Still my mother's quiet theme was strongly evident. When she asked me how it was going, she didn't mean my courses. She meant had it been found out yet: the world. Now I could tell her something. I explained about the newspaper story that was going to appear.

"It was bound to happen, Mom. We knew that. So don't worry. I feel pretty good here. In place. I've made friends." But nothing would reassure her, not that she was without perspective.

"Could you get a copy of the story before it appears? Just in case?"

"In case of what?"

"Mistakes. Distortions."

"What's going to happen has to happen. The readiness is all."

"Three weeks in college and he's quoting Shakespeare to me."

"Hey, Mom. I read Hamlet when I was four. Remember? I'm the smartest guy in the world, maybe in the history of the world."

"Yes, sweetie, but what you need to learn isn't in books, right? And remember what happened to Hamlet, Nicky."

"He got killed. So what? They all get killed in the end or how else could you get a tragedy?"

"It wasn't getting killed, Nicky. That wasn't the point. He was betrayed. Do you have enough clothes? Should I send up your sweaters yet?"

My father had been listening on the upstairs extension. He didn't have much more to say. There was an interesting article in *Cruising World* about Narragansett Bay that he was saving for me. The computerized typesetter that he had bought for his business was getting debugged. Yesterday it started to set everything backwards. But they were getting it straightened out. He reminded me that there was a transit of Mars that night. Not that I could get to a telescope, he understood, but at least I should look up. It was in the constellation Sagittarius. He gave me the coordinates, the meridian and azimuth, even though the constellation was in the ecliptic and therefore Mars would be easy to find.

"You won't be able to see it very well without a telescope, but you can know a lot of things about the stars that you can't see, Nicky, even when you're looking right at them."

"Eleven o'clock, Dad. I'll look up."

Mike and Sara were waiting for me down the hall from the phone. She knew I was sixteen. She had not asked. She would have known that for certain. Her source would have known. My file in the registrar's office if she had access to that. And without saying so, I knew that she would have to report my age in the story she was writing. Now, walking toward her, I resented my age, was embarrassed that my mother had called, called every week at seven on Thursday to see if I needed sweaters, socks, underwear. Protection. What could Sara Logan think? On the other hand, I knew more than she about most things. But not about some things. So maybe what I had here, or could have, was a reasonable quid pro quo: we would teach each other what the other knew. Unless, of course, after this supper, she never saw me again. Tonight was business, after all; she could excuse being seen with me. But after tonight? How could I even begin to imagine love? But how could I not?

·10·
=

At eleven o'clock that night I did not look up to Sagittarius in the northeastern quadrant of the sky. At eleven o'clock I was in Dr. Culver's lab alone in interior space with Sara Logan.

Show me where you work, she had asked. Show me Culver's lab. It was a campus legend: the infamous lab of the famous Culver, the lab that no one ever saw in which who knew what shadows lurked. But there were no shadows.

"Oh, it's marvelous!" She danced about in the great white cubed space, spun and leaped. The capelike deeply woven shawl in tones of amethyst she wore against the chill, she swirled with, mixing within it her ballet runs and jetes with contemporary grind and thrash and slither. To one far wall and back and then across—the shawl, her hair, her body bending to her inner music, her voice aiming at me and leaving me as in a Doppler effect, "Oh Nick Burden, Nick Burden, how do you ever get any work done in here? How can you stand still in space like this? Come on!" She grabbed my hand and yanked me stumbling after her.

"I can't." I tried to anchor myself, but she was stronger now and hauled me. "I'm no . . . dancer. I've never danced . . . like this. At all."

"Of course not. Of course you haven't. But that was before." She stopped suddenly. I flung past her, tripping, but she pulled me back and up. "That was before me, Nick. You'll have to dance now." And then she dropped my hand and moved away from me

*so quickly that I could not at first convince myself that she had
said that. But I had faith. I knew too much to not believe in mira-
cles. With a mind like mine, I was likely to trust in it. I followed
her. Whatever she meant.*

"What's this?" She stood before one of the large pads upon which
I had been doing some calculations earlier. Around the room five
of the large pads were worked on, the other thirty-five were blank,
ten thirty-six-by-forty-eight-inch pads of paper on each wall.
Culver had them made up specially for this use. I explained about
my sensitivity to chalk dust.

"And this," I said, pointing to the calculations. "This is. . . . "
But what could I say? How could I explain? It required so much
mathematics, and even more than that. "This is part of an idea.
Not an idea, really. More a thought. You see, I've been thinking. . . . " But she moved to the next pad.

"That's another idea. Thought," I said. "That one's about. . . . "

"It's in black." She touched the lines. "Some sort of black grease
pencil. A kind of lithographic crayon." She pointed to the next pad.
"Is that another idea, too? And that one and that one?"

"The third is another idea and so is the fourth. The fifth is part
of the same idea."

"Four ideas but only one color. Black."

"Right."

"Here," she said. " Now I've got an idea." She went to her bag
which she had left on the writing table in the corner and came back
with it. She rustled around in it and then pulled out a fistful of
Magic Markers. "Red, blue, green, and a hot orange. Here." She
pulled out more markers and pushed them into my two cupped
hands. "Now you can do each idea in a different color and that way
you won't get confused."

"But I don't get confused," I said, sorry at once to have said it,
sorry to shift the point from her to me, to the Nicky Burden who
could remember everything, to Nicky Burden, the sixteen-year-
old super genius in her newspaper story.

"Never?"

"I mean with stuff like this. I sort of file it. I guess. I think. I don't
know why. That's just the way it works."

"It?"

76

"Me. My head."

"Which?"

"Is there a difference?"

"Oh Nick Burden. *Of course* there is a difference." She put her hand on my arm. I dropped the markers. We both bent down at the same time to pick them up. I banged my head on her knee.

"Ahhh." The bruise was tender still. I pulled away from the pain and fell back into a sitting position.

"You stick around with me, Burden. You won't have any brains left. Sorry."

"It wasn't your fault."

"I know. I meant I was sorry for your head." She smiled and then sat down across from me. She tucked her legs in and smoothed her skirt. I thought how nice it was, the skirt. Besides the female professors and staff, she was the only person at Cobbton who, after the first two days of orientation, wore a skirt.

"Nick. Tell me. What's it like? These ideas? Or any of your ideas? What's it like having them? What's it like being you?"

"I don't know. I mean I've got nothing to compare it to, do I? Being me just feels like being me. But from what I can tell, I think I'm pretty normal. From what I've seen, and from all I've read, I think I'm probably just like anyone else except that I've got this powerful brain. But the power is a function, it's not *me*. You see what I'm saying?"

"Sure. But the power must have its effect. Any one of us is who he is at least partly because of who he can be, what he can do. Do you want to hear one of my ideas—with no math? I think that people probably have an actual physical predisposition that attracts them to their future. I mean a musician probably actually hears better, something like that. A painter is more sensitive to light. Some people are wired to deal with abstractions like numbers. Big strong people like to use their strength. They become football players. People with delicate little fingers sew quilts." She started to laugh, to hoot. "Is that nutty, or what? But honestly, I believe it."

"It sounds reasonable enough to me," I said. "I sort of believe something like that myself." I almost started to tell her about my theory about how metaphor creates us, what I was saying in Appleton's class. I considered telling her about Aristotelean or Bergsonian vitalism, but what would be the point of that? If she had said that she believed the earth was flat, I would have agreed to that as well. To hear her laugh again, I would *prove* for her the earth was flat.

We sat quietly. The white, seamless cube in which we sat pressed my heart into an atom as dense as a quasar, as hot as it was with ancient heat, primordial radiation. Then I began to explain a little of what I was doing with the black crayon on the white pads. I began to perform.

"I've always sort of known that eventually whatever I did, I would begin at the outer limit of what was already done. It was unavoidable. I would just simply know everything about any subject I wanted to know about and then go on from there. Only I didn't know what that subject would be. My ultimate subject. But since I've been here at Cobbton and working with Culver, I've read so much physics and math you can't believe, and that's where the ideas are coming from. It seems to me that everyone in physics is working within the limits; everyone is trying to find the next subatomic particle or to come up with a unified field theory that unites the four forces. To find the superforce. O.K.?" Did she understand that? But I pushed that away and shook my head as if I did not need to know that. And then I said, my voice falling away from myself as if afraid of my own thoughts, "So I'm beginning to get ideas that go beyond the limits. I'm imagining a universe altogether different from the one we've got although it includes the one we've got."

"What can I say," she laughed for me. "Wow? Double Wow? *Triple wow?*"

"That's what I say," I said.

"So you should be delighted."

"Yes. No. There isn't a physicist in the world who would accept any of this."

"But you've only started."

"The concept," I said. "Even just the concept itself will be rejected. Once I can ever give some shape to the concept, no one will pay it attention."

"Then they're narrow-minded."

"No," I said. "They're O.K. They're working to expand the limits of knowledge by working within those limits. I'm thinking of redefining the limits themselves. They're working within the rules of proof. Maybe what I'm doing will get rid of proof itself, or at least how we think of proof."

"To take the chances the rest of us can't take. What Mike said," she said. "That's fabulous."

"Yeah. Fabulous as in fairy tale."

"Yes. Fairy tale as in poetry. The poetic, Appleton would call it," she said.

"Appleton? You know Appleton?"

"I have him for a course this semester. And I've had him before." She stood up.

"I've got to go. I've got a story to write."

I walked with her to the door hidden in the wall.

"You'd never find the door without me. Without me you'd have to say here forever."

"Or until the handsome prince came and saved me," she said.

"Listen. Sara. You won't write about what I just said, will you? In the story? Please? About the work I'm doing?"

"No. Of course not. I never would. I know on the record and off the record when I hear it, Nick. You can trust me." In the doorway she turned to me. "Will we see each other again, Nick?"

"What?"

"After the newspaper story, you'll be hard to get near. Every girl on campus will be after you."

"Me?" I said. "Me?" Then, "Hey Sara. Hey. No. You're my buddy, right? Come back here again and we'll even go dancing. I promise. You're my girl." Had I said that, all that? Had I said it right? Like in the movies, TV?

For twenty minutes after she was gone I sat in the glow. Her slight, fine scent was everywhere. I drew my knees up to my chest and hugged them tightly. Surely she could not imagine me as I imagined her. She was simply being friendly. A buddy. Exactly. She must be twenty-one. She probably dated *men*, not even the college boys her own age. In a few more months she would be gone, out into the world, out into her own world. What could I possibly mean to her. Sixteen. Whatever else, I would also mean that. Even though I looked older, firmer, and could pass for more, the point was I was not more. Four or five years her junior. *Five years!* Of all the arrows of time, two or seven or eight, only that arrow of time truly mattered to me, the arrow to which I was irrevocably strapped. But why should she be attracted to me at all, even as a buddy? As a subject for her interview, yes. But she seemed friendlier than just that, as if she wanted to know me better, to be with me more, for her reasons if not for mine. But what were my reasons? Sex? Preposterous. Love? What did that mean, if it meant anything more than this feeling itself, a condition without sufficient definition? Maybe it is simply that she has never met anyone like me. No one, after all, has ever met anyone like me. Maybe she is attracted to me the way the professors are attracted—by curiosity and amazement, and maybe she likes the discovery that there is a person inside of the me, the me inside of the function. And does she see my feeling for her? How could she not? With her experience. But what could I tell about that without my own experience? To have read so much about life and yet not to be able to direct it, which was, of course, what much of what I had read had taught me. Unlike physics, the heart had its reasons, that reason would never know.

Or maybe it could. Maybe the difference between physics and the heart was not so great as reason had made it seem. From where I sat on the floor in the center of the cube, looking up out of my heart to the calculations on my pads, I noted an odd permutation that had earlier escaped me. From it I could go on in a great bound to a deep question about sequence itself. I got up and, with the red marker, stabbed the figures in between the black lines. Immediately two variations appeared. I placed them on the sixth pad, one in orange, the other in cobalt blue. Complementary colors; next to each other, they vibrated, the blue and the orange pulsing intensely as if in a struggle, as if only one of then could be correct, or else together they could make light itself into a new thing.

By three o'clock in the morning I had filled the ten pads of one wall. In red and blue and yellow and green and orange and purple. It did not help me as she had suggested it might, the color coding, but it delighted me, and I did try to match in some way the idea with a color and to develop a continuity from pad to pad that way. If not for me, it might be a help for others through the arcane forest. Like a trail of bread crumbs. And indeed, my ideas did take on a kind of structure like the graphics on a computer that can turn a figure around and inside out or any way at all. Thought made palpable, the fretwork of my mind. I leaned back on the opposite wall fifty feet away and looked at what I had done. I looked at the line of my thought as it was emerging, actual lines and colors now and not just numbers and symbols. But if what I was starting to think on those pads was true, then nothing in the universe was true. The bubble of that excitement pressed against my bladder. I had to pee.

Crossing the campus at 3:30 in the morning, at the juncture of Hardin Avenue and Smith, I had a cadmium yellow thought. I stopped and in my special notebook carefully scribbled it out. But what could that mean? What it could mean was that I was finally very tired, too tired to think clearly. Or it could mean that the steady state theory had credibility after all. How much credibility? But the implications were what mattered. If the theory had any credibility at all, *any at all*, then space did not begin after all, nor time. Some thought. A cadmium yellow thought. A cadmium yellow thought in the dark blue night. I closed my book and hurried on.

There would be time. Time enough to sleep a little. To dream. Perchance to dream of Sara Logan in a swirl of amethyst in a white ground, in colors I would create for her out of the spectrum I was about to enlarge. Let the universe seek its own equilibrium. Let me seek mine.

⇥11⇥
=

"But what do you mean by 'beautiful?' " Appleton screamed at the girl. He stumbled down the aisle to her desk as if he would attack her with his fists, which even now he held clenced and shaking above her head. His wire-rimmed glasses had slipped even further down his nose. The girl sank down slightly, her mouth twisted in a little rictal smile. Even after four weeks of such histrionics, the whiff of madness that Appleton cultivated kept us on edge, ready to duck if he threw something at us—a chalky eraser or a pencil or a tough question and always an attack, not on our ignorance directly but on the arrogant laziness from which the ignorance came, like the babel out of Delphi, he had said, a blinding faith in the drug-induced fumes of intellectual vanity.

"The beautiful is what is desirable," a boy on the other side of the classroom said, out of Appleton's immediate reach, though not very far. There were eighteen of us. The best of the freshman class. The butter made out of the cream skimmed off the cream.

"But if I punched you in the eye and the eye turned black and blue, people would say what a 'beaut.' Does that mean that a black eye is desirable? No. You see, you've gotten into a circular definition. Beauty is desired, what is desired is beautiful. That won't do, but there's a hint within your comment. Sniff it out, sniff it out."

He had allowed his fierce hands to drop slowly to his side. I watched them descend, float down like the leaves falling all over the October campus. They were elegant hands, thin and long fingered; they suggested a musician's hands or what we imagine a surgeon's hands must be like, though Appleton did nothing with his but peck at a keyboard.

"What about that?" he said straightening and shuffling back to his desk, his knees poking through his ragged jeans, the selvedge of his tweed jacket frayed. "What about what I said to what whats-his-name over there?"

"So beauty is relative," someone replied.

"Beauty is in the eye of the beholder," another said. "It's all relative."

"Beauty is truth, truth is beauty. So that's all we need to know," another said. We all laughed.

"Then should I just dismiss the class now that we've settled that?" Appleton said.

"Yeaaaaah," we shouted in unison.

"Down, down. Back you beasts." He cracked an imaginary whip at us.

"Beauty is the ideal. The ideal is what is perfect. What we desire or admire is the perfection itself," I said, "not the object."

Everyone fell quiet, as if they knew this would happen. It always did. This was what the course was turning into, me in some kind of combat with Appleton, but not a fight, not a struggle, more like a fencing match. It was never mean or angry. It was terrific. And Appleton was willing to be bested. Or maybe he couldn't prevent it. And I could sense the admiration. That Burden, wow! Talk about having it upstairs. And did I ever get off the hook. They settled back. En garde.

"Then the black eye is capable of being beautiful as it approaches the ideal of black eyeness? Do you mean that all conditions, all objects and events can be measured against ideal configurations? But where are these configurations, Burden? And what about cancer, Burden? What about pain?"

"Pain is easy to answer," I said. "The ideal in every case in the universe is order. The more order, then the more perfect, and the closer we come to the ideal. But pain is the result of disorder. Cancer is disorder. Disorder is the opposite of beautiful. Disorder is ugly."

"But how does this apply to humans? Different societies in different ages have defined physical beauty differently. Rubenesque stoutness in women is very much out today. Thin is in. The Elizabethans found pale skin beautiful, now we admire a tan." Appleton folded his arms across his chest.

"Those are particulars," I said. "Specific attitudes. They don't affect the idea that the ideal represents perfection."

"Then you *are* saying it's all relative, that every age, or any one person, can define beauty. Equally."

"No. They call something beautiful but that doesn't define the ideal. The ideal isn't affected by personal definitions."

"Wait a minute. Wait a minute. You're cheating. That isn't Plato." Appleton turned to the class and gave them a quick synopsis of Platonic thought. He explained that basically this was what I was arguing for. But now I was going astray, on a tangent. I wasn't following the traditional Platonic line.

"It's not a tangent," I said, "it's a chord. I'm cutting straight across the curve of Plato's idea to the other side of it."

"Balony," Appleton shrieked. "You've not answered the basic question. Where is the ideal? And the corollary: how do we know when we get there? And don't start giving me physics, they upset my somach." He stopped to explain quickly the pun on physics— the science, the purgative.

"But physics is a good example of the search for perfection, for the ideal," I said. "And we'll know when we get to it when we come up with an explanation of the superforce. It will be an explanation that will explain everything."

"Everything?"

"Everything physical."

"Balony, balony, salami," Appleton said. "Physics doesn't explain. All it does is measure the motion of particles."

"It also explains the measurements it makes," I said.

Appleton went on into a burrowing pursuit, but I was no longer listening.

I was changing my mind.

The ideal was not perfection. Perfection was too small an idea. Einstein's words and my own words returned to me. If I were God the universe I would imagine would have to be infinite, beyond anything reducible to human thought.

A perfect and simple inconsistency.

A perfect and simple inconsistency where only transformation was always real. Sequence. Death following birth. Only motion was real. And was not predictable. Only the eighth arrow of time was real. Contemporary physics could not comprehend that, or, rather, would not allow itself to comprehend that. Contemporary physics had to argue that time could go forward or backward or even sidewards. The odds against time reversing itself were ten to the tenth to the eighty-fourth. It would take all the printing presses on earth printing books full of nothing but zeros for a hundred years to print that number. But there was never any experimental evidence to support the theory. Never once even any attempt to do so. Faced with absurdity, physics ran scared. *Physics only measured what it could measure.* The finite. But the universe was infinite. But even more to my immediate point was the click that went off in my head. In my notebook I scribbled out the math of my answer. I pictured it in blue and yellow and green as it twisted and turned through the work on the pads in Culver's lab. I had figured out where superstring went wrong. A self-contradiction so subtle that it had escaped anyone's detection, so subtle that the system could run without it, the way a train can go on powerfully until it passes through a gate that should have been shut and so into a disaster.

"Burden?" Appleton was saying. "Burden?"

I looked up at him, around at the class. "What?"

"What have you got to say to that?"

"To what?"

"To what I've just been saying, you *ninny*," Appleton said.

"What I've got to say is this," I said. "If delta [aY] is less than .2, then G is off by a magnitude of at least 7."

"Which means?" Appleton prompted me.

"Which means that light does not always move at three hundred thousand kilometers a second. It is not constant."

"And?" Appleton coached me. "And? Go on. Go on. And what does *that* mean?"

"It means—or it could mean—that everything, except time, is always relative and positive," I said.

"Exactly," Appleton said. "Exactly. Just what I've been saying all along."

"Yes," I said. "Yes. I guess you have."

We returned to a more pertinent topic but soon Appleton ended class.

What a unit we had turned into, I thought. But it seemed like a comedy team—Oh, Mr. Appleton. Yes Mr. Burden—an entertainment. But did Appleton get it, or was our art more that of provocation. Maybe I was just an instrument that he was quickly learning to play, a learning resource to be used in his class, just a teaching aid. Still, in ways I had not thought about, I believed I sensed in him a need for me greater than my need for him, and if that were so, then I would be sorry for it. I would rather have thought of him that all he knew or seemed to know was sufficient. Sufficient? Sufficient to what? But what did I mean by that? Did I think that knowledge equaled contentment, that knowledge and experience equaled contentment?

▸12▸
=

Two days later I received a note from Culver: "I see from the
pads that you've been hard at work. Wonderful. At this rate
you'll soon need your own lab. And what you're doing is very exciting. It's provocative and brilliant, but not rigorous enough.
You've left yourself vulnerable at a dozen points. Gauth and the
guage theory boys would eat you alive. Stop by and I'll give you
some suggestions on how to cover your rear end. Also, pad nine
(mauve? puce?)—your fiddling with superstring dimensions
seems murky. But then, so does superstring theory. By the way,
Lionel Kreutzer is going to visit the campus next week. Would
you like to meet him? Would you like to go to supper with him
and a few of us other mere mortals?" The note was signed Tod
Culver. It was the first time he had used his name this way. Tod,
as if to a colleague instead of just a student.

I also received a note from Appleton. All it said was "Look'd up
in perfect silence at the stars." I recognized it immediately. It was
the last line from Whitman's poem, "When I Heard the Learn'd
Astronomer." Why did Appleton assume that I would know
Whitman, know the poem? Because Appleton assumed that I
knew everything. And nothing.

When I heard the learn'd astronomer,
When the proofs, the figures, were ranged in columns
    before me,

When I was shown the charts and diagrams, to add, divide,
   and measure them.
   When I sitting heard the astronomer where he lectured with
   much   applause in the lecture-room,
How soon unaccountable I because tired and sick,
Till rising and gliding out I wander'd off by myself,
In the mystical moist night-air, and from time to time,
Look'd up in perfect silence at the stars.

And from Sara Logan I received a Magic Marker in a shade of
orange I had never seen. Tangerine Tango it was called. "I couldn't
resist it," she wrote. "Save it for the big breakthrough. Sara."
   I sat before my computer. On the monitor was the third page of
my report for the twentieth century philosophy course. I was
writing about David Hume and skepticism. My assignment was to
see if in any way classical philosophy prefigured anything in the
philosophy of Hume, or of Locke and Berkeley. It was a straight-
forward enough assignment, nearly pedestrian, but I found it
difficult because I saw connections that were not legitimate; that
is, I saw through into the subsumptive similarities of thought itself. X-ray vision. It was often like this: instead of looking at the
metaphors in a poem or the characteristic images of a particular
poet, say, or the writing in a particular age, I would examine the
nature and function of metaphor itself as it bound and linked all
poetry together. Or language itself. And that to everything else.
Always the connecting. But not the applications. Not at sixteen.
Only the shadows cast upon the wall of the cave of my head. But
I was beginning to see some glimmering up over my head, too.
   In one of my meetings with Appleton I had spoken about this
tendency. It's because you know so much, Appleton had said. Too
much. But it's natural enough. We all go at our life with our
strengths. Your strength is to know. But sometimes knowing gets
in the way of figuring out. Appleton told me the story about a
scientist at the University of Pennsylvania who became so ob-
sessed with the idea of the enormous distances that exist between
the electrons and protons and so forth that constitute matter that
he began to fear he would fall through substance. He started to
tie tennis rackets to his feet when he walked through the halls.
Like snow shoes. Only instead of snow it was the insubstantiality

of the molecules that he could no longer trust. You think that's me? I had asked. It's a danger to anyone who thinks that the parts of something are more important to knowing than knowing the thing as it appears to be, Appleton said. Psychoanalysts, sociologists. Astronomers. Be careful of statistical frauds, he had warned. Never forget that appearances are more real than the thing it itself, Appleton had proclaimed. Kant would have fits, I had said. So will you if you're not careful, Appleton had said.

I cleared the screen after saving what I had written.

An invitation to supper with Lionel Kreutzer. Unbelievable! I would have something indeed to tell my parents tonight when they called. I jumped up from my desk. "Son of a bitch!" I shouted. "Holy shit! Lionel Kruetzer." I went to my desk and wrote on my list, my gridded life, an instruction to read up on Kreutzer, get up to date. Oh what a chance was here. Culver was coming through for me. Then I thought, what should I call him – Tod, Thomas, Dr. Culver? What would I call Kreutzer? Dare I ask for an autograph?

Next to the list of my day and week lay Appleton's note: "Look'd up in perfect silence at the stars." But what was perfect silence? Was it a way of looking, something equal or superior to the way the astronomers (those counters! mere measurerers!) looked at the stars? Counters. Measurers. (I knew what Appleton was up to.) Or was it a way of responding to the stars *and* to the astronomers? Not a poetry *about* the stars but a poetry out of the cosmology itself? But I could imagine what Appleton would say to such questions: "Don't be a schmuck, Burden. Don't be a schmuck all our life, O.K.?" But what did he want from me?

I should have smiled at the implication or at least taken some pleasure in the flattery of his special regard, but in fact I was disappointed. It was too obvious a gibe, too glib. The astronomer knew the wonder of the stars as perfectly, maybe better, than did the censorious poet. Didn't Appleton know that? Didn't Appleton of all people know that knowledge, information, enhanced wonder and did not destroy it or maim it? He must. So then what was the point of his sending the poem to me? Was he trying to tell me something or warn me? Or was he asking for something? But again, as after our last class, I was beginning to irritate myself with this vague and insubstantial doubting of the man.

Back to the computer I fed into it a random function and six lines and set the machine to work. Let it write the poem that I could not. Suddenly Mike pushed into the room. I closed down the computer. "Till human voices wake us and we drown." I laughed with delight at the quick aptness of the allusion and at my perception. If great poetry is great because it reaches across time, then certainly it must also be able to reach across technology. I clapped my hands again at the wit of my insight. Now *that* was an application.

"What's funny?" Mike said.

"It's not the funny, it's the feeling good. I'm feeling very good today."

"Yeah. Well, roomy, *partner*. Today I'm going to make you feel even better. Look at this." Across his bed he splayed out a deck's worth of four-by-six index cards. Next to them he tossed down a smaller pack of cards with a rubber band around them.

"What are those?"

"These cards list all the fraternities, sororities, social clubs, and bars within fifty miles of Cobbton. A card for each one. On each card is a schedule of events—parties, that sort of thing. In this pack is the name and specs of every band within fifty miles of Cobbton. It's taken me three days. So do you get it? We match up one with the other. We're agents, but on a very big scale. Ten percent right off the top." I looked at the cards.

"Do you know how much information there is here to correlate?" I said. "Do you know what kind of time you're talking about? And a phone? What about that? What about college? Do you ever study, Mike? Are you going to bust out again?"

"College is too easy to do. You've got to be really stupid to flunk out if you really want to stay in. The first time I didn't care. I didn't want in. Now I want to stay. This is a gold mine, Nicky. So it depends on what courses you take and who you get to do the work. It's like any other business. You work, so you get something for your work."

"Right. Something. It's called an education."

"No," Mike said, "it's called a profit."

"You don't do your own work? Is that what you're telling me?"

"I took courses that I didn't have to do too much work, and not the kind of courses that I'd have to work alone. I took multiple choice courses—Psych 101, the odds are working for me; a lab science designed for business majors, we do the lab assignments in groups of six; big enrollment courses with section men doing the grading—The History of Western Civilization; bullshit courses—The Detective Novel."

"But the papers you've got to write? When do you do that? I've never seen you writing a paper for any of your courses."

"I buy them."

"You what? You buy them?"

"I don't make the market, Nicky. The college makes the market. I'm just a consumer. There are consumers and suppliers. For ten bucks I can get an old paper. For thirty bucks I can get an entirely new five to ten page paper. I even get a guarantee. If the paper gets less than a B, I get my money back."

"You've done this?"

"Three times already. Three times I got As. They were good papers. I read them close. So I balance the high grades for the papers against the low grades on the essay exams. The short answer tests are a wash. So I figure I'll end up with a C. And I always go to class. That's important. Profs love that. And I ask questions. It doesn't matter what. They love that, too. Asking questions. You can pass just by showing interest."

"Oh Mike. I mean. . . . "

"What? I learn. I learn more from the papers than I learn from the prof, Nicky. We all learn in different ways. And different things. And different amounts of things. But do you want to know what is the most important thing to learn, do you want to know that?"

"What?"

"The most important thing to learn, my friend, is to learn what the fuck is going on. What the fuck the score is."

"Socrates couldn't have said it better," I said.

We settled down to the idea Mike had smeared across the bed, our room, my life. T&B Enterprises had rented a one-room office with a desk and telephone with a machine to record messages down in the village. It had also hired part-time an undergraduate at minimum wages, but with the promise of a percentage if things went well, to handle the calls. Mike himself would visit each of the organizations to make the initial contact, to present the musical groups he represented, to get more of an idea what the needs would be. To do the agenting.

"This could grow into something huge," he said.

"You'll have to go out of town. Fifty miles around. You'd need a car," I pointed out.

"I got a car. Did you think I can't think at all? What's with you? You alone are smart?"

"You've got a car?"

"Thumper's car. I made him a good deal. He only uses it to get to practice mostly. Some other times, too. So I'll use it when he doesn't. And once I get the basic work done, I won't have to be on the road that much."

"And me? What do you need from me?" I braced. Not to resist but to matter. I could not resist Mike Tremain because I did not want to resist. It was like being on a pirate ship, a mate to a corsair sweeping the seas. Or maybe only a chicken hawk plucking the chickens. And early on I recognized my guilty pleasure in Mike's ethical audacity. And this. Whatever Mike cut out of life, he used a sharp knife and a steady hand to do it. He didn't club and rip and mutilate. And this. I could hang on for the exhilirating ride through moral space and yet be safe. In on the con but not the crime.

And this. Mike Tremain was the first and closest friend I had ever had.

"What do I need from you? Well what have you got? I'm the T and you're the B."

"Nothing. I've got nothing."

"Hey come on, Nicky. You've got money and you've got brains."

"Money? What money?"

From his own desk Mike took a financial records book and turned pages. "There," he said pointing down. "From the posters, $250. Me," he turned a page, "after expenses I cleared $985. It's all here. Between us we've made $1230. Minus the two bills for Thumper's car plus his first payment. Some other expenses." He flipped pages and mumbled, "That's our capital, $972.34." From his desk he took out a check book. "Right on the button, see?" he showed the balance to me, $972.34. He was keeping strict and honorable account. I was surprised but delighted.

"That's good," I said.

"Not so good. Not good enough. The office and phone and expenses, we need altogether about two thousand dollars. The posters are still selling nicely but it's slowing down. Anyway, what we make on the posters we need to pay for them. Thirty days we get since the last shipment. And right before Christmas the poster sales should pick up but then nothing over the break until the semester starts again. We've got the classic small business problem, Nicky. Undercapitalized. We are sound. We've got potential. We've got a service to sell. And a market for it. What we need is capital."

"Well you can take what my share is," I said. "I mean I always thought of it as yours anyway."

"No. We're partners. We'll use the money *we've* made and we'll use our brains. I've used mine. Now you've got to use yours."

"What do you mean?"

"We need the computer to crunch all this stuff. Make us a program. I'll get our employee to do the typing."

"O.K. That's easy."

"There's more," Mike said.

"More?"

"Next week your interview comes out in the paper, O.K.? Next week at this time you will be the most famous man on campus. It's as simple as that."

"What? Simple as what?" I had been seated. Now I stood up quickly. I looked at my hands, at my arms. I looked down at my feet. My pants seemed short. My arms stuck out farther from the ends of my shirt. Was I growing? Why was I thinking this now? Taking this leap? I raced through the process in a nanosecond, the amino acids building into structures that the DNA ordered it into, the nucleic explosions, the synaptic spasms. Why was I thinking this? No, not thinking: processing.

"Tutoring. You'll tutor," Mike said. "Anybody having trouble with a course comes to you. But because it's you, they pay more. We've got to figure out a rate. Maybe five bucks a lesson. With your brains you could do, easy, four lessons an hour. If you work only two hours a day that's two hundred a week."

"You're nuts. I can't. I won't."

"Only a month. In a month we'll be covering our expenses out of the commissions."

"No."

"Why no?"

"Students can get academic tutoring for free. Why would they pay?"

"Because you're the best. People love that. It gives them confidence. They'll learn more from you because they think they can learn more from you. And you'll probably be able to see what their problem is better than the graduate students who do the academic advising. Half of them don't understand what they're doing anyway. With your brains you could do any of it. There's nothing you don't know more about than these people. You're doing them a favor for Christsake. It's nearly an obligation. In this world, Nicky, did you ever think of giving back something, sharing this gift? So this is a chance."

"At five dollars a lesson?"

"No one ever said that charity had to be free."

I smiled. It was a day for happy phrases.

"What?" Mike said. "You're smiling."

"What you said. It's something my mother would have said. The *way* she would have said it."

"So of course. With a son like you she must be smart too. So you'll do it? T&B Enterprises rests on you now."

"All my life, Mike, my only real problem in life has been being me. Being Nicky Burden. The brain. The freak. But now, so far, college has been terrific for me because I've had a chance to be me. Next week that's going to end. If I become a tutor people will come to me not because I'm a better tutor. They'll come because I'm Nicky Burden."

"But you are Nicky Burden," Mike said. "You *are* Nicky Burden. Don't you see? There's no escaping that."

▸13◂
=

When I lived at home I always knew when my day began and ended. It started with the sounds of my father at 6:30 preparing for work. It was not that there was a noise that woke me but rather an interior clock that was prepared to respond. On Sundays when my father slept later, so did I. If during the week my father rose earlier or overslept, so did I.

I would wake to the shower. My father always showered in the morning, winter as well as summer. I would hear the muffled rush of the water and rise up out of the deep blue submarine equation into which I deeply slept. My eyes would pop open. I was immediately awake. But I stayed in bed. Even when I was much younger, I would not get out of my bed and go down after my father to share a breakfast. Much as I wanted to.

Now in my dorm room I wondered at that, here where my day never began or ended clearly, where the heat of the young men all around me was only banked and through the night embers flared until dawn. Why had I not gone down to my father in the early morning?

For one thing, my mother would have objected. She would have insisted that I sleep longer. But that could not have been my reason for staying in bed. If I had gone down, padded after my father in my Doctor D's, followed the scent of his aftershave lotion into the fumes of the coffee in the kitchen, it would have been to present my love, for which I had no terms, neither words for my own condition and estate nor those that I could hand over. Why? Why could I say I love you to my mother but not to my father? It was because my love for him was in a different dimension, not larger exactly, but of a different nature. As in superstring theory, where there were different spaces in the universe all jammed into each other and not just one space. Perhaps what I should search for was metaphor. Not a metaphor for this love, but for metaphor itself, metaphor as a direct condition of experiencing and not just as a way of expressing the experience. Metaphor. It seemed to me that everything I was doing now had more to do with that than anything else. That even the mathematics of my physics was like the images of poetry.

I lay abed watching a small, scrunched-up homunculus taking shape. I could recognize myself, and yet the organism did not even look altogether human. An anomaly. Which was itself a kind of metaphor.

I had spent nearly two entire days and evenings in the libary and in Culver's lab. Except for my meals and the delivery of ten posters on the bus, I had stayed at my task: the examining of the work of Lionel Kreutzer. I had even skipped my workout with the cross-country team, but I could do that. John Lambert had come to an agreement with the coach, who would accept no absence from practice except for illness. But Lambert had worked it out, a compromise: I could be on the team, the freshman team (I was not a starter anyway), but not actually *be* on the team. Like Schrodinger's cat. An anomaly. Lambert was delighted that I had gone out for the squad and that I had stuck with it; it was at least one clear triumphant sign of my normal development, and Lambert was not going to lose it. He had been prepared to haul the coach into President Turner if it came to that, but it had not. The coach was reasonable. Besides, I looked good for the future. In a year or two I would fill out, maybe even grow another couple of inches. I had the right build for the sport. Long muscles, a lot of chest. And I had a good attitude: disciplined, a hard worker, and a terrific sense of time, a clock in my head. In a year or two maybe I could be the rabbit, the runner who kept a race fast and tough. Honest. So was it my fault if I had this problem with my school work, (which is what Lambert told him), if I needed the extra time? Not altogether a lie.

But I did not want ever to miss the practice. It had become important to me, the feeling of my body turning transparent as I ran on and on, as if the flesh was purified by the sweating and the clawing of the lungs for air. And I liked the run through the fields and hills around Cobbton, through the green September corn and now into the late October old gold fields with the red-tailed hawks and the kestrels in their deadly patrol over the stubble for their winter fat of mice and voles and chipmunks. The whip of November coming soon to beat the land flat.

Part of the trail went through an apple orchard of a late variety, Northern Spies, a hardy apple that did not fall easily in the autumn storms. For weeks now I ran through them, first the trees full of apples and leaves and then only the apples hanging on the trees like decorations.

I had invented a problem. Instead of the apple falling from the tree into gravity, suppose the apples were constant and it was the trees and earth that rose up to them. As if, as Ptolomy had thought, the earth was still and the sun revolved around it. If a hundred trees each bear a hundred apples and each tree is ten meters from another and each apple is a thousand centimeters from another, then the gravitational field it would form, the space it would create would be . . . but by then the running had driven it all out of my head and all I could want to think of was the running, the sky and fields, the sight of my body like crystal, my blood pumping through my arteries and veins like Venetian glass.

I had come to count on that in my day and seldom allowed myself to miss it, but I knew that where I worked, on the dazzling edge of my ideas, that even I had to stay with the calculations at certain points. Not unlike poems, I imagined, where the real inspirations, the inspired choices, came out of the work itself and from nowhere else. And only once.

Now I was working up Lionel Kreutzer, who was, if there could be one, the heavyweight champion of the entire world of physics—particles or cosmology. He had won *two* Nobel prizes, and his work had generated at least three others directly, but who could measure the indirect influence? He had been into everything at one time or another in his long career, and showed no slowing down except that he had to spend more and more time meeting with Congressional committees and the major foundations as he led the charge for more research monies. Presently his great campaign was for the supercollider, the "greatest atom smasher ever," as the popular press had styled it. Still, he managed to stay up with everything that was going on. No quark faltered strangely in Switzerland, no neutrino appeared in unexpected numbers in Japan, no new cluster of quasars but that Lionel Kreutzer would not know about it. Einstein's heir, except that he had, perhaps, found the Holy Grail of physics that Einstein had sought for most of his life: the absolute field theory that united the four forces of the universe.

Perhaps.

By the middle of Wednesday afternoon, I thought I had discoverd an anomaly in the center of one of the important supports of Kreutzer's major idea. Kreutzer had established G prime $[^=56AV=D<]$ as a magnitude of all antimatter, but that was wrong. But this was not a simple mistake with the math; it was a conceptual error. I had not begun this study of Kreutzer to find error, but after a day and a half I had. No one else had seen this because to understand it sufficiently one would have had to understand superstring theory sufficiently, and it was unlikely that the ruling Kreutzer school of conventional physics did know superstring theory sufficiently. To conventional contemporary physics superstring was a wild mathematical speculation, a brilliant expression of a truly brilliant man, Edward Witten. But it had never been tested experimentally and, even more to the point, there was no way *that* superstring theory could be tested experimentally. The most fundamental anomaly of all.

The Kreutzer people did not know enough superstring theory, and the superstring people no longer looked at the universe in neoclassical terms. Maybe because it would take two lifetimes to do both. But I could do both.

What I stiffened to was the implication for all of physics. What I found was that in the seventh dimension of superstring there was also a profound anomaly, and if pushed far enough, Witten would have to commit the cardinal sin of superstring theory: he would have to break the absolute topological unity of a string in the seventh dimension rather than expand it. And that you cannot do. Absolutely. You cannot break a string and continue to have what is left function like a string. That is the fundamental axiom.

I remembered my cadmium yellow thought on that night when I had shown Sara the lab. I remembered stopping that night on my way back to the dorm at the Hardin Circle and writing down what I had suspected: that the speed of light in the universe had not always moved at three hundred thousand kilometers a second. Back from the library now, with ten books and monographs and thirty journals spread out across the floor, I went to where I had been on pad eight. I tore off the page and began again, first redrawing what was on the page, but smaller now, to give me room. Then I put in what I needed from Kreutzer. I moved back and forth between the paper on the wall and the material on the floor until at last I did not need the thoughts and formulations of others. Now, free to move at my own speed, I moved at my own speed, moving like light in my own universe. In two hours I stepped back.

Bang. A big bang indeed. Talk about a super collision. Matter and antimatter annihilating each other. Left spin and right spin symmetry. What I came to was this: in their own terms, at this juncture where all of physics would eventually have to go either north or south, neither Wittenn nor Kreutzer could be right if one of them was right. That is, each was, alone, right. But not complete. I had made the two great areas touch each other; I had made superstring touch contemporary physics at the point where each proclaimed the unification of the forces constructing the universe. But I had shown how *both* explanations would have to exist in the same universe for either of them to exist at all. And yet both could not. Finally, they needed each other (though neither had seen that), but they could not have each other. And there was more: my own possibility. My early idea could be right after all. No particle of energy/matter could fit across a Planck duration. It would have to have started on the other side of the beginning of time. So time would not have begun. And only *sequence* would be real. The eighth arrow of time. Time moving constantly and in only one irreversible direction. Just what I had told Culver, though then that had been more an instinctive guess. Now I had more to show. Now I had the anomalies themselves.

For the first time in my life I could adequately imagine not only my own power but the supremacy of it. I went over my calculations carefully. Twice. I was correct. I could play in this league. Einstein, Planck, Heisenberg, Witten, Kreutzer. Nicky Burden.

I removed the last two sheets I had been working on and folded them over again and again until they were a small, thick bundle. I tacked up on the pad the sheet I had removed. I did not want Culver or anyone to know where I had gone, how far. Not yet. Not until I could go further with my calculations, and further still than precedent. Not until I could strike across the universe with Tangerine Tango.

I unlocked the drawer that was mine in the writing desk and put the wad of folded paper into it and locked it. Then I gathered together all the books and journals and periodicals and put them into a special bin outside of the lab. One of Culver's arrangements. A student who worked in the library would come and pick them up.

I sat down in the middle of the white room to review my work. I faced my first worksheet pad. Then I read slowly across the wall and into the second wall. I had once asked Culver where he did his work, whether he was being forced out of his own lab. Culver assured me that I was free to go as far as I wanted, that he, Culver, was that semester busy finishing a book, didn't need the wall space. I looked on, the reds and yellows and purples and greens, the numbers, symbols flowing on into a tighter and tighter idea. In the middle of the second wall of paper pads, I closed my eyes and reconstructed the worksheets I had locked in the desk. And then further ideas began to drift into me, take shape. I was not nearly finished. All I had done was only prelude. I could not stop what was happening, I did not want to. For fifteen minutes I waited in the tension growing between what was on the wall and what was in the drawer, and then I took a deep breath and stepped off into a space no one had ever, ever, ever imagined before.

I opened my eyes. What I had come to was more than a challenge to the two prevailing attitudes regarding the workings of the universe. Indeed, many of the applications of the Kreutzer system would always be valid within practical limits the way that Newton's ideas and methods were still valid in the immediate applications of, say, sending a rocket to the moon or throwing a slider. That was not my challenge. What I had come to was more an epistemological challenge. What had fallen out of the collision of Witten and Kreutzer was the anomaly of proof itself, the possibility of the existence of the limits that proof sought to define. The collision of Witten and Kreutzer that I had brought about left the idea of empirical proof floating away like smithereens of cosmic dust, particles smaller than Hume could ever have imagined. *Ka-pow! Zap! Splat!*

So now I knew what I could do with my life, what maybe *only* *I* could do: create a mathematics that expands, *constantly changes itself*, even as it can be used to describe physical phenomena, and thereby be able to imagine a physical universe similarly but which yet cannot be experimentally proven. The ultimate anomaly. It would be a mathematics that could take quantum theory two, eight, twenty steps further, a hundred leagues further, but it would be into a universe that did not yet exist in that form. So Blake was right: what is now real was once only imagined, and the extension – what I am now imagining will someday be real.

I went back to the writing desk and removed the worksheets and recopied them giving myself yet more room and sketched out the possibilities that began to create themselves. My hand could not move quickly enough. The universe is always here and here and here, but it is never – was never – even for an instant static. Time was the same stream which you could not step into even *once*. The universe was in constant flux before 10(-43), which I would show meant that everything in it was also in motion and that included the means by which the universe was explored and described.

Every change in the universe continues to change everything else in the universe, including, of course, all of space and time, but even, and especially, the rules and laws by which we observe and measure the change – and thus is eliminated the possibility of a one permanent past but not the infinitude of the past itself. Sequence is what is not refutable. I wrote that down, words in the midst of numbers.

I contemplated the major dominoes of contemporary physics and with a thin-line felt tip pen, explored them, pushed them a little until one by one by one they all came tumbling down. Oh I was into magnitudes now nearly beyond the reach of mind itself, unless it was my mind. And now if I could find the principle of the endless changing, if I could at least begin to show how change itself changes the way change can occur, how the values in any measurement of any phenomena must at least include this variable. If I could. If I could, then all the books would have to be rewritten, the face of heaven redrawn.

Thumper McGuire passed, and I felt him go by like a gravitational wave. I could stay in bed for another hour. Sleep again. This was the Thursday. A fulcrum day. After today, my life would never be the same. I closed my eyes. The papers with my last statement locked in my desk drawer opened again before me. I thought of Einstein. If he were God, what kind of universe would he have created? Now I thought I knew what kind of universe I might create. Perhaps.

→ 14 →
=

But there was another universe I had begun to create about which I had no doubts or uncertainties, although surely no conclusions.

On the Sunday past in the slack hours in the afternoon when people had not yet returned from a visit home or to a girl on another campus, and when the noise in the dorm had been drawn tight and centered in the TV room before the football game, Mike and I had settled into the lazy hours, into Mike's construction, a universe, a firmament not of time or space or superstrings but one as hard and solid as the gold into which time and space could be turned.

"So this is where we are," Mike said, pushing the ledger at me. "We're O.K. Nothing to cheer about, but nothing to worry about. But we're in position. We're poised. Once we generate some more capital, we're going to take off. We've got a couple of services to sell, the tutoring and the agenting. Already I've gotten four pretty sure commitments from the fraternities for bands. This is a great idea. We're going to go places with this. And I'm thinking of a way to expand the tutoring, like turning it into a kind of organization."

"Two hours, Mike. Two hours a day is what you said, and that's it." I rose up on the bed onto my elbows.

"Right, but maybe instead of tutoring the individual, you tutor tutors. Get it? We hire some bright people. You teach them, they teach the student. Maybe these bright people don't even need to be taught what to teach, but we've got the organization, we attract the customers." Mike sprawled out in the one soft chair in the room, his leg thrown over the armrest. Against the sharp edge of his ideas, he could be as relaxed as the fakirs in India who lie undamaged upon a bed of spikes.

"But the students can get it free. I told you. You know that. They could probably get tutored for free over at the college counseling service from the same guy they'd be paying for. That's crazy, isn't it?" I flopped back. Over my head, papering my ceiling, my interior sky, a long-legged beautiful woman rose up out of a crimson desert in a crimson dawn. Phallic straight. The newest offering of our firm.

"Listen, Nicky. Did you ever hear of H&R Block, the tax people? So do you think Harry and Roy actually look at tax returns? Of course not. So all their customers can get help for free from the government, can't they? There are pamphlets they can send for. There are telephone numbers they can call to ask questions. The United States government even sets up tables in shopping malls. And a lot of communities have similar help at night in the high school or the church basement. But (a) you've got to wait; and (b) you've got no real faith in who's telling you what. H&R Block is selling faith. Your advisor even signs the form. If you get hit by the IRS, H&R Block goes with you to explain. Faith, Nicky. That's what people want. That's what a good salesman is selling. You go into a store and you ask the salesman for his opinion, and if he's smart, if he's really good, what he sells you is *assurance*. What he sells you is the idea that *you* have made a very wise choice.

"Did you ever hear the questions people ask when they go to buy something? 'How will this car start in freezing weather? I've heard some bad things about fuel injection.' 'And that,' the salesman says, 'is exactly the right question and this is the car with exactly the right answer,' and then he goes into some bullshit rap about how Ford has come up with a heater that vaporizes any water or ice in the fuel jets and blah blah blah as if he knew what he was talking about and as if the customer knew what was going on but is unwilling to admit he knows dick about. Especially after the salesman says, 'Hey, are you kidding me or something? You're a mechanic, aren't you? The kinds of questions you ask, you really must know cars. So you probably know better than I do just how good this car is.' "

104

Mike was up on his feet, the afternoon no longer lazy. He was making the pitch, closing in on the sale. Reaching for the pen in his pocket.

"You know Mike, that sounds like the kind of joke people always make about car salesmen. That's a parody. I don't believe it happens that way, at least not any more," I said.

"Yeah? Is that right Nicky? You've sold a lot of cars? You've bought any?"

"No. But that's not the point. There are other ways to look at things. Experience isn't everything."

"Right, but experience isn't nothing either."

"So how many cars have you sold, Mike? Except to Thumper?"

"My father sells cars, Nicky. Among other things."

"Oh. Listen, I'm sorry. Nothing personal, Mike." I sat up quickly. Offense was not my manner. Never. "I didn't mean. . . ." But Mike stopped me.

"No problem. You think I'm sensitive about something like that? No way. My father is the greatest salesman in the world. His problem is he's got nothing to sell. He's never had anything to sell, nothing terrific. He's like a gypsy. He picks up something here, a line of something there. Like a month ago he bought five hundred cases of a Romanian wine, a dollar a bottle. The last of a shipment an importer wants to clear out of his warehouse. So my father hustles it and makes fifty cents a bottle, $250. He's got to put up six thousand to make $250. That's about 4 percent by the time he's through with everything. So he gets lucky. He buys the wine in the morning and he's sold it by the afternoon. He makes 4 percent on his money in a couple of hours. Terrific. But he's *got* to be lucky, because he's got no warehouse, right? So he's got to sell the wine so it can be moved directly from the importer's warehouse to the distributor's warehouse. Or else he's got to rent a warehouse, which, if he does, he ends up with no profit or maybe even a loss. Ha," Mike clapped his hands. "You should see the shit we have sometimes had piled up in our house. Blankets, dog collars, boxes of knives. Orange juice squeezers. Insect repellant. Jesus, Nicky. I remember just two years ago he had eleven cars. My job every day was to go and move the cars around the neighborhood, park them somewhere different so people wouldn't get pissed and call the cops. Eleven cars! Do you know what a thousand pair of shoes look like, Nicky? Six refrigerators?

"But he's got luck. Some days, some weeks, more luck or less luck, but he's never got *no* luck. What he doesn't have is a warehouse. What he doesn't have is a major franchise."

"Couldn't he get a warehouse? Or a franchise?"

"To tell the truth, Nicky, I don't think he wants to. I think he likes the action. I think that's where the luck comes from. You make come true what you want to happen. He's a terrific guy. I want to be just like him. I swear to Christ I do. He's terrific. Only I want to sell big things, O.K.? Like the Brooklyn Bridge. Or maybe Manhattan Island."

I had never seen Mike so animated. He had come so quickly out of repose. Now he turned in a circle in the room in the small space between the beds and the desks, turned as if he were going to grab something and make me buy it, anything—the lamp, a pencil, a package of used index cards, paper clips. Action incarnate. The luck. And I did believe. You make come true what you want to happen. Not unlike contemporary physics.

"Five weeks and we've never really talked about our families," I said.

"Five weeks," Mike said. "That long? It seems like less, but you know, it seems like a lot longer too. You know what I mean? Why is that?"

I could have told Mike about time, what it was and/or what it was not, but that was not the time that he meant. He meant human time, the great time, the only time, in which we lived. The shell within which we lived, against which all the arrows in the quiver of physics were helpless.

"Because we're having so much fun." I shouted it. My voice surprised me, the leaping out. "You know. Like when you're playing a game and you look up and you wonder where the time went? This has been a lot of fun for me, Mike, these last five weeks. You're the best friend I've ever had. The only friend."

"We do get along pretty good, Nicky. Partners, too. It's a shame you're going to go where you're going to go. We could make a fortune together. Team up after college. With your brains. Look what we're doing already, with nothing. We're making money out of nothing, nearly."

"Where am I going to go, Mike?"

"Into the history books, Nicky. Without a doubt. Into the history books. How can you miss? This stuff you're doing in Culver's lab. You spend half your life there already. It's what you're good at. You like it."

"Maybe it's too easy. Maybe it's that I already know that whatever there is to find I'll find."

"So is that bad? We should all be so fortunate. Hey, poor little smart boy. Have *you* got problems." Mike smacked himself aside his head and rolled his eyes.

But if this was true, then what would it mean to live a life with doubt? Courageous, I thought. My father came into my mind.

We had sailed together, just the two of us, two years before, two weeks in the Narraganset Bay region, to Newport and up into Bristol and Warren and around the islands. At the end of my father's vacation, we were going to sail from Point Judith at the tip of Rhode Island, forty miles down the coast past Watch Hill and around Napatree Point and across Barn Island, up the Pawcatuck River to Westerly where we would haul the boat and drive the long way home.

Our day to sail dawned mean even though it was August. We had watched the approaching front dawdle and dwindle and then strengthen as it lurched up the eastern coast. Even the night before NOAA could only tell us that it would not be a good day and that the wind could easily build to twenty knots. But they had issued no small boat advisory. Not yet.

The wind came at four o'clock in the dawn and stayed. YARPS swung into it. The boat was well anchored, but it swung into the wind and dropped back tightly on the anchor rope. I went forward and payed out another thirty feet of line to increase the scope. We were well up into the inner harbor of Galilee. We could have stayed out a hurricane there. We did not have to leave. An extra day or two or even three would not cost my father his business. We could even take the dinghy to shore to call home so Sally would not worry. And spend the day kicking around the fishing trawlers or hiking down the weather-scoured beach.

"What do you think?" I asked my father. "Stay or go?"

"What do you want to do?" My father said.

"Well, I want to stay *and* I want to go."

"Then we go," my father said.

"Why?"

"Because to stay is safe, which is O.K. Being safe is O.K. But to be safe when you don't have to be safe, that's not O.K." And so we sailed.

Twenty miles down, off the breachway at Charleston, twenty miles to go, the wind freshened. We had to put in a second reef in the mainsail and go down to a storm jib to keep from being over-powered. But now, with shortened sail, we could not move fast enough to overcome the leeward push of the weather as it bore us down toward the Rhode Island beaches. It was the classic trap. Off of Ninagret we had about two miles of sea room, by Charleston In-let one mile, within sight of Napatree point we had a thousand yards. And this option. We could still turn and run all the way back before the wind into Galilee, duck into the harbor of refuge behind the barrier jetty and then work back through it to the original an-chorage.

"What do you think?" my father said.

I took a bearing on Stonnington and off of Napatree Point and called out the heading. The heading required an adjustment to the trim of the sail. "We have to fall off a little more, get on more of a reach," I said.

"That will take us closer to shore," he said.

"We'll go faster. We need the power now. We've got a hundred yards to play with. I've figured it." I had taken the bearings and measured the wind, the estimate of the speed the boat was making over the bottom, the leeward drift, the angle of the waves to the boat, the position of the sails, the slight crack in the blue squall of blown sea and the heavy, singing wind, even my father's steady helm. The calculation of my life. Our lives. And my decision. Two hundred sixty degrees west north west.

And now, over two years later, what I remembered most was the sweet taste of the uncertainty, an actual taste, sweet and sour. A mortal taste. I remembered that and my father with me. How splended he had been. How brave. And wise. Tears came to my eyes.

"What's the matter?" Mike said. "Something wrong? Hey. Come on, Nicky."

"Nothing wrong. Honest. Nothing at all. I was remembering something. Something wonderful. My father. . . ." but I couldn't say more. Not then. But it was my resolve to someday say more. Someday.

"Let's get out of here, Nicky. Let's take a walk. I want to show you this field in back of the Phi Delta house. I've got an idea for the spring. And we can get an early supper. Come on."

"Sure," I said. I got up from the bed. My clothes were tight. I was growing, I was sure. Up. Out. Maybe it was the running. Or maybe only that my time to grow had come.

We kicked across the piles of broken leaves on the lawn of Jameson. The day was darkening quickly now.

"Daylight savings," Mike said. "That's what happens. You turn the clocks back and you lose a billion hours of light. A fortune."

"You don't like it? You want daylight savings all the time?"

"It's dumbness is what I don't like. When it comes to things like that. If we all got up with the light and went to bed with the dark, or at least were home by then, it would save all that electricity, all that money. That's the way it used to be, you know. Before there was electricity. Candles were expensive. A candle in 1600 in England cost about a dime, which back then was a lot of money for a farmer."

"You know that?" I said. "I'm impressed."

"It's what I'm interested in."

"The price of candles in Elizabethan England?"

"Nah, nah. I'm interested in what's going on."

"In 1600?"

"No. In light. Where it comes from. What it costs. You think it's different? Light? In 1600 or now? Same problem, Nicky. People can't see in the dark." He stopped walking abruptly. I had to turn and come back to him. "Did you ever think that the work day got set up the way it is by the electric companies, by GE and Sylvania, the bulb manufacturers? Is that why they turn the clocks back just when it's getting darker?

"Think about it Nicky. If we used the light at the start of the day here in the dark at the end of the day, we'd save a lot of money, but the electric companies and bulb people would lose a bundle."

"I've never thought about it." Now I thought about it. In my head I projected an analemma. I compared sun time with sideral time and factored in the time the sun rose before and after noon during the period on the analema either side of where the months crossed over themselves. In a few seconds I had a result. The differences in available light to usable time at or near the equator or above the fiftieth parallel were either too narrow or too extreme to be used, but between the middle parallels in the northern hemisphere, where 70 percent of the world's population lived, maybe Mike's idea was right.

So even on earth, light was not a constant. I hollered and slid across a pond of damp leaves as if over ice. "Hey, Mike. You could be right."

But Mike had already moved on, ahead. I ran up to him and we loped off. And then we started to sprint across the Jameson field and around it until, heaving for breath, we stopped, steaming and puffing like old locomotives.

"You know what we need, Nicky?" Mike said, bending over, his hands on his knees. "What we need is a commodity. Something to sell, a product. Something elegant. Something equal to our distribution system. Something we can handle easy. Buy, sell quick. Turn our money over and over. Something that's both goods and a service at the same time."

"Like what?" I said.

"Like I don't know yet."

"Like dope, Mike?" I said, the thought, the possibility, and my words coming all at once. The liklihood. "Oh Jesus, Mike. No."

"Dope?" Mike said. "Dope? Hey, what a great idea. What a brilliant idea. Now why didn't I think of that? But that's the difference between us, isn't it Nicky. Dope. Fantastic."

"Mike."

"Don't 'Mike' me, Nicky. Where you get your ideas, huh?"

"It's a feeling. Suddenly I had this feeling. It makes too much sense to me for it not to make sense."

"Come on, Nicky, for Christsake. What do you think I am?"

"A great salesman, Mike. You're a great salesman looking for something worthy of your talents. You're like me."

"I'm like you?" Mike said.

"Yeah," I said. "You're trying to find your ultimate sell. A good and a service. From where I stand it looks like it could be dope. So that worries me." We had started to walk again, but then Mike stopped.

110

"T&B Enterprises will never do dope, Nicky. Never. O.K.? You've got nothing to worry about. You've got my word. Never." He put out his hand and we sealed each other in our love and faith. Whatever representations Mike Tremain might put upon the world, I knew that he would not lie to me.

▸15▸

=

I had never written down anything I wanted to remember. It had always been easier just to remember it and easier to find. And what little I had written for others to read was analytical. There had been a limited correspondence with some mathematicians, but that was when I was seven years old. And other letters on occasion. I had written some essays for Sorenson and Lyle, but those were specimens, data for their study, and my mother had soon stopped that. The fact was that until I had come to college I had not even had school work to write, papers, exams, that sort of thing. No classes and so no writing.

Not until Appleton's class had I ever written out of the personal self, used writing as a tool of self-discovery. Appleton had driven and poked me. In class and out of it, in private conferences, Appleton had dragged me by the ears into confrontations with himself.

"Come on, Burden. Pay attention to your life. Look at something. See it. And for godssake, think about it. Use your noodle." Appleton, flailing away at whatever air he was in, his boniness jumbling and thunking in an unsyncopated dance. The threadbare aura he assumed or projected, he used for self-mockery, getting to himself before you could so that only his ideas, finally, were on the table to be negotiated. "The style is the man, Burden. So what's your style? What's it going to be?"

"*Le style est l'homme meme,*" said Buffon when he entered the French Academy in 1789. I knew that but did not know what that meant. That the character, the soul, of a man was revealed in his writing sytle? Yes, but more. It must also mean that the style created the soul. Plato was right. We become the object of our contemplation, and the tool of that contemplation is our lanaguage. The stronger our command of language, the greater our capacity to contemplate complexity. But the most important point was this: the greatest complexities required a language that was as wide and various and molten as were the complexities it hoped to describe and understand. It was unlike the mathematics of physics which, like physics itself, was based upon a fundamental assumption: that the physical universe was ultimately knowable. Given enough time, its secrets and mysteries would be resolved. But about that already I had a different speculation. Maybe the universe was infinitely forming. And maybe it was the limits of the analytical style that created the cosmological limits: if you describe a universe along x and y axes, then that would have to be the universe you got.

The style is the man. The style is the universe.

But I did not write about that for Appleton for this assignment. Instead, I wrote a character sketch of Appleton, arms and ideas akimbo, a Rozinante more than a Quixote, a swaybacked nag instead of an ironically heroic knight. Appleton had loved it. He had read it with flourishing emphasis to the class. And he gave it an F.

"Do you know why I flunked the essay?"

"Yes."

"You do? Why?"

"If you know, then you don't need me to tell you. If I know, then all you need to know is that I know. If you don't know why you flunked the paper then you shouldn't be judging it. If I don't know, then I should ask."

"That's quick, Burden. Quick, as befits a smart lad. But I'm calling your bluff. You don't know, do you?"

"Sure I do. You want me to understand that you can't fail me. I can't fail any assignment you give me. I can't fail at anything like this." And then I said, "That's my problem. I think. Sir. You've probably already got me down for an A in this course."

"You know so much, Burden. So why don't you know more than you do?"

"I don't know. Why don't you tell me. Why don't you tell me

something for a change. Billy. Billly Billlly Billlllllly," I shouted, and flew out of the door on the manic winds we two had come to blow around in.

Appleton. This incessant playing off against each other. Was there substance to this, some point at which I would be able to say *this* I had learned or *this skill* I now had more control of? What had any of this to do with freshman composition? But if nothing, or nothing much, then were these conscious and directed intentions in Appleton or merely his way of avoiding me? Odd thought, that, that Appleton was using all the fussing and fuming as a kind of smoke screen. But why should he want to escape from me? What was he afraid of? Was that it — he was afraid of me? But that was an idea I could not manage at all and so dismissed. The notion of anyone being afraid of me was just too absurd.

I lay in my bed and felt the dorm begin to rise. At first it had surprised me, but delighted me, that I had adjusted to dorm life so easily, I, who had never been away from my home except for Camp Gingacook. Except for the camping trips and *Yarps*. But those were homes, too, carried on my back like a turtle. But I had slept well in the dorm from the start and did not feel embarrassed to use the commode or be naked out of the shower in front of the others. I did not shave yet, but neither did many others even older than I. And I was taller than many of them, and now there was the whisper of the jock about me. I took to wearing athletic department-issued sweats in the dorm. And I was Mike Tremain's roommate, silvered by Mike's golden light. I had fit in, maybe not enough to engage in the shaving cream fights in the corridors, but enough to feel no discomfort. I had rooted quickly, and growth was all in me. But now I was not going to sleep for the extra hour because of these ideas that pulled me into consciousness.

"Consciousness, Burden. What about consciousness?" Appleton had screamed at me in class last week. "What can be more evident in the universe than consciousness, and yet is more absent in the concerns of the physicists? Ha! Truth? Jesus! What contemporary physics does is refuse to look at what it can't reduce to mathematical measurements. Give me Newton any day."

"Sir. I respectfully submit that you don't know anything about contemporary physics," I had said. The class stamped its collective feet, but it was O.K. This was what Appleton encouraged, as long

114

as you had a defensible position, an argument and not just a pot-shot. As long as you smiled when you said that.

"Wrong, Burden. Wrong. I know plenty about contemporary physics. Don't confuse knowing about something with being able to do it. I can't do a lot of things that I can understand. I can't compose music but I can understand it, and more to this point, at least, I can understand the process of composition. No. What you mean is that I don't know as much about contemporary physics as you do. But then maybe nobody does. Anyway, that's an argument, or a defense, based upon authority. 'I am right because I know more.' But that's an assertion, not a proof." The class assumed an irony here, sarcasm, and stamped its feet again and waited. My turn. But I looked into Appleton's eyes and understood, of course, that there was no irony here. Was this a threat to expose me? Had I actually pushed Appleton too far?

"Not fair. Not fair. You're taking advantage of privileged information."

The feet were silent. What did that mean, what I just said? What the hell were these two fighting about now?

"O.K. You're right, Burden. Stay on the subject."

But what was the subject? The subject always got lost in Appleton's class. It was only the point that mattered, and the point shifted. It was worse than quantum mechanics, where energy could be a particle and a wave at the same time and in different places. Schrodinger's cat again. But with Appleton even the point did not matter. What mattered was that between the urgency of Appleton's insistence on the use of language as the source of "human plentitude" (he called it) and Mike Tremain's pride in his father, I had that Sunday afternoon past come to my decision to write a journal. Much as my father kept a journal. And this: I would use the journal to say all those things I had not said because I had not followed my father down to breakfast, because I had not said them in the cockpit of *Yarps* when my father brought the boat around the shoaling point and on to the course to Stonington because I had said that it could be done and he had believed me. All those things I had not said and I could not say and might not ever be able to say. But needed to say.

The sublime. The ineffable.

Journal Entry, October 20. Father/Print Shop.

I think I remember the first time you took me to the print shop. Maybe I was three, although it is very hard for me to place myself at specific ages in my life because I was always so far ahead of myself intellectually. I have always lived in two times: the time of my daily life and the time of my power. But I think I was three because it was easy for me to walk, easier than it would have been for a two-year-old. And I remember you holding my hand. A print shop can be a dangerous place, especially for a little kid, what with the presses whirling and clanking, all those levers and arms and gears and pawls. And thirteen years ago you would still have had the linotype machine. Hot lead. I remember you holding my hand and my not being afraid. I think that is my first clear recollection of you. I mean of course I knew you long before that, but I remember that moment in the shop when you took my hand with a specific, located clarity unlike anything I can draw out of my amorphous feelings and awarenesses about you before that day.

Maybe courage is something we learn. And what does it mean to be brave? If we are brave are we brave only in certain moments? Is courage something we store away and draw upon in a circumstance? Or are we always brave (or not) in all we do and only pay attention to that capability at certain critical instants? I think it is the latter. I can remember you being courageous in a crisis as in the stormy, leeward drift off of Rhode Island. But more importantly I remember you in your daily rising to your responsibilities. You taking your shower, shaving, making your breakfast coffee. Going off to print wedding announcements and business cards and raffle tickets and the menus for restaurants.

I know you have not read Proust because you told me you did not. Too long, you said, for you. But not for me. With my power nothing is too long for me. I read Proust in two days. Whatever else, Proust is often referred to as an example of the nature of olfactory memory. The kickoff for the entire work is located in a memory that occurs when the adult Proust smells a madeleine, a small kind of French cake that takes him back and back and back into his life. I have such an experience. For me it is the smell of printers' ink, or, rather, the smell of a print shop, the mixtures of smells of ink and paper and heated metal and the oil and grease of the presses. But I do not have to actually smell that smell. I can think about it and return to that moment when I was three and you held me safely as I walked through whatever dangers there were. And maybe whatever dangers there are to come.

I wrote more. How wonderful I felt. I would have to tell Appleton about this. I would show him what I had written. Look, I would point out to Appleton. Look how I can write about myself. See how I can refer to my power. Give it a name. And, oh, what a region is this that I have entered into.

I ran off a copy on my printer and gave it to Appleton on Tuesday.

Mike stirred and grunted; soon he would get up. Quickly and all at once. Ready. In action. All his life moving continuously like a progress in a fiction, Mike's life a narrative, a story like Stevenson or Kipling might have written. The curtain would go up in the room in Jameson and he would take the stage. I knew Mike's habits. He would be awake in ten minutes.

Time enough for me to think about Sara Logan. She had called me Monday night.

"The story's in print, Nick. I've just gone over the galleys. It looks great. Thursday. Thumper's story too. Two bylines, Nick. I'm finally doing something." She had explained to me how, until these opportunities, all she had done was work as an unnamed reporter gathering information for the editors and more experienced writers. Now she had gotten this chance. "This is really important for me, Nick," she had said. "For people like you and Thumper McGuire, everything is already yours, or will be. For people like me, we have to scramble around."

"Oh Sara, no," I had said.

"I'm not complaining, Nick. I'm not afraid. Life's a kick. It's going to be. I've got a lot of confidence. I just want it to get started, you know?"

"I *do* know, Sara. I do. Me too. I want my life to get started too."

"It's not the same, Nick. Saturday there will be NFL scouts at the football game looking at Thumper McGuire. And Thursday you are going to have supper with this Lionel Kreutzer. Your doors are open already, I'm still knocking."

We had been walking together in the Cobbton College art gallery, Cassidy Hall, a splendid gift. Cobbton, despite its small size, had one of the strongest art history departments in the country. The accident of a large special bequest of an industrial family, the local Cassidys. Sara had told me about them. A typical nineteenth century American success story. Irish immigrants who in a generation had become wealthy, in two generations powerful enough to own whole eastern forests and to buy and bribe state legislatures to build railroads into their holdings. Lumber, lead, garnets, graphite. In the third generation they returned to Europe and brought back crates and crates of art. And a hundred years after the first Cassidy tumbled dirty and half-starved into America, the Cassidy family deposited their art into little nearby Cobbton College, close enough for the family to feel that it was still theirs; close enough to keep a still suspicious Irish eye upon it. The endowment had grown. It had attracted other money. It had all turned Cobbton into a college not unlike Dartmouth. A pocket university, like a pocket battleship – great firepower but less of it. There were selected graduate programs at Cobbton: English, physics, mathematics, and art history. The Cassidy money had even generated a successful sports program, a football team that might produce an all-American interior lineman, the college a Nobel laureate.

"Not bad, huh?" She said to me. She had taken my arm as we walked about. But I didn't know which she meant. The current show? The college? Or did she maybe mean my life just at that moment? If that is what she meant then I could answer.

"Yes. Not bad. Great, in fact."

"Oh look. Look!" She stopped me hard before the painting. "A Bruegel. *The* Bruegel. Well, one of them. One of the most famous. How did they ever get *that* out of Belgium? Landow is a genius, a miracle worker." Landow was the director of the Cassidy Hall gallery, its programs and its own special funds.

Sara let go of my arm and swirled around before the Bruegel as she had swirled around before in the white cube of Culver's lab. Her skirt flung out. She became one of the dancers in the painting. Even the color in her cheeks, still bright from the crisp day that we had come out of, glowed like the skin of the peasants chasing pigs four hundred years ago in a north European autumn. "Oh, Nick, oh, Nick. I love this painting. I love Bruegel." And still she danced. And then all the figures in the painting began to move. I watched them come alive, attend to their business, their lives, their joys and fears and ends. The painting was still, the figures in the painting were not. And the colors and lines and shapes were

118

not still either as they turned into each other and out again, the sky becoming blueness itself, a tree becoming a hole in space.

When she touched me, I jumped, startled.

"Hey? Where did you go, Nick?"

"Into the painting."

We turned a corner into one of de Kooning's ikon paintings, the woman series.

"Ahhagh," I exhaled as if I had been hit.

"Right," Sara said and began her lecture about de Kooning and the abstract expressionists.

It was some more of what had begun shortly after she had interviewed me: my education, she had told me, was sorely lacking. I was like a blind man. She would have to do something about that. She had given me Sewell's *History of Art in the Western World* and demanded that I read it. And Gombrich's *Art and Illusion*. She would talk to me about Byzantine roots and Hellenic principles – Myron and Phidias. The grandeur of Rome. Michelangelo and Titian. And sweepingly onward into the present. She was indeed very knowledgeable, and her passion seemed genuine.

But I would not have cared what she talked about as long as she talked to me at all. And this was an excuse, was it not? A reason to be together? An excuse for me to be with her? Because there still had to be an excuse, right? An explanation? There had been details in the feature article she was writing about me, things to check out – my favorite food, my favorite rock group. And the chatter and sniff of life she brought to me, the crumbs she scattered for me to peck at, oh how they sustained me. And in my art appreciation lessons, I was, as in everything, a dutiful student. What would I not do to please her?

But this had happened too. My interest in the art itself was very great. The Bruegel. The de Kooning. Vermeer, Rubens, Rembrandt, Van Eyck, Apel. Others. The Flemish Heritage the remarkable show was called. That afternnon had for me the quality of revelation. If I closed my eyes later, I could summon up the intensity of Bruegel's peasant life and feel myself come near to weeping at the thought that all of this was dead, all that life so fiercely evoked was gone.

And I could not do it quickly. It was the first experience of that different pace that I had ever had. I could still read and comprehend the words written in the text, the history of the ideas of art. But I could not go quickly through the paintings and the photographs of the sculptures. In the Cassidy Hall art library I had taken books with larger reproductions and detail studies and read them, but I could not make them move faster or quickly. The Bruegel paintings I had examined figure by figure; I held them as if they were pieces in a jigsaw puzzle, each with its own unique shape and yet all interlocked. It was as if these objects had nothing to do with time at all except that the painting altogether measured conclusion and made a statement: that even time, that took survey of all this bustling world, must have a stop.

But Sara's lecture about the de Kooning just then did not matter to me. Much as I had wanted to listen, all I could do was look at the violence of the woman, at the infinite transitions between the ravenous teeth and the slashing legs, the colors and shapes twisting and grasping my eyes until I had lost choice and finally volition and accepted the domination as Sara Logan, beast and beauty, ravening, for here indeed was an ontology recapitulating a philogony, the breasts of all of history, the legs battering at equilibrium, funneling into the vagina, terra incognita, flowing into her, into the woman, into Sara, into my own body, into a euphoric explosion as my body and the body of the painting and the body of all painting become one. A vast oceanic oozing, an ambiotic sea. Sea. Man. Sea man.

"Nicky. Get up. You've got to get up. Remember what I told you, get up fast."
"What?"
"Thursday. Remember? The big T day?" He bent to tie his shoes.
"What?"
"What do you mean, what?" Mike was already half-dressed. He would get his pants and shoes on before he went to the steamy cluttered bathroom down the hall. It saved him time. "I've got to get things in order. I've gotten a good set up for the tutoring. Maybe. In the basement of the eco building. But I've got to finish up that deal this morning. And I've got two guys so far who are interested, but I haven't told them how much yet. They look good for the job. Both were Phi Beta Kappa in their junior year. But by this afternoon, bingo." Mike jumped in the air and clicked his

heels. Or tried to. He could never get high enough or stay up long enough, but it always seemed as if he thought he had.

"What?"

"Hey, Nicky, are you all right?" He came and stood over me in bed.

"Thursday? This afternoon? This is Thursday?"

"Thursday, October the twenty-ninth. Two days to Halloween. Also the first day of the rest of your life."

"But what happened? The dream? I was awake. I was dreaming."

"Yeah. Well, right. That's the way it happens. You sleep, you dream, you wake up. It can't be helped. So was she beautiful? Was it kinky? Did she suck you off? Come on Nicky, goddamn it, get your ass out of bed. Let's go, let's go!" and Mike left me.

I was wet between my legs. It was not the first wet dream I had had, but the euphoria of this dream was different. And in the past I had not entered a woman. Then the fantasies were more masturbatorial, more like the perfectly posed photographs that papered the room. *Real* fantasies, but fantasies, the body bending and pumping to its own personal music. But now there were real women, Sara Logan, whom I had entered. I was no longer a virgin.

▸16▸
=

I consulted my grid. I had so much to do this day. Topology at nine. At ten I promised myself I would check out the references I had made to Berkeley in my philosophy paper, at least an hour in the library for that. Then a delivery of poster tubes to Joe. Who was this Joe who now kept showing up at the bus stop to accept tubes? I had meant to ask Mike. Then Appleton's class in the afternoon. This was a special class; I was especially exicted about it. Appleton had asked us individually to suggest poems or stories that we wanted to discuss. I wanted Auden's "Musee des Beaux Arts," the poem about the Bruegel painting that depicts the fall of Icarus into the sea. Appleton had accepted my suggestion and assigned it to the class. Then I had to get to Culver's lab. I wanted to go over my own ideas so I could be intelligent about them for my dinner with Kreutzer, just in case an opportunity arose for me to say something. But would I dare? Kreutzer. Still I couldn't believe it. The meeting had the feeling for me of pivot or fulcrum: the balance in my own life might shift across that dinner table.

But it might shift sooner than that, at noon, when the Cobbton College *Chronicle* appeared with Sara's article about me. I tried to submerge the thought of that in the busyness of my day. There was no place to indicate it on my grid. What, after all, could I put down. Twelve to one o'clock, the end of my new world? Seven P.M., the beginning of a newer one?

122

But I could not submerge it. Wherever I pushed it down, it popped up somewhere else. I remembered from the past summer trying to run around a squall. There was a formula for doing it. If your compass bearing to the left side of a squall moves left while your bearing to the right side of the squall moves right, you are on a collision course with it. But whichever heading I took that day, the storm shifted with me. From ninety degrees east to 270 degrees west the squall moved as if to block me, as if it had intention, volition, a determining energy of its own. I tried to maneuver around it up to the last possible moment. I even sailed a little into the forward shadow of wind that surrounds a squall, the grey cat's-paws of wind roughly scratching the surface of the water. At last I had to give in and scramble with difficulty to get my sails down and take the storm full and solidly on. That is what I felt now, that there was no dodging what was coming at high noon. But at least in this case I had a chance to reef in time. At sea I had had a chance to miss that squall, but not this one, so I prepared in the only way I could: I allowed myself to expect what would happen. I imagined what it would feel like.

I was not without experience. I had been through this sort of thing before. But not exactly either. Cobbton College wasn't Camp Gingacook. Maybe it would be better this time, less antagonistic at least. Maybe no one would care, at least not for long. But a deeper thought reached up and clenched in me until I actually gasped for breath. Everything would change–for better or worse was not the point. It wasn't even a point that could be made. Nothing good could come of this for me. The fabric I had woven myself into since coming to Cobbton would be torn apart. I would be raveled out. That would happen, and I did not want that to happen. What was approaching at noon was not a squall. Squalls were violent but quick; they were all wind and no waves; they knocked you about and then they were gone, the air and the day scoured clean and bright in their wake. But this was not a squall. This was a hurricane that was coming my way. And after it the coastline would be changed forever.

"It is not true that Nicholas Burden, a member of this year's freshman class, can read at the proverbial mile a minute, but he probably can read at a hundred words a second, which means he can read a three hundred-page book in twenty minutes and remember it almost verbatim.

'Novels take less time, philosophy more,' he says."

So it began. Then I skipped around. After the first paragraph, I tried to read the article from the start but could not, only the pieces I felt I had been cracked into.

"Nicholas, or Nick as his friends call him, has the highest IQ ever measured. Quite simply, he is the smartest guy in the world, probably the smartest guy who has ever lived. He is able to solve quadratic equations in a glance. He can learn a language in a week."

The article went on more or less repeating what I had told her about my prodigious powers. Sara had kept it pretty straight and stayed close to the brain power theme, recounting the incredible feats. But she also stressed the normalness of me as a person. Indeed, that theme emerged: The smartest guy in the world was just like you and me, only smarter. She was doing her best to protect me.

"But there is nothing about Nick Burden that would make you think he was any different from any other collegian you might pass on campus or sit next to in the library or in the commons. He is a New York Giants fan and he loves the Rolling Stones. His main interest is sailing, and he has his own twenty-four-foot sloop that he often sails alone. He is a member of the Cobbton cross-country team."

My eye flickered over the page. The courses I was taking, my dorm, my roommate Mike Tremain quoted ("A terrific guy, just terrific. And a great buddy to have when you need something explained. Like living with an encyclopedia. What every dorm room needs."). I had not noticed my photograph. I looked at it closely. It was O.K. Even good. I didn't look goony. And I didn't look young. But eventually she would have to make the point about my age. And the future.

"But for a guy who knows everything, or can if he wants to, there is one thing he doesn't know, just like a lot of the rest of us. What does he want to do with his future? What does he want to be?

" 'I'm very interested in astrophysics at the moment. Some very exciting things are happening in that area,' Nick said when asked about a further course of study. Astrophysics by the way, for us mere mortals, means theories about the creation of the universe and the beginning and end of time and space. Wow, right?"

There were pieces and chunks of my close past, my home town of Steffanville, my father's business – The Burden Printing Company, Inc. – (she made it sound like something much more than the modest printshop that I had described to her), my mother's fine work as a reference librarian in the town library.

"When asked about his formal schooling, Nick replied, 'There wasn't any. I never went to school. I had tutors when I was very young, but after awhile I just read at home.' And what did the school board think about that, I asked him: 'We worked out an arrangement. I took tests at the end of each year. And passed them. I could have passed them earlier, but my parents decided to spread them out to avoid further complications. The only real problem was gym. Health. It's a state law. I took private tennis lessons, golf, archery, that sort of thing, and the school board accepted it.' "

And then she did what I knew eventually she would have to do.

"And it's not over yet, his dealing with the health credits, because Nick Burden, though a freshman at Cobbton College, still has to fulfill his high school health requirement. He never graduated from high school. Nick Burden is sixteen. And although he is not the youngest genius to ever go to college, he could have gone at the age of twelve or even ten or maybe even eight, but his parents felt it was better for him not to start too soon. They wanted him to be able to fit into college when he went. And the Nick Burden we have here at Cobbton today is a good indication of what a wise decision that was. Normal as can be, pleasant and polite, and not at all overly impressed with himself because of his superior intelligence – he is not only the smartest guy around (for sure, for sure), but maybe the nicest as well."

Only after the third try could I read the article from start to stop. It was not a bad job. She had made me look pretty good, considering the problem.

On the facing page under the shared banner NEW STUDENTS TO WATCH was Sara's article about Albert "Thumper" McGuire. I read it easily. Quickly. A hundred words a second. It was also a good article, perfunctory, direct. She tried to downplay his size and strength or his jockness. The theme in the story was what was

125

waiting for Thumper. All-American status (maybe even as a freshman) and eventually the Pro Bowl. His life was all before him. The progress of a champion. Only Thumper's picture was not so good. He came off menacing even though he had said cheese when Sara snapped his photograph.

I looked at the full centerfold spread and at the two photographs. NEW STUDENTS TO WATCH. It was meant as praise. But what could people know who had never had fifty thousand people watching you and screaming your name, cheering you for your power and success, but ready always to curse you for failing their dreams? I looked into Thumper's eyes and felt a compassionate bond. It wasn't menace in Thumper's smile but a plea that he could not utter, just how any prisoner might respond to a command that he dare not refuse: say cheese.

Mike slammed into the room carrying a bundle of newspapers. "Help me," he said. "Cut out the article. We can use them for direct advertising. Would you believe, I've got people who want to learn things already, want your services. In thirty minutes." He kicked the door closed behind him and thew the papers onto the bed. There was a knock. Sam Pelton.

"The phone is ringing for you, Nick. It hasn't stopped. Not in the last half hour."

"See," Mike said, "see. So maybe now we can put in a private line? You think this is going to stop? This is the beginning. Just the beginning. Give us a phone."

"Maybe it would be easier to move Nick out," Sam Pelton said.

"What? You're nuts. No way. What for?"

"For his own protection."

"Protection? Bullshit. Protection from what? What kind of shit is that?"

"Protection from whoever wants a piece of his ass. Something like that."

"Yeah, well don't worry about his ass. I can take care of his ass. Right, Nicky? Tell this fucker." Mike was standing up and facing Sam Pelton. His fists were actually tight as if whatever battle had to be fought would be fought right now and this way.

"No one's moving me, Mike. Relax. He's kidding you," I said. "You can't move me out of here, Sam. You know that. And the

phone will stop ringing in a day or so. Come on, get off our backs."
But would it stop?

Sam Pelton smiled and gave us a thumbs up and moved to the door. "What about the phone calls? Maybe when the phone rings you should be the one to answer it, it's probably for you. Why should everyone else in the dorm have to answer your phone? Think about it."

"Maybe leave it off the hook. I don't want to talk to whoever's on the phone."

"Or get us a phone," Mike said. "The solution is so obvious." He started to cut out the articles. "And what about Thumper? What about his phone calls?"

"Bye-bye," Sam Pelton said, and left.

In twenty minutes we had cut out all the articles. One story Mike had cut and pasted into a border around a neat small sign. The NICK BURDEN TUTORING SERVICE. The relevant information followed. The phone number was the one Mike was using for the agenting busines. "But now," he said, "maybe we're going to need a full-time secretary. More expense. We've just got to get some capital, Nicky. But I'm working on it. I think I got the answer. Don't worry about it, O.K.? I don't want you worrying about this. I'l take care of it. Let's go eat. These articles I'm going to use until I get the sign reproduced. Let's go."

But I stayed.

"What?"

"I haven't been out yet. Since the newspaper."

"So? You're going to spend the rest of the year in here? You think I'm going to bring you food for the rest of the year? Jesus, Nicky, it's nothing bad you did. People are going to love you for being so smart."

"You think so, huh? Yeah. But it's not that so much. Not *so* much. It's being sixteen. If I was twenty-one, it wouldn't matter. If I was twenty-five I'd be a professor. But at sixteen I don't belong."

"There are other people who are sixteen at this school, I'll bet you. It's not such a big deal in this day and age. Kids start school at three. Everybody reads already in kindergarten. I saw this thing on TV, mothers showing little tiny kids, they could hardly sit up, cards with words and numbers on them. Sixteen is nothing."

"But I don't belong here anyway. I shouldn't be here. I'm not here for what everyone else is here for, a college education. I have a college education. I've got a graduate education. A postgraduate education. I've got any education I want, any level of it. I don't belong here for any of that, not really."

"So do you know why you are here? I know. Your parents know," Mike said.

"Why?"

"To get laid, Nicky baby. To get laid, just like the rest of us. Only I don't mean get laid just as in get laid. I mean something like what-do-you-call it? He talked about it in class. About poetry."

"Metaphor?" Nicky offered.

"Yeah. Right. Metaphor. Get laid like a metaphor for learning about life. So no one is too smart for that. None of that is in the books, Nicky, right?"

"Yes. Of course. I knew that. I know that."

"Sure you do. It's not the hardest thing to know or figure out, not even for a sixteen-year-old kid." He punched me gently on the arm. "Not even for a sixteen-year-old kid going on sixty." Then he put his arm over my shoulder and whooped me down the hall and down the stairwell and out of the dorm to get laid.

Waiting for me was no metaphor. Instead students had started to gather as if they were getting ready for a parade or a spectacle. Some began to point at me. Then I was approached (rushed?) by a knot of about ten young college women squealing at me as if I were a rock star. Three of them ran up and put pieces of paper with their names and addresses on them into my pockets. One of the girls shouted at me, "Oh Nicky, I want to bear your child," and another girl said, "No, no, me." Others began to collect, like particles in a solution, a charge attracting other particles. "It's him," I heard someone shout. Mike and I began to run. Maybe this was a joke, all of them. The girls did not follow.

"Hey," Mike said, "I'm thinking. What she said. What a great idea. Sell your sperm. Breed super kids. I saw about that on TV, too. You jack off into a test tube and they freeze it and charge people a bundle for a little bit of it."

"Jesus, Mike. Jesus."

"But for Cobbton College coeds, you give them a better deal, out of a sense of school spirit. Instead of jacking off you just fuck them directly and only charge them half."

128

"Oh Mike," I was laughing now, for nothing seemed unreasonable; laughing hard.

"What do you think, a hundred bucks a fuck? Of course they'd have to sign papers relieving you of parental responsibility. Shit. A hundred? Shit. These girls, they spend that on a sweater. Five hundred. Take it or leave it."

He spun it out further and further in a great entrepreneurial swirl, until, by the commons, we both believed in the venture. Or wanted to.

In the commons it was different. Everyone had not yet read the newspaper. Most, in fact, were just now reading it with lunch. And then one at a time and then more and more, people looked up and the separation of awe began and deference began to seep into the air like a poisonous gas. I muttered to Mike in a soft voice. I looked down at my plate when for the past weeks I had looked around.

"You are imagining too much, Nicky. You are paranoid about this. Cut it out." But even Mike could feel the contours shedding down and off from where we sat. And then we were approached.

"Nick Burden?" the student said. He didn't put out his hand. He did not want to intrude on my eating, only on something more.

"Yes."

"I'm Carl Sullivan. I'm the president of the MENSA chapter for this area. Centered here at Cobbton. I'd like to welcome you and offer you membership. I'd have contacted you sooner if I knew you were . . . who you are."

"Thanks," I said, "I'll have to think about it."

"We meet every third Tuesday of the month, but sometimes more often if we have a special speaker or project." Carl Sullivan went on as if he had not heard what I had said. He had not heard.

"I'll let you know. I'll have to think about it."

"You . . . will?" Sullivan heard that and was surprised. "But you of all people. It would be such an honor for us." He might have taken a chair at the table to discuss the point, but Mike stopped him.

"He can't decide right now, O.K.? He'll let you know. Me too."

"Who are you?"

"Mike Tremain, Nick's roommate. What? Do you think they'd let him live with just anyone? I'm his trainer. I keep him in shape.

129

He'll let you know. I'll let you know." He waved Carl Sullivan away, and Sullivan left.

"What's MENSA?" he asked me.

"It's an organization of people whose IQ scores are in the top two percent. They've been after me to join for years. My mother forbids it."

"Of course," Mike said, slicing into his Jello.

"Of course?"

"Sure. It's for anybody in the top two percent, right? So she doesn't want you mixing with the riffraff."

When I left the commons, I felt as if I were in a progress, the multitudes opening before me. Before Mike left me, he said, "Come on, Nicky. Don't make too big a deal of this. And how would you want it, anyway? Would you rather *not* be so smart? So what would you want it to be?"

"I'd want it to be yesterday, Wednesday instead of Thursday," I said.

"Yeah, but Nicky, time doesn't go that way. Time only goes *what's next?*"

▸**17**▸

=

Appleton never began a class by asking it what it thought about the topic of the moment, and he told them why. Often.

"Suppose you don't think anything? Or suppose what you think is trivial or insignificant – thoughtless? Or suppose everyone has a different opinion?"

"But isn't that how we learn? By discussion? By comparing our ideas and by argument?" a student asked.

"That might be a way. One way. But why assume it is the only way or the best way? Besides, the aim of education isn't to teach you how to learn so much as it is to teach you something. Maybe the best way to learn something is to listen to the person who knows the most."

"But what about the idea of learning by doing? How can we learn thinking unless we do thinking, even if imperfectly?"

"But even if you accept that Deweyish mishmash," Appleton contiued, "at what point do you start the doing? Do you start at the beginning? Why not start as far along as you possibly can? So instead of sorting out a lot of flabby overgeneralized babblings, someone establishes a particular idea. Then the other ideas have, one, a high level to start at, and two, an idea against which to bear. An idea to displace. Besides, you need an editor. A boss. When it comes to thinking, democracy doesn't apply.

"For instance. Let's take the Auden poem that you were assigned. I'm going to read it.

About suffering they were never wrong,
The Old Masters: how well they understood
The human position; how it takes place
While someone else is eating or opening a window or
    just walking dully along;
How, when the aged are reverently, passionately waiting
For the miraculous birth, there always must be
Children who did not specially want it to happen, skating
On a pond at the edge of the wood:
They never forgot
That even the dreadful martyrdom must run its course
Anyhow in a corner, some untidy spot
Where the dogs go on with their doggy life and the torturer's
horse
Scratches its innocent behind on a tree.

In Bruegel's *Icarus*, for instance: how everything turns away
Quite leisurely from the disaster; the ploughman may
Have heard the splash, the forsaken cry,
But for him it was not an important failure; the sun shone
As it had to on the white legs disappearing into the green
Water; and the expensive delicate ship that must have seen
Something amazing, a boy falling out of the sky,
Had somewhere to get to and sailed calmly on.

Reading the poem, he became someone other than Appleton. The shaggy bumpkin, the scarecrowy discombobulated lurch disappeared under the cloak of his voice, which was as dense and muscular as he was not. I looked at him more carefully than I ever had before. I tried to imagine Appleton now not as an actor, not giving his clownish performance, not entertaining us with his intellectual slapstick, his comedia del'arte outrageousness, not coating the rim of the cup of medicine with honey to get us to drink it. I had had no teachers. I could not make comparisons. The only teachers I knew about were those I had read about–Mr. Chips, Mr. Antolini from *The Catcher in the Rye*, or Mr. Grandgrind, *Tom Brown's School Days*, that sort of thing, or some of the sweet duddies on TV. Fictions. And Appleton, too, had been a fiction: a real-life fiction. Now he took on a substance. Or was it the poem he took on? Was that the substance? Was that what poetry was for–it made us real? A lovely irony. But I did not know what to do with ironies. All I could do was understand them, figure them out as I might do with any complex notion–a math formulation, the subjunctive case in German, the Kasparov variation of the Nimzoi defense, the inverted theme in the second movement of Mendelssohn's Scotish symphony–should I care to. But what to *do* with what I could understand? The ironies? I signed. The problem of my life.

But not the problem of the moment.

The old Appleton returned (or had the real Appleton slipped back into his disguise?).

"Right away there is a problem that has to be solved for us to understand the poem, which is? . . ." He looked at us. No one responded. "See? So what do we do now, go home? So now you see what I mean. A system can't wait to work, it can't depend upon what you know or don't know. It needs someone who does know. Like me, O.K. The problem here is allusion. There are at least two major important allusions, which are? . . ." Hands went up.

"Bruegel's painting."

"Yes."

"Icarus. The Daedalus myth."

"Right. Good. Now what?" Nothing. "Now we have to interpret the painting and the myth before we can experience the poem. A little like Chinese boxes. What's within what's within what's within. I assigned this poem so I assume you read it before class– ho, ho–so when you read it, did you go and find a reproduction of the Bruegel painting? Let's see hands." Nothing. "Look around. And did you go and read the Icarus story, or did you just vaguely remember it? Sit up, sit up. Don't slink away. I've told you a thousand times I know you're there, you can't hide. You can cut the class and then you'll flunk this course. You can hide that way. But once you're in this room on Thursday afternoon, *you are mine.* So who is Daedalus, goddamn it? And what, in truth, is the real subject this afternoon?"

But we all knew the answer to that: me.

Appleton left the poem.

After nearly two months in Appleton's class, this star section of freshman composition, we had been melded by him into a pliable unit. We were bright enough to be quick, and we had a self-assessment we had to defend–valedictorians and salutatorians all—without being defensive. And Appleton did challenge us where we lived: in intellectual pride. And with me as the lightning rod or the point man at the front of the phalanx, Thursday afternoon had been a pretty good time. But honored too. Pummeled but petted. Now something had happened. Who was running the show? Suddenly they were playing in the minor leagues, and this Burden, once their Hector, had turned out to be a ringer. He was sitting on the wrong side of the big desk up front.

Appleton spelled that out for them. I wanted to scream.

"But let me tell you this. About what I'm teaching you and what you've got to learn here and elsewhere, Burden doesn't know shit. In other words, about the miraculous he doesn't know any more than the rest of you. Now let's get on with class. I brought a projection of the Bruegel painting. We'll look at it. You," he pointed at anyone, "turn out the light. And you," he waved his hand over us, "You run the machine." Someone who knew how to do it got up and did it.

The Bruegel filled the room. It filled me. It pushed everything out of me except the colors and lines and volumes, the baffling distortions of perspective, the nearly naive stylization pushing back against the delicate and perfectly drafted details—the expensive delicate ship. Against the painting I pushed the poem—Something amazing, a boy falling out of the sky.

"Now here is what to think," Appleton said.

"I can't see to write anything down," a voice complained.

"Then don't write down. Good. Remember. *Look* at the painting. *Hear* the poem. The power of a truly great painting or poem is that you remember it."

"Or a truly great insight." A voice in the dark. Some general laughter.

We left each meeting feeling that we'd maybe been taught something, but certainly been honored for being so smart. Pummeled but petted. And still, again and increasingly, I thought that Appleton lived more in the light we reflected upon him than in the brilliance of his own generation, that we were the foil to his diamond, and without us his own light would go out.

"Yes," Appleton said in the voice with which he had read the poem. "Of course. So here we go. Hang on. First of all, what is the first thing you look for in the painting that is the last thing you see that once you see it you can never not end up by looking at it?"

The legs of the boy splashing into the water. The white legs disappearing into the green/Water.

Whatever else Appleton told them about the painting and the poem in the remainder of the class – the melted wax, the refusal to obey the father, the failure of technology (as Appleton put it) – all I could focus on was the way Bruegel had structured the experience. Appleton was right. Though I had looked at the painting in the books in the art library I had been consuming since Sara brought me there, I had not thought about what Appleton had pointed out. The subject of the painting was hidden by the painting until it was precisely revealed by the painting. All the diagonals moved to the left and upward. The plowman plowed to the west and the expensive delicate ship sailed to the west, running before the wind astern. Even the sheep looked away, the shepherd gazing upward. Force and counterforce. Nobody saw a boy falling out of the sky. Except for us. No one heard the forsaken cry.

Moving out of the classroom, Appleton called me back.

"Your noteriety? Has it gotten bad yet?"

"Nothing specific yet. Just . . . it isn't what I wanted to happen when I came to college."

"It was bound to happen. It had to happen. You must have known that."

"Sure, but it doesn't make it any easier when it does happen. It's going to be a real pain in the ass, that's all. Sir."

"Well, maybe not all," Appleton said. I waited for him to say more, but he did not. He turned the subject. "Do you know when everyone *did* look at the boy, did notice him? It was when he was flying around up there near the sun. Can you imagine their amazement at that?"

"Am I supposed to be Icarus? Is that your point?"

"You did choose the poem."

"I was interested in the painting. In Bruegel. He knocks me out."

"Poem or painting is not the point, Icarus is. If you don't want to be different, Nick Burden, if you don't want the world pointing

at you while you fly up around the sun, then fall into the drink."
He started to gather up his papers.

"Fall?"

"Right. If that's what you want."

"Fail."

"Fail *significantly*. That's the only failure worth anything." He
started for the door of the classroom. "By the way, the essay you
gave me, the journal entry? It was splendid, Nick, just splendid.
You have your own copy, I assume. I'd like to keep this, if you
don't mind. And please continue to write these. Let me see them.
Splendid. Just splendid."

And now who was *this* Appleton, a third Appleton? It was the
first praise I had gotten from him, an unadorned, untheatrical
Appleton speaking to me as if to another mortal, a mere mortal,
sensibility to sensibility. And just then I felt his capacity for the
vulnerability I had sensed in him before and the chance he was
taking in this small movement, this small gesture toward me. For
how else could he make his words authentic except by taking what
for him apparently was a risk? How different we were, I, who
could *only* care entirely and openly (my center and my surface being one), and he, who, until this moment, did not seem able to care
or even exist except by indirection and through masks.

◂18▸
=

"Go on, go on. Give him some wine," Kreutzer said. "What is it? Ach. Yes. You are underage. I have been in this country forty years, a citizen for thirty-five, and I still cannot remember that rum is a demon here. In much of Europe, of course, it is a beverage, a food. A joy."

"It's not the drinking so much, it's the driving," Ian Menlow's wife said. "In Europe, if you're young and you drink too much, you still have to walk home or ride the tram. In America you get in your car and kill yourself."

"Yes, yes," Barney Tobler said. "That is true. But even before you all had automobiles here in America, drink was still considered a curse, was it not? Prohibition must have come from somewhere."

"It was a young and optimistic nation. It believed it could do something right. Avoid all that old, evil, godless Europe had done wrong," Jacob Cravitz said.

"What an idea," Lionel Kreutzer said. "No wonder it drove you all to drink." They all laughed at that. "So what is it now, eighteen that you must be to drink?"

"Twenty-one in this state," Eunice, Tod Culver's wife, said.

"And you are sixteen," Kreutzer said to me. "Five years to wait. Ach. There is so much you must wait for. Are you not impatient?"

"I've been drinking a lot of beer since I've come to college," I said.

"You like that, then?" Kreutzer said. "The beer?"

"Not particularly. But if you don't drink it, then they pour it on you. Or even if you do drink it." All at the lavish dinner table smiled.

"Ach. But now look what you've done. Your confession has made all these professors accessories to your crime. See. You've compromised them," Kreutzer went on.

"Well, then," Jack Kelly said, "let us drink to our collective guilt."

"Here, here," they all said, and raised their glasses, me too.

It had been a wonderful evening for me so far. Kreutzer had been very easy to be with and not intimidating at all. Indeed, I saw that the others seemed far tighter than he, more self-conscious and accommodating. They, like me, wanted to make a fine impression, which would be natural enough. But they, unlike me, wanted to make a lasting impression. They wanted Kreutzer to remember them, to connect a face and a clever comment at a good dinner party to some paper that they might write that he might referee or to a grant proposal that he might kiss or kill. But as Culver had pointed out to me at our very first meeting, I had no reputation to defend, no career to protect or further.

And in fact, I was nearly as much the central theme of the dinner party as Kreutzer, partly because Kreutzer was so directly interested in me, and partly, too, because of some things he had said as early as the predinner avocado dip and the brie and Jarlsburg and the shrimp empaled with toothpicks whose ends were dressed in swizzles of colored cellophane. Or maybe not a theme. More a vibration, the oscillation of a plucked chord that went on and on, like a harmonic high on the E string.

I had walked to the Culvers' house, which was only five blocks away from the campus in what amounted to a compound of faculty housing, especially the more senior faculty. I had dressed as my mother had doubly-checked me to dress for such occasions. My blue blazer, freshly cleaned and pressed; a light-blue Oxford cloth button-down shirt (Sally Burden hated those contemporary shirts with white collars and colored bodies); a regimental rep tie (circa 1950) whose time had come again. On the back of the tie there was a little tag that read Barclay's Bank. I had wondered what that meant. No one in the dorm knew. I wore dark grey flannel slacks. For shoes I wore my buff-colored bucks, a concession to my college

138

student status. My mother thought it would be a nice touch: don't be older than you are, she had warned me on that first day at Cobbton. And when had that been, it had been so long ago. I carried a present. When I had told my parents about Culver's invitation to dine with Lionel Kreutzer, and had received my instructions from my mother, she had also told me to buy a very small box of something like Godiva chocolates, four pieces in the box. Only four pieces! I had protested. It's not the candy, Nicky, she had explained, it's the gesture: a little of the very good is better than a lot of the less than the best. But what about a *lot* of the best, I had pointed out. Wouldn't that be better yet? My father on the extension had laughed. Go get her, kid, he had said. She had answered that too much of a good thing was showing off, flaunting what you had – or pretended to have.

Eunice Culver greeted me at the door. She was tall and pleasant, a pleasant looking woman dressed in a long, full dress that touched the carpet. I gave her the small box even as she opened the door. A mistake, I sensed at once, not that she gave it away.

"Why thank you, Nicholas," she said. "Come in, come in." I was the only one there. I glanced at my watch. Seven o'clock exactly. Was this the right night? A burr of panic circled me like a mosquito and was gone. She was dressed for an occasion, and I could see the platters of food set around the living room. I could see in the dining room the long table set and glistening with glass and silverware and thick linen napkins and even two heavy, branched candelabra, their candles already lighted. I had come on time. Too early. Another mistake. But Eunice Culver carried me easily, even as a woman dressed in a white uniform came in from the kitchen twice to ask questions.

"Let me show you around, Nicolas." She walked me about the living room pointing out some objects she and Tod had gathered on their travels. "Extraterrestrial evidence," she explained. Inside finely wrought cubes of clearest plexiglass, the edges bound in silver, rested stones, pieces of fabric, bones, shells, coins, chips of wood. There were twenty boxes in all.

"Extraterrestrials, Mrs. Culver?" I said. But had I made another mistake, the clarity of my skepticism? (Not about the objects. That was too evident to need expression.) But about her own gullibility?

"It's a game for us, Nicholas. A little joke. We have found items for which there is no apparent explanation. This coin, here. See. It was minted by no identifiable country or community, present or past. We've shown it to leading archeologists and numismatists and they are baffled. It even has a very high gold content, so it's not a fake. Or it wasn't a fake to someone. And this bit of cloth? Under a magnifying glass you can't find any weave. It's like a piece of fabric punched out of some material. But what material? And this pebble? It's probably from a meteorite, except that its weight is wrong. It seems like it was made from a meteorite but it couldn't have been made on earth."

"There are probably reasonable explanations," I said.

"We're *sure* there are reasonable explanations, Nicholas," she smiled. "But for now we're happy that there aren't any easy ones. It's more fun that way, don't you think? A touch of the mysterious? A little unscience in the scientist's house?"

"Yes, ma'am," I said. "I really do."

She took me into Tod Culver's study.

"Perhaps you'd like to mull around in here. I've just got to get into the kitchen for a minute or so or else we're going to end up eating out of cans. Feel free." She waved around the room and was gone. For ten minutes I read the titles on the spines of the books on the shelves all around the room. What I might have expected. And an old well-preserved leather bound book. I took it from its place on the shelf: Isaac Newton's *Philosophiae Naturalis Principia Mathematica.* I opened it: 1687. It was a first edition. Perhaps Newton had even touched this book himself. Why not? Only five hundred copies had been printed. Newton was twenty-three when he had written it, writing it all in an incredible six months while he was home and away from college, which was closed because of the plague. But he must have started three years earlier, at nineteen. Only three years older than sixteen. But I was embarrassed that I had remembered that from Newton's life.

Then I heard the others arrive. First Jacob Cravitz and his wife and Ian Manlow and his. A second group came almost immediately after: the Kellys and Barney Tobler, who was a widower. I had met Tobler once, but not the others, but I knew who they were by reputation and because I had seen them three times when visiting professors had made presentations on the campus. For its size,

Cobbton had a powerhouse physics department; these men were heavy hitters. And Tod Culver was the cleanup batter.

I waited. Had Eunice Culver forgotten me for the moment? Should I wait for her to come and get me, or should I just walk out into the living room? Everything was a decision, and so far I hadn't made a right one. But what, after all, was at stake? I entered the room.

"And this," Eunice Culver said without missing a beat, "is our other guest, Nicholas Burden." But weren't these people also guests?

Everyone made their introductions. Immediately the talk was about the article that had appeared in the newspaper. They had all read it. Of course. But the tone of their comments and questions wasn't gawky. I was an event, and they were discussing it with me, that was all. I was surprised that my true identity had been maintained for so long by those who knew all this.

"It's going to get you a lot of attention," Ian Manlow said.

"It has already," I said. "I guess it will get worse. I mean more."

"But worse, too, I'd suspect," Kelly's wife said. "Privacy is at such a premium these days. Who's in? What's up? How is it new? The Warhol syndrome."

"What's that?" I asked.

"Andy Warhol said that in the future everyone would be famous for fifteen minutes," she told me.

"Warhol was a famous pop artist," Jack Kelly offered. "He painted the Campbell soup can?" he urged. "The multiple silk-screen of Marilyn Monroe?" But I shook my head. Pop Art? Warhol? The name was familiar, but I hadn't gotten that far. I would have to ask Sara. Sara. I clenched my left hand softly around her name, holding it like a lucky charm.

It's not going to be easy for them, I thought. I know so little. A small pang of apology went through me as I considered all the adjusting they were going to have to go through for me this evening. On the other hand I thought about all that I *did* know that I would not allow myself to say or talk about, all the adjusting that I would have to do, and I remembered what my mother had said: don't flaunt what you have. And I did appreciate the directness of these people. It was easier this way than it would be to pretend that I wasn't there or that I was not what I was. I *was* there in the

Culver's living room exactly because I was the person they had unquestionably by now heard about from Culver and who they had now, this afternoon, read about. I was sixteen and I had been invited to this dinner with Lionel Kreutzer because maybe I was the future. Maybe I was going to be their future. And if I was right, if the theories and calculations that I had already taken a purchase on were right, then I was absolutely going to be their future, though they did not know that then.

They talked to me about me some more, but also about the experiences of my home and parents and larger interests too. My current courses. Activities and friends. Jack Kelly had been a cross-country runner in college. The Cravitzes sailed in the summer out of Castine in Penobscot Bay. They stayed away from physics.

Then Lionel Kreutzer arrived. Tod Culver had picked him up at the airport.

He was a warm and jolly man and quick to make all of us easy; his generosity was the sort of gift you must be a king to be able to give, if you are a nice king. And he was expansive, a discursive, rambling storyteller. Soon enough they were all exchanging greetings from colleagues and bantering around professional news— who was the new chair at MIT, who had inherited the laboratory of Miles Crane who tragically died in that terrible air crash over Los Angeles. Upcoming conferences. The fate of the supercollider. The fission-fusion debacle. They talked of the wonderful autumn weather, the spectacular success of the Cobbton football team and the chance that it might even get invited to a bowl game for the first time ever since it had moved into division one football ten years ago. They talked about Thumper McGuire, Cobbton's first possible all-American. And Kreutzer waded right in.

He fancied champagne, and Culver, who had researched that, provided. With a constant glass in one hand and something or other off of a tray in another, he hooked on to whatever anyone was talking about. The marvelous art exhibit in the Cassidy gallery that he wanted to be sure to see, all that splendid northern European painting—Rembrandt, Vermeer, Ensor, Apel. The old masters, the new pretenders. Kreutzer was very well informed. He told them something recent about Van Megeren, the famous forger of Dutch art. They had heard of him of course, he said, but did they know that there were still two works attributed to Van Megeren that were now being reconsidered. Maybe they were, as the authorities had first maintained in 1946, early Vermeers after all. And Bruegel, I wanted to say. Don't forget Bruegel. De Kooning. But held my peace.

And so it went on, quickly, fluidly, the pitch and tempo certain and exciting to me, everything new. I bobbed happily along like a cork, content to now have Lionel Kreutzer be the current and tide. Until Kreutzer turned to me quite specifically.

"So. Nick. Yes. You are the Nick that Culver speaks about? And physics is it? Where you are going? I envy you, I envy you."

They all fell silent. What did Lionel Kreutzer envy in a sixteen-year-old, even a sixteen-year-old super genius? But what could they say to him? Nothing. Except me.

"Me?" I said.

"Yes. Physics. We are getting to a new beginning, so much is happening. I'm an old man. My work is over. These men, even their important work is now almost in the past. Their own past. The past of physics. But you. Ach." He raised his glass abruptly, spilling a little. "Culver, he tells me a little of what you are doing already. Challenges. New ideas. Excellent. And superstring? You are exploring, eh? You have thoughts?"

"There's too much I don't know yet. Sir," I said.

"Yes, yes. But not for long. Already you make trouble."

"Trouble? No sir," I said. Panic buzzed again, now a swarm, a battlion and not a single dart.

"Ach, ach. You think a Planck duration is too small to account for time. You are worse than Culver, this time before time thing. And this eighth arrow of time, the irreversibility of time?" He laughed, but as a compliment. "You do not call that trouble? The implication? That the speed of light is not a constant? *That*, my young colleague, is trouble. Trouble for us all. Yes? Trouble for the universe." He looked all around him and again he laughed.

I was appalled and delighted. Colleague, the mighty Kreutzer had called me. And how quickly he had seen into what I was doing. How much could Culver have told him in the ride from the airport? How much could Culver even have known about my work, even with what was spelled out on the paper pads on the walls in his lab? No. Kreutzer must have intuited it.

The others murmured. They took Kreutzer's drift. No doubt the kid had it. Even to be *wrong* about light, to play in that game already required a pile of chips few others possessed.

"But what do you do with my G, Nicholas? If the speed of light is not constant, what do you with my G?"

"Your G, sir?" O my god. I wanted to run.

"Come, come, Nicholas. *You* know what I mean."

"G is off by a magnitude of three alphas. If you push it far enough the formula will break down." I said it all in a single breath. But now I was not frightened. It was not a matter of a social situation now, a rudeness, an insult. This was different. Three alphas, possibly. G would not hold. If there were four pillars that supported contemporary physics, along with Einstein's $E = MC^2$ and Planck's theory and the Schrodinger equation, there was Kreutzer's. But it was wrong, or at least slightly askew, but enough to make any further configurations of the big bang universe wacky. And I had my arguments. *This* I could handle. I braced myself, but Kreutzer did not swing his kingly mace at me, his Emperor's scepter.

"Maybe more like two alphas, or a little less. Yes. G is a serious problem to me. The skeleton in my closet. So, Nicholas. You see what I mean? You do not accept. *We* accept, but you do not know enough yet to accept. You reinvest. Wonderful. Wonderful. Physics is in good hands."

"You question G?" Ian Manlow said to Kreutzer.

"Alas," Kreutzer said with a shrug. He smiled and drained his glass.

"Dinner is served," the white-coated servant announced. And even after the second call no one moved until Eunice Culver, a touch pale, began to urge and then actually push us into the spangling room. She pointed out the name cards she had carefully placed. Me she put on Kreutzer's right.

But Kreutzer hung back a moment and took my arm. "And there is more, isn't there, Nicholas? Not only G is in trouble, yes?" he said in a low, private voice.

"Sir?" I said.

"Come, come, Nicholas. I am old and busy, but not yet altogether lost. Witten's seventh dimension is very weak, is it not? It could bring superstring down like a house of cards. Good, good," he smiled with mischief. "But it could bring down a lot of physics, too. *My* physics. *Our* physics." With his chin he indicated those who had passed on into the dining room. "We must talk. Later." But now I could say nothing more. Had I been threatened or praised? I should not have said what I did in public. Even if I was right, I shouldn't flaunt what I had. So all I could do was turn red as Kreutzer walked me into the sumptuous meal awaiting us.

Only after we had gotten through the shrimp in the curry-tinged aspic did the party, that had begun so well, regain some of its happier momentum as Kreutzer regaled us with an anecdotal history of this century's physics, so much of which he had attended to. He had worked with Einstein. He had been at Chicago with Fermi when the controlled chain reaction had been produced under the football stadium. He was one of the signers of the famous bottle of chianti they had drunk at their dinner after the great event. Neils Bohr, Feynman, Rabi, Bethe. He called the role of the great warriors, evoking for us Valhalla here in Cobbton at Thomas Culver's table. Evoking and embodying the grandeur and the glory. Even so, the men all wanted to run home and do calculations and make telephone calls to California and Cambridge and Zurich and Karachi and Tokyo. $[G=\{6+^{\wedge}\}]$ was in trouble. Light in the universe was flickering. What had gone on here, a coronation or a beheading?

At last they were all gone. In the general leave-taking, Kreutzer had told me that he would like me to stay longer for a little chat. Now Lionel Kreutzer took me into Culver's study with Culver in attendance. Eunice Culver supervised the clearing away of the fine evening that had increasingly softened and mellowed after the spikey shock of what Kreutzer had said during the hors d'oeuvres. The coffee and the cake still lingered. I tasted it over and over. In the study Kreutzer loosened his tie and kicked off his shoes. He had carried with him a freshly charged snifter of brandy, which he carefully set down on Culver's richly polished mahogany desk. He gestured for me to do the same with my tie and shoes, but I would not.

Kreutzer seemed endlessly energized. He had not stopped drinking through the evening but was as certain and quick as he had been when he walked through the front door. He took out of an inner pocket an enormous cigar.

145

"What do you think?" he said to Culver. "What about Mrs. Culver?"

"No, no. Please. Go right ahead."

"And you?" he asked me. "May I smoke?"

"Sure," I said.

"Everything today," Kreutzer said. "You can't drink, you can't smoke. You can't eat the wrong food. You must run in the streets in the morning. Ach." He stopped and lit his cigar langorously, the odor of it brilliant and right.

He began to tell us – but me, actually, Nicky Burden – more tales of his adventures in physics, for adventures they had been; not excursions but bold voyages. It was as if he had been saving this just for me, a rare vintage, a special gift. Then immediately Kreutzer asked me about my topology course with Guzman, what he was doing.

"Guzman?" I said, surprised. "Inversions," I answered. "We're turning enclosed spaces inside out. Right now we're constructing a three-dimensional Moebius strip that we'll then invert."

"It could be a model for the present idea of the universe, yes?" Kreutzer said. I considered for maybe thirty seconds.

"Yes, but no," I said.

"Explain please."

"There's a twist in the construction. The three-dimensional strip would have to end up looking like sausage links. The inversion wouldn't work unless you got rid of gravity. Or included it."

"Guzman taught you this?" Kreutzer asked.

"No," I said. "I figured it out."

"Just now, yes?"

"Yes." I said. "I mean I'm not sure about it. It's just a quick idea, that's all."

"Ach. So," Kreutzer said. "Then you will see my point, I am sure. Why are you studying this subject?"

"Why?" I said. I looked at Culver. "Because I've got to take something. I've got to study something, don't I? I'll need credits to graduate."

"Why bother?" Kreutzer said. "Why not just get on with your life's work?"

"But isn't that what I'm doing? Isn't this my life's work, the start of it? Getting an education? I'm getting confused here. Sir."

"Yes, yes. Of course. But why study for weeks what you can learn in a few days. Like here with Guzman's inversions? Too simple, too simple for you."

"But there are a lot tougher problems than that. There are some real killers. Professor Guzman told us about some of them. We won't even get near them this semester." I was talking quickly, as if I were making an argument, but what was the point?

"Listen to what you are saying. In one moment you are telling us that light is not constant, that superstring theory and my own work and half of physics is verging toward a massive redefinition. In the next moment you are telling me about schoolboy exercises that take others weeks and months to perform, for you hours or minutes. Is there not a confusion here? What about fractals? What do you know about that, eh? Or the elusive nutrino? Or the gravitron? Tell me, tell me Nicholas," and Kreutzer leaned forward out of his chair toward me in a conspiratorial slouch. "The truth, now," and he poked at me with the great cigar. "You have had enormous ideas, yes. Things you tell no one. Ideas you are almost afraid to have?" But he did not wait for an answer. He leaned back and smiled at his assertion. It was enough for him. He lifted the snifter to me. "I was once young and brilliant, Nicholas. More than all the rest. But never as brilliant as you. So, eh? Tell me."

What could I do but flaunt what I had?

I told Kreutzer and Culver about my chromium yellow thought and the implication that the steady-state theory of the universe was to some extent still intact, which would mean that physics, both particle physics and astrophysics, should be thinking of transformations and amalgamations and not searching for limited universes or discrete atomic particles or even for a unified field theory, a superforce.

But I did not tell them about what was in my drawer in the writing desk in the great white cube, my Tangerine Tango ideas.

"And that you will pursue at Cobbton College? Ideas like that? Of such dimensions?"

"Not now. Not yet. Or a little. I don't know. Maybe. I mean I've got other decisions I've got to make." I looked at Culver for help. Did I need help? What about art? I thought I might say. Bruegel? Or Mike Tremain? Or Sara Logan? Still, I did not know what question I was trying to answer until Kreutzer waved the wand of his cigar like a sorcerer.

"Yes yes yes. Of course. But nothing like that need change in your life. An education? Of course. Believe me, I know better than you that there is so much more to life than physics. But that is not my point. Here is my point. Cobbton is my point. I would like you to move to Princeton."

"We considered Princeton. Harvard. Yale. All the Ivy League."

"I do not mean the university," he said, not so jolly now. I mean the Institute for Advanced Study. To be a fellow there."

Kreutzer shifted and was silent to allow what he had said to have its effect. He waited for a full minute, letting me dissolve in the acid of my confusion, then he began again, expansive once more. "You should come to work there. Then you could argue with Witten in the next office. Or get deeply into fractals with McNeice. Or catastrophe theory. And study everything else—literature, music. Ach. *Yes*. Join an eating club if you want. Dance with the girls. Drink beer. Fight duels. Be young. But you must also be who you are. You must not deny yourself. Or us. Think of the contributions you might make. Think of the effect on others your work might have. In one month Meyrhoff will publish his work on the molecular rearrangement of genetic material. It will make gene-splicing look like the Middle Ages. The eradication of diseases. The extension of life could come from this. This is the future, but it needs people like you. And soon. Quickly."

"But I've done nothing, nothing at all. I couldn't go there," I bleated.

"There are perhaps exceptions that I can cause to be made. Exceptions for exceptional people." But it was clear that there was no perhaps to it.

"But now, not another word. This is not a decision to make now or alone. You must consult your parents. Yes. I will be in touch. I will write to them. We will visit." He got up from the deep chair. He was a portly man, and deep into his seventies, but even now he moved with lightness and agility. He got up easily, steady. He put his arm around my shoulder and walked me directly to the front door. "Go home. Taste the pleasure of your life. Ach. What a feast awaits you." At the door, Culver trailing, he said, "And I have this little gift for you." He gave me a piece of paper with an equation on it. In a quick glance I saw that it related to G. "You see? A small key to a great puzzle, eh? You see? Old Kreutzer has not stopped thinking yet. Ha." His arm stiff around me, his cigar in the other other hand, he squeezed me tightly. "He does not understand," he said, gesturing with his head at Culver. "But you understand, yes? *You* understand. Come to the institute, Nicholas. We will do this all the time. You will think about this?" A question? A command?

►19►
=

It was eleven o'clock in the evening and cold. Orion was standing upright in his winter stance. Sirius sparked like a diamond cutting the sky. Rigel, Aldebaren, Canopus, Fomalhaut – all were in place. How confident I felt in these heavens. I could have navigated *Yarps* by the stars and the moon around the world; to Jameson was easy. I stopped for a minute and looked across the sky. I remembered back to the challenge I had once posed myself, to memorize all the stars on the Norton star atlas down to the fifth magnitude, those just at the edge of unaided sight. I still knew them all, from great Betelgueuse, larger than a hundred thousand earths, down to the merest galactic smudge of M98 in the constellation Drago. And there were stars and galaxies, billions and billions beyond. I thought of Vernaux's paradox: If the universe was infinite, then why was there not a heaven full of the light of all the stars? But if I was right, if, as I was coming to imagine, the universe was already infinite and had always been infinite, then there was already an infinity of galaxies, and given a powerful enough receptor, the universe would appear to be all light and never ending, a universe without dimension or direction and certainly beyond any available concepts that limited time or space. But not beyond the concept of sequence: event followed event, and must absolutely follow event regardless of the position in space-time of any observer of the event.

Like Newton and Liebnitz, Poincare and Driac, and now Witten,

I would also create a mathematics to describe this vision, a language sufficient to create my new cosmology. But what language would I have to express my astonishment? To express the Cosmos itself? And if there were two languages—the language of the learn'd astronomers and the language of Whitman, then why should I, of all people, settle for only one or the other?

I had worn nothing over my blazer. I hunched into myself and walked fast, and now I did not think of the evening that had just passed or what had just happened. Not even of Kreutzer's parting gift, a wonderful line of thought that opened the problem of the three—or two—misvalued alphas in $[G + [6 + a]]$. What I thought about now was Bruegel. Instead of Princeton, I thought about Antwerp. Instead of the twentieth century, the fifteenth. I imagined myself as one of the skaters on Bruegel's ponds, how red my cheeks even now must be, how my scarf must be flying in the hard North Sea breeze (but I wore no scarf) as I labored after the heavily padded woman in the white kerchief binding her head, how I was one of the puzzle pieces into which Bruegel had fractured the world in order to rebuild it. Why was I suddenly thinking of Bruegel? Too much wine? The thick befuddling cigar smoke? The precipices of exhiliration I had leaped about on all evening like a young goat? The star light?

But in Jameson it was another kind of scene from Bruegel, the Bruegel of nightmare and madness and the punishments of hell.

"Fuck you, asshole," someone was shouting at someone else, or at everyone else.

"Yeah? Well fuck you, too, scumbag."

"Suck dick."

"Up yours, cunt mouth."

There was a crowd, a gang. A mob. Sam Pelton stood in the middle of it keeping the traffic of invective moving from one side of the room to the other and not allowing it to boil into a maelstrom, as it threatened to do.

"What's up?" I asked at the edge.

"A lot of us have come here to talk to Burden. The Jamesons want us out. Too much noise. Fuck them. Hey," the young man said. "You're Burden. *Hey*," he screamed over the general rubble of argument, *Hey hey. He's here. Burden's here.*"

Sam Pelton got to me first, maybe fortunately.

"Get into my office, Nicky. Now. and fast."

"Wha . . ."

"*Now.*" He grabbed me and thrust me through the bodies into the small front desk/office and closed the door. Through the plate glass window, I watched everyone looking in, pushing in, rising up the glass as if it were an aquarium filling with water.

"You have visitors," Sam Pelton said. "And phone calls. And we all have this." He stuck his thumb over his shoulder.

"What's happening? I don't understand."

"Well, some of these people out here have got business with you they say, and some just want to see the action. Half the girls want to fuck you. The other half want to attack you for being a sexist pig."

"Me? Sexist? I don't know what sex is."

"There are a couple of religius organizations that want your soul. And there are a few goonies who want to kick your ass."

"Kick my ass? What for? What did I do? That's nuts."

"Right. Nuts. And this place has been like election central in the nut house from about nine o'clock on. And then there are the people who live here, who are complaining they can't study, they can't sleep, they can't get to the candy machines, the coke machines."

"Can't you just order the others out?"

"Technically, yes. Practically no."

"So what can you do? Call security?"

"I've got a better idea. I shoot you and give them your body."

"Good," I said, "good. I like it, I like it. Come on, Sam. You can't blame me for this."

"It's not a matter of blame, Nicky."

"So what is it?"

Then the glass halfwall of the office leaned in and shattered, but it was safety glass, dormitory glass built to anticipate, and no shards flew around. The crowd had pushed too hard, the pressure. Sam Pelton pointed now. "*Out. Right away,*" he shouted. "Two minutes and out or I call the campus police. *Move.*" To the residents of Jameson, he ordered them back into their rooms for the next half hour.

"Hey you can't do that," someone argued, as someone always argues. "That's against the fucking law. Suppose I got to take a shit? Suppose . . . ."

"Wartime powers," Sam said. "Emergency law. So suppose you shut the fuck up, Bickle, and do what I say."

It took five minutes, and only after the milling thinned did I see Mike Tremain. Mike was talking to a guy here, one there, then another as they left, writing things down. With him was Joe, to whom I had delivered tubes of posters over the past two weeks. twice and three times a week. What was Joe doing here? What was Mike doing now?

"Business," he said with Joe beside him at last back in our room. "This is Joe Casper, Nicky. You've met."

"Sure," I said. "At the bus stop."

"Right," Joe Casper said. In the dorm room he looked older than he did under the bus stop cover where I would quickly get off the blue bus and give him the posters and then get back on the same bus back to campus. And he looked hard. The muscles around his neck sloped down from his ears to his shoulders. Across his back, I could see Joe Casper ripple. His shoes were hard and shiny leather, not campus shoes at all. For the first time I saw that a finger on Joe Casper's left hand was missing. On the next finger he wore a gaudy golden ring with a bright veridian stone in it. Emerald.

"You're looking at my finger," Joe Casper said.

"Sorry," I said looking up into Joe Casper's eyes. They were green like his ring.

"No problem. It don't bother me. I got nine more, right?" Then he looked up at the ceiling and along the walls at all the posters. "Fantastic," he said, "fantastic. You could fuck your hand to death in here. Who's your favorite?" he asked me. But he answered for himself. He looked up and down. "Her. That, my friend, is the best cunt I ever saw. She is unreal. Un*real*. You think she is like that, a cunt like that? Christ, I hope so. Man, would I like to boff that." He seemed caught. "I would like to boff that right here with all the other broads watching." He flopped down on my bed, his feet up on the covers. "Come on, baby. Swing on this." He grabbed his crotch.

"Here," Mike said. He came from his desk. He handed Joe Casper a thin white envelope. Casper held it up to the light. Sam Pelton knocked on the door and came into the room.

"Hello. Who's this?" he said to Mike.

"A friend," Mike said.

"Just leaving," Joe Casper said getting up from the bed. He snapped the envelope to his eye in a salute. "See you tomorrow, Nick. See you around, Mike." He turned by Sam Pelton and left the room.

"Who?" Sam Pelton said. "Who? You know the rules, Mike. No strangers in the dorm after eleven unless they're signed in as guests. You think I need this shit, *more* shit, right now?"

"He's not a guest. He's a business associate of mine and Nicky's. He sells our posters over at Greenfield and Charlton. He's a sub-contractor.

"Your distributor," Sam Pelton said.

"Yeah," Mike said, "sort of. But we don't do business here, O.K.? We deliver. Off campus"

"I know about your delivery system."

"What, you've got us under surveillance? So then what's the problem, Sam? Are you breaking our balls because the guy is in our room for a couple of minutes? Jesus."

"Why is it always you, Mike, but then it turns into *us?* 'Me and Nicky?'"

"Because that's the way it is, Sam. Me and Nicky. We're partners. Didn't I ever give you a card? Sorry about that. Here." He reached into a pocket.

"You gave me a card. You gave me a hundred. You wanted me to pass them out at the RA council meeting."

"Oh yeah. Yeah yeah. Now I remember. Sure," Mike said. "So how did that go? You need some more cards?"

"Just watch your ass, Mike," Sam Pelton said, but as if he were saying more.

"Yeah. Sure, Sam. But like what have I got to watch my ass about?"

"Here," Sam Pelton handed me a list of my phone calls. "This is some of it. We couldn't keep up. Tomorrow we've got to have a talk, Nicky. You, me, and the dean of Student Affairs. Don't leave town." He winked and pointed his finger at me like a gun and left the room.

I looked at the list in my hand. I recognized none of the names, only quickly and hard as a punch, my mother. Thursday night. I had forgotten to call. I was supposed to call before I went to the

154

Culvers'. Now she had left a message. Call me whenever you get in. The second name I recognized was Sara Logan's. Call me.

I sniffed the air.

"Joe Casper," Mike said. "I think maybe it's something he puts in his hair."

"Are you all right? You seemed pissed at Sam."

"I'm all right. Sam's all right. He's got a job. I dig it. We've all got something to do. And you especially."

"Who's Joe Casper?"

"You heard. A business associate. A distributor. Why, what's the matter? You don't want to sell to Greenfield and Charlton? And maybe to Fort George, too? Casper can handle the expansion. We've got better options now."

"He didn't seem to have ever seen the posters. What does he know what he's selling? He seems kind of old for a college student. And, you know, tough."

"Maybe it's because you're kind of young for a college student," Mike said.

And then we were silent at that. And neither of us knew how to turn away.

"I'm sorry," Mike said. "I'm sorry, Nicky. You're right. I'm kind of edgy. So much is happening. And now more than ever. You." He came to me and took me in his arms and hugged me and patted me on the back. "I'm really sorry."

"Forget it," I said. I stepped back from Mike's embrace and extended my hand, palm up. Mike slapped down on it. "All *right*. Now I've got to make some phone calls, Mike. My mother. What was happening down there? So I can tell her."

"A lot of fraternity people. They want you."

"I told them before. At rush week. No fraternities my first year."

"That was before. Now they want the great Nick Burden. Some say you can come right in. No pledging or nothing. Immediate membership."

"No way."

"A lot of invitations to parties. Saturday night is Halloween. The whole campus. Big business. We've got six of our bands working. Wild. And Saturday we play Colgate. We win that, we could win

155

the east, the Lambert Trophy. There is a crazy weekend shaping up, my friend. Cra*zy*."

"I'm not a party animal, Mike. You know that."

"This is different. I sold appearances."

"What?"

"Like with celebrities. You know, like at benefits and important weddings and bar mitzvahs? You think Don Rickles or O.J. Simpson show up for nothing? You think Tony Bennett is an old friend of Gino "Thumbs" Babinozambino and that all he's got to do on a Saturday is to go to Gino's granddaughter's sweet sixteen party?"

"You sold appearances? You sold *me*?"

"Five. A hundred bucks apiece."

"Jesus. A hundred bucks. What for? Why would anyone pay me to go to a party? It makes no sense."

"Sure it does. You go to the Pi Lambs, say, or the Dekes, and some guy says to his date he brought down from Smith, you know who that is, that's Nick Burden, the smartest guy in the world, the smartest guy who ever lived. And she says what do you mean, and then he tells her the whole story, and maybe he drags her over and says hey, Nicky, this is Mary Sunshine, say hello. So he feels like a big deal and she feels this is some great fraternity. There are sixty Dekes, which means it costs this guy one dollar and sixty-six cents. Which is like nothing, am I right?"

"I can't believe this. Maybe I should do some tricks, Mike, earn my money? Maybe I should add up a list of ten-digit numbers in my head, or name all the kings of England and France with their dates and their major wars. Something like that. Jesus. Holy Jesus."

"I hadn't thought of that. That's cute, Nicky. Cute. But we'd have to charge extra for that. Like in working in the movies, you know. One rate for walking around or falling off a horse, a higher rate if you say something."

"Fuck you, Mike."

"Fuck you, Nicky, we make it while we can. Next week who knows what you'll be worth. A market like this is very unstable. Who knows how long it can last."

"Fifteen minutes, Mike. Only fifteen minutes, I hope."

"People, Nicky. Celebrity. I'm telling you this over and over. People want to worship something. They want to touch you. Grab

156

a piece of the glamour. So you go to a party for half an hour. So what's the big deal?"

"Do the Dekes know that? The Pi Lambs? Suppose their girlfriend doesn't get a chance to see me? They'll be pissed, right? At me. So what do I need that for? Or any of this . . . this shit?"

"For the money, Nicky. Five hundred bucks is 250 each and no expenses at all. It's like picking up money off the floor."

"Suppose I like the party, Mike? Suppose, just suppose I actually like the party and want to stay?"

"So you stay. So what's the big deal. What's another fifteen minutes. Twenty."

"You *know* what I mean. It's not the extra fifteen minutes, Mike. It's a principle here. It's me having the right to do what I want."

"O.K. Fine. So what do you want to do, Nicky? You keep saying that, one way or another. So what do you want to do? Do you just not want to go to the party? Do you not want to make some money just for walking into a room? You listen to me a minute. You see the trap you're making for yourself? If you start thinking about the things you won't do now that you're out in the open, you'll end up not doing all kinds of things you would have done before. You'll be hiding. I've told you this before."

"Yes."

"Don't hide, Nicky. Run but don't hide. And if you've got it, flaunt it. Better yet, sell it. Go on, my buddy. Go call your mother. We've got more business to talk about. The tutoring is flying. I've got you scheduled for an organizational meeting tomorrow at one. Is that good for you? Also, we should pick out some costumes. Down in the village there's a place with all kinds of stuff. We can drop off an order of posters to Joe and then swing by for costumes. Halloween. Trick or treat. You ever do that?"

"Sure. Of course."

"Make your call. We got business. Oh have we got business."

So for a little while the universe would have to wait.

◂20▸
=

"Calm down? Calm down? *No*, I won't calm down. What do you mean, calm down? What I'm going to do is call Dean Roskov. Now. And even then I won't calm down. There is nothing here to be calm about."

"The dean? You're going to call the dean now? It's midnight Mom. Come on, Mom. It's midnight."

"If I'm not going to sleep, why should he sleep?"

"Dad? Speak to her. Dad? Are you there?"

"I'm here, Nick. I'm here."

"So tell her."

"Tell her what, Nick?"

"Not to call the dean."

"Do you mean not to call him ever, or not to call him tonight?"

"Tonight. Not tonight. Just not tonight." But he knew I was stalling; I meant never.

"But what difference would that make, Nick? If we call him tonight, we make a point."

"What point? What point?"

"A point about urgency, Nick."

"And about anger," Sally Burden said, and as if that was the last necessary word.

I had called and filled them in in broad and attenuated strokes about the general response to the article about me in the newspaper. The heavy seas that were making up around me would crest

158

and some would break over me. I might take a couple of knock-downs, but every storm subsides. I would weather this, however it might permanently change the shape of my life here. Hurricanes wash islands away, but they deposit them somewhere else. My parents did not need alarm. Of course, I did not tell them about the scene in the dorm, only about the more expected attention: the interest from the fraternities, the MENSA man, the outrageous girls who wanted my children. At any rate, I felt sure I could handle my own apprehensions better than I could handle those of my mother.

But that is not what made her angry. I told them about the supper at the Culvers' and my meeting with the immortal Lionel Kreutzer. She wanted details; I gave her the menu. And yes, I had to tell her, as she would have understood anyway, that I was fairly central to the dinner party. But that was O.K. by Sally Burden. She didn't want me not to be a part of the world of which I was already a part. She did not object to the creative attention of Thomas Culver and the physics department of Cobbton College or of a Lionel Kreutzer. It was a position that I was going to have to accept sooner or later, sooner than later. She understood that I was a prince and that this might be my kingdom to come. This was a nice, socialized way to begin. Reasonable curiosity and interest. O.K. It was why they had finally sent me to college.

But when I told her about Kreutzer's offer of the Institute for Advanced Studies at Princeton, my mother had reacted as if she had been robbed, had come home from the movies to find the house broken into and her most valuable possessions taken – not the expensive stereo system and the twenty-one-inch TV, which money could replace, but the fragile, old family silver, the multifaceted lead crystal bowl that an aunt had brought from England in her youth, the tiny Faberge egg. A violated history. I could hear her grind her teeth and bite.

"The offer's not for you, Nick. It's not for you, it's for him. Them. But that is not the point. The point is that we had a deal. *For sixteen years we had a deal.* You, me, your father. The world wants to use you in every way it can. The dean was supposed to prevent that. The dean snookered us."

"The dean wasn't even there, Mom. He didn't know anything about it. He couldn't have. No one was there, except Culver. And nothing's happened, has it? No one is driving up in a truck with a cage on it and a net to drag me away."

"Don't be so sure," she said. "But something *has* happened, Nicky. Something we didn't want to happen. Temptation, Nick."

"A lot of other things are happening, too, Mom. Temptations. They're bound to happen, aren't they?"

"I don't know about the other things, Nick. So I don't worry about them. If you tell me about them and I have to worry about them, *then* I'll worry about them. I don't worry about things in the abstract. If the dean didn't know, then who's running the show down there? Someone's supposed to be. . . ."

"*Mom. This all took place like two hours ago.*" I looked over my shoulder. The telephone was in the hallway at the end of it. Behind me what looked like the entire second floor of Jameson was listening. I dropped my voice to a whisper.

"What's the matter?" she said. "Why are you whispering?" I explained. About my sudden celebrity.

"When I breathe, somebody watches me. When I go to the toilet, somebody watches me."

"Well *that* I can understand. *That* we expected." She paused. "Nicky baby? Just tell me this. When Kreutzer made his pitch, what did you think? What did you really think? Did you think you wanted to go there? I mean right now?"

"No."

"Then what?"

"Antwerp. Belgium. I want to go to Brussels. Bruegel," I said. "I thought about Antwerp and about Pieter Bruegel, the elder. And that's the truth."

"Bruegel? Antwerp?" she said. I had caught her, but "O.K." she said. "Bruegel, then. Good. I want you to call me tomorrow at seven. Here's your father. He's got something to tell you."

"Nicky? Some not such good news."

I braced. What now?

"*Yarp's* propeller shaft is twisted. That's what the vibration was. We've got to have it pulled. It's going to be a big job. The strut has got to come off too."

"When?"

"Sometime over the winter. And that's not all. The gearing in the self-furling mechanism on the jib is shot, top and bottom. It's got to be replaced, which means the mast has to come down to do it. Expensive. You'll have to work this summer. Make some money. You want to work in the shop, maybe run the typesetter? Learn a trade so you won't go hungry in this world? I mean who knows if this physics stuff will last. Bosons, quarks? Hula hoops? Think about it."

"Dad?" I said. "Dad?" No whisper now. "This summer. *Yes*," I said. "*Great!*" And we hung up. Then "*yes*," I shouted for all of Jameson Hall to hear, for the heavens to hear.

Then I left the dorm to find a private phone to call Sara Logan, whom I also loved, even as I tried to discover what that meant, this love that was growing by itself like a root system of a tree in winter, preparing for the green effusion of spring. Or maybe more like the unshaped silent mycellium spurting and diving without direction through the detritus of the forest floor. "My vegetable love shall grow, vaster than empires, and more slow," the great poet Marvell had written. If there were world enough and time. The perfect poet, Appleton had called him. "To His Coy Mistress" the perfect poem. If there were time.

Sara did not live in a dorm. She lived in an apartment with two roommates. She lived on the opposite side of the campus from where the Culvers lived, where the college town economy of book and record stores and cafeterias and bars and pizza parlors was slapped down like cards in a child's game. The dry cleaners and laundromats, McDonald's and Taco Bell, a photography store, CVS Pharmacy. At least one of everything for every demand. Guitars. Downhill or cross-country skis. The gentle dishabille and affected seediness that was a foil to the gem of academic life.

"Sara? It's me. Nicky."

"Where are you? What's happening? Oh, Nick. I've called and called. I've been worried about you. What's happening? Is it rough?"

"I'm fine, Sara. And it's not so rough, just crazy. More a pain in the ass, you know? But there's a different problem. A bigger problem."

"Where are you?"

I told her.

"Come here. To my place, 210 Oak. Second floor. You're only a few blocks away."

"Now?" I said. "Tonight?"

"Yes. Now. Right away." She hung up before I could say anything else.

Into the night again. I had not changed my clothes or put on an overcoat. Cloudless, no wind, winter clear though it was only October at the end. Very high pressure. The fumes of the leaves that had been burnt through the days lingered low to the ground. Tomorrow would be perfect for the kids tricking and treating. For the football game the day after that. All weekend, I could tell, it would be fine. I was a mariner. I had to know such things.

In the apartment Sara's mates, Ricki and Janie, were watching the last of the Johnny Carson show, preparing for David Letterman indifferently. They were ready for bed, pajamas and housecoats. Other than my mother, I had never seen women close in the things they wore into sleep. And the odor of women pervaded. I was stirred, but then, I was stirred by everything. They clicked out the TV and turned to me. Did they expect me to sing to them, to these daughters of Lesbos? Orpheus, my head floating across the sea?

From the upper north corner of the room, where the ceiling trisected with two walls, I watched myself watching myself. The perfect symbol of my life: this *detachment* from my enormous knowledge, from my collossal sack of information, from my strength with procedures and the processes of thought with which I examined Nicky Burden. But what I saw was like what you see in a mirror that reflects a mirror with you in between—a seemingly infinite regression that fills the field of vision, but what more do you know after the first reflection? What did all I know about Orpheus and Freud and Leda and Zeus and Masters & Johnson and Cassanova and prelapsarian eve and the mating rituals of sticklebacks and the rites of sexual passage in Babylonia or the south side of Chicago mean to me within the swirling olfactory vortex of Prell shampoo and Jergen's lotion and the pink pop of Bazooka bubble gum? How trivial did the curvature of outer space now seem compared to the gentle roundness of Ricki's ample breasts or Janie's rump. I looked up at myself in the corner looking down at myself looking up. Both of us shrugged at each other.

"Hi," Janie said to me.

"Hi," said Ricki. "I read about you today."

"It was a great story," Janie said. "Sara is just so good. And Thumper McGuire, too, she wrote that. She wrote half the paper, you know what I mean?"

"The half that was interesting," Janie said.

"The quarter that was *most* interesting," Ricki said. They giggled together.

"Out," Sara said to the two of them and pointed to their room. They had a double, she the single.

"Good night," they said together.

I walked around the room examining it, but as if I were afraid to look at Sara now sitting on the sofa before the blank TV, her legs tucked up under her, under the heavy tweed of her skirt. The makeshift shelves filled with books from courses they had taken, the canted piles and sloped columns of records and cassettes. Memorabilia, the artifacts from social life – old-fashioned beer mugs, college pennants, stuffed mascots, sis boom bah sort of stuff. Bumper Stickers: MAKE LOVE, NOT WAR. Posters on the wall of men with glazed bodies and skintight leather pants, but not nearly as good as the posters sold by T&B Enterprises. In a special place a thick block of art books – Carravagio, Mantegna, Monet, O'Keefe, Corot, Raphael. I twisted my neck sideways to read the titles. On the top was a smaller book, *The Principles of Art*, R.W. Collingwood. I picked it up, opened it, and read the scrawled inscription: "A curse I put upon, the borrower of this book, who after six months mistook, the scholar in the crook. William Appleton."

Appleton.

"Have you had this long?" I said. "You had better be careful. The curse looks serious. Appleton could probably make it work." She ignored my question.

"Come here, Nick," she said. "Come here and sit down." I did. "Tell me your day. Please. I want to know. I have to know. Maybe if you tell me, then I can sort of share it with you. Maybe it will be less painful." She was as close to me as she had ever been. Her

hair was loose and longer than I remembered it, and full of highlights from a light in the room that I could not precisely locate.

"It wasn't so painful, Sara."

"For me, not you. Painful for me, Nick. Just tell me. No. Don't
tell, *show* me it wasn't so bad. I tried to find you. I thought maybe
I could do something. I called and called. I started to get a little
frantic. I started to imagine all kinds of things."

"It's O.K., Sara. I'll *show* you, O.K.? This is what happened." I
recalled it for her, chapter, verse, line and syllable, detail and nu-
ance. Up to Lionel Kreutzer's offer. "See? Not so bad. Maybe more
funny than bad. Annoying."

"Bad enough, but not so bad." She softened and fell toward me
another inch. "But there's always tomorrow. Maybe it will get
worse." She poked me in the ribs so I would be certain to know
it was a joke. "So what was the big problem?"

I told her about the Institute for Advanced Study. And then she
went blank. She grasped my hand but then released it.

"When?" she said. She looked up at me as if she were reading the
answer across my face, her eyes moving from left to right. I tried
to look at her, but she was too close. I went cross-eyed and looked
over her head.

"I don't know. He didn't say. I guess whenever I want." She took
my hand. She had reached for me.

"So when do you want?" she said. "When Nick? When?"

"Sara. To tell the truth. Sara . . . it's hard for me to talk when
you're holding my hand. It's very . . . for me. Sara." I thought
how I had closed my hand around her at the Culvers' party, and
in the same instant I remembered a tract by Origen on the differences between the forms with which we understand things and
the forms with which we feel things—that they were not different
because God was immanent in ideas as well as matter. Fourth century Origen believed in such a God as that, but I did not, although
I thought that Origen was in this instance right. But that did not
prevent some forms from being *superior* to others: earth was the
proper place for love and the warm hand in mine.

And being frightened. The only word for it. Until now I could
be in love with Sara the way you can love when distance is a buffer,
especially when any action, any acting out of a specific fantasy, is

impossible. But now there was less than an inch between us. And a touch.

"I don't care," she said. "I'm not going to let go of your hand. I've just gotten to know you. I've just gotten to. . . . " She reached across me and took my other hand fiercely and turned into me. She had tears in her eyes.

"Sara?"

"You said you couldn't talk if I held your hand. So don't talk. Don't say anything. Then you can't say you're leaving."

"I'm not leaving."

"Yes you are. Yes you are. Oh yes you are. You'll leave."

"I'm not. I haven't even thought about it. I don't know anything."

"You'll leave."

"No. I won't."

"You will."

"I won't."

"You will. You will. You will. You'll have to leave. You're Nick Burden."

"I am not," I said.

She started to laugh at that and cry too.

It was as if I had turned into the vehicle for the ventriloquist, only it was not words but my soul through which she was speaking. And my fear mounted. Not a terror, not that sort of fear, but rather the paradoxical fear that what I wanted to happen could happen.

We sat together and she subsided. When she released my hands she took my arm and put it across her shoulders and burrowed further into me. Then she started to talk. I heard her as vibrations through my body, as if she were talking into my body, which had turned into a stone cavern. Her head was on my chest.

"Ever since I met you, I mean when I started to talk with you and think about writing the story, I wanted to write the story. And I didn't, too. I'm glad I wrote it and I feel guilty about writing it. Can you understand what I'm saying?"

"Yes."

"No. I don't think so. I don't think you understand about my feelings about you. See? I feel how you tighten at that. You don't know anything about me, but I know about you. The more I worked on

165

the story, the more I began to feel . . . this way about the guy in the story. But we never talked."

"About all the art," I protested. "We talked. That's been wonderful. It's the best thing this semester. Sara, I've . . . every minute in the gallery and the library and walking."

"Not the art," she said. "I want to be the best thing that happened to you this semester, Nick. Me, not Bruegel. *Me.*" Then she pushed away from me and went to the stereo and put on a record, a soft nondescript music. She came back and sat down beside me and showed me a photograph in a large book. It was a picture of four handsome young men. They were dressed in Civil War officer's uniforms, Yankee blue. Their pants were stuffed into cavalry boots and were puffed out about the knees. Across their chests were elegant and unusual sashes, flowing and loose. Over the left pocket of one of the soldiers a large, floppy rose was pinned. And they were smiling.

"This is a Matthew Brady photograph. We're studying him in this course I'm taking, the Photo History of War. I look at this picture, Nick, and it makes me so sad I want to cry. Just look at them. The bravado. You can just tell they've not seen any fighting yet. You can just tell. Oh Nick. They were probably all killed."

I turned to her. There were tears in her eyes. How could I comfort her?

"I wrote a poem," she said. "It's how I dealt with this photograph. They must all of them have had sweethearts back home."

The moon looks over us in the trenches of our love.
The howitzers keep us apart.
Our love is like a history of war,
Lost from the start.
We began under lofty banners in strife,
And ended with this junky truth of life:
It is a battlefield.

"That's a fine poem," I said, handing it back to her. "It really is."
Then suddenly she pushed herself away.

"Is it because I'm older than you? Is that it?" Now she had risen and was standing in front of me, her hips at the level of my head.

"Is *what* it?"

"Why you keep me away from you?"

"I don't. I'm here now, aren't I?"

"Then bring me close."

I reached up and took her hands and twisted her down beside me. I thought that none of this could be happening. Or did I mean that none of it should be happening? My mind started to shift as it always did, grabbing at allusions, references, books, essays, learned treatises.

In desperate haste I began to jerk into defensive position, a picket line of information; I marshaled what had always been my effective safeguards. But it was a Maginot Line. Immobile, inflexible, all my guns locked into one position expecting the enemy to come from only one direction.

But the enemy came from elsewhere. And there was no enemy.

I tried to find the switch to shut it off, but I could not. Jung started to form, D.H. Lawrence, the hormonic pattern of the chemistry of the organic compounds of sexual arousal, the lymphatic path of testosterone. She reached behind my head and stroked my neck and the windows upon windows that had started to open all closed down and all I had to deal with was the girl in my arms and the aching shaft between my legs. And the softness of her lips.

"What's wrong now?"

"Nothing."

"Yes. Your kisses are hard."

"Sara."

"Don't. I'll show you. It's O.K. It's wonderful. Do what I tell you. Open your mouth."

I opened my mouth like at the dentist.

"No, not so wide. Like this." She pushed my mouth together.

"I'm so dumb," I said. "What a dumb thing. Open your mouth and I . . . . "

"Shush. Now. Pout a little. Like this." She showed me. "Make the inside of your lips turn out. Good. Close your eyes. Now." She took my mouth upon hers and held me until I could not breathe. But I did not want to breathe.

"O.K.?"

"Ah yes." But she felt my body arch.

"So now what's wrong?"

"Your roommates? Suppose they come out?"

"I'd kill them," she said. Then she took my lips again. She stroked my neck and sometimes bit my ear. Sometimes she put her tongue in my ear. Then she said, "Put your hand on my breast." I did. "No, Nick. *Under* the sweater." I could not move. She took my hand and guided me properly. "Good, Nick. Good." I groaned. We continued. My hand found its rhythm, gentle and exploring, her nipple hard as an acorn. I knew what to do. Animal reason, Santayana would have explained it, but Santayana shattered into a spasm of exploding star stuff.

The moon looks over us in the trenches of our love.

"Sara," I shouted as she rocked with me as my body threw me around.

"Here," she said, rising, "in here." She took my hand and led me into her bedroom. She turned on a small light on the dresser across the small room then faced me and raised her arms out from her sides. "Undress me. Slowly." I did, her tweeds and woolen sweater falling like gossamer veil. O Salome.

My hands were shaking, badly out of control. She saw them and took my hands in hers and the shaking stopped. She transfused her certainty into me. What was there left for me to do except believe?

"Now pick me up and lay me on the bed," she said. And I did. O prince's daughter.

I was erect again, one of the few but considerable blessings of being my age, but what was my age now between the thighs of Sara filling me with her? She had had to explain about the condom. I understood the mechanics of it, of course, but she knew far better than I how to do such things quickly and well. And more than that. "Here," she guided me. And, "*Here.*"

"Sara," I said at last. "Ah Sara. I love you so much. I love you so much."

And then I fell asleep, plummeting as if I had rolled off the sharp edge of flat earth.

When I awoke it was still deep into the night though close to dawn. She had touched me and I had sprung up. She straddled and then rolled off. "Put on a condom." I reached for it. "What are you doing?" she said. I had taken the used condom and was trying to fit it. "Stop that. Get a new one. It's right there."

"A new one? What's wrong with this? I only used it once."

She laughed and bit me on the chin and then licked my chest. "Oh Nick Burden. Oh, you are so wonderful. Oh, you are a story, you are."

And when I was ready, she straddled me and off she went and I went racing after her beyond Alpha Centuri, beyond M81, beyond the furthest quasars, further even than the last possible photons could be. And before I fell asleep this second time, I was certain that I felt in her a subtle change; it was as if I had become less her student and more a partner. What I wanted to believe, I believed: that my love was now reciprocal, that the sex had somehow beaten us into love the way a nugget of purest gold is beaten into a sheet of airy thinness. I had extension, now—we did—and had all the glory of well-being that I could imagine ever wanting.

►21►
=

"Mike," I said into the phone, "how did you find me?"

"You have got an appointment with the dean at ten o'clock. Did you forget that? Everyone's running around trying to find you."

"The dean of Student Affairs, right? What Sam Pelton was saying? The trouble in the dorm?"

"No. Dean Roskov. The big dean in the sky. Ten o'clock. And me at one o'clock. Don't forget, Nicky. It's very important. A lot of important shit is coming together today. Don't forget."

"Right. Ten o'clock."

"No, no. Not that. That's nothing," Mike said. "Me. One o'clock. I'll meet you in the room," and he hung up.

Janie and Ricki were watching me. They were still in their bed clothes. All I had on were my pants. My feet were cold on the bare, hardwood floor. In the bathroom I heard the shower running. I tried not to think of the water coursing over her body, between Sara's breasts. And I tried to think of what I was supposed to do now. I slapped at my pockets for my grid sheet, but I had no more clothes on, and I had not coordinated this day yet. But I did not have to. I would have to remember what I had learned last night, starting at seven o'clock at the Culvers' front door until the phone rang just now, that I was the gravitational center whose movement gave planetary motion to others, to Lionel Kreutzer or to the readers of the college newspaper, to the Tod Culvers and the deans and the Janies and Rickis and even the Sara Logans. *The* Sara Logan. I felt splendid and adored.

"Breakfast?" I smiled. "I've got to get to the dean's office by ten." Both Ricki and Janie rushed to do my bidding.

Schwartz, Lambeth, Roskov, and Culver. I thought it sounded like a law firm whose job it was to administer me like a trust fund. And Appleton. He had been asked to attend the meeting. They had assembled at nine to discuss the situation that had developed, but what was the situation? Was it that Kreutzer had attempted to raid Cobbton of Nick Burden? Or if there was now a question of serving Nick's best interests, then should Cobbton not encourage me to seek my fullest potential and go to Princeton? But how was that potential defined? Or was that even the point? My parents' desire was clear: I had come to college to discover more about myself, to discover what my *direction* was. They weren't worried about my potential; potential was the least problem I could have. And they were not in a hurry. Dean Roskov agreed with that position. He also pointed out that those were the terms under which I had chosen Cobbton.

"He came to us for nurture," Roskov said.

"Development," Lambeth seconded him.

"By whose definition?" Culver said. "Do you think he is not being nurtured, not developing? It just happens quickly with him. He learns and develops exponentially, at a logarithmic rate. That's the point here, really. His parents' definition and maybe ours isn't sufficient in this instance. People develop at their own rate. And there is no way of measuring his."

"But they all need to go through certain stages," Lambeth said.

"Yes. In the first six months of life," Culver answered to answer back.

"Or the first six years," Andre Schwarz said, his contempt for such distinctions barely registered but yet not adequately hidden. They had been talking and talking—about what?—for the better part of the hour. All had given their testimony. The boy seemed happy enough, adjusted enough. In the four times he had dutifully reported to Schwartz, he had not indicated even the slightest difficulty. Not of any sort. The mother was a hysteric.

But before Lambeth could get into a defense of his professional judgment, Roskov pushed them all, as best he could, into a focus. His own calendar on his desk pushed back at him.

"Please. As I see it, the immediate situation is this. His mother is waiting for a phone call from me. What I tell her will determine whether Nick continues in Cobbton. He could be gone by this afternoon. But not to Princeton. Just away from here. I'll work on the assumption that none of us wants that." He looked at Culver, but could find no agreement in his face. "The mother understands that Kreutzer's offer had nothing to do with us, and that it was not and is not supported by us." Again he looked at Culver.

"Why are you looking at me?" Culver said. "Do you think I set this up? I do think he should go to the institute, I've not hid that. I've seen his work. Which means I've seen his destiny. But I didn't know what Kreutzer was going to do."

"I'm sorry if my looks implied suspicion," Roskov said. "But you're a critical voice here. You can have a serious influence on him. His mother believes that. You were with Kreutzer when the offer was made. In your home. I accept your statement, but I'd like to be able to say to his mother in good faith that we all think he should stay at Cobbton for the foreseeable future. Frankly, I think he should. But his mother needs our assurance that we are trying to keep him here and not otherwise. Can I give her that assurance?"

"You can, but you shouldn't," Appleton said. At last. He had been invited into this special committee because Roskov knew how closely he worked with his students in the star section. His insights might be useful. Now inwardly the dean groaned. "I agree with Culver. We shouldn't get in Burden's way. Maybe we shouldn't encourage him to go where we want him to go. But we should encourage him to get on with his life wherever it takes him. That's what we try to teach all our other students, isn't it? So let's not make such a big deal about it."

"You want me to say that to his mother?"

"Not in so many words."

"Then in what words, pray tell?"

"In his own words, in the boy's words." Appleton said. 'Maybe he is content for now to be here. Maybe he has no desire or intention of leaving. Why don't you ask him?"

172

"No sir," I said to the dean. "I love it here. Nothing would make me leave."

I sat before them in the clothes I had worn last night, although without my semen clotted undershorts. I had had no time to get back to the dorm to change. I had showered at Sara's and eaten a breakfast with her, served by her maidens. I might have had time to run back to the dorm to change if I had not lingered, but we had things to discuss, she had said.

As I ate my scrambled eggs, she wanted me to promise not to talk to other reporters. From the Cobbton College *Chronicle*, I asked? From the *New York Times* or the *Daily News*, she said. NBC, CBS. What? You're kidding, I had said, though of course it could happen. It had happened before in my life. They have stringers on campus, she explained. She explained what a stringer was. Above all, she instructed me, be careful of the *National Enquirer*, which would be sure to show up in some guise or other. She wanted me to get solid-colored socks and not the argylie things I favored. And let my hair grow just a little longer. She would give me my next haircut. Free? I asked. Nothing's free, she said. I had a second cup of coffee. A third. She had green eyes with little flecks of yellow and black in them. Amazing eyes. Her skin was lustrous. She was queenly here, attended to by Janie and Ricki, advising her young courtier. What self-assurance. Then Kreutzer's equation suddenly buzzed in my head; like tectonic plates, two great ideas were pushing against each other somewhere down, down, down in me where the earthquakes occurred. And quickly passed. The poetry of *Battlefield* replaced it: We began under lofty banners . . . . She held out before me a jam-smeared morsel of English muffin to which I rose and ate out of her fingers. She walked with me to the door. There she lightly touched me behind the neck and touched her lips to my cheek. Call me at seven, she said. At 7:30, I said.

There was my mother to call at seven. If I was (was I?) Sara Logan's lover, still I was Sally Burden's sixteen-year-old son.

"Last night, Nick. That was very special for me. You. Well?" I started to speak but she put her finger on my lips striking me dumb. "No. I'm saying it for both of us Nick. I am. More than I had imagined. Before." She kissed me again.

What might Culver think seeing me still dressed as I had been the night before? Though now slightly rumpled. And unshaven (did I need to shave everyday?). But what did I care? I worried about nothing except that whenever I thought about Sara I started to get an erection.

"I think your mother would be very relieved to hear you say that, Nick," the dean said.

"I'll tell her tonight when I call."

So that was that. They spoke to me a little about the impact of the newspaper story. I told them what had gone on.

"It's just started," I said. "But I'm O.K. I was a little apprehensive. A *lot* apprehensive," I smiled. "But it's not going to be so bad. I've got a feeling."

And then we all left, splitting off along the angles and paths that cut the campus up like the ancient charts of the sailing lines of ships that sailed by astrolabe and Polaris. Culver walked along with me.

"Kreutzer won't stop, you know. He'll contact your parents. He's very persistent."

"My mom's a tough lady. Her life has a lot to do with protecting me."

"Right. But Kreutzer isn't an enemy. He's not some curious jerk. He's a friend."

"I know that."

"Maybe you could make that clear to your mom. Soften all this. All she sees right now is Kreutzer as a threat, rather than a promise. Or a future. Do you see what I mean? Let her reject his offer for what it really is and not because of what she is afraid it might be–do– to you."

"O.K. Sure. But sir, I'm not leaving Cobbton."

"Someday you're leaving Cobbton, Nick."

"Not soon," I said, and turned with a wave off on my own path.

"But what's time to a physicist?" Culver shouted after me.

Along my way I was encountered, examined, stopped for autographs, pointedly ignored, hooted at, cheered. But more often just simply passed by.

"Nick Burden?" a young man stopped me. "I'm Alex Smith from the college chess club, and I'd like to invite you to become a member of our club." He picked up my brisk pace beside him.

"I don't play chess," I said.

"You can't play chess? Wow. That does surprise me."

"I can play, I just don't."

"Is it because it's too easy for you. Is that it," Alex Smith said.

"No. I don't know. I've never played against someone. I've never really played the game, I've just studied it."

"Ah ha."

"Ah ha?" I said, getting ready.

"This is your chance. You could play in actual competition here. You could represent your college."

"No. Thanks."

"Don't you want to represent your college? Don't you think maybe you've got some responsibility here?"

Alex Smith stopped walking, but so did I. We faced each other. It was not an aggressive question, though bluntly put; it was honest enough. I could feel that: it was everyone's question, and maybe my own. If I was an accident, then did I have a right to withhold what was not, after all, my own, not something I had earned? Whose coin would I be spending, anyway? I thought of Kreutzer's argument that the world should not be made to wait for what maybe I alone could give it—a unified field theory? a possible molecular solution to AIDS? a national collegiate chess championship to Cobbton College? Mike's tutorial service? It was easy enough for me to say to myself that as an individual, like any other individual, I had personal rights. But what were they, especially if I was not like any other individual? What happens when the hypothetical turns into the actual? When what you do *not* do has as wide consequences as *what* you do?

"Do you know the king's Indian opening, if you are white?" I asked Alex Smith, who nodded. "And do you know absolutely the very best defense against it?"

"Ah . . . uh," Alex Smith said. "Uh, Ruy Lopez. Or no . . . no, the Nimzois counter. Yes. That's it."

"No," I said. "It was Cabablanca's response to Alekine in Cuba, 1936. Do you remember what happened?"

"Sort of. I think. I mean I don't actually remember the actual. . . ."

"He didn't show up," I said. "He forfeited the game." I started off again toward the library. A car of students drove by us braying its horn. Alex Smith fell in next to me.

"But that's not a defense. Alekine won. Cabablanca lost."

"Maybe not," Nicky said. "Won, lost. That's a score, that's all it is. There was no game. Not even a single move. No annotation. No discussion. Right? Nothing to analyze in the chess history books. So what was it Cabablanca lost? The championship, but not the game. So what could Alekine have won?"

"Yeah, but there's something wrong with what you're saying. It sounds right but it's wrong. It's like one of those philosophy tricks, you know?"

"You're right, Alex. It's a trick. What I did was change the meaning of defense."

◆22◆
=

The poster delivery system worked this way. Under our beds, stored in large flat cardboard cartons, were the posters, each in its own large foam core folder. In the closet the tubes were stacked like unsplit cord wood or artillery shells not yet loaded. One or the other of us would fill an order, carefully extracting Panther Puss, say, and rolling it and sliding it into a tube. Mike or I would consult the bus schedule taped to the back of the door and, by appointment, make the run into the shopping plaza and back. It had become a casual routine. Mike did all the ordering and selling.

Today. One o'clock. A very large order. Presents for the big party weekend. Art and gifts. Waiting for me when I returned from the library were twenty-eight tubes. On eighteen of them the customer's name written on a red-bordered sticker. Ten tubes were bound tightly together for one customer: Joe Casper.

"Let's go," Mike said. "There's a 1:15. We can just make it. We've actually *got* to make it. Joe doesn't like to be kept waiting, or haven't you noticed?" He took up the ten-tube package and pointed to the eighteen for me.

"Why do we both have to go?" I asked. "I mean one of us could make the delivery easy. You want me to do it? I don't mind."

"No," Mike said. "It's not just the delivery. We've got to get costumes, too. Remember? Halloween? Come on. Let's go. We've got a three o'clock appointment with the tutors. And messages."

"Messages?"

"About the bands. There is always something fucking up. We've got to check in with our secretary."

"The one in the basement of the eco building?"

"That's her."

"I was joking. You really have a secretary? You're incredible, Mike."

"Us. *Our* secretary. And I hope so, Nicky. I'm going to need something in this life. So incredible might help. But you learn, right?" With our arms nearly full, we scurried down and out of Jameson. "I mean providing a service is much more complicated than selling goods. Selling posters is easy compared to agenting, for instance. And did you know that repairing and servicing cars is a larger part of the gross national product than the profit made from the actual sale of cars? This bus ad course I'm taking, it makes some interesting points. So we'll see what tutoring is like." He was nearly jogging. "Stanley J. Kaplan makes a fortune tutoring SATS, so why not us? But that's why you can charge more for services than goods. My old man is always selling goods. So you're only in business as long as you've got some *thing* to peddle, but with a service you're always in business. Like a lawyer, for instance, or a dentist. You've always got your dentist even if he isn't always working on you like at that exact moment. And he's always got you as a customer. You're always his. He can usually count on you. You know what I mean? He divides you into his gross so he can figure what his per capita expenditure is. Get it?" He was gulping slightly for air.

"I think so."

"I'll give you an example. If you have a medical practice or a law practice, you can sell it. But you can't sell being a salesman. All you can sell is *something*. If you sell a store, you sell the inventory and fixtures, and that's it."

"I hadn't thought about it."

We had swung quickly out of the dorm and down toward the bus stop, Mike talking quickly and high, a manic note even in his usual allegro.

But was it Mike or to myself that I was responding, resonating to my own internal tuning fork now that it had been struck? Spinning faster now, faster and faster.

No one had been waiting for me by the boarded-up window of the reception desk in Jameson, but a pile of notes and envelopes for me were in a mound. I swept them up as I swept by. But no *bodies* were lurking about; it was Friday afternoon and a big party weekend was coming, a ridge of high pressure, plans to make, fraternities and dorms to be prepared for serious partying – the kegs of beer rolled in, the bhangs fed, the decorations flung about, the trysting plots to be strung together, niches found. Tricks to be imagined for Halloween. And treats.

In the bus I went through the papers. Many invitations to every conceivable event, assemblage, meeting. Offers to sell me things across an enormous range – a cat for a pet, a machine for making juice out of vegetables, a complete layout of an HO-gauge model railroad. Exhortations to join clubs and particularly campus religious organizations, but many off-campus churches as well. How could the religious have all gotten to me so quickly unless they had delivered the messages directly? Such effort. Amazing. Was God so impatient? Was my soul in such immediate danger? And if so, why?

"You shouldn't be surprised," Mike said. "There's only one of you, right? There's never been another. Maybe never no one like you after you. So how do you think people are going to react? Look at Elvis?"

"That's different. He did something."

"And you *are* something."

"Maybe," I said.

"What's that mean? What's a dumb thing like that mean?"

"Look." I showed Mike a letter asking me to run for the head of student government association. And another similar letter. Each letter was signed by a committee. "Faction," I said.

"Democracy," Mike said.

"But why me? I'm a first semester freshman. I'm sixteen."

"Just what I said. Capitalism."

"What you said was 'democracy,' Mike."

"Same thing. Democracy, capitalism. You can't have one without the other. And if you have one you *have* to have the other."

"Like Witten and Kreutzer," I said.

"What's that?"

"Nothing. Just a stray thought. Democracy and capitalism, is that from bus ad, too?" I said.

"Right."

"But what does capitalism have to do with me running as the president of SGA? Am I a product, a set of goods? Or a service? What do they want with me?"

"Right now I'd guess they have in mind a trademark. You know, like Betty Crocker. Only there never was a real Betty Crocker. The idea was you set up a trademark that everyone felt good about so they'd feel good about the stuff she was selling. It's like Bill Cosby or Ed McMahon. You see them selling everything, right? Only all they are really selling is what everybody feels about them—good. Product identification."

"A figurehead," I said.

"A trademark," Mike said.

The bus lurched to a halt. Waiting at the stop was a group of Cobbton students. "Tube Call," I shouted to them as I hopped down and led them away. Quickly I called out their names: Kleiner, Doyle, Petersen, and on. Three of the eighteen posters I gave to two young women. One of them glared at me, her jaws set, her hair short and punky, but the other, who identified herself as Celia Petersen, took me by the sleeve of my blue blazer.

"I'd like to ask you something, Nick," she said. "Why are you doing this? Do you know what you're doing? Why is a person like you supporting this sort of thing?"

"What?" I said. "What sort of thing? Doing what? Making money?"

"The worst sexist act next to rape," the other young woman burst out. "Isn't that just predictable?" She was raising her voice, turning some passing heads. "The highest intelligence in human history turns out to be a hard-core porn-selling sexist shit-head. Some brain." She spun away, her disgust and anger coming too close to an action. Celia turned back to me.

"I apologize for Angie, Burden. What I wanted to—"

"Don't you apologize for me to that piece of dung!" Angie said, turning back into battle and approaching us. I thought of running. What if she swung at me? How would I defend myself? Are you allowed to hit a violent feminist, even in self-defense? But again she suddenly broke off.

"Look. This isn't the best place to talk about this," Celia said, "but will you talk about it? A person like you has a lot of influence. Right now it's not hopeful to have someone like you selling something like this. What about humanity? What about the future?" She held up the tubes. "Do you have a girlfriend?"

"I think so," I said. "*Yes!*" I said.

"Would you want a picture of her, one of these kinds of pictures, up on some guy's wall?"

Angie broke in shouting, "*While he jacked-off on it?*"

I shuddered. Everyone must have heard. I thought about Sara stretched across an azure sky with crimson clouds blurred into it, her skin tawny and alizarin and smooth, her nipples vermillion, peach highlights on their tips as bright as Venus when she rises as a morning star. Between my legs my penis began its rough assent. I still had not gotten into new underwear. The grey flannel rubbed me the wrong way. Oh Sara, Sara.

"No," I said, "I wouldn't."

"Then don't do this," Celia said. "Don't do this."

"I'll think about it. I will. I promise."

"Good," Celia said.

"Then why . . . . What are you buying these for?" I asked.

"We burn them," she said. "At each meeting of the woman's coalition we have a symbolic burning."

"And we're running out of symbols, pig. Soon the real thing. Soon the merchant pimps,"Angie said as the two women finally turned and climbed back into the bus.

A person like you. Someone like you. Brain. I was a little depressed.

Markum had not come for his poster. I looked around, but no one else was waiting. Across the small plaza where the bus came in I saw Mike talking to Joe Casper. I walked to them.

"Hi," I said to Joe Casper. "Markum didn't show up," I said to Mike. "Do you want another poster, Joe?"

"What poster? What's *another* poster mean?" He said this to Mike. Sharply.

"Nothing, nothing," Mike said and took the tube from me. "A poster. You know? A naked girl?" he said to Joe Casper. Joe Casper grunted and nodded.

"Nick the brain," Joe Casper said. "You're in the paper. Here."

He took the local newspaper that was folded under his arm and swatted me with it. "Right on the front page. So I got a famous friend, huh?" He punched me high on my arm, not so lightly. Then he turned back to Mike.

"So we got everything straight, O.K.? No fuck-ups? No problems?"

"Right, right," Mike said pulling away, stepping back, moving. But Joe Casper put out his hand and took him.

"You know what I mean, hey? My customers are not patient types. Me neither." His face was blank and full of hard edges. Then he smiled. "Go on, g'wan. And you, brain, you got to be something else. Some piece of work." Then he walked off.

"What's that about, Mike?" I asked.

"What's what about?"

"Him. Joe Casper. He's not a college student."

"Why? Because he's so rough? So who do you think goes to community college? Not the Nick Burdens, my friend, on full scholarships. The Joe Caspers go to community college. And his customers. I was there. I know. Come on, come on, we've got a lot to do."

"But it's something more," I persisted, not moving. "He's older. I mean I bet he's near to thirty."

"In the community college you've got a very wide age span. You've got college age kids right up to grandmas. No kidding. People who work in the daytime take college courses at night. All that. Wives. Fathers."

"There's something tough about him, Mike. Look how he dresses, how he talks. He even sounds dangerous."

"So what's your point, Nicky? What are you trying to say? I shouldn't sell him posters because he doesn't fit your idea of a college student? I don't ask him a lot of questions. He's a very good customer. Our best, in fact. I don't have the time to care about who buys and sells. I'm a bottom line man, Nicky. Now will you please come on? What do you want to be?" He pulled me toward the K-Mart where the largest selection of costumes and masks were, and where the prices were best.

I wanted to dress up as a giant white rabbit, but Mike argued against it. "Jesus, Nicky. No one will see you in there. People have got to see you. For a hundred bucks a party, remember? They don't want a rabbit. Something more dignified."

"Product identification," I said. "Nicky Burden and Alpha Beta Gamma."

"Right, right. Now you've got it," Mike said.

We settled for the Mad Hatter. All I needed was the wing-tipped collar and the cravat and of course the exaggeratedly high-crowned beaver hat. Mike got a pirate costume. A buccaneer with a black patch over one eye and a huge loop of an earring. "Me," he said. "Me to a T."

On the ride on the bus back to campus he told me about his newest scheme. During Thanksgiving break we would go to Atlantic City to play blackjack. He explained how blackjack gambling worked, and how you could beat it if you were a counter. If you could remember what was already played in a stack of cards that the dealer pulled out of the shoe, five decks of cards, then you would have a better and better chance of figuring what was likely to happen. In the casinos the dealer has to hold at seventeen.

"If you know what's left, you've got the dealer at your mercy."

"It sounds too easy. Lots of people could remember that sort of thing."

"Sure. Not lots, but enough. So it's against the law. The casinos watch for the counters and throw them out."

"Then we can't do it." But I was laughing. "Mike, you're going crazy. This is the looniest scheme yet."

"What is driving me crazy, Nicky, is how to maximize you. I think of ways to make your power worth something, you know?"

"Yes. Me too. Exactly."

"So what kind of ideas do you have. You never tell me," Mike said.

"They're not money ideas, Mike."

"You've got something against money? You're rich? I didn't notice."

"Not rich at all. And money's fine. I've got to make some serious money this summer to fix my boat. And in another year I want to take a major cruise somewhere, probably to Maine, and that will cost."

"And don't forget Sara," Mike said.

"What? Sara?"

"Girls. They don't cost nothing. Even today, they cost the guy more than they cost themselves."

"Did you learn that in your bus ad course, too?"

"Don't get sore."

"Leave Sara out of this, O.K.?"

"I'm not talking about Sara. I'm talking about money. Relax."

"And forget the blackjack idea."

"Why? You miss the point. Other counters have to count. Even the fast ones needs some time. That's how they get caught. You don't need time to count. You just look at the flow of the game and you *know* what's been played, what's left. Besides, we hit the casinos just this once. We take everything and parlay it and don't. . . ."

"No. *You're* missing the point. You said it yourself. It's against the law."

"Not the *law* law. The casinos' law, Nicky. They set things up to suit themselves. Well, fuck them."

"No," I said, "forget it. The idea is definitely out. I'm not going along with this one, Mike. Gambling isn't business. Anyway, I've got to be home for Thanksgiving. I want to be home for that. My parents would expect it. And maybe Sara . . . maybe Sara will . . . invite me for the weekend. Or something." Where had that come from? But where was so much that was occurring to me coming from – particular eyes and noses and tree limbs from Bruegel and paragraphs that I wanted to write in my journal and Sara reaching down between my legs – where was that coming from? So why not every other possibility or hope or dream?

Why not fly at the sun?

►23►
=

It was nearly dark down in the gullies and in the shell bursts of trees I ran through, but I knew the way exactly, where the crown of the dirt road rose or broke off and where the shoulders flattened or disappeared, where the larger limbs of the broken apple trees had not yet been cleared, the curves and dips and cant of everything. Where to expect the dogs. Nearly every day I had run along this path out beyond the campus since I had first gone out for the cross-country team. Out from the gym on Morrell Street toward the river and then over the small footbridge and up the rise to Custer's farm, through the apple orchard and then swinging in a wide arc first east and eventually veering westward and back across the traffic bridge, route 7, until at last I turned into the neighborhoods, two streets over from Tod Culver's house, and at last back to the gym, where I would shower.

I thought of my running now as I thought of my sailing on *Yarps*, as my own time, as an exquisite compression. Here in the dark umber end of the day on this trail as in the indigo conclusion in *Yarps* behind Cole Island in Lake Champlain, I felt indivisible. I remembered my father's words, that I would have to be taught—"or for him to teach himself, to be one person." Now, at least in these moments, I felt like that one person. But did that mean that I was always to be a runner or a sailor? A Flying Dutchman?

The end of daylight saving time had fallen down hard on cross-country running; it increased the danger of falling, for one thing, to run in the dusk. If you fell and hurt yourself badly enough, a severe ankle or knee sprain, or even a break, so far away from help if you were running alone, you might not be found in time. Hypothermia would claim you before you could crawl out of the apple orchard or across the corn field to a farmer's house or out and across the bridge to the highway. None of the others ran in the dark. But I accepted the shape of these physical risks because of my single-handed sailing. I had experience with danger, something I could count on that I hadn't been born with. Something I had earned. Now I could navigate my course on land as well as I could navigate at sea. The cold came down quickly, already at a half past five as clear and hard as black ice or as a force-five wind.

And I thought about my life just then and laughed out in the dark and burning air. I began to run faster, faster than I knew I should run in the dark and against my pace.

There are moments in sailing on a close reach in hard but steady wind when the boat hits a slot in the air and the water and resistance seem to end. You can take your hand off the tiller, cleat down all your sheets, and rise, it seems, almost out of the sea itself and into the air. That is what I felt now running through the orchard and past the fields, further into the darkness in the east before I turned into the slight remaining spray of light in the west-southwest sky and to the lights of the college and the town.

Rapture. I would run on into the darkness, stay in the slot. I had read of mariners who had succumbed to such a rapture, who had gotten caught in the perfection of their life in the sea and who never returned to land. That is what I felt now, that I had reached a kind of perfection, not that all (any) of the fundamental problems that I would have to face were resolved, but rather that now I *had* these problems, the simple problems of first love and a best friend (and a business to be a part of) and indecisiveness about the future. The abstract me had become a specific me. Pinocchio had turned into a boy. I had become, was certainly becoming, perfectly human. At least for now, in this instant, with my breath rushing through me in the dark. And even if this perfection, this perfect moment, did not last, there would be other such moments, I felt sure. For the first time I was certain of something other than the power of my brain.

I felt the dangers in my feet, the swiftness with which my knowledge of the trail was coming up to me through my running shoes, the mistakes I was averting by inches, the rock, the hole, the hay wagon that had collapsed maybe twenty years before but whose rotted whippletree of locust wood still made a low hurdle that I took in full flight.

I dropped my pace down and down, and fell out of the slot. I thumped out onto route 7. At the corner of Elm and Beech the fat and wheezy Labrador challenged me. I could probably outrun the old dog, but I bent to an imaginary stone and threatened the dog and it stood back. It was always this way, by now a game the dog had come to wait for.

At seven I called home.

"So that's the end of it," I told my mother after I had described the meeting with the dean and the committee.

"Don't you believe it," she said. Then, quietly, "Your father has something to tell you."

"Nick," my father said on the extension phone. "John Sebering."

"What?" I said, quickly attentive.

"He was killed in an automobile accident. We thought you should know."

"But," was all I could say. Then, "How?"

"An accident," my father said, "just an accident. He lost control of his car. He wasn't speeding. No drugs or anything. He ran into a light standard on the highway. I'm sorry." There was nothing more he could say.

John Sebering had been one of my closer friends in Steffanville. Because of him, I had not been torn apart by the pack.

We would run together, just the two of us. He was on the high school track team, as I could not be, but sometimes on weekends or early or late in a day, he would come over and we would run, not saying much. I tasted the irony of my now daily running, and now alone. John Sebering was the first person my age to die, the first person I knew who had been like me in being young. Now he was gone forever, and in that moment I was truly angry and for the first time contemptuous of the absurdity of contemporary physics that argued that time could move backwards as well as forward. But there would never again be a John Sebering.

And then I was flooded by an emotion that I could not name. Not simply a sorrow or a sadness for John Sebering and his family, and not the simple elegiac, carpe diem response either: be absolute for death, seize the day. No man is an island? *No. All* of us are islands, I thought, just as the planets and suns and galaxies are islands, but the distance between the islands is not empty, is not an emptiness; it is not a void. Space is what we are and live in. So once again I had no language to express what I felt, first love for my father and now for this grief in which John Sebering was now dead and in which, in this moment in the sequence of time, I lived.

Images. Perhaps undifferentiated emotion exists just as eukaryotic cells exist, cellular structures of undifferentiated material, cells with out nuclei. Emotions without names.

Back in my dorm room I wrote down that idea in my grid notebook. Across the evening of October 30. I did not need the grid to remind me of what remained for me to do. Call Sara. And work in Culver's lab.

"How was your day?" she asked over the phone. I told her about it in general terms, but she wanted details. About the dean's meeting, the actors and their lines, how they delivered them. Their performance. "It's so exciting, isn't it? I love it. It's so gossipy. So insiderish."

"It's all confidential, Sara. You understand that."

"Of course. For now."

"For now? What does that mean?"

"Well, someday when you're *really* famous and *I'm* really famous, I'll have to write about all this. Us. Won't I?"

"Will you? Why?"

"I'll have to. We'll belong to the world. Public domain."

"I don't want to belong to the world. I want to belong to you. I want you to belong to me. Last night. All that we said, Sara. We weren't talking biography, were we?" She heard my voice thinning out, getting scared of being sixteen, of losing her to wherever she was going to go before me.

"Oh Nick, sweetie. Come on, come on. Be playful. Everything last night was true and wonderful."

"But you're taking notes? You really are going to write about us?"

"Sure, Nick. But not yet. Someday. That's what writers do, isn't it? Live a life and then write about it."

"Will it be sexy?" I asked, letting go of my fears a little. Trying

188

to be playful. Trying to get everything right, everything she was teaching me.

"You bet."

"Will you sell it to the movies?"

"For a fortune," Sara Logan said.

We talked on. And on. Twining around each other. Nuzzling.

"Come on, Burden. You've been on the fucking phone a half hour," a dormmate said behind me.

"I've got to go, Sara. Someone wants the phone. Where are you going to be tomorrow? I've got to hang up."

"Wait. Wait a minute," she said. "I forgot."

I signaled to the guy with the quarter in his hand. One more minute.

"I'm really busy tomorrow. It's a major weekend. I've got assignments for the newspaper and deadlines. And you've got all your parties. But listen, listen. I almost forgot. Appleton has invited you to his place for Sunday brunch and afternoon. His address is in the book."

"Appleton? Me?"

"And me, too," she said. "Maybe it's some sort of thing for students."

"But why didn't he invite me himself? Yesterday in class?"

"I don't know, Nick, but please be there, O.K.? I'm going to be there. We'll go somewhere afterwards. We'll welcome in November. Bye, sweetie."

➤24➤
=

In the bright white cube on the last pad on the wall, Culver had written a note: "Where you are here can go in three different directions. Two of them have been explored, as you probably know, by Guth and Lester respectively. Also, look particularly at Hawking's most recent paper in *Astrophysics*. The third direction looks promising. See how far you can pursue it before you fall off a cliff. Your value for delta pi looks a little small to me. And you need more rigorous work on your math. Your proofs are basically right but not yet elegant—Tod."

Culver always used the black marker, never any of the colors. I looked at the pads. I had not worked on this line of my thought for a few days, not since my study of Kreutzer and the subsequent smashup with Witten. And not since I had further refined some of my own strongest concerns wrapped up in the writing desk drawer.

I sat down on the floor and followed myself around the walls. It took me thirty minutes to pick up my patterns. At Culver's note I got up and went to the pads and began to work. He was wrong. There were not three directions. There were five. Yellow, blue, dark green, crimson, and black, with grace notes in veridian. On a fresh pad I carefully described them, more for Culver than myself. And I dutifully worked out the math in elegant completion. It would satisfy Culver. It was not an unreasonable demand. It was just not necessary for me. Beyond a certain point, I could know what would work in my equations. And these were sketches anyway. When the time came for me to form all this into a presentation, then I would consider the details.

If the time came for me to do this. Was this what I wanted to do? It had never occurred to me otherwise, not that something else had.

But what I was doing here in the narrow, cold, complete light of the cube did not interest me as much as my ideas about the infinite changing of the fundamental physical laws of the universe. The shifting speed of light. The absoluteness of sequence. Next to that, this on the walls was chopping wood. At least for me.

How did Appleton know that Sara knew me?

I stopped my work. It stopped for me. The marks on the pad might as well have been the language of the northern tribes of Sikkim, which I had never seen enough of to learn, all cursive and never printed. But it also looked like the brush work in the de Kooning paintings I had been studying, Woman No. 1 and on to No. 5. She was taking a course with Appleton. What course? She had not mentioned it. She was an art history major, what would she study with Appleton in English in this her senior year? Of course, she was also a writer. Maybe she was taking a writing workshop with him, but did he teach one? I stripped my questions away as if I were peeling a complexly leaved fruit. I got to the center. Did they talk about me? Appleton and Sara? I flushed with rage. It banged inside my head. I held my ears. I had known so little of rage in my life. Nothing. The mildest of anger. I was too smart for anger. My quick understanding of predicament and its process always prevented me, always got in the way. And even now, not anger or rage, but a spasm of jealousy was what had happened. I pushed the key. It computed. I looked at the fruit in my hand. It wasn't exotic at all. All it was was jealousy.

Jealousy. But it wasn't of Appleton, it was of the thought of any male in any stance near her. Nothing complicated at all, but, oh, the complication. I looked down. My hands were shaking.

"Wow," I shouted. "Wow *wow wow wooooowwwww.*" My voice pinged off the hard walls of the room like a stone hitting a large water tank, the sound running on like an impulse through a nerve rising and amplifying before it died. "This is terrific. This is great."

◗25◖

=

Journal Entry, October 25. Father/Garden.

I remember your gardens, how patient you were. I remember when you gave me a piece of your garden to be my garden. I was eight and had no patience, but neither was I impatient. I think that is because I have never had to wait for anything to happen in my mind. But if at eight I could comprehend any mathematics then extant or construct the most complex of conceivable benzene rings or read Aristotle or Aquinas, still I was eight and wanted the seeds to spring up overnight like the beans of Jack's beanstalk. I wanted the magic, but I thought the magic was only in the plant, in the harvest. You knew that the magic was in the tilling itself.

You showed me that when you squeezed a fistful of dirt and it stuck together in a mass that the earth was still too cold and wet to plant. And when the dirt fell out of your hand as loosely as when you had picked it up, that was the proper time. I remember how you would put a small piece of dirt on the tip of my tongue every Sunday for a month, and how each week the dirt did taste sweeter than the week before. An odd Eucharist for an eight-year-old. But maybe not so odd at that.

We worked in your garden and we worked in mine, but once mine was planted, I could not return to the weeding and the watering, the caring for it. Not untypical, I'd guess, for an eight-year-old, even for an eight-year-old like me. Still, I did not forget the garden, even then, but certainly not now. I remember you coming home from work in the spring as it grew milder and you changing and then going out into the yard to

192

dig and putter, and when you came back into the house, you would smell wet and sour, so shapeless and different from the smell of the print shop.

I have been thinking recently of the namelessness of emotional states and how limited the language of emotion is. I have this idea that the location of the feeling of a garden or of *YARPS* in a fog bank or of a father making his breakfast alone in the early morning kitchen is where our truest language is, but not all of us can speak it. I know or can know every language on earth, and the languages of all the sciences, and mathematical languages. But I do not know this other language, what I heard in the scrape of your shovel in your garden, the click of the rake through the unlimited stones that rose up through the soil through the winter. The frost had pushed them up, you explained; that is why there were always more stones in the spring for you to rake. But now I imagine wildly, you all winter hearing the stones ascending, just as I imagine you listening to the epithelial cells forming on the tips of the root hairs as they trust down through the grains of the dirt with a force once calculated at an incredible eighty thousand kilograms per millimeter, a force three times greater than the thrust of an oil rig grinding through rock with a diamond bit. Greater than the power of the rockets that lifted the satellites into outer space.

You never tended my garden for me, but you did not plow it in either. It must have been an eyesore and maybe even a source of diseases and a haven for destructive insects. And maybe it offended your aesthetic sense, my ragged patch on the edge of your neat and sturdy garden. I did not feel guilt. I allowed myself to forget my garden easily. But I do not think I forgot you in your garden, and now I surely remember you with vivid recall, the glint of light off your hoe, my mother calling you in to supper, and the great adventure of the cucumbers, the peas, the melons and corn and squash.

More and more in these past very few weeks I've tried to conceive of my own adventure, but all I come up with is the adventures of others, the painting of Bruegel and de Kooning and now each day more painters. And your garden. And you.

→ 26 →
=

Saturday night did not work out well, at least from a business
point of view, a Mike Tremain point of view. By nearly eleven
o'clock – and after three fraternity parties – it was clear enough
that the idea of selling me as a celebrity had limited possibilities.
Perhaps enough people hadn't heard of me or maybe it was more
that the context was wrong. We were all wearing costumes; none
of us was who we were. Any of us was someone else, grander,
more exciting, different, odd, so why should my oddity be more
than their own, or any more believable? And our costumes were
themselves out of the ordinary range of literary allusion. I was the
Mad Hatter, but there were far more creatures from the cabaret
in Star Wars or Hulk Hogans or people in Michael Jackson masks
or often just the simple androgynous smear of boys and girls looking unisexual, being natural. I was a freak, all right, but the wrong
kind of freak. A high IQ, the smartest guy in the world – that was
too abstract. You had to think about what that meant, the implications, but implications have no substance, no tangibility. My freak-
ishness didn't have the impact of, say, the two-headed man at the
circus, something that had image to it, and impact. For a man with
three eyes and two noses and a chin cleft deeply into his mouth
who lived his life under a paper bag until you paid him fifty cents
to lift it – for a man like that you could feel anything from revulsion
to pity, but whatever you felt it would be felt searingly: you would
remember what he looked like for the rest of your life. But not me.

194

And in the swelter of bodies and the swill of beer, the room full of the loud music of Bon Jovi or U-2, in the inebriation of the sexual pressure that bore upon us, squeezing us into a singularity indeed, breaking us into fractal repetitions out of this sexual chaos, what place was there for the appreciation of such an idea as intelligence, and only raw intelligence at that, an enormous reservoir of potentiality? Try that as a line to impress some girl in the Walpurgisnacht of a fraternity Halloween party. O wow! Out of this primordial chaos of pure undifferentiated energy, there was only one big bang that everyone was interested in, and for that you didn't need a Nicky Burden, whoever he was. Which is what I told Mike.

"But the other parties? We've still got to put in appearances at the Delta Upsilons, the Theta Chi's. . . ."

"Forget it. Give them back the money. Or tell them I was there. I've had it. It was a dumb idea."

"But we're talking a hundred bucks, Nicky. Even if it's not such a good idea, a contract is a contract. They paid, so now you show up. Jesus, Nicky, two quick stops is all."

Mike was pushing hard. There was an urgency to him, although maybe it was just his way of responding to the roaring situation.

"Come on, Mike. It's a bust. Forget it. Pick up a girl, they're all around."

"I don't want a girl, Nicky." He took my arm in his hand and held it hard. "I want my customers."

I pulled my arm free. "What's with you, Mike? Forget it." And I left.

That I was such a bust as a celebrity heartened me. Maybe the more important excitement of this weekend – the defeat of Colgate this afternoon, the intense partying going on – had broken the wave of the campus's interest in me. On Monday that tide of interest would still be high, there would be aftershocks and maybe small susumis, but maybe the energy had gone out of it and I would be, if not entirely accepted into this world of mortals as happily as I had been before the revelation, then at least allowed to bob along as a small unintrusive oddity. Sure. My mother and father and I had lived behind our barricade so long that we had developed a seige mentality. But when at last we had bothered to look over the ramparts, the enemy had departed. If Cobbton could win two more football games, especially the season finale against

Syracuse, then the chances of a bowl bid would be very good indeed. That, I felt certain, would draw the community interest away from me as well. When I saw Thumper McGuire, I would have to tell him to play especially hard. But I did not think I would encounter him as soon as I did.

I left fraternity row and headed for the library. It was the proud vaunt of Cobbton College that the library kept itself open for more hours than any other comparably sized school in the country. In the age of energy conservation there had been some good arguments to close earlier and more often, or at least on Saturday night (when only the geeks might be about, though no one said *that* of course). But it was a tradition that the president felt worth the cost. An expensive but valuable symbol.

Into the main library building, I wound my way through the empty halls to the art library that had been built as a link between the main building and the Cassidy Hall complex of art center and gallery. I entered the art library in costume, but the young woman on the desk did not bother to look up, even when I said, "Hurry up please, I'm late." At that she did look up at me and said, "No. You've still got half an hour," and turned back to the book she had been reading.

What had she thought she had seen? She had missed the reference completely, but how? How had she missed the outlandish beaver hat, the wing collar, the velvet lapels on the antique frock coat, the furled cravat? I couldn't resist it. I stopped.

"Listen. I'm expecting a friend. A white rabbit. Tell him I'm in the ND section, ND 3987.4 to be precise. O.K.?"

"O.K.," she said again not looking up. "A white rabbit. I'll tell him."

I hurried on.

But before I got to ND 3987.4, I passed ND 725.8 (Fishing– watercolors) and a figure so large, his bulk emphasized by being wedged between the stacks of books, that it could only be Thumper McGuire.

"Thumper?" I said. "Is that you?"

"Hi," he said. "Yeah. Me. Look at this." He thrust the book in his hands at me. "This is terrific. I've never seen anything like it. It's better than any photographs. Why is that? The paintings of the fish look more real than photographs." It was the most Thumper

196

McGuire had ever said to me all at once, and the tone of his voice had changed from its more usual tough monotone; now it was enspirited, lively. "And look at this, will you. You see the shine in the eye? Every one." He thumbed through the pages of the book – brown trout or giant blue marlin, spotted weakfish or green-yellow dolphins. "They all look alive, you know? That's how you tell a fish is alive, really alive. The eyes are the first thing to go, they get dull and filmy. And then the color goes out of the body. But Jesus, this guy must have known fish. I mean you couldn't paint one of these fast enough before it died to get the eyes right, you'd have to remember them."

"What are you doing here, Thumper? Why aren't you partying?" He looked at me with what I thought was a sorrowing glance, as if it was *my* eyes that were filmy and dull.

"I couldn't find a gorilla suit big enough, O.K.?" He snapped the book shut. I had broken into his mood, and I had broken it. He made to move off.

"Hey Thumper," I said. "I'm sorry." I was backpedaling down the aisle. There was no possibility of us squeezing by each other.

"What for, Burden? What are you sorry for?"

"For interrupting you."

"No big deal."

"For ruining something for you," and then, inspired insight, "and for locking you inside your body." He stopped.

"What's that mean, locking me inside my body?"

"I just assumed something about you, because you're big, a football star. You had a big day."

"I didn't have a big day. What I did was a good job. It's what I get paid for, a little now, a lot later in the pros. What's the matter, Burden, don't you read the papers?" He started to move again. But I did not move backward. Maybe I owed him this. All his life everyone must have moved out of his way. On line in a supermarket or walking down a sidewalk, people must have unconsciously deferred to his size assuming that he would act here as he did on the football fields that he had grown up on, where if you didn't move out of his way, he moved you out of his way. But I stood still, and when in two steps he was upon me, he stopped. He did not threaten or gesture or even tell me to move. He did what most people would have done: he stopped and waited for me to make my decision. He did not automatically assume that he had a superior right to the space we shared because he could take that space if he wanted to. It was I – and the rest of us – who projected that assumption upon him. So Thumper and I, we were just alike.

"We've got to talk," I said to him and laughed and gave him a little shove, a backward push.

"What's with you, Burden?"

"Nick, " I said, "not Burden, Nick."

"O.K. Nick, then. What's with you?"

"Suddenly I'm feeling pretty good, Thumper."

"Al," he said, "not Thumper, Al."

"Al, then," I said. "I'm feeling pretty good."

"Also, you're a little crazy." He smiled and indicated my costume. "The Mad Hatter, right?"

"You've read the book?" I said, too late.

"Yeah, Burden. Imagine that. I can read." He was ready to move again.

"Well you could have fooled me, *Thumper*," and I shoved him again.

"Hey. Cut it out," he said, "I'm school property. You can't do that. What happens if you break it? The coach will have your ass, *genius*." He stepped back and started to laugh.

"I'll have to take my chances," I said, laughing too. Delighted. "You're in trouble now, *football player*," I said advancing upon him, a belligerent character out of a fairy tale. Then he reached out and knocked my beaver hat off. "Oh now you've done it. *Now* you've done it," I said and pushed into him hard. He put his arms up to ward me off and started to shout for help. Loud.

The girl who was on duty at the desk appeared.

"Stop it," she said. Sternly. "Stop it. You. In the costume. Stop it. Leave him alone." And together we hooted at that.

We walked back to the dorm together, a giant and a smaller man in a beaver hat out of the nineteenth century. The closer we got to the dorm, the more we waded through the revelers, knots and clumps of them. In Jameson, the building seethed and shuddered like a building in a cartoon. Al McGuire asked me to come to his room. He wanted to show me something.

He lived alone. Cobbton did not approve of a football dorm. Athletes lived as randomly as the rest of us, although they did eat at a special table in the commons. But Al McGuire lived alone; I did not ask why. Perhaps it was the one special request he had made for whatever personal reasons. Or maybe he was just too big to fit in comfortably with another. Or maybe his assigned roommate had moved out earlier in the semester. Whatever, he had made of his room a domain that seemed more personally his than many others. On his walls, instead of pictures of girls or football players or rock stars, he had pictures of fish or of people fishing or of fishing situations. And two stuffed fish, a large brown trout and a western trout, probably a cutthroat from Wyoming. On his bookshelves he had maybe forty books about fishing and related subjects and piles of fishing magazines. At the second desk, the missing roommate's desk, he had set up a fly-tying bench.

"After a game. Like today. You know, a big game? So I don't want to party. I want to relax. I want to come down. I play pretty intense, you know what I mean? It's like I'm a little out of my head. Not crazy, just . . . *intense*. So I don't want more of that, and that's what the parties get into. I go to those parties, by the end of the night I'm about ready to explode. And nobody leaves me alone. Everybody's suddenly my pal. 'Hey, Thumper, great game.' You know something, I can't ever remember anybody ever talking to me about anything but football. I mean complete strangers look at me and think of football. And there's nothing I can do about it. I can't change the subject. I *am* the subject. Or what people think I am, that is the subject. But you know what I mean, don't you?"

"Indeed I do," and I told him about my own life, from eighteen months on, Lyle and Sorenson, private tutors, Camp Gingacook, *Yarps.*

"Yeah. Your boat. O.K. So for me it's fishing. You know something, what I really want out of life? I want to fish. I want to fish every major stream in the fucking world." Out of a filing cabinet he pulled a thick sheaf of maps—road maps, atlas-type maps, elegant topographic maps of New Zealand, Great Britain, Vermont, the Yellowstone region of Montana, the legendary Merrimack in Nova Scotia. "I want to fish bonefish in the Florida flats. Maybe someday become a guide. That's all. I get married, have kids, that's O.K., too. I want that, yeah. But even that's going to have to fit into the fishing. So I got things pretty well figured out for

199

me, you know? My only problem is that I got this body between me and what I want. I could start my life tomorrow, no shit. Leave college and everything. Look."

He went to his closet and opened it. His few clothes were pushed back deep inside. In their stead were carefully placed fishing rods broken down into two or three pieces, aluminum cases holding rods, plastic boxes with reels in them and stacks and stacks of lures. Tool boxes of paraphernalia.

"But when do you get a chance to fish now?" I asked.

"I don't. I just keep this stuff around. I look at it. I play with it. The big stuff, for surf or deep sea, that I keep at home. Here, you want to see something beautiful?" He assembled one of the rods and removed a reel from its case and placed it. "You know anything about fishing?"

"Yes. A lot," I said. "I love to fish."

"Yeah? Trout? Surf?"

"Both."

"Yeah? You want to go fishing? Someday? This spring?"

"Sure."

"Great. Look at this. Is this beautiful or what?"

He handed me the lightest spinning outfit I could ever have imagined. The rod was about five feet, six inches, the reel the size of a walnut.

"I fish trout almost always with a fly rod, but sometimes you've just got to get into spots that spinning's the way to go. But light. With that rig I can just about throw a streamer maybe fifteen feet. Incredible. Can you imagine? Casting a streamer with a spinning rod? Fantastic. This rod is pure graphite fibers wound on a hollow amaroid core. There's no real butt to it. It's just one long taper. Watch." He bent the rod so that the tip of it touched the heel of the cork grip, a perfect circle, and then he gave it to me to hold. "And see this reel, see? It's a Bellingham." He indicated an elegantly etched inscription in a smaller silver plate attached to the side of the reel. "It's made in Glasgow, Scotland, by John Bellingham himself. Three ounces for fucking Christsake, but it's built like a fucking Rolex, you know? *Better.* Bellingham machines every part himself. Every reel is one-of-a-kind, too. He makes about thirty a year." He took the rod and put it away. The reel he put into its special case and that into a drawer

200

in his desk that he had fitted with a padlock. "That's why I'm here. At Cobbton College."

"I don't understand."

"The Bellingham reel. It was a bribe. I could have gone to any college in the country, you know? Big Ten, Pac Ten, Alabama, Harvard, Yale, Princeton. But my parents liked the idea of a really good small school with a good football program. I was scouted out of high school. I could go to the pros maybe now if it was legal. So my father said I'd look good anywhere but I'd look even better at a smaller school. As long as we played enough division one competition, it didn't matter. That made sense to me, so I decided to stay in the northeast for the trout streams and the closeness of the coast—blues and stripers in Rhode Island. So there was Penn State or Pitt or Syracuse, or Maryland and a bunch of others. But they were big. But someone gets onto my being a fishing nut and one day this sucker takes me to lunch and offers me the Bellingham reel. Just puts the fucking thing on the table next to me. I look at it, I know what it is, I know what he's saying. I put it in my pocket, eat a good lunch, and sign a letter of intent."

"Is that illegal or something?" I said.

"Fucking A it is," Al McGuire howled. "*Fucking A.* But for a Bellingham I'd kill, so coming to Cobbton was easy. Besides, the NCAA only looks for heavy stuff, big money, cars, you know?"

"You're a lucky guy," I said.

"Yeah," he said, "once I get through the problem of this body."

"My problem is my intelligence. I've got to get through that."

"It's when I read that newspaper story on you. I thought, I'll bet he has the same bullshit to go through like me. You got any ideas? I mean about your future?"

"Everything is saying the sciences. Astrophysics and or quantum mechanics. The heir to Einstein, that sort of thing."

"That's heavy. Einstein. So is that it?" he asked.

"I guess so," I said. "It's exciting, the stuff I'm doing. But it's also like I never had a chance to think about why I do what I do. It's like my power to do it takes over, and whatever I do generates a demand to do it again, more. So who's in charge here? And sometimes I think, does that even matter? Do we determine our own lives, or does the larger life we live in determine us? I mean what really stands between you and your dream? Between what you want to do and what you can do?" I didn't say that I also did not know how to find out what was important, what counted, and that until I did I couldn't understand how I was going to do what my father had said to his journal I would have to do, live both of who I was in one person. How was I going to become human? A real boy?

"For me I figure it's about 206 more games," Al McGuire said. "I figure two games this year, thirty over the next three years, maybe two bowl games. Then ten years in the pros is 160 games. I'll probably go to a bottom team as a top draft choice, so out of ten years maybe only five play-off games and two more for conference championships. No Super Bowls. And say I make the Pro Bowl five times. Without serious injury that's 206 games."

"That's great," I said. "That's terrific. You really do have it figured. But why ten years? Suppose you play longer?"

"No. I've made up my mind. Ten years I'll have more than enough money to support me the rest of my life. But it's not even the money. By then I'll have paid off whatever fucking debt I think I've got to use what I've got. Ten's enough. Lots of good players retire with ten years, or even less. I can live with that. I won't have to eat any shit anymore about being me. Thirteen years to go. I'll only be thirty-two. And then I'll be free." He slapped his hands together and the air in the room bounced.

"So what I do," he said "is after a game I come back here and tie flies." He turned to his desk and showed me. "Now this," he said, "*this* is something I'm really good at. And it's nothing I tell about. I didn't tell the girl reporter who wrote the story. Fishing, that's my secret."

His tools were all before him, sharp as a surgeon's, his fingers as delicate and sensitive. "This is a number six Quill Gordon. I just got this terrific cape of blue dun feathers, see, and some great peacock feather spines, very flexible. Nice." As he worked he talked me through the process. I understood it well. I had tried my hand at tying flies without great success, though the flies resulted and I even fished them with mixed results. But what Al McGuire produced were marvels, more jewels than dry flies. The spiral of the hackles was perfectly even and didn't require trimming, the head was shaped and sloped exactly, the wings were as precisely split and balanced as any natural mayfly that the Quill Gordon imitated. When you threw the fly in the air it landed head up, hook down every time. And he worked quickly.

"I could do this for a living," he said. "I'm fast enough and good enough. Now here is my modification of a royal coachman." And there it was, the bits of feather and thread and yarn seemingly lost for a few moments between his ponderous fingers and then, like in the best of magic, the object appeared out of the air resting in his huge palm as if there could be no explanation except the magic itself. "Now watch this," he said. "This is really tough. A number twenty-two green gnat." A number twenty-two-sized hook is three-sixteenth of an inch. It is hardly large enough for it to be held in the fly-tying vise. "Some tyers need an illuminated magnifying glass to do this, but not me," he said. And presto, there it was. He gave the tiny lure to me. He sank back against his chair into his great satisfaction.

"Now that," he said, "is something. Football is shit compared to that."

In my life till then, I had never had such envy for anyone as I did at that moment for Al Thumper McGuire.

Jameson boiled around us, sometimes like a riot but increasingly quieter as young men and women, two by twos, lingered down into the night that they would share. We talked on, about our mutual problem, but more, and increasingly more, about fishing and boats. He was also a camper and had spent good days deep in the Adirondacks. He told me how his strength was an advantage, that he could portage his canoe and kit into ponds and tributaries too difficult for others to reach. I told him about my canoe trips with my parents, but mostly I told him about *Yarps*, the good sails, and the hard chances. He was seriously impressed and listened intently to my descriptions. He thought that what I did in *Yarps* was some of the gutsiest stuff he had ever heard of, single-handed sailing. Storms. Not as gutsy as leading the blocking against two linebackers nearly as big as yourself, I almost said but did not, for that would have been to say the expected, to measure him against some notion of courage and achievement that robbed you of courage and achievement. For courage, I learned, was playing 206 games and then no more. Courage was tying a green gnat on a number twenty-two hook in the dorm on Saturday night. But I did not learn that then, only later.

And I felt a great need to give him something, a kind of payment for the green gnat, but more, a payment for the openness of his uncomplicated friendship for me, for the quick bonding of our mutual sympathy.

"Al. Do you remember when we first met? The stuff about the different angles to take?"

"Yeah."

"Let me show you what I was telling you then. Let me work it out in detail for you."

"I told you, Nick. I've got to fit what I do to the rest of the line."

"Right. But maybe I can work that out, too. Or maybe it's something you can use someday in the pros. Let me give it a shot, O.K.? Please?"

"Why not?" he smiled. "Sure. But not tonight. I had enough football for today. Another time."

"Where were you?" Mike said as I came into our room.

"In the library."

"It's after twelve. The library's closed."

"Hey, Mike. Come on. What's the problem? Do we have a problem here? Then let's talk about it. I've got my own life to live. Don't I? Why do I always have to be accounted for? I'm sorry about the fraternity thing, but somewhere in my life there's a line that I've got to draw."

"Where's that line, Nicky?"

"I don't know, Mike. I'm trying to find it. Since Thursday – three days, try to imagine what's happened to me."

"Opportunity is what's happened to you, Nicky."

"Yeah, Mike? But whose opportunity?"

He let that go. He was on his bed looking up at the ceiling, although he was not focused on it. On his desk was a small package from his mother. It had been there since yesterday, still unopened.

"Aren't you going to open your package?" I said. "Aren't you curious?"

"I know what's in it. I don't need it yet," but he offered nothing more.

204

"Is something wrong, Mike?"

"Nothing with us, Nicky. I'm sorry if I was on your back. Just some business pressures, is all. I'll handle it. I'll work it out."

"You always do, Mike. You always do."

"Yeah," he said, and rolled over toward the wall.

◆27◆
=

I did not realize how much I was looking forward to this visit to
Appleton's home until I got there. At some unconscious level I
think I must have imagined it to be a refuge, a place where I –
great soaring eagle? fatigued pigeon? – could alight. Which means
that at some level I must have been searching for such a haven.
When I sailed for any distance in *Yarps*, especially in unfamiliar
waters, I always spotted out on the charts the possible holes to
hide in against the sudden thunderstorm or a racing white squall.
Small plane pilots are taught while in the air to constantly consider what could serve as an emergency landing area – a plowed
field, an interstate highway, a shopping mall parking lot. But
though I expected the aftermath of the *Clarion* story on
Thursday – the general fact of it but not the bizzare forms, I had
taken no special care. It was as if I had decided to battle through
whatever the storm might present rather than to duck and run.
I had made no provisions. So I made a mistake here on land that
I would never have made at sea. Because storms are full of sur-
prises: it is not the strength of the constant wind or the height of
the prevailing waves that do you in but the rough wave, the wave
that comes from an unexpected direction that adds itself to another wave and builds to a catastrophe. It is not the boiling sea
that breaks you but the sudden disappearance of the water, the
sudden absolutely unpredictable hole that forms in the water into
which you actually fall as if you had toppled off of a two-story

building, snapping the stays to your mast, cracking your hull. So who could have imagined what Kreutzer had offered. And even less, how could I have imagined my new life with Sara Logan, for that, I felt certain even against the odds, was what it was or might become. But even then I had left that condition as amorphous as it was: a waking dream. I let it be a fume that seeped in and around and through my every other thought and motion. The common image of heaven as clouds was right–angels drifting around in heaven on gossamer wisps while listening to the music of the spheres that was created by the cosmic zephyrs wafting through the Aeolian lyres. Ah yes. For I on honeydew had fed, and drunk the milk of paradise. So even as I bumped and scraped over the uneven terrain of these past days–caught out, as a sailor would say–I did not suffer so very much or maybe not at all, but I was tired nonetheless, and sore and bruised beneath a knowingness.

"Come in," Appleton shouted to my knock. "It's open. It's always open." I turned the ornate brass handle to his apartment door and entered.

"Twelve o'clock, Burden. Prompt. You're always on time, aren't you? Do you know why?" was what he said to me as if we were in the middle of a conversation, as if more than three days had not passed since last I talked with him.

"I guess I am. I've never thought about it."

"Then why don't you think about it?" he said.

But thinking about his apartment was just then much more important, certainly more interesting. It was a splendid clutter, an old curiosity shop raised at least to the third power, far more scattered and interrupted even than his office at the college. Books and magazines and journals in profusion, paintings, sketches, ceramic vessels, restaurant-sized mayonnaise jars full of buttons and pins and plastic charms and rings that you got in cereal boxes or Cracker Jacks. Pieces of clothing, pipes, musical instruments (quickly I saw two violins, a concertina, a flute, a clarinet, and shoved into a corner a small piano), cardboard cartons full of tools–wrenches, screwdrivers, pliers and the like, or utensils that I could not identify, old cast iron things that might have been used to peel apples or pit cherries. I counted four cameras. Everywhere, scattered like potato chips, were phonograph records and cassettes and computer disks. Nothing was arranged, and there was no principle of organization that I could detect, much less even imagine. Snaking through it all were anachronistic rivulets of electronic equipment. Against one wall was a massive music system, speakers mounting up like pillars supporting the ceiling, and then a bank of receivers and equalizers, two turntables, dual cassette players. A CD player. A studio-sized reel-to-reel tape deck. Three large TVs and two video-cassette players, Beta and VHR. An oscilloscope. An electric keyboard and some sort of synthesizer. A video camera. In a corner extensive shortwave radio equipment. Other pieces of equipment that I couldn't identify, perhaps electronic editing machines for the video. In one corner was a table with two computers and what looked like a laser printer between them. A telephone answering machine and another machine attached to that. Wires seemed to run from every mechanism to every other one. It gave the feeling of one of those wizard's workshops that you find in the old cartoons, where everything is puffing and boiling and bubbling. Somewhere there must be a master switch that, once thrown, would bring Appleton's room (and what else was there in the rest of the apartment?) to blinking, buzzing, clicking, flickering life. A contemporary alchemy in the midst of the flotsam of the near and older past.

And Appleton himself. He was wearing what I guess was once called a dressing gown – as distinct from a bathrobe. He wore slippers that curled up at the ends into sharp points, the footwear of a caliph in *The Arabian Nights*. He wore a kind of sleeping cap that you saw in old illustrations, long and soft and floppy with a tassle at the end. He took it off and threw it over his shoulder. He was smoking an enormous pipe, a calabash. The room was as heavy and thick as I would picture an opium den in old Shanghai to be. Around his neck a long black ribbon was draped attached to spectacles. He and this room looked like each other. And he and it looked like what I would have imagined them to look like had I thought about it before. And it *did* bear me up. The claustrophobic *isness* of it all pushed against me; the intense materiality of the room bound me up as if in swaddling and made me feel as secure as an infant must feel. If the scientist at the University of Pennsylvania who came to believe that he was in danger of falling through the insubstantiality of matter had spent some time in this room, he would have cast off his snowshoes and danced across such density as this.

The style was the man. And yet here Appleton was different from the actor/bumpkin of his classroom. As playful as ever, yet now his voice was different, more like those times he read poetry or other people's words. In class he was what he appeared to be, angular and gawky, a deceptively agile clown. Here he did not seem that way. It even seemed that he had put on weight. Without his glasses (were those he always wore in class just a prop in his performance as a teacher?) his face seemed fuller, his eyes more focused. All in all he had become better looking, nearly handsome, his gestures and movements more languid and exact, a master here of more than mere college boys and girls in a course in composition. So maybe he *was* a sorcerer. Or perhaps (or more likely?) a necromancer. He swept me into his room and chatted me around it, wooing me with his embrace of authentic affection, Appleton, this living oxymoron, this courtier of paradox.

"So what do you think?" he said at last. He indicated a chair in which I might sit; I had not seen it until he pointed it out. He eased down into his own seat.

"Think? About what? The apartment?"

"You haven't seen the apartment. The rest is nothing like this." He stood up. "Come," he said.

It was true. The bedroom was as neat and spare as the other room, the living (?) room, was not. It was all white. Even the knobs and handles of the dressers were white. The bedspread. The floor was covered completely by a white carpet. The walls had nothing on them, no pictures. Thick white curtains over the window. And the kitchen was a design for efficient use—brackets for an array of pots and pans, knives in canted blocks of wood. An island in the middle with its own shelves and drawers. Cuisinart, microwave, blender, can opener. More. Gleaming clean. It all hardly suggested use even though it was so finely honed and ready. He led me back to the great room. There were two other rooms that he did not show me.

"Well?" he said once more. "What do you think?" By his hand on a small cleared spot on a side table was a box with buttons and levers. So there *was* a master switch. He pressed one of the buttons.

"What's that?" I said. He pointed across the room. The large reel-to-reel tape recorder was turning. "You're *recording* this? I don't believe it. Why?"

"I record all the conversations in this room. Sometimes something particularly worthwhile gets said and I don't want to lose it. More importantly, I want to savor it. It's no different than recording music, is it? Or filming important events? It gives you a chance to keep the past."

"But why don't you just remember it and write it down afterwards?"

"We don't all have your powers of retention, Nick. Besides, after the event all you can do is make a note of the experience, you can't recreate it because it's not only what is said but why and how, like good drama. The timing is so important."

"But how can people talk if they know they're being taped? It's inhibiting. I feel it right now. How can anything intimate or private get said? I'm just about ready to shut up for the rest of the afternoon. Come on. Turn it off."

"I don't trick anyone, Nick. I always tell people that I'm taping them. And pretty quickly no one cares. Actually, I think there may be some pleasure in it, the feeling that your words are not being lost. It makes what you say a little more valuable. It makes you a little immortal."

"But it's an invasion of privacy," I said. "It's immoral."

"Immoral? Not likely. It's not a moral matter at all. Privacy is a myth," Appleton said. "A convenient social myth. A mere legality. A matter of definition, that's all. Not an innate right. Not a moral matter at all. It—privacy—is not even anything we much want or value. At least not any longer. Besides, it was never more than a mere romantical, narcissistic moment in human history, and now it's fading away. Just look at all the adulation we spill out on our celebrities—a Cher, for godssake. Look at all the kiss-and-tell books. *People* magazine. "Entertainment Tonight." Etcetera and so forth. Are you hungry?"

My head roared with refutations, constructions I could build that would wall him in, squeeze him into contradictions. Defend privacy. Defend myself. But before I could answer, he said, "Good. I've got in some wonderful stuff. Sara will be along shortly to prepare it for us."

"Sara?"

"Yes. But you know Sara. You knew she was coming this afternoon, didn't you?"

"Sure. Yes."

"Do you know why I'm dressed this way?" he said without any pause or shift in his rhythm.

"Huh?" The inertial mass of my juggernaut of information kept me in a motion away from where I was, though I was slowing down. Sparks of my argument continued to pop and fuss in the darkness, in the void—a paragraph from Wittgenstein, a notation from Descartes, morsels of Hume, Whitehead. Buber. Partial lines of attack formed, salients developed. Oh what an offense I could have mounted for the rights of privacy.

"Why I'm dressed this way?" he repeated. "Like Sherlock Holmes?" he said. I could think of no suitable answer. I shook my head.

"It's like acting out. It helps you to intensify the literary experience, to get closer to some actuality that the fictional character is itself only the sign of. Also, it's lots of fun, being someone else. Today I'm Holmes."

"Do you do cocaine?" I said.

"Cheeky little devil," he laughed. "But of course. Not now, though. Too risky, too expensive."

"There's crack," I offered.

"Too dangerous, in every way. Besides, I never thought it was worth it, the cocaine. I used to sniff it a while back when it was fashionable and chic, but no more."

"You don't strike me as fashionable and chic," I said.

"Oh but I am, I am. I just don't show it around. But it's only one more costume. Just another way into life."

"You get into life by wearing costumes. Disguises? I don't figure that," I said.

"I get into literature by wearing costumes, assuming other identities. And *that* way I get into life."

"That seems indirect to me," I said.

"By indirections we find directions out," he said.

"That sounds glib to me," I said. "And you're not Hamlet."

"Nor was meant to be! Am an attendant lord. Full of high sentence. At times, indeed, almost ridiculous." He looked hard at me, and then he said, "Go on, Nick. Say it. Say it. Finish it up."

" 'Almost, at times, the Fool.' " I finished the line from Eliot's poem.

"Good," he said, "good for you. We're going to be great friends, only you mustn't hang back. You mustn't be afraid."

"I'm not exactly afraid. I feel pretty good here. It's just that I'm uncertain. I'm always uncertain, but if I know so much, if I'm so smart, then why am I so often uncertain? That's what it is."

"Experience?" he said.

"Sure. I've figured that in. Still, it's not that I don't know what experiences I'm going to have. You see what I mean? Even there I know what to expect. I've read about all the experiences. I understand what kinds of impact experiences are likely to have. It's like everything else. My life has a kind of inescapable inevitability about it. There is me and there is it."

"Does that bother you a great deal?"

"No. Not really. I mean I'm not depressed or anything like that. I'm not unhappy. I feel pretty good about myself. I'm enjoying Cobbton. It's just this . . . sense of something waiting for me. I'm not afraid of it at all. What I'm afraid of is missing it. It's hard to talk about. What other characters have you been?" I veered away from me.

"Little Dorrit's father, Heathcliff, Falstaff, Madame Bovary . . . ."

"Madame Bovary? Come on. How did you do that? Jesus, did you dress up like Madame Bovary?"

"Certainly."

"Oh god," but it was more funny than shocking.

"It was a profound revelation. You can't imagine how it deepened my understanding of Emma but of women in fiction – in life – as well by seeing what a woman's body was like, how different than a man's."

"I guess," I giggled.

"Don't be dumb, Burden," he said in his classroom voice, but then returned. He got up and went to somewhere near his table of computers and pulled out of a pile of printed matter an offprint. "I wrote an article about it. Here. Read it. Learn something." He flipped it onto my lap.

212

"How about *The Metamorphosis*? How about Gregor Samsa? Did you ever do Gregor?" I yipped with delight.

"Good, Burden," he said. "Very clever."

"Hello hello," Sara Logan said. She had entered the apartment unannounced. "Here's the *Times*," she said dropping the ream of paper on top of me as she passed, "and here are the bagels. And I'm off to work." At the entry to the kitchen she stopped and turned, only now pulling herself out of her coat. "Did you start the coffee?" she said.

"No," I said and stood up, the newspaper and the offprint sliding to the floor. "I didn't know, . . ." but it was to Appleton she was speaking.

"Sorry," Appleton said. "Got busy with Nick, here. Forgot."

"Oh Billy," she said. "Oh, really. Sometimes you're just, . . ." but she turned and went into the kitchen. "Impossible," she shouted out.

Billy!

I waited for his fit, but nothing happened. He had forbidden me Billy but now allowed her to snap it reprovingly at him like a wet towel. Unless he had changed his mind and Billy was now O.K. With Appleton, I was quickly learning, anything goes where/whenever he wanted it to. Maybe his names were like his costumes, more masks. Sara popped out of the kitchen. She had found an apron and was tying it on. The touch of this domesticity walloped me. Maybe this was a costume for her: coed in the kitchen. The start of a porno film. You start with this beautiful, vibrant young woman going about her womanly chores and eventually you got her down to just the apron, which covered everything but an occasional flash of her lovely butt as she busied herself preparing the meal. But all of her is moving inside of that apron. All the mounds are shifting and jiggling beneath the little, dainty piece of material which is getting smaller and smaller, lacier and lacier, until it is suddenly gone and – backlighted, the light glimmering through the wreath of her luxurious hair – she is offering you . . . .

"Lox?"

"What?" I said.

Appleton laughed. He had been reading my mind. Sherlock

Holmes. Of course. Elementary. That is why he had chosen
Holmes this afternoon: to find me out.

"Lox?" she said. "Do you like lox? I've got lox, whitefish, kippered salmon, Swiss cheese, cream cheese with chives, Greek
olives. Danish. The bagels, onion and plain. And eventually some
very good coffee." She gave Appleton a look. "But maybe you want
something else. Bacon and eggs? Wheaties?"

"No. I've never had kippered salmon, whitefish. That's great."

"A Bloody Mary?"

"One for me," Appleton said.

"Nick?" she said.

"Me?" Then, "Sure," I said. "I always have a Bloody Mary for
Sunday brunch." It was, of course, said as a joke, but they did not
seem to take it as such. Sara turned back into the kitchen. She was
fully clothed. And again she was wearing, as she always did, a
skirt. I wanted to rise and go into the kitchen with her and help
her, or watch her. I wanted to thank her over and over again for
Thursday night and Friday morning. For having launched my life.
In the midst of my uncertainty, I had, at least in her presence (in
her presence in me), escaped from any nervous and irritable striv-
ing after facts and answers. I was simply in love.

Appleton rattled the *Times*. "Here," he said. "What do you
want? I always read the book reviews first, myself. You?"

"Whatever."

He put down the paper and looked at me with one eye closed,
squinting as if he were taking aim.

"Do you read the Sunday *Times*, Nick? Scout's honor."

"No," I said without guilt. I didn't have to lie to people, only
to myself. "I mean I'll read some of it. Sometimes. It depends if
I'm interested. I read about sailing. The outdoors. Science. I'll
glance at the chess game. Or if my father shows me something,
I'll read that."

"And the world? Life in the streets? Khmer Rouge? Bangladesh? The budget deficit?"

"I know what you're driving at. You think I don't know about
that stuff, but I do."

"Stuff?" he said. But I ignored that. I was learning how to talk
to Appleton. He was a fencer; he got you to parry him; he got you
to use your own motion against yourself. But if you went straight

ahead he would have to let you. And I wasn't a fencer; I had no fine and elegant moves. I was better with a mace. Raw power. A smasher.

"My attitude is this. The news is unrefined ore. It needs to be processed. It needs a book, say. Some distance. So I read the books. News is superficial. It's about what just happened. It's not very deep. I read the books. They keep me informed. I can read books pretty quickly." A calculated boast. "And I never read book reviews. It's easier just to read the books." A little threat of my own.

"Yes. That's right. The fabulous Nick Burden. How fast did Sara's article say that you could read?"

"She made that up," I said. "I've never tried to figure it out. But it's very very fast. I read Proust in two days. In the French, of course."

"Good grief," he said. "And did you 'get it' all in two days? Did you understand it?"

"No. But that's because I'm too young yet to understand a lot of things. I mean I understand a lot of things generally. It's what I was saying before. I know how to put all the parts together. I know what things are supposed to mean. I understand the experiences that people are having—love, hate, confusion and so forth. But there's something else going on that I often can't get into."

"The suffering in Bangladesh?"

"No. I can understand that too, at least the way everyone else does. But Proust. Conrad's *Victory*. Axel Heist. That's what I mean. I can't experience the limitations. It's hard for me to explain this right now, or simply. It's just . . . just that I don't know what it's like not to think that I can work things out if I put my mind to it."

"The traps people can't figure themselves out of?" Appleton offered.

"Yes," I said, "something like that."

"You put a lot of faith in reason," he said.

"Well, yes. But . . . look. It's not that I don't know about unreasonableness. I'm telling you, I understand what I read. I have sympathy. It's . . . it's *empathy* that I'm missing. I can't put myself in the places of the characters." Then I said, "Here's what it's like. It's like the characters in the books are more real than I am. It's like they live in the real world and I don't. That makes me uncertain about a lot of things I think about, so far. But it doesn't make me unhappy. Maybe a little nervous," I laughed. Yes, I thought. That's it. Good. I'm making my own progress. I looked at him closely, watching for a sign, a nod of approval, but all he did was stare at me; his grey eyes seemed almost white, his light hair hung down straight as coarse flax near to his shoulders. I had not realized how long his hair was. And his Adam's apple. I couldn't find it. What had he done with *that*? Again, he seemed younger than in class. His flesh was smooth and firm and full of color, which vibrated against the pallor of his hair, his white eyes. To me right at that moment he looked different even from when I first entered the apartment this afternoon. He was a chameleon, physically and intellectually.

Sara came out of the kitchen with the Bloody Marys, three of them. She handed them around. "Cheers," she lifted her glass.

"Cheers," we chorused her.

Then she looked and quickly found a table. It was, as was everything else, covered with something, in this case a jumble of books and pamphlets and offprints.

"Here it is," she said. "This will do just fine," and she tipped the table so that everything on it slid off onto the floor, sliding a little into the stream of books and such that was already flowing there. Then she picked up the table and placed it between the two of us.

"Oh not that one," Appleton said, too late.

"It's the only one there is. It's the only table light enough to move around," and back she went into the kitchen. "Be here in a sec."

How did she know about the table, that it was the only one light enough, or even where it was?

"Pick those up like a good fellow, Nick. Please." He indicated what she had dumped.

"Sure." I put my drink on the table after I had taken a sip. It was delicious. I could taste the vodka. At least I was fairly sure that was what I was tasting. Vodka! Great! Sally Burden would have a fit. Picking up the books and papers, I saw Appleton's name on all of them. William Appleton. *Thematic Structures in Paradise Lost* was one book. *The New Historicism* was another. But one of

216

the books was a collection of short stories. And three of the pamphlets were collections of poems. The other sheets were a mix of literary essays and poems and stories, many from prestigious journals whose names I recognized. There was a lot of everything. He was impressively prolific.

"This is all yours?" I said.

"Yep. You sound surprised."

"I am, a little."

"Is that because you only thought of me as a whirling dervish, so to speak? A peripatetic?" he said.

"Yeah, sort of. I never thought you couldn't write, I just never thought about it at all. I never thought of you that way, that's all. But just now I guess I was surprised that you could be organized enough to write anything. That you could be serious enough to write. But then there is your bedroom and your kitchen, they're pretty organized. You're a surprising man, Mr. Appleton. Full of twists and turns for sure. Yeah, I think you're smart enough to write. I just never knew, that's all. The seventeenth century is your area, huh? It was a great century." I drank deeply at my Bloody Mary.

"Mr. Appleton?" he said.

"William," I said warmly. "Billy."

"Billy?"

"Billy," I nodded.

"I thought I told you never to call me that."

"But Sara called you Billy." Had I betrayed her? Maybe he hadn't heard her clearly. Bill is what he heard. Or maybe he would correct her later, personally, and not in front of me.

"Sara can call me Billy, but you can't," he said.

"Ta-ta," Sara announced as she approached the table bearing a large platter of dishes with our food.

And soon enough we were at it. I ate with relish these new things. Kippered salmon. I wondered if my parents had ever heard of it. Bloody Marys. Danish so large and light and rich the butter in them oozed out. This cave of an apartment that Sinbad might have discovered. The filagrees of thought, the convolutions everywhere. Sherlock Holmes chewing on a bagel. The new historicism. And my paramour (oh precious word) serving me. Surely. Surely, I thought as I skinned the purple flesh off of the largest olive I had ever eaten, there must be an image for all of this, this moment, what I was experiencing now and for these past four days on earth. A metaphor. Yes. That is what was required; that alone could do it. Could do anything? Metaphor. Some great mythic statement. But just then I could not think what that metaphor might be. I poured another ambrosial cup of the thick, slightly bitter coffee. I felt my hold on the cosmos loosening, that pearl in my hand richer than all my tribe.

We ate and talked on and on about everything – about Bruegel, Rembrandt, Egon Schiele (my most recent discovery), the astonishing Cobbton football team, about the increasingly successful worldwide effort to save the whales, about the ethical problems raised by extreme prenatal care – about shoes and ships and sealing wax and cabbages and kings. I regaled them with Mike Tremain stories, embroidering here and there, touching up the drama of this daring entrepreneur. I asked Appleton about his writing, there was such a range – fiction, poetry, literary scholarship.

"They're not incompatible. Every English professor began as a writer of poetry and/or fiction, after all. Did you ever think of that?" he said.

"You make that sound like a fact," Sara said, "rather than a wild opinion."

"Not at all. It is a fact. Think about it. Every professor I've ever known has a great love of literature. Or did. When did that start? As a kid, of course. Now how would a kid who loved literature get closer to it? The same as with sports or anything else. He'd imitate the heroes. Little Leaguers want to be like the reigning stars. They fantasize hitting game-winning home runs or striking out the side in the bottom of the ninth of the last game of the World Series. Just so do little readers want, in time, to be writers. *Never* have I ever heard of some youngster wanting to be a literary scholar or critic. They don't even know what that means. You see what I'm saying? So you go to college and you write stories and poems, but increasingly you get your rewards – your good grades, your peer approval – from the term papers you write *about* literature. And you also find out that that's a lot of fun, too. And by then you start to think about the future, which means graduate school, which means the professional scholar route, especially if you are also thinking about marriage and a family."

"Hostages to fortune," I said, remembering my Francis Bacon.

"And you didn't give any hostages," Sara said to him.

"Not yet," Appleton said.

"Not yet?" I said. "But you're. . . ."

"Too old? That the fires of passion are banked? Do you really think it's too late for me to take a wife, to father children?"

"It sure is," Sara said. "No woman in her right mind would have you. And can you imagine a kid crawling around in a place like this." I listened for more of a tone of humor, a comic banter, but I didn't hear as much of it as I would have expected.

"I might very well not prefer a woman in her 'right mind,' as you put it. And as for a child, I'd have a nanny and send it away to boarding school when it was seven. Let those whose business it is to raise children do it. The English have been doing that for years, and now more and more than a few of the increasingly wealthy Americans. The boarding schools seem not to have done a less good job than many a kid-raising home. What do you think about that, Nick?"

"Terrible," I said without a doubt at all. "Where would the kid get love?"

"A schoolteacher might love a child with greater intensity than a parent," he said.

"Some teachers and some children, but in the main I doubt that very much," I said.

"But what about you?"

"Me?"

"Yes. You've been sent away to school. Ordinarily you'd be at home with your parents for another two or even three years."

If I had implied that he was too old, then he was implying now that I was too young. For what? For women, what else. For Sara? No, no, no, I couldn't believe that. It struck me as obscene, he and Sara. But I *could* believe it too. He was, at least this afternoon, young enough, physically attractive enough. Accomplished enough. The green-eyed monster started to nip at my balls, but instead of shriveling up, I got a hard on. Thom's catastrophe theory validated. I started to giggle. Thom's theory was that systems, when stressed beyond a certain point—when faced with catastrophe—instead of continuing to fall in a predictable and accelerating curve of collapse, would reverse themselves. Stars collapsing, at a certain point explode. A stock market, if it falls fast enough, will suddenly rise. Beat a cur hard enough and eventually it will spring up at you. I had sprung up. I giggled into laughter even as I pulled myself a fraction further under the table. My jealousy detumesced, but I was still leery. Was there nothing about myself that I could own?

"What's so funny?" Sara said. But I disregarded her and answered Appleton.

"I'm a different case. And the point is we don't know if my coming here to Cobbton is a mistake or not. We'll have to see, won't we?"

"It's not a mistake," Sara said. (O my beloved, I quivered.) "Nick's being at Cobbton has made—will make—an important and good impact on all our lives. So people will like him for that, love him. His teachers, the students. He'll make them happy just being who he is. And people who make others happy, get made happy back." (O prince's daughter!)

"Yea? Say you so?" Appleton said. "Is that the response you sense to your story in the *Clarion*?"

So here we were, back on me again. No more shoes and ships and sealing wax. Only kings. Emperors, for Christsake.

"There are some crazies taking shots at him, sure. But mostly what I hear is admiration," she said.

"It's not as bad as I anticipated. Not so far," I supported her. I told them about some of my encounters.

"But you won't be Nicky Burden to them anymore, will you? So have you thought about who you will be to them?"

"Not in so many terms," I said. "Not exactly."

"You'll be authority," he said. "You've been indicted. Everything you say from now on will be held against you. Or thrown up to you. You see, from now on everything you say will be accepted as right, as true. And if you say things that someone doesn't want to hear or to believe, he'll get angry because he's got to accept that you are right even though he doesn't want you to be right. But because you're Nicky Burden, you can't be wrong. He can't even argue with you. You win from the start. You offer an opinion about world events and people will react like you're the Delphic oracle."

"But I can't be right about something I don't know anything about. That's absurd," I insisted, but I knew what Appleton meant.

"People will think that because you *can* know something that you *do* know it."

"Then let the world look out for itself," Sara said.

"Oh, it will. It will," Appleton said.

"It's sort of what Thumper McGuire told me," I said. "Thumper's six-four and 285 pounds, but quick. Fast. Not fast for a big man, just fast in itself. He runs forty yards in under five seconds. So all his life his coaches have played him at all possible positions, even quarterback for a while in high school. And in high school he was also the punter. He's been a wide receiver, a defensive end, a full-back, a linebacker. Now he's an interior lineman. People look at him and say, he can play that position or that position, and so he does. I suppose I'm like that, too," I said. How could anyone doubt me if I couldn't doubt myself.

"Yes," Appleton said, "like Proteus, but on a much wider playing field." He stood up. "But I wouldn't worry about it, I mean the campus reaction. That will die down soon enough I predict. Your more important disturbance will be the national press. Have they gotten to you yet? Be careful there. They'll savage you for sure. I've got to go." He walked out of the room to the bathroom.

That had been Sara's warning, too. The *National Inquirer. People* magazine. The *Daily News*. The *New York Post*. I imagined my face plastered across from the checkout counters of supermarkets throughout America. But for what lurid sins or escapades I could not imagine. That I was the love child of an alien visitor from space, or that I had been manufactured by mating in a petri dish the egg and sperm of two high IQs? Jesus, I thought. I would have to be careful. That kind of notoriety would really be painful. That kind of attention would really start the pack baying after me. And then they would never stop. I'd always be good for a feature when there was nothing else around. That's what happened to William James Sidis, the world champion smartest man until me. He collected trolley transfers and worked as a low-paid clerk, quietly and alone, his entire life an escape from what his intelligence had forced upon him. But the less he did with his life, the more he was described as an oddity, a freak. That's what could happen to me.

If I got a traffic ticket (after I got my license) I'd end up in the funny papers. In Johnny Carson's monologues. Appleton was right, and Sara. They would all be after my story now, whatever that story was. They'd pay a pretty penny for it. I was on my way to becoming a commodity. Then with alarm I thought about Mike Tremain. Would he? I'd have to alert him. Don't talk to strangers. Or warn him not to. Threaten him? Plead?

"Wait a second." She pressed another button. The tape recorder, halfway through its enormous reel, stopped. She pressed another button and music just at the edge of hearing came on. She knew her way around the control panel pretty well. "He tapes everything," she said. "He must have told you."

"Yes."

"I hate it, but you do forget about it."

Indeed, I had. So all this afternoon was preserved. How odd. How pointless.

"Now," Sara said, her voice all conspiratorial laughter, "tell me something. Let's have a secret from him. Quick." But I could not be quick, not quick enough. The time out was over. The teams were lined up in scrimmage position. What secret did I have to give her?

"I love you," I said. "And the other night. Together. We've got that." Did she hear me? She had turned back to the game. The music moved through the action on the monitor. Later. I would tell her again. She would hear me then. At least Appleton would not know.

We clattered down out of Appleton's apartment and Sara slipped her arm through mine. We began to run and whoop, like kids out of school, giggling as if in retribution, stumbling against each other. It was dark now; the end of daylight saving time had reclaimed dusk, or, as Appleton would have argued, at this time of the year it was Demeter drawing herself down into bitter sorrow as Persephone returned to the lord of the underworld. The grieving earth mother, her sighs the wintery blasts, her tears the icy storms. But Appleton would have insisted upon accepting the myth as a literal truth. He would have demanded an actual belief in the mythic tales at least for the moments in which we participated in them. Like Peter Pan. What we believed was what made reality. Metaphors were more real than molecules. He was a literalist of the romantic imagination. Real toads in imaginary gardens. Culver, on the other hand, was a romantic literalist: he sought imaginary particles of space-time in a literal universe. And I, I was the power, the magician with no tricks to perform, nor need of them. Not at this moment with Sara Logan touching me, at any rate. The air that we breathed glowed and swirled around us in the ambient light, glowed like phosphorescent organisms in the seas that break into light in the turning and tumble of waves against a shore or in the slow-furrowing wake of a sailing ship.

I did not even think about where we were heading until we arrived at Sara's apartment.

"Come on up," she said.

"Janie? Ricki?" I said.

"Gone," Sara said. "Gone home for the weekend."

Later we sat in front of the TV with the sound off as if watching a strange planet through the porthole of a spaceship. Sara had prepared some quick food, sandwiches and tea, while I had sat like a king in my counting house counting up the largess she had flung at me.

"You know, Sara, I never was certain what you were actually majoring in. Art History? I mean with what you're going to do. At Appleton's, we never talked about you. With me and you, we never talk about you."

"You're much more interesting, more exotic," she said.

"No one's more interesting than herself to herself," I said.

"That's true, but Appleton is an opportunist. You're his opportunity.

"His opportunity?"

"Sure. Don't you get it? You're everyone's opportunity. Appleton, Mike Tremain, Culver."

"You?"

"Me." She nodded and bit into her sandwich.

"Opportunity for what?" I said.

"See? We're talking about you again, just like Appleton. You're hard to resist."

"Then let's talk about you. What are you going to do after you graduate? Are you going to get an advanced degree in art history? Or work in a museum? Or for a newspaper? Do you think about it, the future?" Now I was talking about her – or was I still actually thinking about me trying to imagine her imagining me as I was imagining me being imagined by her?

"I've studied art history and taken art courses and journalism, it's what most interests me, but what I'm really into is adventure, Nick. Adventure is my game. It's not what I want to be, it's want I want to do."

"Which is?"

"Travel. I want to travel the world writing about it and photographing it for the great magazines and agencies and important newspapers. I want them to send me on assignments, all expenses paid. I want to be someone like Jodi Cobb, beautiful and daring, and do work for the *National Geographic*. I want to ride a camel train to Timbuktu and sail in a dhow across the Indian Ocean to Sri Lanka. I want to be like Catherine Leroy and cover a war at the front end of it. I want to discover Paris in April as no one else has, at least not for my generation. That's what I want. I'm writing features for the *Clarion* so when I go for job interviews I'll have a portfolio of stuff to show around. And photographs. And I've got to show them that I'm smart, and tough, too."

"How do you show them that?" I asked.

But she got up and went into the bedroom and returned with a camera and started shooting at me, the flash rapidly bouncing from different angles as she moved quickly around the room, sometimes climbing up onto a table or squatting down on her haunches. And all the time she was ordering me around, telling me to move an arm or a leg or to stand up or to pick up a book or to laugh or wave a hand or stick out my tongue. Just like a fashion model.

"Enough," I shouted and dove at her, but she was quicker than I and stepped aside deftly and got me in midflight, my arms outstretched like Superboy.

"You know what else I want, Nick?" she said putting down the camera.

"Let me guess. You want to, . . . " but she put her finger on my lips.

"I want to go to New York this Thanksgiving. I want to go with you. I want to take you to New York and show you some of it.

224

You've never really gone there, have you? I mean as a grownup. That's what I want to do. I'd love to do that."

"Thanksgiving?" I said, and my heart sank under the weight of Sally Burden's turkey. "That won't be easy," I said. Impossible, I meant.

⇥**28**⇥
=

Appleton proved to be right. The news of me subsided quickly. Within the week the gawking, flaring wildness had lessened to an easily tolerable level. And by the end of the second week it had nearly disappeared. It was as if it became important for the more sophisticated student *not* to be (or appear to be) overly impressed by my advent. There were still incidents, phone calls, people showing up in Jameson who wanted me to do or be or buy something, the fraternities still made a daily pitch, but between Sam Pelton and Mike Tremain and my dormmates, they were easily deflected.

Of course there was still the nakedness I carried within myself, the knowledge that no one now did not notice me. I was a celebrity, after all, and once out in the light there was no longer the possibility of protective shadows of anonymity to duck into. But it wasn't a battering nakedness as in the past. And that, I think, is because as a student amongst students, as students all, I was now part of a group itself singled out by society. The best or worst of what we did was focused upon as an entity and amplified by the good people of Cobbton. Boys became college boys; girls became coeds. Unlike Camp Gingacook where it was me or them, here it was us or Cobbton. Town/gown? Something of that. I had heard that in semesters past a gang of village kids would occasionally spring onto the campus and get into a fight. But I had seen none of that so far and felt no animosity as a Cobbton student when I would wander down into Cobbton town. Which I began to do more and more. Maybe because in the village I was even less recognized (entirely unrecognized) than on the campus, merely a student and not Nicky Burden. Whatever, though I would have preferred my immediate nameless past, the present was not as painful as I had anticipated. Against the buffeting of the storm I had expected, my anchor had held.

Not the least of this was due to the firm ground into which my anchor had deeply dug. There was the increasingly miraculous work I was doing in Culver's lab, both the work on the pads and that on the papers in my private drawer in the desk. The two lines (dimensions?) of thought were related, but they were distinct enough to be kept apart. What was on the wall would expand physics enormously, but what was in the drawer might change it altogether.

I did not meet much with Culver through the semester and now, but he would leave me frequent notes about my work on the pads, though from his comments and increasingly his questions, I sensed that he was starting to struggle. That was partly because of the complexity of what I was doing, but also because the work on the pads was like a sketch of what was in my head, like the preparation for the large view of time and pretime, of the universe and gravity that someday, I supposed, I would present. And this: without the critical work I stored in the drawer, the forging of the steel of my ideas about sequence, it would be harder yet for anyone to figure out all that was happening on the walls: it was like a kind of Rosetta stone. But about sequence, which would challenge relativity, the uncertainty principle, Kreutzer, and superstring theory—about that I wanted to be certain. If I was going to slay giants, I wanted to make sure that I could do it with one stroke. Against giants you didn't get too many chances. It was best to kill them while they were sleeping. I had never written a paper, never submitted anything to any of the learned journals, but that was as much because I had not until these past months focused upon any particular line of thought. All I had done till now was learn what was; now I was making what would be. So I wanted to get it right before I made my debut (and won the Nobel Prize?).

And Culver and I never did much about fashioning a course of study; unlike what he had suggested at the first meeting in September in Dean Roskov's office – that I would learn what I needed in the sciences as I discovered for myself what those needs were – all I really did was this physics and the math I needed to do it. Which made sense enough. But it had always been that way. All my life, as much of it as I could remember (which was plenty), if I encountered a blank spot, I got to the books that would fill me in and filled myself in. I had never needed a teacher. I couldn't remember learning anything from anyone, at least nothing analytical, or anything that had to do with the facts of situations or the record of them. Whatever was in print was mine. Which made me think that Kruetzer was probably right. What was I doing in Guzman's course? Or in Culver's lab? But then, what did that matter either? At Princeton or at Cobbton, I would have my own way. Only here at Cobbton I had some friends now, and Sara Logan. And William Appleton. Maybe from him, or through him, I was learning something important. Not information or the complex ideas, but more about the nature of complexity itself, the complexity of experiencing, at which I was a novice, as distinct from the complexity of knowing, at which I was a master.

My writing for Appleton was increasingly expansive and supple, specifically the journal pieces (or so I styled them) to my father, which I showed to Appleton with the understanding that they were not to be read in class as were the papers of the other students. Now *here* was a discovery, like the young colt finding more strength in his legs every day. And Appleton encouraged me to write poetry. When I asked him why, he said because I couldn't do it. But look, I had said, showing him the few poems I had written as class assignments. Exercises, he had said. You're a good boy, you do what you're told. Poetry is for taking chances. Write the poems you won't show me. Write the poems that you won't even show yourself. At least not right away.

Mike Tremain began to enter new manic reaches, swinging with ferocity at every pitch, good or bad. Now he did not seem to study at all, and when I mentioned that to him, he dismissed me sometimes with a shrug, or sometimes with an intensity that seemed like anger, though he was not angry. I'm learning plenty, Nicky, I'm studying like crazy, he would say. Finals are coming,

I've got to be ready. Then he would muss my hair or punch me on the arm or push me down on the bed, but he seemed somehow fragile to me, like a good blade that can be ground to so sharp an edge that though it can cut deeply and easily, it can't do so for long before the edge crumples and curves over on itself. But I could not worry about Mike; it was nearly impossible to do so. He was so totally certain about himself that there was no place to enter him with concern.

I spent more time with Al McGuire, in what little time he had between his studies and his football practice. I helped him with some of his school work (free, I told him, like a joke). He was a conservation and ecology major ("Somewhere between a bird-watcher and an ornithologist," he had himself described it. "Somewhere between a fisherman and an icthyologist."). I didn't know whether he was an average or better-than-average student. I had nothing to compare it to in my own experience. He got mostly Bs on his tests, but then so did nearly everyone else in college. But some As. He was a diligent student. He did his work. With the genetics section in one of his courses he had some trouble, and there I helped him. And I read his written work and corrected his grammar and syntax and spelling, though he was far from helpless with the written word. Mostly we talked about our life in the wind and the water, and about fishing. There were some adventures that he had had in trout streams that had a beauty in his telling of them as authentic as any I had knowldge of, the evocation of a soul doing its proper work. And again I would envy him and wonder if someday I would have such a music of my own.

But above all I spent my time with Sara, with Rembrandt, Bruegel, de Kooning, Schiele and the volumes and volumes of art that I poured myself into. One day I tried to invent, or figure out, a corellation between colors and their temperatures. I worked out a system for the visible spectrum. If a crimson red, say, was 2000 Kelvin, then its compliment, viridian green, would be 400 Kelvin, and so on around the color wheel, from the warmest yellows to the coolest blues. Then I took a painting in a book (a still life by Zurburan) and traced it and filled in each island of color with its temperature. Then I put it through a rough computer program that I threw together which digitalized everything. But when I was through, what did I have? Nothing. I had reinvented

229

a kind of esoteric painting by numbers. The Kelvin temperatures were measurements of light. But they were not light.

I spent much time in Sara's apartment or her bedroom. Ricki and Janie came to accept me easily enough, especially when I insisted on contributing some money to the food fund and because I was always willing to wash the dishes. And I would entertain them, willingly perform for them the feats of astounding intelligence that I had resisted and resented in my other life. Jester? Clown? What did it matter to me? I would let them quiz me from a volume of the *Encyclopedia Britannica* ("Metterlinck," Janie would say, picking a name at random, and I would rattle off his dates and accomplishments and some little curious nugget if there was one) and they would squeal with delight. I seldom did that when Sara was present; she disapproved. But often I was in the apartment without her, waiting, for she had courses and her work on the newspaper and her research in the library to do and other strings in her busy life to pluck, while I had nothing to do that I did not want to do, and time enough to do whatever that might be.

We had one close call. A reporter (if that's what you could call her) from the *National Enquirer* showed up one evening at the apartment.

There were, as Sara had told me, stringers on the larger college campuses who worked, if there was ever anything to do, for the *New York Times* or one of the news services like the Associated Press. When my story broke, they swooped in on me at once from Syracuse and Cornell and SUNY Albany, but what they reported and what was finally printed about me (here and there, deep into the back of the paper buried in the features) was merely innocuous detail. At sixteen I wasn't even young enough to be a prodigy. It wasn't as if I had come to college when I could have at the age of six or seven or eight. It was as with Mozart: at four his prodigy was an entertainment, by sixteen he was nearly forgotten, or at least ignored. So even with my astoundingly high IQ, managing editors saw that all I was was smart, even if very very smart, but that in itself wasn't news enough until I did something with it. Or against it.

But the *National Enquirer* person was different. She worked from a different premise altogether. Not facts but titilation was her goal, and hardly truth. It must have been easy enough for her to find me at Sara's. All she would have had to do was trail me from Jameson. When she knocked on the door and identified herself, Ricki innocently invited her in. Why not? The reporter wasn't much older than the girls, maybe a couple of years out of college herself. What did she see or invent—*a ménage à quatre?* Was the sexual appetite (requirements?) of this sixteen-year-old super genius equal to his intelligence? What could her angle be? Maybe that is what saved us, there was no angle here, no perspective, just three coeds and a guy, who was probably sleeping with one of them. Her editor would have scoffed at so green a story. So she put me away until I was ripe for picking, though I, in my own invincible innocence, imagined the the world would maybe dismiss me after all.

"Damn," Ricki said, "my big chance," when it was clear that the reporter would make nothing out of us.

"Oh Jeez," Janie said, "my mother would just about die." They hugged each other and laughed and howled.

Sara said nothing at all.

I continued to run through the countryside, though the outdoor track season was over. Fingers of Indian summer still reached into the coldness coming on. Some days there were slight flurries, but on others it could have been early April as much as mid-November. The ground was hard now, and all the flowers had turned into the skeletal weeds except the hardiest asters and the witch hazel which had just begun to bloom. Running through this landscape, often I would, as in sailing, find the slot, and on a surge of well-being, the joyous rightness of my life just then would sweep me up, and I would rise toward apogee. Fly. And I believed that, unlike Icarus, I could safely reach the sun, or unlike Orpheus, I could descend into the underworld and return unscathed, for I was Nick Burden, and I, unlike all other men, was marvelously blessed.

▸29▸
=

"One day? You'd only be home one day? Thursday, and that's it? We haven't seen you since you went away, and all we get is one day?" my mother said.

"Ah come on, Mom. You're putting guilt on me," I said.

"Right. You're absolutely right. You are guilty. So you're putting it on yourself. We looked forward to your visit. You must have known that. We've missed you badly and we were hoping to spend some time with you. We've also got a lot to talk about. This Kreutzer thing. He called. He writes. He is very polite, charming, but insidious."

"Kreutzer we don't have to talk about. I told you before. I'm staying at Cobbton. Nothing could get me out of here. I love it here. But let me say it again. I've been invited to New York. Sara Logan is going to take me to museums and galleries. I told you about her. She's an art history major. She knows all about this, where to go, what to see, how to get around the city. It's a great chance. Good for my education. I've discovered art. I told you all about that. It really excites me. So here's a great chance to see it. Don't you want me to learn things, to expand my horizons? You don't want me just to be a physics geek, do you? I need these kinds of experiences. This is more important than college itself, isn't that the point?" I rattled on. I would babble her into submission.

"And Sara Logan?"

"She's a good friend. A *girl* friend."

"A girlfriend."

"A friend who is a girl, Mom. Come on."

"Not a girl, Nicky. A *woman.*"

"O.K., then the first person of the opposite sex I've ever known *at all.* Is that better?"

"What about Selma Kaplan," she said. "She'll be home from Wellesley. You could see her. You'd have a lot in common to discuss."

But now I knew she was weakening. If she had to resort to Selma Kaplan, that frog of a girl I had taken out a couple of times, my first (only) date(s), then I knew she was coming around.

"I'll come home Wednesday early. There's no reason to stick around here. I'll be home Wednesday and Thursday. Friday I'll go to New York. Oh, and listen. I nearly forgot. There's a meeting of the northeast chapter of the American Physics Society. I've been invited to attend, or at least to drop in. Professor Manlow. Just last week. He told me about it. Drop in if you're in town, Burden, he said. That's kind of an honor, Mom. I'll probably do it."

"And where did you say you'll stay?"

"At an apartment of Sara's friend's parents."

"Who will be out of town for the holiday, right?" she said.

"No, no," I said. But yes, yes, I prayed. "I'll get their telephone number. You can call." I was overplaying my hand. Sally Burden might very well call. She might even decide to visit the city herself. Have leftover turkey with me and Sara in the Big Apple. Jesus. What a thought.

"I don't know, Nicky. I just don't know."

But, "Let him go," my father said, and then I knew that I had won.

We argued and poked a little longer, more for form's sake, I suppose, the old momentum of her concern carrying her on, and of course her desire to be with me as much as she could before. By degrees, I would less and less belong so exclusively to her. And I was learning to protect myself, to meet the dreaded world on its terms and survive. Maybe even triumph. She and my father had done a fine job. The list on the refrigerator door had worked. But now, greater than her defensive strength, what she needed was the strength to let up. Not that she did not know that about herself. She was too smart not to know—or not to want—that for me, this emergence. It was the pace that was troubling her, the speed with which my life was overtaking me. Along that line I might have had a few doubts myself but I was not now in a doubting mind about anything. Besides, I was a fast learner, was I not? The world's champion fast learner? So why should I not be as quick at working within the quotidian and mundane spaces of life as within the gigantic and eternal reaches of the universe and maybe beyond? Why indeed.

I told Sara. It was go. Go and go and go. I got a bus schedule and worked it out. I could leave Steffanville Friday morning as early as 7:45 and get to the port authority by 11:15. Great connections. The gods were smiling. She would meet me and we'd go directly to SoHo and NoHo and TriBeCa. Saturday we'd do MOMA and the Whitney and the Frick and the Met and Fifty-seventh Street. She swirled around as she always would when she was excited.

"And what about after lunch," I laughed. "I mean we wouldn't want to miss anything, would we?"

"Oh there's plenty left. Plenty." She showed me copies of the *New Yorker* and *New York* magazine, circled and underlined. Movies. Off off-Broadway productions. Poetry readings. Musical events as large as Lincoln Center, as small as a jazz trio on Eighth Street. We rolled around in a giddy fit of mouthwatering pleasures.

"Oh this is going to be so much fun for me, Nick. Showing you. Showing you everything."

I told Mike I needed to make a draw against my share of the profits: two hundred dollars. I told him about Thanksgiving, Sara, the museums and galleries. The city.

"Is two hundred enough, Mike? I mean I've got a place to stay. But what about food, transportation? New York's really expensive, isn't it? What do you think? Maybe I should take an extra fifty just in case."

"Yeah, well, Nicky," he said leaning back in his chair. "I think it's time that the board of directors had a meeting." He was sitting at his desk in our room fiddling listlessly with papers full of numbers. He pushed them aside and took out of the center drawer the business ledger of T&B Enterprises. I was sprawled on the bed.

"What kind of clothes do you think I'll need. And shoes. Jeez, I never thought about that. All I wear is jogging shoes. Can I wear jogging shoes into a gallery or a. . . ."

"We're broke, Nicky."

". . . restaurant? Broke?"

"Broke, partner. Flat. Zilch."

I sat up. "But I thought we were doing terrific. What about the posters? We're still selling the posters, aren't we? I'm still making deliveries. And I've been tutoring. How's the agent thing? Is it the expense? Maybe if we didn't have the secretary. Is that it? I mean, Mike. What do I know?"

He was waving his hand slowly in the air as if to push out of the way what I was saying, or erase it.

"It's worse than flat, Nicky."

"Worse?" I just could not understand this at all.

"We're in a hole. No. *I'm* in a hole. Not we, *me.*"

I waited. What else could I do, what question could I ask? How deep a hole?

"How deep a hole?" I said.

"Five thousand dollars."

I stood up. "Five *thousand*? Dollars? Is that what you said? Five *thousand*?" He nodded. "That's impossible, Mike. Impossible. We don't do that kind of business. We don't make enough money to get into that kind of debt. How? What? On what? . . . Mike? Mike? *What?*"

I had never known this kind of alarm. I had been frightened at times in my brief life, mostly while sailing. But that fear had a specific location and a size to it. A thunderstorm once coming at me and I couldn't get the mainsail down: the halyard had jammed in the sheave at the top of the mast. Once deep in the Adirondacks a black bear had gotten into our tent while we were out hiking but couldn't get out easily, and we came back to find the animal growling and tearing its way out, perhaps as angry and frightened as were my father and I. The storm itself jerked the halyard free. The bear broke out and ran off dragging the tent that had stuck to a hind claw, fled in its own terror from the flapping creature that had attacked it and was pursuing it still until the tent was pulled off by a bush. But this was different, an anxiousness of another kind altogether, dry and not full of adrenalin.

Unlike the stuck halyard and the trapped bear, where something I had planned had gone accidentally wrong, here was something that had come out of nothing. It was like some of the Big Bang theories that postulated a nothingness out of which the universe pulled itself, a nothingness so absolute that it could not be described, named, or even imagined. It was a concept in physics that I found so repugnant that it made me react physically, a tinge of sweat around my temples, a tensing of the muscles across my shoulders. That is what this was like, not terror but a massive collapse of the rational, what Mike had just told me. Perhaps I did begin to tremble.

"Hey, Nicky baby. Relax," Mike said. He stood up and gently eased me back down onto the bed. "O.K.? O.K.?" he soothed me. "I'm sorry about your plans for the city."

"Not important," I said. "I'll get the money. My folks will lend it to me. I think."

"And I'm sorry for the rest. Your chunk of the profits. But I didn't steal it, Nicky. A bad investment, that's what it was."

"I know you didn't steal it Mike. Don't even think I think that. So what happens. Bankruptcy? Is that a possibility? Were we actually incorporated? T&B Enterprises, Inc. Was there really an Inc.?"

"Yes, Nicky, there really was an Inc. For tax purposes. But this is different Nicky. It's a different kind of bankruptcy. So now I'm going to explain. You O.K.?"

"Yes."

"So this is the story, Nicky. I was dealing dope."

It was simple enough. Mike bought small amounts of cocaine from people in New York and supplied Joe Casper who sold even smaller amounts to individuals in the Cobbton area. The posters, our distribution system, was the means of transfer. Who could suspect anything? Mike would get the cocaine actually mailed to his home in Flushing, New York, and his mother would forward it to him: the small boxes. Then Mike would load the cocaine into the poster tubes that I would often deliver to Joe Casper. A neat operation. Very safe. A middleman operation, somewhere between wholesale and retail. Instead of selling bundles to dozens of people, anyone of whom could be a narc, all he had to do was do business with Joe Casper.

But what about me? Where was I in this equation? I sought for anger, but it wasn't actually anger that I wanted. An accounting, rather, and not of the dollars and cents. What did I mean to Mike? How did he truly define me? Was I only a tool for him to use, or did he simply make no distinction between the two of us, simply assumed that our partnership entailed the both of us equally. I hoped for that and remained silent; under those terms I could accept the danger he had thrust me into, maybe even enjoy it the way I could enjoy a squall after it had passed.

"So Casper stiffs me," Mike said. "At first he pays right up front, but more and more he's always a little short and then a little shorter. And now he tells me to go fuck myself. Go call the cops, college boy, he says. So I can't call the cops, right? And I can't break his leg? And I can't afford to hire someone to break his leg. But that is not the problem. The problem is that I'm five thousand into my supplier. It's not a lot of money to them, but they're a very small outfit themselves, so it's not no money either. Also, it's nothing they can allow to pass. It's not the way business is done."

"Business? Crime," I said.

"Crime? I don't know, Nicky. Crime is what you call crime." I remembered what Appleton had said. "Now murder, rape, armed robbery, that's still crime. But this, this is what I'd call cost accounting. Black ink, red ink. My people have got expenses. They sold me goods. At first I used T&B money to make up the short fall from Casper. But I kept getting behind. So then they extended me credit. So now they want their money. But Casper won't pay me and I've got no one to sell to. And nothing even to sell. I'd say they've been very patient, actually. If we were talking a car here, or a house, they'd repossess. So what have I got to repossess?"

"What?" I said, hoping he had a five thousand dollar answer.

"Nothing, Nicky." He glanced around. "Some barely used textbooks?" He smiled. "Nah. My people, I don't think they can read."

"What's going to happen, Mike?"

"For sure? I don't know. I've explained, but they don't want to know that. I'll talk to them again. I'll try to make a deal. Maybe I'll borrow money to pay them off."

"Borrow? How can you borrow that kind of money? Your father. He'll lend it to you."

"I'd never do that, Nicky. My father's got his business. I've got mine."

"So? Who?"

"Them. My people. Shylocks."

"That's true? That really happens?" I said.

"All the time, Nicky. All the time."

"So you borrow the money and you pay them off. That's it?"

"Well, yes. But you never really pay them off. They get interest. A lot of interest. and it compounds. If you don't pay them off quick, then you end up paying them forever, interest on the interest. After awhile you never even get to the capital."

"I can't believe it. It really happens."

"It really happens, Nicky. Just like in the funny papers. TV."

"Don't do it, Mike. Don't. You're talking your life here, the rest of your life. Or a lot of it."

"That's right, Mike. My life. One way or another. So? You got some other ideas?"

"Me." I said as quickly as that. "Sell them me."

"What?"

"Sell them me. You've been selling me all over campus all semester, so now sell me to them. Figure out what they need that I could do for them."

Mike got up and came and sat down beside me on the bed and put his arm over my shoulder.

"Oh Nicky. That is beautiful. That is so beautiful. I can't think of anything so beautiful ever happening to me." He hugged me. "Thank you. But Nicky, right now in the real marketplace, you aren't worth shit. Except to me, Nicky. Except to me. To me you're gold."

I had to tell Sara. To tell her and to ask her advice. Not about Mike Tremain. I didn't tell her anything about that. Just about the sudden money problem.

I'll call my parents. I'll explain. They'll lend me the money. I'm sure they will. I think. I'll call them tonight."

"But how much money do you think you need?" she said. "Besides your bus ticket?"

"Two hundred," I said. "Two fifty." But a question more than an answer.

"Oh Nick, sweety, no. Nothing near that."

"But it's so expensive. New York. Isn't it?"

"Not the way I do it, and you're with me."

"Then what do I need?"

"Nothing," she said. "A few bucks for chewing gum, Nick. Nothing. I'll handle it."

"But. But you can't just pay for me. I mean. . . ." But she put her hand on the back of my neck and I shuddered to a stop.

"No? Why not? So let's say it's a loan. Someday you'll pay me back."

"With interest," I said.

"Yeah," she said. "With interest. Lots of interest." And then she kissed me.

⇥ 30 ⇥

=

I could not forget Mike's problem, but I could not live within it either. Nothing outside of myself had ever seemed so real to me; it was as if a thin fine crack in the pleasure dome inside of which I had lived had opened and I had glimpsed a coarse reality through it, a reality that I had only seen vaguely through the softening scrim of the dome itself. Now instead of real toads in imaginary gardens—or real vipers in real jungles—I had to consider the possibility of actual violence, the possibility of harsh consequences that were as hard and dull as rock, not metaphors at all. But—and yet—Sara Logan was as real. My new sexual existence, such a fantastical notion just a few months ago, was now as real as anything else in life could be. My work in the lab and in the desk drawer was as real. Appleton's impact was as real. If the pleasure dome of my life had been cracked by my fear for Mike, the pressure of my life kept the crack from widening. Sometimes I even felt guilty at not worrying more, but whenever I started to slide into his anxiety as I might imagine it, as if to share the weight of it, my life just now would hook me up and out.

And Mike himself was not drowning. After his disclosure, for the remaining two weeks before the Thanksgiving vacation, he said no more about it. There was no apparent panic in him, no thrashing about. It was as if every day I expected him to say, I've got it! The solution! Salvation! Only this: I tried to imagine what it must feel like to live with a constant and ineradicable ex-

240

perience. Whatever the immediate outcome, Mike Tremain would forever after have to live with the wound of this mistake because it seemed to me to be more than just a question of business, an error of judgment. It had more to do with some deeper notion of himself. Would something break in him, some small cog of his confidence that would in all his years to come take a toll which, however small, eventually total to a great sum? Maybe it was Mike Tremain more than I whose destiny it was to take the chances that the rest of us could not. And now, after this experience, maybe he could not. If this was so, or would be so, then I grieved not as much for Mike Tremain as for the rest of us.

But I did not grieve much at all just then. Cobbton beat Syracuse in the final game of the season and went undefeated. Al McGuire was selected as the outstanding player of the game, a rare thing for a defensive player, rarer still for an interior lineman. We—the Cobbton Revolutionaries—were offered a bowl bid, the Apricot Bowl in Arizona. Not a major bowl but our first bowl ever. We. Our. I was beginning to think like one of us, a xenophobic Cobbtonian. Into Thanksgiving week, the weather was as fine as November can sometimes be, and the prediction for the rest of the week was excellent. Tuesday night Sara and I made our final plans, checked over our times and places. She even pressed forty dollars upon me. Just in case. Give it back if you don't need it. But all we would need she assured me was bread and wine, good walking shoes, the gritty atmosphere of the city. The art of northern Europe. The latest hot, flickering, jokey ephemera of the contemporary scene. My willingness. Each other.

My mother picked me up at the Steffanville bus station. The depot was freshly painted in blue and gray, and it was as neat and arranged as the Cobbton bus station was disheveled and indifferent. Steffanville lived on the narrow edge of having a bus station at all instead of only a part-time agent who sold tickets from the counter of the diner where the buses stopped on their way to Boston or New York or Montreal. Cobbton, for all its college charm, was more transient, its population more importantly dependent upon the come-and-go economy of the school; it had a collegiate scruffiness to it. Steffanville, however, lived on the dissolving verge of American life where it could still be personally concerned about the trees that lined its streets (it required a town ordinance for you to cut one down) or the addition of a room to the public library. Or to the presentableness of its bus station, believing as it still did in the importance of first impressions upon visitors, not that it had many visitors. But like so many other small towns, the metropolitan ooze was seeping toward it like a giant amoeba, a phage that would someday engorge it, and then its energy and life would become a part of something larger and more exciting, more profitable but less distinct. Not altogether unlike me, I thought.

I had expected my father to meet me because his business was much closer to the station than was our house, but he was busy with a last-minute printing job. I would not see him until evening.

"So," my mother said even with her arms still around me. "So." And then she stepped back. "Look at you. Just look at you. You really *have* grown. In only three months. You're filling out. You look great." She rubbed the back of her hand across my cheek. "And shaving every day now, I'll bet."

"I could, I guess." We got to the luggage compartment of the bus and I hauled out the L.L. Bean duffel bag I used for traveling, what little I had done. What about New York? I thought. I couldn't lug this huge thing, three-quarters empty, down there. I could use a gym bag. But what if I brought a suit or a sports jacket with me? But should I bring a suit? I should have asked Sara. Maybe I could call her.

"Nick," my mother said. "Nick. Where are you going?" I had walked off away from her in the wrong direction.

"I was thinking," I said, "of something."

"Of New York?"

"No," I said, "yes."

"It's O.K., Nick. It's O.K. You don't need to feel guilty."

"It's not that, Mom. Not exactly. It's not a guilty kind of guilty. It's more like having two obligations at the same time, two appointments and you don't want to miss either one."

"I understand, Nicky."

"You do?"

"Better than you, sweetie. Better than you. It's nothing you can know yet. Wait till you're a mother." She grabbed one of the handles to my bag and together, the bag between us, we carried it out to the car. "You've always been the center of our lives. For over sixteen years you've lived there. Now, for us, you're moving out of that center, for you too. But for us, you'll never move out of that center." She walked quickly, which was characteristic. The bag twisted and banged against us at each step. "You'll always be there, long after you're gone from it. That's the way it is with parents, Nicky. So whether a parent lets go gracefully or not, for the parent you'll always be there, right where you've always been. In fifty years that won't change. Now let's go to the mall. I'm taking off the afternoon from work."

"The mall? What for?" By the time I got into the car beside her, the motor was running and she was nearly moving off. I slammed the door closed quickly.

"To get you some clothes."

"Clothes? I don't need clothes, Mom. I'm only going to New York for a couple of days."

"For the winter, clothes for the cold, not New York," she said. "Is that all you can think of, New York? Believe me, after a couple of days in New York, you've still got to face the winter."

"Oh Mom," I laughed. "You haven't changed at all. You still can't handle the enthymeme."

"The what? What's an enthymeme?" She looked to her left and then pulled out into a hole in the traffic.

"It's . . . . Well, it's like going from A to C without passing through B. Or it's like adding A plus B and getting five."

"Nine," she said. "A plus B equals nine. Any fool knows that."

"Oh Mom," I said. "Oh Mom." And now I was back in the happy center again. Our center. My center. But only for a little while.

Before college (so recently as that) I had lived most of my life contentedly literally inside of my house and alone, partly out of the necessity to do so imposed by what I was. When other kids were in school, where was I to go? And both my parents worked, so a lot of my life I spent within the constructions of my mind and its inventions. Which was not such a bad place to be. And the after-their-school and weekend friends that I did have were never very close, with maybe the exception of John Sebring, now dead. I could not enter fully into their conspiracies on a part-time basis; the gossipy urgencies generated by their social life at school could not be mine. Too many references would have to be explained to me, too many insider jokes illuminated. So I didn't ask. I just hung around on the periphery, not resentful, even a little grateful, but not contented either. And girls had remained at a distance because though my friends made contact with girls on a daily–hourly–basis in classes and hallways, after school it was only us boys flailing at baseballs or shooting hoops talking about the girls, snorting and sniggering with adolescent bravado at the chimera born out of our nervous lusts.

My parents noted this as much as I. As strongly as they wanted to protect me, they certainly didn't want me to become a solitaire. There was nothing that said I was to be protected from girls. So my mother discovered Selma Kaplan.

Selma Kaplan was something of a prodigy herself. Not in my league, of course, but at least in class double a. She was able to go to Welleseley at a young sixteen and apparently hold her own. But she was working at the outer limits of her ability. A friend of my mother's had told her about the girl. My mother urged me to meet her, to do something together. Like what? I wanted to say. Shout. Do what together, Mom? Calculus problems? Or fucking (whatever that exactly was)? But of course I never said that. But here it was again as always, even from my defense-minded mother, the notion that my interest in someone should depend more upon me rather than upon her or him, that I, or what I was, should be accommodated.

Why had my mother's friend not called to tell her that she knew of a beautiful girl with the chest of a *Playboy* centerfold in whom I might be interested? Did they think I could not relate to that? Hardly. My mother knew that with my ranging mind I was certain to know about all that even if I didn't know anything *important* about all that. But there it was, as ever, as always: if they provided me with the books that they did and the computer and the telescope and other equipment that such as I required, then why not a smart girl, a *very* smart girl, a girl smart enough for me?

Poor Selma Kaplan. She was not at all attractive. When she would someday shed her heavy eyeglasses for contacts and let her finespun and abundant hair flow free and donned tightfitting jeans and billowing peasant blouses, nothing would change. And as it turned out we had nothing in common, not even our intelligences, because just then in her life all she had was her intelligence; it was important to her and she depended upon it. It was all she did. In

244

the two times I met with her I had the feeling that she understood that about herself, that her future would be made good because it would have at least that to sustain her. And though I did not think it then, now, on this Thanksgiving eve, in my own bed in my own room in my own house, I thought that she, like Albert McGuire and even Mike Tremain, had made her accommodation and I had not. But I was getting close, or closer, or so I thought. In three months I had come to face the world without my parents running interference for me. I had fallen in love and had actually (incredibly!) *become* a lover. I had made two good friends in Mike and Al who had helped me toward discovering myself to myself. I had found the universe of visual art that was expanding in me at quasar speed. And maybe I had discovered my future work in physics or wherever else that would lead. But about that I was maybe not as at ease as I thought I should have been. Because I had also discovered Appleton. I remembered his most recent words to me, just two days ago: "So, Burden. Three months and nothing important has happened to you yet. So what have you to be thankful for?" "Are you kidding?" I had protested. "*Everything* that's happened to me in the past three months has been important." But, "Not that way, not that way," he said. "Those are all successes you're talking about, just good old Nicky Burden rolling on as might be expected. But what about enigma, eh?" "I'm getting there. I'm getting to that, too. Give me a break, will you?" But he dismissed me with a wave of his hand before I could begin to answer him more fully. But then, provocation was Appleton's game.

I softened into sleep, rising and falling as if on the small waves rocking *Yarps* at anchor. A thought about Mike's problem spiked me awake a little. I thought of Sara and my cock grew hard. I thought of the indigo of Bruegel's North Sea skies, Rembrandt's compassion, Velasquez's contempt. The collapse of Kreutzer's G. Superstrings tied into Gordian knots. Appleton reminding me that I had not failed and still could not. So maybe I was not approaching enigma after all.

In the morning my father and I set out for a sturdy walk.
"Go on," my mother ordered. "I'll cook, you guys fraternize. It's very healthy. I read it in a book about fathers and sons."
The air was clear and clean but cidery, too, touched faintly with

245

the flavor of the terrain just before it would be finally locked up until spring, just the faintest sourness as the leaves and the grasses started to rot. We hiked out straight north of town toward and then up Steuben's Knob.

Steuben's Knob was a sacred place to me, something like what American Indians have, an exact location where the present and the past can meet, a place to which you came in moments of great sorrow or great joy to weep or sing, to draw strength from the ancients and to deposit your share of strength in the future. Steuben's Knob was a geological oddity. It was a hill about eight hundred feet high. But it was not natural to the predominant shale of the region. It was instead a solid chunk of basalt. It was the core of an ancient volcano that had been sheared off and pushed over from Vermont, nearly fifty miles away, in the last Ice Age. Near the base of the hill you could pick up everywhere slabs and slices of slate. But suddenly you bent and picked up a hard, glassy stone, surprisingly light – the texture, the weight, the fracture planes entirely different from the shale.

Steuben's Knob was so special to me because it was my first clear memory of awe and wonder. My father brought me here when I was five and told me about the volcano and how the knob had gotten here. By five my range of information was enormous, but for all my precocity, I had no great emotional reach. The awesomeness of the cosmos had not yet enthralled me, its very vastness a prohibition. But the idea of an eight hundred foot hill being pushed intact fifty miles by a mile-high mountain of ice, that I could apprehend, that was a scale of wonder that I could manage. I remember perfectly the rush of emotion when what my father told me penetrated, the exhiliration and terror of the idea of such forces. I take that moment and that place as having holy implications for me in the sense that something greater than myself was born in me then, or maybe it was I who was reborn into it, and all my life since then has become a pursuit of the ramifications of that informing act. The ramiforms. The ramifictions. The metaphors.

Steuben's Knob was named for a soldier in the American Revolution, not the great Baron Frederick von Steuben but a lesser officer, an artillery man who had hauled a couple of cannons up the hill to threaten and harass General Burgoyne on his march toward Saratoga and defeat. Thereafter nothing much had happened to

Steuben's Knob. It was almost entirely rock, too little dirt to grow anything upon, too hard to break up to build on. Only scrubby oak and pine, hawthorne and shadbush and various dogwoods had gained rootholds in the cracks and crevices and a thin skimming of weeds. If it was used for anything it was by young lovers or picnickers. Or by fathers to teach their sons.

We got to the top of the knob by one o'clock. It would take us about two hours to get down and hike back into town. Dinner was set for four. Then we would watch what was left of the Washington-Dallas game.

In our times like these together, hiking or canoeing or sailing, often with my mother too, we didn't speak until we were stopped. At anchor. Hauled out for the night. At the peak. We were all easy in each other's company. But I never could say all that I felt about my father because I had no definition of that feeling, only *a* feeling, an intensity like a wave of quantum energy. I thought of it as love because that is what it was, but it was more than that word could encompass. I suppose all love is more than the word for it, but despite all the other words I had, love was all I had for this. In the past three months, in my journal essays, my father work, what Appleton said was the best thing I was doing ("The only good thing that you're doing, Burden."), I had begun to approach some definition, but I had not gotten there yet. I had only gotten to the top of Steuben's Knob.

We talked about the summer to come.

"I was thinking," my father said, "maybe you shouldn't have to work this summer." He tossed a banana to me and peeled one for himself.

"What does that mean? There's the money I need to fix *Yarps*. And if I don't work what will I do anyway? Hang out? Hang around?"

"Well, maybe you should study. Go on working on what you've been doing, what you've been telling us about. You're in college, but you're not really connected to a college year, are you? I mean from what you've described and what Kreutzer explained . . . you're already well into your career. You don't really live by semesters or courses, do you? So maybe your job is just to go on doing what you do."

"Stay at Cobbton for the summer? No way."

"Or Princeton," he said.

"Princeton?" I said. "No."

"They'd even pay you. Pretty good. A lot more than you'll make around here. You could fix *Yarps* easy."

"No," I said, "not a chance. Whatever I'm doing, the universe can wait. I'm coming home. I'm going to work for you. I'm going to fix your typesetting computer when it goes wrong. I'm going to learn how to run a press. I'm going to print restaurant menus. In September I'm going back to Cobbton.

But there was no argument here. All he was doing was offering me my options. We sat quietly eating our bananas looking out over the gray-blue late November land, farm buildings and silos breaking up through it like small, cresting whitecaps in a force-five wind.

"I never finished college. Did I ever tell you that, Nick?" he said.

"No. You never did. I just assumed. I'm surprised."

"It felt as though I finished. It seemed that way. But actually I dropped out even though I continued to live around the campus. I stayed involved. Your mom stayed with it, but I didn't. And we were going together by then. I'd sit in on courses I was interested in. And we'd all talk and read and argue. Marx, Marcuse, Fanon. Camus. But I just stopped caring about the degree. It was in the air, that sort of rejection of institutions. Civil rights, the heating up in Vietnam. Some of us felt that we should not accept college deferment as a way out of the army. If we were against it, then we should be against it directly."

"That was brave," I said.

"Well, honest, maybe."

"Maybe honest and brave are the same thing."

"Yeah, well, sometimes honest and brave can be dumb, too, but we weren't always honest, not about everything. Not as honest as we thought we were. When you're young you lay claim to a lot that you have no right to. And you make a lot of noise about it. Back then we substituted a lot of noise for a lack of knowledge and ex-perience."

"But you were young, you didn't know better. You had ideals. Your heart was in the right place."

"No. We knew. Most of us knew. And a lot of us were lying. We were getting off on the moral posturing more than the issues. In fact in a lot of ways it was a way to escape from the issues, escape from the responsibility of thinking. It was easy to be against sin, to make vicious cracks about Johnson and Nixon. It was a terrific high. *Relevance.* That was the key word. That was the touchstone. We'd sit around and make these judgments about whether what we were asked to study was relevant. But we never bothered to define relevance except in the murkiest terms. For a lot, for many, all irrelevant meant was that they felt justified in not writing a term paper for that course. If they flunked an irrelevant course, they'd wear the F like a badge of honor."

Then he turned and looked closely at me and put his hand on my leg. "But not me, Nicky. I didn't lie to myself or anyone. And I never gave up on my ideals, and I'll tell you why. I discovered that the issue wasn't as simple as the right and the wrong of Vietnam. It was more about the failure of the human heart. What wars are about is the death of gentleness. So what I saw was so much moral arrogance that the leadership in Washington and the leadership on the campuses didn't look that different. Did you ever hear of SDS? Did you ever hear of Abbie Hoffman?"

"A little," I said. "Some stuff I've read."

"Everyone thought he was terrific. But I got to spend a little time with him, a weekend in fact. He was a posturing jerk, an ego freak on the joy ride of his life. And that's how I got into printing, did you know that? I thought that there could be no spokesman for me except me. I got a job and started to learn the trade. It was a good apprenticeship. I learned from setting type by hand to running an offset press. At night and in between jobs I'd publish statements I'd written or that friends I respected had written. Mostly what we tried to do was print information that we dug for. We got a lot of information from the foreign press, the *Manchester Guardian*, for instance. A lot of what never got into American newspapers. I printed information and I pointed out the implications. For instance, I printed about the atrocities of the North Vietnamese as well as those of the South. And I had this guy who used to write beautiful and thoughtful essays. I remember once I printed an essay of his called "Just and Unjust Wars." He didn't take a side, he examined the idea. But nobody liked it. And nobody wanted information, all they wanted was a position and the propaganda that supported it. I stayed with it for two years, and then I stopped. It was like it was breaking my heart. I felt myself getting angrier and angrier at the angriness, at the clenched fist. At the breaking down of any kind of civility. I stopped. But I never lost what I believed in. I just got quieter about it."

We had never spoken this way before. Perhaps it was my going to college, the shifting of me in his perspective, his own memory of going to college, a lens, a catalyst. Suddenly on top of Steuben's Knob, another revelation for me. I had become, if not equal to him, then in his eyes equal to the possibility of certain kinds of thoughts that had nothing to do with that barrier, the intelligence of Nicky Burden.

"You know," I said, "you've never lectured to me about conduct. You've never told me how to behave. You never hit me. You've never even shouted at me. Or scolded me. Or punished me."

"You've always been a good kid," he said. "You never needed to be scolded."

"But you're not born that way," I said. "You've got to learn to be what you are. And I've had to learn all of that from you and Mom. So if you haven't lectured me, then how did I learn, assuming I have?"

"You absorb it, I guess. You reflect what you get, what you see."

"That's right, I think. That's what I think. You become the object of your contemplation. Plato. So you and Mom and the life you've given me, that's what I've had to contemplate. It seems to have worked out."

"Maybe," he said, "but you've got to feel good about yourself, is the point. But so far it's pretty abstract, isn't it? Plato?"

"Yes. The test is when I've got to do something."

"Like what?" he said.

"Like being honest. And brave. And maybe dumb. And never to lie." Then quickly, "This is great," I said, "this is fun. Talking like this. I love this. Talking about this stuff."

"Stuff?" he said, laughing.

We hiked back into town and then home. Me, my mother, and father.

Afterwards, we called my grandparents, the Porters. My father's parents were both dead, one from disease, the other in an automobile accident. They were only photographs.

The Porters were not much closer. They lived in California, in

250

San Diego; they visited us once a year. But it was only more recently, only in the tales of the Porter sisters, that my grandparents became more real, but mostly as the butts upon whom the tricks of their daughters had been played. After our supper we called them. It had been planned. After our supper and just before theirs.

I was the last to talk to them. We said the usual things.

"So how's college?" Grandpa Porter said. "How do you like the coeds?"

In the background I heard my grandmother say something like Now stop that George.

"Just fine, Grandpa. I like college, and the coeds too."

And that sort of thing.

"Oh, you're growing up so fast," my grandmother said.

Yes, I thought, but how fast was that? Maybe tomorrow I would begin to find out.

⇥31⇥

=

I was up at half past five; but my mother had already arisen, although she had nothing to do before driving me to the bus station
but worry and fuss.

"It's such a terrible place," she said as she hovered around and
patched together a breakfast.

"What? New York?" I said.

"The Port Authority. What a way to enter the city. Eighth Avenue and Forty-second Street. The gates of hell. That's what worries me more than anything.

"You're kidding," I said. "What? A gang of thugs is going to jump
me and drag me off to a life of degradation and crime? You'll never
hear from me again?"

"Something like that, yes," she said without a trace of humor.
"It's been known to happen. Drugs. Addicts. They get crazy.
They're everywhere."

Including Jameson Hall, right in your precious son's room. In
the tubes of dope he carried on another bus to another bus station.

"But that's part of the challenge, isn't it? The young Galahad
passing through the perilous forest in search of the grail? Danger
is part of the game. It's what gives life its zest."

"What grail? What game? Mad dogs drooling down their chins,
peeing in their pants? Hardly the stuff of romance, Nicky." She
slapped at the toaster, which had been sticking and burning toast
for as long as I could remember.

"And Galahad had the strength of ten because his soul was pure," I continued.

"Yeah, well Galahad disappeared. He didn't come back. What's wrong with you, you can't remember what you don't want to remember?" There were tears in her eyes. I rose from the table and went to her and hugged her.

"Come on, Mom. Don't worry like this."

"No? So how should I worry? You're sixteen. You don't know crap about what's waiting for you, it's all in your head. And you sure don't know Eighth Avenue and Forty-second Street."

"Sixteen and two-thirds," I said, but she pushed me away.

"Grail?" she sniffed. "What grail?"

"Knowledge. Involvement with life. Art," I said.

"Sara Logan," she said.

We didn't say more until I was ready to board the bus. Before I left home my father had come down. He gave me a hundred dollars. That's a lot of menus, I said. Experience isn't as cheap as you think, he said.

"You call me right away, you hear. Twelve o'clock. I'm sitting by the telephone, Nick. If I don't hear from you, I'm calling the police and then I'm driving down to the city. Do you hear?"

"The truth is, Mom, I'm not really going to the city. I've dropped out of school and Sara Logan and I are going to New Mexico, to a Hare Krishna type of cult in Taos where we sit and stare at the sun all day and sing mantras and get enlightenment. I didn't know how to tell you. I thought it was best this way. Try to explain it to Dad."

"I don't find any of this funny, Nick."

The door of the bus hissed closed and I was on my way.

My mother was right about the Port Authority. But it was hard for me to gauge the degree of actual danger I might have been in, although everything was ominous and threatening. But nothing clearly alarming was actually happening, or nothing that I could see—or could interpret as danger; it was more the idea—the feeling—that control was minimal here, that anything could happen, anything at all: that these people had slipped out of the restraints of the cerebral cortex and had floundered down into the limbic and reptilian systems where only the reflex of appetite ruled, and ruled completely. What it made me think of was scenes I had so recently studied in Bruegel and Hieronymus Bosch, the phantasmagoria of the hell of self-mutilation, of spiritual annihiliation – people blowing their lives out of their assholes, people who had turned into their own demons.

Nothing of this surprised me. Besides the lurid fears of my mother and her descriptions, I had read enough and heard enough about this world below the nether world of mortal corruption to know what to expect – the bag people, the destitute in general, the beggars and their stench, the black pimps and the white teenagers from Indiana, the jittery pushers, the addicts nodding off, the occasional ranter or screamer locked in a furious, seething inner diatribe striding through the boiling and eruptive landscape of what was left of his mind, the homosexuals still searching out even within the reach of the sweeping knife of AIDS. What did surprise me was the monochromatic quality of it all. Prepared by the colors of Bruegel and Bosch, I expected a similar intensity, but instead these characters in these scenes were drained of color and of sharp shifts of values. They were all in grayed umbers and blunted siennas. It was as if their color had drained away with their lives, that only the outlines of their lives were left, and even those were dissolving. But isn't that the way it is with death, at first a pallor, and then an icy blue whiteness as all the systems cease to function?

So there was already something to think about here, another start to the end of my heretofore sentimental education.

I had been to New York three times before with my parents. We had driven in and gone directly to the American Museum of Natural History including the Hayden Planitarium. On another trip we went to the top of the Empire State Building and then to the Statue of Liberty. On a third trip we took a boat ride around Manhattan Island and then went to a Broadway show, *Chorus Line*. We had on those trips walked into Central Park, walked down Fifth Avenue, visited Greenwich Village, eaten in Chinatown and loitered in the area of Washington Square. And that had been New York for me except for what I read. Until today, what I had seen of the city, its inhabitants, had been flickered through quick, faceted glimpses, my mother filtering on one side of me, my father on the other. Now here I was, not only present but for the first time aware of the requirement that I think about what I was seeing, or more importantly, that I think about how to think about the whirligig of a molecule that these atoms constructed. Where was there a mathematics that could consider that?

"Nick. Over here, over here," Sara waved. We had arranged to meet in front of the Greyhound ticket counter on the main floor of the terminal. I had decided on a backpack, which I slung over one arm. We grabbed each other. She kissed me quickly on the cheek. "Been mugged yet?" she said as we swung off toward the Eighth Avenue exit.

"Once getting off the bus and once outside the men's room. It wasn't so bad."

"There. You see? New York. More bark than bite."

"I've got to call my mother at twelve."

"Sure. No problem."

I had nothing to compare New York to except its own legend. If Paris was more beautiful and London more effective and sedate, if Rome was full of a boisterous gaiety and Athens bright, I had no real, no personal, sense of that. For all my superiority of intellect, my knowldge of this physical world was as much a result of the *National Geographic* as was my knowledge of Antarctica and Nepal or Ecuador. But against its own legend New York faltered. Baghdad on the Hudson? Hardly. (Or maybe exactly, for what was Baghdad on the Tigris like?) What we swept through, what Sara pulled me about in, was unremittingly filthy and cacophonous, grey and mostly sunless, the air thick and gritty, sulphurous and hard to breathe. And nothing was built to human scale. It was a city designed by a murderer. Everywhere it seemed the people who probably lived or worked here hurried through it, rushed through it, as if to avoid it. Or rather they struggled to move through it quickly, but the taxis and the buses were often stalled, large groups of people clotted at the corners barely held back from crossing the street against the traffic. Eating anywhere during the day was an energy-consuming ordeal, excepting the hot dog and falafal carts.

And none of my observations were original. Not unlike Hesiod in his *Georgics* or Cicero inveighing against the urban, extolling the suburbs. Shakespeare's Jacques. Prospero. Tolstoy's Levin.

For more than two millenia the city broke the heart and buried the soul.

But it was full of a fierce, attractive energy, too, like the strong force that kept the core of an atom together – the ideas of wealth and power bubbling in the cauldron, hags of ambition chanting magical spells around it, offering deals. Even I, who knew so little of that, could sense it in the profusion itself, the magnitude of the sensuousness of it all. The materiality. That such a place could be, could function, go on, continue to exist at all seemed to me to argue for an engine driving it that was fueled by more than the struggle merely to survive. If you came to New York, if you put up with it, then you were like a gambler or an adventurer. You were playing for high stakes. Or at least you were trying to get into the big game. For which you had to take the risks. Maybe the highest risks. But if you came to New York for any other reason than to *triumph*, then you came as a fool.

Art. The scene, as Sara styled it. Not the art scene, just the scene, by which she meant what was mostly going on in the galleries of lower Manhattan and those on Fifty-seventh Street. A scene in a dramatic production, something larger than the paintings themselves, maybe something that had nothing to do with the paintings at all. I cannot recall (Me. Not able to recall.) most of the specific visual experiences – the structures, the paintings, the conceptual statements, the textures and colors (or the lack of them), the vitality and the urgencies or the lifelessness, the articulate exhuberance or the stolid and the dumb. What I remembered more than any unique work was the shout and blare – the proclamation – of art itself, the existingness of it. In and out of everything we twisted and dove, darting like swallows indiscriminately feeding. All the rest of Friday and all of Saturday we plundered. Giddy in our exhaustion, what was I to make of this? Or of the exhaltation?

"It's a new approach," Sara said. "The Sara Logan school of art appreciation. It's called the saturation method." We were sitting on a bench in Central Park just near to where the skating rink was waiting. Over us rose the Plaza Hotel. We had visited the Metropolitan and the Frick and then the Whitney, from which we had walked back to Fifty-seventh Street. Now it was four o'clock and, even as fine for November as the weather had been, getting chilly.

It works," I said, "I'm saturated. Drenched. Drowned."

"Not much more to go, " she said. "There are the Marins you have to see at the Kennedy and the Leonard Baskins. Then we shoot over to Madison and the Wildenhain to see the old masters if we're not too late and if they'll let us in. Upstairs."

"Why not? We could go into every place else."

"Upstairs at Wildenhain is different. Here's what we'll do. We'll tell them you're Nicholas Burden of the Steffanville Burdens and you're thinking of buying your grandmother something for Christmas. Only twenty-nine shopping days left."

"A Bronzino for Grandmother Porter," I said. "She'll love it."

"Sure," Sara said. "She could put it right over the fireplace."

"She lives in San Diego."

"O.K. Right over the air conditioner, then."

We howled and leaned into each other.

"Next to the Norman Rockwell," I said.

"A little to the left of the Kean," Sara said.

"Who's Kean?" I said.

"Forget it," she said. "Nothing you want to know about."

Four college kids kicked and scuffed by us, crossing by a tall black guy carrying a large music box, only playing it low, even softly. Brahms.

"So what do you think, Nick? What do you make of this? The art?"

For all the saturation, this was actually the first time we talked about art separate from it, while not standing in front of something. Last night we went to a movie and ate in a Cambodian restaurant (upstairs, back, hardly more than a large room). In the apartment we ate great gobs of ice cream and watched TV till two o'clock and eventually fell into bed too tired even to think about sex. I had called my mother at noon as she had demanded, and, ever the solicitous son, had called her again at six. Surprise, I reported. I'm still alive and kicking. Lucky me. Good, she said. Don't press your luck. Sara said she sounded like a great mom. Maybe you'll meet her someday I said. Sure, Sara said. Someday. And in the morning we were off again, strong as only the young can be. And Sara vibrant and radiant, lighted my way, her pleasure in mentoring me, my pleasure. My Beatrice.

"It's hard to put a beginning and an end to it. What I've seen. How to talk about it. You've been here, Sara. To New York a lot. Into art. The city. It's all so new to me."

"Start with thinking about what you liked the most and the least. What did you hate?"

"I didn't hate any of it. It's all exciting, one thing after the other. It's like it's all part of one gigantic canvas or . . . or like an endlessly changing kaleidoscope that's being recorded on film and the film is being played in an endless loop. It's not the individual pieces that I can think of just now. Mostly. So *that's* what I like. All this *going on.* It's like what I like so much about Bruegel, the action everywhere. But no one thing of all I've seen is like Bruegel. But what I don't understand, you remember those plywood boxes by Donald Judd? You remember the black paintings by Yves Klein and the white paintings by Ryman, square white paintings?"

"Yes."

"Well what I don't understand is this: How much fun could it be to do something as simple as that? And it couldn't have taken much skill. And no imagination. And it couldn't have taken very long to do. So how much fun could it be? And what did the painter do for the rest of the day or week or whatever? You know what I mean? How can you go on painting a white square? What's going on in your mind? What kind of life is that? Or the stripes by Nolan?" But before she could answer I said, "Am I being very conservative?"

"You're being very honest," she said. "That's what's important."

"Honest? Yeah," I said. "And dumb."

"You read those books I gave you?"

"Sure." In a couple of hours. "And a decades worth of *Art in America* and *ArtForum.* I understand the overall rationale. The history of the art. The contemporary theories. That's the easy part for me – aesthetic theory from Plato to the present. I could quote you pages of Ruskin or Meyer Shapiro. I could do that right now better than anyone. Sure, maybe I question some of the premises. And very often just the basic logic itself, the thinking, is simply wrong. But those are technical objections. Most of what people say about most things isn't logical anyway. But what I'm asking is at the individual level. I just can't understand what pleasure someone gets in painting something pure white or black. Or green or yellow. Anything so simple. That's what I don't get. And there's something else I think of. Why are all these contemporary people doing this, making all this art? I don't mean that as a judgment. Not at all. It's admirable in a lot of ways. But it's got to be more than hoping you hit it big, getting discovered, don't you think?"

"No," Sara said. "I think that mostly that is what it is and that is all it is. Hitting it big. Fame. Fortune. Adulation. Making it. Bright lights. Big city. Bigger World. Getting to drive a Lamborghini, or at least a Mercedes, by the time you're thirty."

"You make it sound kind of ugly," I said. "Vulgar, meretricious."

"And you're maybe thinking it – art is – a little holy? Or should be? Poets as priests? Painters as priests?"

"Yeah," I said. "Sort of. Holy vessels through whom the gods speak. Doesn't Appleton talk to your class about that?"

"Appleton?" Sara said, as if startled. "Appleton?" like, what's he doing here? "Oh. Right," she said. "Exactly. But who are these gods? Define your gods? Mammon is the only one I can think of, but that's only because I don't know the names of the others. You'd know them. Are there names for the gods of making it?"

"Yes. Garthra and Solmar," I told her right away. "Norse gods. Gods of pillage and violent victory. Holtar," I added, "the god of theft."

"So there you are."

"But what about Bruegel?" I said. "Reubens? Velasquez?"

"Then was then and now is now," she said, "But even Reubens was a wheeler-dealer. He was a millionaire. He made a fortune. Built the best house in Antwerp, didn't he? He was an emissary for kings. Ingratiated himself and got terrific commissions. He ran a painting factory. And Velasquez wanted to be a nobleman."

"But the painting itself, their best work?" I persisted. "It must have engaged them. It must have been their whole life just then."

"All I'm saying is they were worldly men. Their painting was still a means to other ends."

"Vermeer, then," I said.

"Vermeer's a tough one. We know so little about him."

"But the paintings? The incredible paintings? Think of the joy he must have had making those paintings."

"What can I tell you, Nick. Maybe gods come and go – the gods of joy in painting and the gods of the joy of making it. You're old-fashioned though anyway. You take it serious. But you're not supposed to, not now. It's not a postmodern attitude."

"So the gods are not immortal?" I said.

"Only in the sciences, maybe. In physics where it's safe. That's for you to say, not me. But right now I'd say that art is like this city, this city is like its art. If you come here, you've only got one church to go to, one shrine to worship at. Whatever you do."

"Physics!" I said jumping up. It was 4:15. "Where's the Van Pelt Hotel? Where's Fifty-fifth and Lexington?" I had forgotten.

"Not far. Three or four blocks. Why? What is it?"

I explained about the meeting of the northeast region of the American Physics Society even as I tugged at her. I had been invited. Sort of. It would be kicky. "Come on."

"O.K.," she said.

"You'll hate it," I said. "It's worse than black paintings or plywood boxes. You won't understand a thing. We won't stay long."

In the lobby of the Van Pelt Hotel the sign was clear nough: American Physics Society, Northeast Region. Under the sign were listings of the two days of presenters; some were individuals, some panels. At 4:00 P.M. in the Pelham Room, Dr. Thomas Culver was presenting a paper.

"Look," I said, "Culver. We've probably missed most of it. Come on." We hurried to the Pelham Room. "I've never been to one of these things," I said.

"Maybe you should get used to it," Sara said. "Maybe someday soon it's going to be you up there."

"Yeah," I said, "that could be. That sure could be."

In the room there were maybe as many as two hundred people sitting on folded chairs. Culver was at a lectern, three large portable blackboards were set up behind him, smeared with the chalk dust of what must have been two days of computations. He was turned toward one of the blackboards and was writing quickly upon it when Sara and I slipped into the room. No one noticed us, no one cared. Quietly we settled down into seats at the rear.

Culver turned back to the room and began to expound upon what he had just added to what he had earlier put down. He must have been talking for twenty minutes I guessed. After two minutes Sara nudged me and raised her eyebrows and, smiling, silently mouthed Greek to me.

"Want to go?" I whispered. No, she shook her head. I returned to Culver. I had already picked up the gist of where he was going, and now I was three steps ahead of him and then five steps. I saw where he was heading, but I didn't think that he did. But mainly I saw that he was rapidly sliding away from his topic. He was getting to the edge of flat space, and if he wasn't careful he would fall over the edge of it into all kinds of monstrous questions about the tachyon particle and the variable speed of light, about the significance of the collapse of Kreutzer's G and the weakness in Witten's seventh dimension and the consequences of that to orthodox Big Bang theory and to much of physics in general. Above all he was getting into sequence. I was watching this like a great chess player would, extrapolating from an opponent's position the only possibilities that were eventually going to be open to him. From what he was saying now, I reconstructed what must have been going on in the twenty minutes before. Now having gone as far as he had into this increasingly speculative ramble, he was going to have to go further. But he wouldn't be able to do that. Only I was able to do that. *Had done that.* I saw it all and saw it all at once. It was as if Culver had gone nuts, was about to hang himself in public. I wanted to stand up and warn him, or maybe even help him, but in the same instant I thought that maybe this was a manipulation by him, that maybe he wanted to happen what was going to happen. But before I could stand up, someone else did.

"Frank Cantrell, Harvard," he introduced himself. I had read three or four of his papers. He was a heavyweight. And immediately he took a swing at Culver, a solid left hook, and connected. If you say this, you can't say that, but if you can't say that then you have to say this. But even if you say this or that or not, you still end up with gibberish.

"Morris Fierkin, MIT." Pow.

"Louis Sorrel, Yale." Bam.

"Marie Keller-Smith, Brown." Splat.

It was like a Roy Lichtenstein cartoon.

"What you've done, Professor Culver, among other things, is gotten yourself into an impossible antrophic bind." Morris Fierkin was being restrained; what he was really saying, what everyone in the room understood that he was saying, was that Culver had made a fool of himself: that the moth who had played so freely with his ridiculous metaphysical speculations about pretime and prespace conditions had finally flown into the flame and been consumed by a fire of his own making. Pity. A brilliant man, really. You could feel that floating in the chalk-heavy air. But of course there was no pity because the positions that Culver had apparently been forced to, slipping and sliding down the greasy slope, were too dangerous to all the rest of them in that room. But what surprised me was that Culver knew even as much of what he had gotten himself into as he did. So much of what he seemed to know, though imperfectly, was what I *did* know.

Then Culver swung back, hitting them harder than any of them could have possibly imagined. He turned back to the blackboards and erased all three of them, then he withdrew a sheath of papers from his briefcase and began to transcribe them onto the boards. The more he wrote down the quieter the room became. Then all around the scientists began to copy what was on the boards, slowly and then more and more quickly. It took him fifteen unbroken minutes of writing. When he was finished he turned to the room. Sara asked me what had happened, what was going on. I told her something very important. We had to wait and see this.

"Any questions?" he said. There were a thousand questions, but none that could be easily asked. The scientists would all have to return to their campuses and for days and weeks ponder the implications of what was on the blackboard. So now there was only silence.

Everything he had written on the blackboards was mine, all that was locked in my drawer in the desk in the white cube back in Cobbton. Mine. My Tangerine Tango thoughts.

And then he said, now a lord speaking to his vassals, "Every change in the universe continues to change everything else in the universe including, of course, all of space and time – but even, or especially, the rules and laws by which we measure the changes themselves – and thus is eliminated the possibility of one permanent past, but not the infinitude of the past itself. Sequence is what is not refutable."

My physics and now my words.

I didn't know what to do. Should I leap up and denounce him? Claim what was mine? But to what end, to what purpose? Because it wasn't the physics that mattered. It wasn't the physics I wanted, the acclaim. What I wanted was not the recognition of the seething room but for him to give me back what he had stolen – not the Tangerine Tango equations but the fundamental decency demanded of all human intercourse. It was for my father that I wanted to shout out. But I had no words equal to my task, equal to my fury. Where were my words? I had no words.

My eyes were tearing, my nose running. The chalk dust heavy air was closing in on me, choking me.

And then, in the second or two before the audience stood up and gave him, begrudged or not, an ovation, I think he saw me. By the time they all sat down again, I was gone.

"What's wrong, Nick? What's wrong?" Sara said. I was almost running. She had to trot to keep up. We were out of the hotel and onto Lexington Avenue. "Wait, Nick. Tell me. Nick!" She stopped. She couldn't keep up. Or would not. She had to stop me from going on. Where? Where was I going? What was I going to go? At last I stopped. She came up to me. She took my hand. "What?" I told her. I explained what Culver had done.

"The son of a bitch," I said. "He stole it all. I can't believe it. He actually went into my drawer and took all the . . . . Incredible."

We had made plans. We were supposed to go down to the East Village to attend something called *The Return of the Happening: An Experience in Improvisational Performance Art.* We were going to eat in an Italian restaurant on MacDougal Street and then walk over to the loft theater for the show at eight o'clock.

"We can go back to the apartment," Sara said. "You can cool out there. Relax. Whatever you need."

"No," I said, "I didn't come here to sit in the apartment and mope. And there's you."

"Don't worry about me."

"I came here to learn, right? Remember?"

"Well, you're learning, aren't you?"

"Damn right."

"Then why are you shouting?"

"Am I?" I said, dropping my voice, looking around. But who would notice me in this city?

Saturday at five o'clock on Lexington Avenue in November, the street already city dark, the flow of the people thin and thick at the same time the way in some bodies of water currents can flow over and under each other in opposite directions.

"Let's walk," Sara said. "Let's walk it off."

At Forty-second Street we cut west to the New York Public Library. It was still open and we went in. I had never been there, but of course I knew all about it, the great citadel of learning and research. We stood just inside the portal doors.

"When you think of it, it's a wild thing," I said. "Right here we're in one of the greatest signs of civilization in the world, but we're only a few blocks away from Port Authority. What would you guess, a mile? Five thousand feet? In here people are writing books. Over there people are ripping their minds into little pieces."

Somewhere in lower Manhattan we sat drinking coffee before we went to the restaurant.

"You're feeling better," Sara said.

"How can you tell?"

"Well, I can just tell."

"He can't go anywhere without me," I said.

"Who?"

"Culver. He stole all my ideas, but mostly they're the sketch of what's to come. But he won't be able to go on, at least very far. He's not in my league."

"No one's in your league, are they Nick? You're really out there in front, way in front. And all alone. Aren't you?"

"I don't know. Maybe."

"I don't know anything about this, but I could tell back there in the hotel, how they all responded. Something very very big had happened, hadn't it?"

"Yes. If I'm right, my ideas, very big."

"So what are you thinking about Culver for at all? Piss on him."

"But . . . what do I do? What do I say to him the next time we meet?"

"Say, 'Kiss my butt, Professor Culver.' "

"I can't say that."

"Why not?"

"Because."

"Because? Is that an answer," she said.

"It's not in my nature," I said. "I've never been angry before, not like this."

"You've never had anything to be angry about. You've never lived with people to get angry at. Even at college it's been pretty good for you."

"I was angry while I was at Camp Gingacook," I said.

"At what?"

"Camp Gingacook. When I was ten. The kids teased me because I was, you know, the brain."

"Did you slug one of them?"

"No. Of course not."

"Of course not? Didn't you even want to? Or is that not in your nature as well?"

"I guess not," I said. "I guess that's not in my nature either. I've never had a fight. I've never been really *really* angry. Even now. Even now I guess I'm more embarrassed for Culver, more worried about how to accommodate him than . . . . " Then suddenly I trailed off into another region beyond Culver altogether, where Culver didn't matter at all.

"Maybe you'd feel a lot better about yourself, about a lot of things, if you did get angry, if you did sock someone."

"No," I said, "that's not it."

What I couldn't say to her, even to Sara, was that it wasn't the theft of my ideas that mattered to me. Easy come, easy go. There were plenty more ideas for me to have, tons and tons more physics to do. I would even get my due, almost all the credit. Kreutzer would know it wasn't Culver who had gotten so far. The word in physics about me was probably already spread and spreading. No, I'd get mine even if Culver horned in a little. There was plenty to go around. And when I worked out even some of the ramifications of my ideas, I'd get my Nobel Prize as well. Maybe, like Kreutzer, even more than one. So that wasn't the trouble. The trouble was that I couldn't locate my unease even now. Instead of physics and Culver stealing my work out of my drawer, I was thinking of the five thousand feet between the New York Public Library and Port Authority. I was thinking about Bruegel. He would have understood. He would have known what to do about that five thousand feet. Why couldn't I?

But above all else I thought about my father. How it was my father whom Culver had violated. But about that, or what I fully meant, I could not say to Sara. Because I did not want to share this anger with anyone. It was mine. Alone.

Well into *The Return of the Happening: An Experience in Improvisational Performance Art*—(You couldn't say in the middle because, as we had been instructed by the conductor of the happening, happenings didn't have a beginning or an end. Just like the universe I was constructing, I thought.)—the experiencers (because in improvisational performance art there were no actors per se) were called upon to respond to questions that were a) actually pulled out of a hat, and b) after the experiencer was given a new name. The new name was supposed to enable the experiencer to be free from her past that was incorporated in her name, a name that was given to her at birth and not chosen by her. A woman sitting next to me was happened upon. She was told her new name was Tamayra Trevalyan. She was to answer her question after allowing the impact of her new name to work upon her. Her question was, "What would you like to say to the person sitting to your right?" Me. Then I was supposed to respond to her. She had ten seconds. "I'd like to suck your dick," she said in a loud, clear voice. Everyone clapped and cheered.

But nothing happened.

Back in Steffanville late Sunday afternoon my mother and father together met me at the bus station. I would stay over and go back to the campus tomorrow.

"Piece of cake," I said and flopped into the back of the car. My father was driving. My mother turned to me.

"It wasn't that we didn't have faith in you, Nick," she said.

"You want to protect me," I said. "I understand that. But you can't."

"I know, I know," she said, turning forward. "There's just so much out there. Not just New York. Too much to protect against."

"Yeah," I said, "And anyway, it's too late." But she let that go.

That night, in bed, I thought about the confrontation that would have to come between Culver and me, and how it would probably have to involve my relationship to Cobbton. Was Princeton the answer? The Institute for Advanced Studies? Sara would be leaving after the next semester. Where was she going? She herself was uncertain. But the point was she would not be at Cobbton. But Appleton would still be at Cobbton. And Mike (I hoped) and Al McGuire. Slowly, others. And the Kennedy gallery and all those art courses and lectures I would attend. The cross-country team. Maybe I would join the chess club after all. Cobbton. It had become a place for me, a physical locus in this otherwise abstraction called Nick Burden. And offered to become even more of that. This house in Steffanville. *Yarps*. Steuben's Knob. And now Cobbton. Why should I let Culver push me out of that?

And I thought of something my father had written in his journal. It was about me when I was first learning to ride a two-wheeled bicycle without training wheels. How I had fallen again and again and how he had picked me up and started me off each time and urged me on. I had started to cry with frustration. As I remembered his written description of that event, the scene came back to me, his voice, his words. He ran beside me with his hand on the seat helping to steady me. You can do this, he kept saying. You can do this. Don't think about it. Don't think. Just keep pedaling. It's the pedaling that keeps you up. Don't think. Just pedal. You can do this. You can do this. After you do this, he said, you'll be able to do everything else you'll ever want to do. Don't think. Pedal.

➤32➤
=

"Hey," I said. "How was Thanksgiving?"

"Good," Mike said. "Great." My father gets hold of a thousand turkeys. Frozen. So we've got only a few hours to move them, right? I mean there is no tomorrow, right? I mean even if you can sell them, who wants them? Who wants to buy a turkey the day or the week or the month after Thanksgiving? You're still eating old turkey, right? Like forever?"

"Right," I said.

"So my father gets these thousand turkeys for nearly nothing. They're part of a trainload of turkeys which is in a small accident in a train yard, you know? A freight car is bumped too hard, the load shifts, some of the crates are smashed, things fall out. They're called breaks. So when something like that happens, they call in the insurance man. He takes a look, estimates the loss, and orders up a check. After that he doesn't care what happens to the turkeys he's written off, and the turkey people don't care because they've gotten a settlement, and the railroad, all they want is to get rid of the turkeys before they begin to melt. So my father buys them for nothing. Which means he can sell them for just a little more than nothing. Maybe a whole big turkey for five bucks. At that price some dealer somewhere can always find room. If you can find a dealer. Which my father can and does. Anyway, he ends up making a buck a turkey. A thousand bucks in two days. We worked like crazy. We rented a truck. Look at my hands. They're still red.

I think I got frostbite." He shoved his hands out for me to see. "Afterwards, we went to the best restaurant in Yonkers to celebrate. Thanksgiving. We had steak and lobster. Who could look at another turkey?"

It sounded like the Mike of old, charged up again, in action. Seizing his day by the throat. If he wasn't going to mention his troubles, then certainly I wasn't. If his troubles hadn't gone, then certainly he was holding them at bay. Nothing like some action to set the world right. Action, an anodyne against danger and malaise. I must remember that. Keep pedaling.

"What about you?" he said.

I told him about New York, me and Sara. All the art in the world. My own terrific two days.

"You're really into that stuff, aren't you?" he said.

"Yeah. Really into it. Art. And Sara." Then I told him about Culver.

"Wow. That's real shit," Mike said. "What are you going to do?"

As in a poorly made play, just then there was a knock at the door. It was Sam Pelton.

"I have a message for you, Nick. It's from Professor Culver. He wants you to call him as soon as possible. He asked me to deliver the message personally."

"Hey, Pelton," Mike said, "is this a special service? What about me? You going to bring me my messages personally. And what about a tip? Does Nicky have to give you a tip?"

"When you get special messages from special people, Mike, I'll bring them, too, O.K.? I promise. And no tip. See you." He left.

"So what are you going to do?"

"Call," I said, "see what he wants."

"He wants to make a deal," Mike said. "I can smell it. You want me to come along? You want me to negotiate?"

I called him at home but only Mrs. Culver was there. She said that her husband left the message with her. He wanted to meet with me at his house that afternoon at five. Or at another time, whenever it was convenient. Five would be fine, I told her.

In his study with his inexplicable objects around him, his book-lined walls, the wainscoted trim, nothing seemed unusual or out of the ordinary, nothing momentous. But to Culver, I could tell, it was a momentous moment.

"If you think it was a matter of simple theft, you're wrong," he said right off. "There is no way that I would be able to pull off something like that. What you're doing is beyond me."

"My own thoughts exactly," I said.

"Then you were right. I've already sent letters explaining all that, all this to a number of important physicists and institutions. Wheels are already turning. Etcetera and so forth. Your career is launched. And in a spectacular fashion. Now you've really got to get down to your work. You've got to develop the blue print, work out the ground rules. It's like when Einstein proposed his theories, or Planck, or Hawking proposing his ideas about black holes. Ideas like that need to be tested, demonstrated, by the rest of us, but it's dependent upon the proposer to show us the ways. You've got to show us how to look at what you've put before us. Who would know better? It's not just enough to test, you've got to show us what to imagine as well."

"But it's what *you* put before them, not me," I said.

"You're talking about the way it was done, not what was presented. The ideas were already there in the drawer."

"Speaking of which. I mean, isn't that what's important here? You went into my drawer. It was mine. I had the key. It was private. It was my secret."

"It was a moral indiscretion," Culver said, "but a small one. And if you want an apology for that, then you've got it. I'm sorry. I can guess that it might hurt you. But there's another dimension to all this. In one sense you made me do it."

"Me?"

"We each serve ourselves, but we also serve knowledge. Suppose you had discovered or developed a cure for some deadly disease, AIDS, say. Suppose you had decided not to reveal it. If I had knowledge of that discovery, would I be morally justified in revealing it to the world? I would be wrong to do it, but I would be more right to do it."

"You could have asked me. We could have discussed it."

"What would you have said?"

I didn't know the answer to that.

"Wait. I would have said to wait."

270

"Wait for what?" Culver said. "That's my point. Wait for what? Until when? Could I allow physics to go on, people to go on constructing their lives, their careers, when it became more and more apparent to me that major readjustments were going to have to be made? People have a right to the best knowledge in their fields. Maybe it is you who has the moral responsibility."

But it seemed so obvious to me. For all his explanation he should have credited me at the meeting in New York. Not because of what I wanted but because that, I believed, was the way life was supposed to be. What was it that I was not able to understand? What was it that Culver saw that I did not? Why did my books always seem to fail me at these junctures?

He leaned back in the heavily padded elegant leather chair. So recently Kreutzer had sat in it while he unfolded for me his exciting history, the burr of his own enthusiasm grinding out the shape of my own possibilities. Now, sooner than I had ever thought, closer than I could have imagined just those few weeks ago, here it was. Culver picked up one of his objects, the coin that had no history, and turned it in his hand.

"So what's supposed to happen now?" I said.

"You continue to do what you've been doing."

"Do I continue to lock things up in my drawer?" I said.

"That will hardly be necessary," he said, and smiled. "What's yours is now everybodies'." He paused. "Nick, I really am sorry about doing it this way. I'm sorry for whatever hurt I've given you. Look, if you really want, I'll let you get the lock to the lab changed. It's your lab now. Totally."

"Unless I go to Princeton." But he said nothing to that. "What else?"

"You'll be getting a lot of correspondence from all over the world. Mainly you'll be getting requests for papers to be given at various conferences, to be published in the journals. Pretty soon I'd imagine there will be a conference centered on your work. Soon enough an international congress. You're going to be busy. Maybe we'll have to get you a secretary."

"You're going to have to tell the dean about this. And Doctor Lambert and Doctor Schwartz."

"I already have," he said.

"And someone is going to have to answer to my parents," I said.

But at that he looked into the plastic cube in which the coin was embedded and gazed at it as if it were a crystal ball in which he did not see Sally or Frank Burden.

So there it was, all laid out for me, Nick Burden becoming the only Nick Burden it was possible for me to become. I had to talk about this with someone who could understand what had happened to me better than I could understand it, although maybe understand wasn't the right word.

Spread across the unused bed in his room were large scale maps of western America. On them Al McGuire traced out for me trout streams that would be dense with yellowtails, western trout, big as this, he showed me, wild as natives. Just two days ago the announcement that the Apricot Bowl was a certainty had been made. The team would go to Tempe, Arizona, the week before Christmas to practice for the game on December 31. But there would be some time off, a little recreation during the two weeks. And time after the game. Already Al McGuire had made plans to get up into the San Francisco mountains west of the city.

"Here," he said, his large finger taking out an entire range. "I can get here and back in a day. Here's how to do it. It's all figured." He showed me the Arizona travel and tourist information, fishing magazines, what looked like private letters. "And after the game I can get a ride to here and then hike in to here." He poked at the map as if to drive his words into Arizona like a claim. It's a done deal. You want in on this, Nick? Maybe I can get you onto the team. Waterboy."

"Do they still have waterboys?" I said.

"Assistant managers, we call them now. And it's Gatorade. And we come off the field to drink it. To the sidelines. You're thinking of those guys running out on the field carrying those little cups of water. That's a long time ago. Before my time," he said.

"It's tempting," I said.

"Yeah," he said, "Trout like this." He showed me again.

"No. I mean waterboy. Assistant manager."

He pushed everything aside.

"So what's the matter, Nick. That sounds no good. You don't sound so good. What, was it New York?"

"Let me ask you, Al. What would happen if you could go into the pros right away. Not even next season. I mean right now?"

"I'm not good enough," he said. "I've still got a lot to learn. And I'm not strong enough."

"Not strong enough?" That hardly seemed possible.

"I'm close. Stronger than most. But I don't use steroids. It's going to take me longer to get up to top weight and strength. So no, I wouldn't go to the pros even if I was offered."

"But suppose you were strong enough and knew enough, what then? Would you do it?"

"Yeah," he said right away, no doubt at all. "To get it over with. Football is not my life, it's my ticket to my life. I told you. The sooner I take the ride, the sooner I get off the train. So what's your problem, Nick?"

I explained.

"I don't know. I mean what can I say to that kind of problem? I got this body, you got that brain. No one will leave either of us alone. Sure. So you know that. You always knew that. So now the pushing is getting to shoving. But this is the difference between you and me. I've got something to walk away to. You've only got something you can walk away from. You see what I mean? You've got nothing you can walk away to. Waterboy is no answer. You'd hate it. So get yourself something. Sail around the world. Something like that. At least think about doing it. Something." Then abruptly he started to finger the maps again, caress the book on western fly patterns. I had asked all I could ask, and he had told me all that he could. Now the bright water rushing through the red rock of the San Francisco mountains in his imagination beckoned him. How could I hold him from his dreaming? And why should he be strayed?

•33•

=

All day Tuesday I wandered around on the campus, tucking into the angles and corners of it that, until now, I had had no time to find, or need. Perhaps I was looking for a way to ground myself, to map a territory in case I had to claim it, or to defend it in order to know where I was. I went to the computer center for the first time, to the kitchen of the commons, the weight room in the gym, the central power plant, the college garage where all the vehicles were maintained. I went to the fine greenhouse, which was divided into temperate, desert, alpine, and tropical zones, and you could pass through almost all the latitudes of earth by walking through a door. I visited the electron microscope and its facilities and the meeting rooms in the union that I had never thought about, the rooms in which the student governments met and the women's coalition and the Black Students League and the gay alliance. The small auditorium in the Fine Arts Center where the poets read or where visiting string quartets performed.

The weather had snapped; there was more of deeper December in it now than late, mild November. By three o'clock a few snowflakes fluttered down. I went into Cobbton and walked about. Despite the pressure from the shopping malls that were ringing Cobbton like encroaching armies, the beseiged center of Cobbton held. Not unlike Steffanville, except that Steffanville was much smaller and not under as much pressure. But both Cobbton and Steffanville had names and faces. Feldman's Clothing, William

274

Pratt Insurance, Dottie's Diner, with a real Dottie running her own show. The streets were called Elm and Maple and Pine instead of numbers like Eighth and Forty-second. I thought about New York. I had read that New York had once actually been a linking together of many small, usually ethnic, communities, each virtually self-contained and clearly identified; like mitachondria in an enormous cell, I thought. But what I had briefly seen there resembled more the undifferentiated miasmic energy of an earliest life form like blue-green algae: energy with no centralizing nervous system. Like the buildings I saw there. And the art. None of it seemed to belong to anyone or anything.

I walked through Cobbton and looked up at the flat-roofed, nineteenth century Italian renaissance revivalist friezes, the narrow arched windows with jambs of carved stone, the patterned brick work. And then at the street level, where the buildings would put on business faces, slap something – anything – across the older original front. And plastic signs – Cobbton Newsroom – with Pepsi medallions on either side of it. I walked looking up and down. It was like walking on a sine curve. It was like walking in two different places and times in the same moment, the present and the past. Schrodinger's cat again.

Maybe that was me, Schrodinger's cat, only instead of being dead and alive at the same moment, I was alive and alive at the same moment.

I walked from one edge of downtown Cobbton back to the other edge, and as I walked I thought again of what my father had written about me: the problem of my life that I would someday have to solve would be how to be the one person I am and not the two – or separate – people the world will see me as being.

I did not think that Appleton could give me answers, certainly not to the questions that I did not have. And he was not the answering kind. Nor much of a comforter. But he was full of views and perceptions. Maybe he would help me because he was, simply, Appleton, and not easily budged from who he was at any particular moment. Maybe what I wanted just now was a dispute. Not about physics, of course, and not with him, but about my own uncertainties.

I knocked on his door but no one answered. I knocked again and then again. I turned the oddly shaped, elegant brass handle and the door opened. He never locked up, he had said. Was that some sort of challenge to or a statement of faith in the good people of Cobbton? Certainly there was a fortune in cameras and electronic equipment, thousands, easily, lying around. I went in.

It was about 6:30, supper time for most, but with Appleton, who could tell anything? He was not here and there was no activity in the kitchen, no sign that he was preparing supper and had left for a moment to get something he had forgotten from the store. Should I wait? But maybe he had gone out to eat, or maybe to a movie or a party, or whatever would keep him away for hours. To a woman? For the night? I smiled at the thought and maybe even blushed, for veteran that I now was (thirty-one times), I still could not divide sex from love. I loved Sara and our sex expressed and sealed that in sanctity. But the thought of what others might do with their appetites . . . it was like my imagining my parents in each other's arms, slightly repugnant.

One of his machines began to softly buzz and hum, the machine connected to one of his complicated telephones, the fax machine. Paper began to ease out of it. I went to it and watched.

First it said, "This is fine, the idea is excellent. But is it premature? What's the rush? What I'm thinking is this, that, given the intimacy of the exchange upon which your essay is based, especially his essays and conversations, once you write this and publish it, then that's as far as you can go. You kill the golden goose, if you see what I mean. But you must have anticipated this. So why now? Why not play out the string to the end? Anyway, I'm faxing back to you my marginal comments."

Here the machine began to send what I soon saw was an essay that Appleton was writing about me. The essay was structured around the essays I had shown to him, the essays about my father that I had told him I did not want read in class. And a counterline was excerpts from my Sunday here, what he had recorded on his tapes. He was putting a *me* together–*some* me–out of pieces of my most private self.

Culver and now Appleton. Did nothing of mine belong to me?

"What do you think?" Appleton said.

I had not heard him enter. I was engrossed in the ribbon of paper rising out of the machine. I did not answer immediately. I could read faster than the machine could produce. I was impatient.

He was writing, from the little I could see, about his fascination with the teaching of such as I. How was his essay going to turn out? But it wasn't going to turn out, not in that sense. It had already happened, for it hardly mattered what Appleton wrote about what I had written or said: I was sufficiently the matter itself, the material, once again the attractive freak.

"I'm quite a goose, aren't I?" I said at last.

"Don't take offense," he said, dropping his ripped and patched book bag and removing his ragged overcoat.

"No? What then? Should I be pleased?"

"Don't take offense where none was intended is what I meant." He flopped down in his chair and picked out a pipe and began to fiddle with it. He pressed a button and the large tape head began to revolve.

"Turn off the tape," I said.

"No." He struck a match and sucked the pipe alive.

"You're unbelievable."

"My house, my rules," he said. "Are you hungry? Do you want something to eat?"

"Turn off the tape or I'm leaving."

"Suit yourself," he said.

"But then how will your essay end? Without me? Without the golden goose?"

"It doesn't matter," he said. "It will go as far as it can and then it will stop. Maybe this is the end, right now."

"It is," I said. "You can bet on that."

"Well, then, good. Good for you, Nick. Made a decision at last, have you?"

Not yet, I thought.

"Why?" I asked.

"Why? Why what? Why am I writing the essay? Or why am I writing the essay now? Is there some reverse statute of limitations here? What, no writing about Nick Burden until . . . until when? After the course is completed? After the semester? The school year? Graduation? Until he is dead? Dead for twenty years? Until someone else has written about him? Who do you think you are to tell me anything about when or how I do what I do? You've got no special rights here. You're a subject, a sustance for me to work with. And you've not been maligned or slandered. You're not even misrepresented. I'm using your own words. It's not even a legal matter." He puffed softly.

"It's a moral matter," I said. "You violated a trust."

"You mean your essays about your father?"

"That, yes. But more. I trusted you. I thought of you as a friend, someone to whom I could open up. Explore myself in safety."

"I was never your friend, Nick. Only your teacher. Well, I have taught you. And I'm teaching you now, if you'll see it. But what you want is to be taught within your own narrow definitions. And safely, as you just said. See? Well learning isn't safe, now, is it? Remember what Stein said to Jim? 'In the destructive element immerse yourself,' So there you are. Consider yourself baptized."

"Experience is the best teacher, is that your point? It's a tired, hackneyed point."

"Perhaps, but true nonetheless."

"But dull and limited," I said.

"Ah ha," he said. "Resentment. A littler anger. Good for you. But don't overreact. You're going to have to get used to this. It's probably going to happen a lot. It's probably even good for you."

"What?" I said. "Betrayal?"

"Betrayal? Oh, that's hard, Nick. That's hard. But I see your point."

I could not argue with him, only accuse him. But he would not be accused. He would not accept my indictment. And what did I expect, remorse? That he would leap to his feet, fall to his knees, beg forgiveness, rip up the pages turning out of the fax machine (still whispering away), erase the tapes? And once again the vastness of my knowledge – my *information* – about life came more to frustrate me than to help me. To answer him well I would need to make the only answer that I could, a large and complex answer. An abstract answer. I could summon up all the history of the arguments regarding moral propriety in such matters as this. I could quote him chapters and verses from volumes he had never heard of, much less read, and maybe he would not be able to understand them as well as I could. But that would not matter. He had his reasons, I had mine, Kant and Maimonides and Santayana would have theirs.

What I did not have was an answering action.

"Look. Don't you see? You can't decide for me what's good for me. You shouldn't do that. And you should have considered my feelings. And my father's. You should have been able to figure out how I'd feel about what you're doing. Even if you think that no one has a right to privacy, even if you think it's O.K. to take advantage of a special relationship, there's still the overriding matter of your hurting me. No one wants to give me my own chance."

"You mean like Culver?" he said.

"What do you know about Culver?" I said. "How?" But he did not have to answer that. How else?

Sara.

In the apartment Janie and Ricki were practicing *Dirty Dancing* maneuvers with each other. There was going to be a contest during finals week. They were entering.

"Want to see?" Janie said over the music, twisting in and out of it.

"Not right now, thanks," I said.

In the kitchen area, spread across the table, were picture after picture of me, the photographs that Sara had taken in the apartment, and others that I didn't remember her shooting.

"What do you think?" she said as she sorted through them. "These three are my favorites."

"What are they for, Sara?"

"I've been in the darkroom all afternoon," she said.

"Sara? What are they for?"

"Right now, they're not for anything. They're just photographs of you."

"They're not snapshots, Sara. They're eight-by-ten glossies. Maybe they're illustrations for Appleton's essay."

She didn't pause or look up. She went on moving the photographs as if she were trying to find some arrangement of them.

"They don't use photographs in the kind of places Appleton publishes," she said still without looking at me, still fiddling with the photos.

All across the table top, there I was, twenty or maybe even thirty Nicky Burdens laughing, smiling, jumping, rolling, reading, thinking (?), eating. I had never seen so large a photograph of myself, eight-by-ten, and certainly not so many of them. She continued to move the photos around like pieces in a puzzle or parts of a montage. Or the shards of a holograph. Was I all of these pieces or any one of them?

"Maybe you're going to illustrate something *you're* writing," I said. "Is that a possibility, Sara?"

"It's a possibility, Nick. I might as well be prepared."

"Please, Sara. Look at me, O.K.? Listen to me. You told Appleton about Culver, about what I told you, didn't you?"

"Yes," she said, looking up.

"And maybe lots of other things?"

"Yes."

"Did you know he was writing about me?"

"Sort of." She was looking at me now, calm and not defensive. "He told me a lot about you."

"And you? Now? Why now?"

"You're hot now, Nick. Or you're going to be. After Culver, it's not going to be long before you'll get compared to Einstein. You're headed for the cover of a lot of magazines. And you may not be here much longer."

"I'm everybody's opportunity?" I said.

Behind me Janie and Ricki writhed within the music nearly against each other. Do this, do that, move here, now here, they instructed themselves.

"Is there something more you should say, Sara? Is there something I'm supposed to say? Or ask? I'm very new at this. Jesus Christ, Sara? What the fuck is going on? I'm in love with you. You know that. You know that. You know that. I thought you loved me. It's what I thought. Am I wrong?"

"I never once said I loved you, Nick. I was careful never to say that."

"Then you don't? Is that it. You never did?"

"No, that's not it either. You can love someone and not *be* in love with them at the same time."

"You can?" I said. "*You* can, maybe. I can't."

"Not the first time, you can't, Nick. Not the first time. It's something you learn."

"Wow," was all I could say.

"We've got a great relationship, Nick. Think of that. Think of all the fun we've had. And still can have. Nothing has to change. We can go on doing all the things we've done together. Hey," she laughed. "We've still got Rembrandt to share. And you're not a virgin anymore, are you? And you're a *lot* older now than you were three months ago. We've had nothing but a great time."

"So what am I doing now, paying for that? Is that why this is hurting me so much?"

"You set your own price on these things," she said.

"What was the price you set on me, Sara? What were you buying?" I said.

"The adventure. The friendship. The love. The things we've done together. The sex—you don't get to score a virgin everyday." She smiled at that and put her hand on mine.

"Are you and Appleton . . . lovers? (But what were such words any longer?) Were you? Are you?"

"If we were, or are, does that matter very much, Nick?"

"No," I said, getting up, "I guess none of that matters very much anywhere you look. Not *very* much. But I guess it still matters to me."

"Are you very angry, Nick? Very hurt?" she said.

But as always, there were two of me to answer, or maybe now several of me, one of me for every photograph, one of me for every time I had held her in my arms and imagined not so much an exact future as the timelessness of the euphoria I had shared with her just then. Or maybe not shared. All along it had only been me within the vial of my innocence and inexperience, the bug in the test tube, the specimen to be examined and experimented with. And I had thought that here I had been different. But that hope—belief—was gone now. And gone in this ugly way. To measure myself in the sea of this vast duplicity. I was a boy again, a mere child. No more able to comprehend than ever before. Or maybe this was the curse, the price that the gods were going to make me pay for being me. Like Cassandra, so, too, no one would ever believe me, *in* me, in *a* me. Sara was only the first. For why should it ever be different? Sooner or later I would always be Nick Burden.

"This will pass, Nick," she said.

"What will pass?" I said.

"What you're feeling now."

"Is that supposed to comfort me, Sara? Make me feel better?"

"Yes."

"Well, I don't think it works that way, Sara."

"Oh come on, Nick. Of course it does. You're young. At the beginning of your life. There will be other girls. And finally *the* girl."

"Wow. Where do you get your dialogue? What do you read, for Christsake, Harlequin romances? TV resolutions?"

"I'm trying to help you, Nick, is all."

"But you miss the point. Of course my life will go on. But what it will look like, who can say? For me? But that's not the point either, not abstractions and banalities. Love is another thing. *My* love. What I felt for you. What I imagined you felt for me. That never changes. That never goes away. The loss. The trickery."

"You'll heal, Nick. You'll heal."

"Sure. But that doesn't mean there won't be a scar."

As I was leaving the apartment, Janie said to me, "Hey, Nick. Look. Watch this. Watch us." And so for a full minute I did. I did not storm out of the apartment to scream and rage and weep. For a full minute I stayed and watched Janie and Ricki shimmy and giggle, for I was Nicholas Burden, and my mother and father had taught me always to be polite.

▸34▸
=

"What a pair," Mike Tremain said. "You and me." I had finally told him the story of my last few days.

Wednesday. We were eating supper early in the commons. After Tuesday, I had continued to wander trying to sort myself out. A week ago I had imagined my life just then so firm that I could not imagine it any other way, as if my state was steady, and though it would undergo changes, they would be of a piece, like the changes that occur in a continuum. Now what I had was the changing but nothing else, no idea of a development, only a sundering. Not the changing of one element into another, lead into gold, but the change that a rock makes when it crashes through a window. All along I had been living in a Ptolemaic universe, traveling around myself in a cumbersome but effective explanation, even if a false one. No wonder they had threatened Galileo with the stake.

Who were these people that I had come to rely on—Culver, Appleton, my Sara? What had what I thought we had between us meant to them? When I was thinking friendship and trust, what had they been thinking? Here was the central question: For all that I knew and understood, for all the vastness of my knowledge, I did not know what I was to make out of what had happened. Where was I to go from here? I mean, had I labored under a complete misreading of human prospect? Or was it me again? Was I the corrupting force here, once more drawing people into their opportunities because of my opportunities? Were these bad people or were they the way we all are, and that only I under heaven had believed the philosophers and the poets? Were the philosophers and poets only for precocious sixteen-year-old boys? Was my disappointment only some sentimental notion bred in youthful inexperience? A male Miranda? Where were my metaphors now that I needed them? O brave new world!

Was my father a great man or a fool?

"What a pair," Mike repeated as he scooped up his strawberry Jell-O and shook his head.

"Of losers?" I asked.

"Hell no," he said sharply as he snapped up his head. "The game's not over, is it? It's not even the ninth inning." He waved his spoon at me. "Sometimes you're ahead, sometimes behind."

"Like a crap shoot?" I asked. "Life's a crap shoot?"

"You ever shoot craps, Nicky?"

"No. Of course not."

"I didn't think so. So in craps, Nicky, it's not so simple as win or lose. It's how you bet. It's when you've got what to bet with. It's being able to stay in the action. Maybe one roll of the dice is all you need."

"So with us, what is that, Mike? You. Me. What have we got to bet with?"

"Everything we always had, Nick, except a little less time. For me. Time is what I'm running out of. If I had more time, I could make this all work out. With you, Nick, it's harder to say. Or maybe not. With a broken heart, maybe all you need is time, too. To, you know, heal."

"It's not just the hurting, the broken heart, Mike. There's that, but there are also large and complicated moral questions. Questions of conduct."

"Maybe not," he said. "Maybe all that happened to you is you got screwed the same way as I got screwed. We thought something was happening, but something else was happening."

"O.K. Sure. But what does that mean, that that's the way life is? That you go through life looking over your shoulder all the time?"

"Sure it is," Mike said at once. "But a guy as smart as you, all the stuff you read, you must have known that. What you mean is that you don't want it to be that way." He returned to the Jell-O, scraping hard at what was left.

"So? Now what?" I said.

"For you, that's easy. You could stay at Cobbton. Why not? You don't need courses. You could cut your own deal. You already have, mostly. Maybe you could even start teaching in college. Why not? Or you could go to Princeton. Start over. You could do anything you want. Go on, Nicky, choose something."

"I don't mean just the practical," I said, still hanging back into my ache for clarity. It wasn't just Culver and Appleton, who would be easy enough to dismiss, and not even Sara, for even in my hurting about her there was a kind of sweetness, the palliative of self-pity. It was more this endless collision between purpose and possibility, the playing off of who I was against who I was, this floundering in the riptide of knowing everything and being nothing. This hunger for an illusive shape.

"There *is* only the practical, Nicky. Everything else is theory. It's only what you *do* with what you've got that amounts to anything. That's what's so great about business." He pushed his tray back.

"Mike," I said, "love is practical, too. Love *is* doing something. Without love there is no point to any of the other things we do."

"Love makes the world go around?" he said.

"Right."

"Maybe," he said. "This Sara problem," he started to say.

"No. Not Sara. Not just Sara. Or Culver and Appleton. You."

"Me?"

"You've used me, Mike."

"Like the rest? Is that what you mean, Nicky?"

But I was silent. But Mike was not.

"You're so smart, but you don't know how to keep books. With me you were always a partner. I included you in everything. The others, what did they do for you? All they did was take. Steal. Culver, Appleton. The girl. Me? I gave. Fifty-fifty. T&B Enterprises, Inc."

"You used me to push dope. You made me an accomplice."

"So along with the good I gave you some of the bad. It's called earning your share," Mike said.

"But you never asked. You sent me into a dangerous situation."

"Generals send soldiers into battles. Some of them get killed."

"You were never good at analogies," I said. "It's different. The soldier has a choice. He can run. He can refuse."

"Then they shoot him," Mike said.

"But that's his choice. His solution to the existential dilemma."

"His *what*?" Mike said, and hooted. "His existential *what*? Jesus, Nicky. After all of what's happened to you, you still think that crap? If the soldier advances he gets shot or if he runs away he gets shot or else he advances and doesn't get shot. So he's got one choice in three, about a 30 percent markup on his life. That's still pretty good, so that's why the system works. You've got no real choice, Nicky. None of us has. We just look for the best percentage. About the cocaine. You. What I'm sorry about is it didn't work out. I'm not sorry that I did it. I wanted to make you rich. *Us* rich."

I started to reply.

"Wait." He held up his hand. "Wait. I got this to say, too. For me this is important. Whatever I did, I never fucked you over in my heart, Nicky. And I never filled your life with shit, not like your professors or the girl. You got to admit that."

And in my own heart I did.

"So?" I said. "So what about your practical problem? Have you got a practical solution?"

"Maybe, maybe not," he said. "But my friends, have *they* got a practical solution. Oh have they ever." He leaned toward me. "Over Thanksgiving I talked to a man who lends money. A shylock. I told you about that. He said he could do better. He would lean on Joe Casper. And he would give me the money to meet my debt."

"Give?" I said.

"Wait. Listen. This man I talked to, he wants me to work for him. He wants me to push on campus, to deliver around Cobbton, upstate. A kind of courier. I earn my way out of my debt that way. I even start to make new money for myself. Or us. T&B Enterprises."

"You're crazy," I said. "Don't do it, Mike. Just don't. You're talking wild."

"Not crack," he said. "Not that shit. Good quality cocaine. All you hear nowdays is crack, crack houses, crips and blues. But there is still a substantial upscale market for cocaine. Quality stuff for the quality people, your doctors and lawyers and bank presidents, right? And their kids who they send to college."

"Don't, Mike. Don't."

"Why not, Nicky? Because it's wrong, bad, against the law? You know better than that. All the best people—big time movie stars, top athletes, guys running the movie industry, they all do cocaine. So who do you think makes what is *is*, Nicky? Customers is who. I was always a demand sider. Supply comes after."

"Don't. Just don't."

"You got any reasons why not? You got a better idea?"

"It's dangerous. Once you get mixed up with these guys, you're in it for good. Eventually you get caught. By them. By the police."

"So how do you know this, Nicky? From the TV? The movies? From your books? You don't know shit about this, now isn't that right? So if it's dangerous, then what do you call what I'm already into? You think a broken leg isn't dangerous?"

"A broken leg isn't a life. Five thousand dollars isn't a life."

"Five thousand dollars and another five hundred dollars. Interest," Mike said.

"Interest?" I said.

"Sure. Time is money. I'm tying up their money. They could put it in a bank, invest it it T-bills. Something. The longer I hold their money, the more they can't use it. So why should they take the loss? They add it to my bill."

"Incredible."

"No, Nicky. You say that because what you see is crime, but what is happening is a commercial transaction. Laws change but not the rules of business. Besides, you can have both at the same time. Look at your congressmen. Look at that guy Boesky. And this Milkin."

There were so many ways to think of what Mike was saying that I could not have begun to explain them to him. We sat silently together. The commons was beginning to fill. No one noticed me. In the world you were either in it or not. And maybe there was only one true way in. Bite the apple. Go out through the gates. Go east of Eden.

"I do have an idea," I said. "A great idea for the both of us. 'In the destructive element immerse yourself.' It's something a character said in a novel."

" 'In the destructive element immerse yourself,' " Mike said. "That's it? That's your idea, the *practical* solution? Great, Nicky, just great. In the hospital I'll remember that. Or what, I should tell this guido with a lead pipe that he should go take a bath in the . . . what? Destruction element?"

"The destructive element. No. Listen. Let me explain."

I told him about Appleton's apartment, about the thousands and thousands of dollars of cameras and video equipment, the state of the art electronics of every sort. The stuff. The easy access to it all.

"Nicky, Nicky, Nicky," Mike said, leaning back and expansive, avuncular. "The business of stealing isn't in the stealing, it's the selling what you steal. Besides the fact that we don't know how to steal, selling hot stuff is a specialized area. You need to know fences, which I don't know. And talk about dangerous, Jesus."

"Not us. We don't sell it. We don't even steal it. You give it, the apartment, to your associates. I make sure Appleton isn't home. That's easy. The door is always open. They drive up with a van and. . . ." Mike held up his hand.

"You're an expert on stealing now? A van? You've got it all figured out, how to do it? Stick to the stars, Burden. But it's not a bad idea, giving them Appleton. It's something anyway. I give them the apartment, the open door, guarantee the owner is absent. Maybe they fence the stuff for more than fifty-five hundred dollars, but all they can make more than that is theirs. I show good will. Not bad. But that puts you in a tough spot, doesn't it? Appleton would know it was you."

"He wouldn't know, but he would strongly suspect."

"Yeah, he would."

"Good," I said. "I want that. I'd even tell him."

"Tell him?" Mike said.

"About the destructive element. That I took a bath."

"I'll think about it," Mike said.

"You don't have too long." I said.

"You're telling me," Mike said.

But we both had less time than we thought.

Walking back toward Jameson, the light fading, just at Haynes Circle, a car swerved up beside us. Even as we turned to see it, two men were out of the car, grabbed us, and shoved us into the car before we could react. In less than ten seconds we were driving off, four of us stuffed into the rear seat. It was not a large car. It was not even new. And not very well maintained.

"So, Michael. Who's your friend?" the man driving said. He was not speeding away. He drove slowly and carefully, relaxed. Except for me no one seemed excited.

"This is Nick Burden, my roommate. Stop the car and leave him out. He's got nothing to do with me in this, with you."

"Well, we can't do that just now. Not till we do a little business."

He drove off campus and then around in the neighborhoods surrounding it. On one circuit we passed by Culver's house. The driver was circling. The men sitting on either side of me and Mike were silent. They were big men, fleshy, probably in their early thirties but already puffy and out of shape. The man driving seemed much older.

"I was waiting to hear from you, Michael. I never heard from you for two weeks," he said at last. By now we were out onto the quiet road that crossed the river to the football stadium and the practice fields.

"I've been working on the problem. I was waiting till I had something positive to tell you," Mike said. He seemed composed, nothing of panic about him.

"Good, Michael. That's good. So what have you got that is positive to tell me? Or better yet, to give me?"

"Nothing yet. I'm working on a couple of things."

The man driving sighed noticeably as if he wanted Mike to understand something by the way he sighed. Halfway to the football stadium he pulled the car over and parked on the gravel shoulder. Carefully he turned on the emergency blinkers and then eased around to talk to Mike directly.

"That's not so good, Michael."

"I need another week. Or maybe less."

"Michael, you think because I drive this car I own it? You know what I mean? This fella here, he does what I tell him, right Jimmy?" Jimmy nodded. "So someone is saying to me, what is happening in college these days? What's going on with Michael Tremain? What do I tell him, Michael? And what does he tell the guy who is asking him? You know what I mean? I've got to show something to somebody else who has got to show . . . and so on. I am not the last word here, Michael. I'm small potatoes. You know what I mean? You read in the papers everyday, ten kilos, street value three, four million. That's not me, Michael. I am working for a living. Five thou is real money to me, very important."

"I understand. I just don't have the money yet. In a week for sure. You know the story. I told you about Joe Casper. You believe me."

"I believe you. We all believe you. But Casper. He is your problem."

"But . . . ."

"Wait. There is more to this problem. It was a bad idea to do business with a college kid. I was told that. I didn't listen. College kids, they have no good idea of responsibility. They don't know how to take things serious. But me, I think, no, this kid, this Michael is O.K. This guy's got a head on him. A future. He is what we need in this country. Jimmy here, and Alvin here, these are fine guys for what they do. But you are different. You are special. So I give you a chance, and see what happens. It's not your fault? Maybe. Maybe you couldn't see Joe Casper doing you. Maybe you didn't know how to handle Joe Casper. Maybe Joe Casper thinks, fucking kid, what's he going to do, he's got no muscle. So here is the point, Michael. We are talking not only money here. We are also talking credibility, you know what I mean? We are talking about my credibility. Now get out of the car."

He had given Michael the lecture. Now he was putting us out. It would be a long walk back to the dorm, but what the hell. I started to feel the release, and the tang of the experience, the realness. This was a helluva story to have to tell someday. But then Mike said, "This is not a smart thing to do."

The story was not over. My heart leaped.

"Get out of the car, Michael."

"No. Listen to me. You're making a mistake here."

"Come on, Mike," I said. "Let's go." Maybe the man did mean what I wanted him to be meaning. Get out and go.

"Shut up, Nicky. Just shut up." Then back to the driver. "Breaking legs is not an investment. That's thinking like the Middle Ages."

"Just get out of the car, Michael. Jimmy," the man nodded. As easily as they had pushed us into the car, they pulled us out. The driver got out too.

"It's the way things are done," he said.

"What are you talking?" Mike said. "You're talking like something out of a movie, *Godfather* shit. Listen to me. I'm taking this business course, it's got a lot to say about the value of extended debt, the uses to make out of it. Listen to what's going on in Brazil, Mexico. Their national debt is the best thing they've got going for them. Poland. Managed debt, it can be a great thing. The debt is what gives them leverage. Or take junk bonds." Mike was going on quickly but not in panic, with great self-assurance. Was it all just a ploy? Or was he actually imagining real possibilities, offering to this man real expansions just as once he had offered them to me? There seemed to be no desperation in him, only his usual confident insistence and fecundity.

"Both of them?" Jimmy asked. The man nodded.

"Oh no, not him," Mike said as if it was his decision, as if there was a negotiation going on here. "What's he got to do with anything? Him you've got to leave alone."

Me? They were going to beat me? Break my leg? Me? The golden child, Einstein's heir? Break a leg? Or was that only a figure of speech, a metaphor? My metaphor at last, the exquisite moment when something true became palpable?

"What's it matter? I've got to show my people something, so this will show I'm serious. Jimmy, Alvin," he nodded.

"Wait. Wait, goddammit, wait. Are we talking business or what? What kind of shit is this? We're talking business and suddenly we're on the side of a fucking back road talking mayhem. That is so fucking nuts I can't believe it. You ever consider what my business connections are worth, what kind of markets I've opened, what the growth potential is? You're talking nickels and dimes, I'm talking actual money. You're talking about the end of something, with me it's beginnings."

"I got to show something, Michael. You've got nothing for me to show."

"Appleton," I blurted. "Appleton, Mike."

"Shut up, Nicky. Just be very cool and shut up. Go think about the fifth or sixth dimension, O.K.? But just shut up."

"Nothing," the man said. "You've got less than nothing. So what does that make me look like?"

"I've got Breslau," Mike said just as Jimmy started to raise a fist.

It was enough to stop him. "I've been to Breslau. He'd take care of the money."

"Bullshit," the man said. "Breslau would not lend to you, not with nothing to show, nothing. A punk kid. I can't even believe you could get to talk to Breslau."

"See?" Mike said. "See how good I am? I got to you, I got to Breslau. And he can lean on Casper. This can all work out profitably for all of us with a little patience and faith."

"Casper's busted, Michael. You didn't know that?" The man seemed honestly surprised. "Oh Jesus. You didn't even know that? You're thinking you'll get your money from Casper and here he is busted and you don't even know that? Jesus."

"My market," Mike said. "What about my market?"

"What market?" the man said, "Casper's market, not your market."

"I've still got market left without Casper. What I got now, but what I'll make. Casper's a creep. His idea of an action is to stiff some kid for five bills. So Breslau sees that. That's the difference between Breslau and you. He's got imagination. He's got a vision of the future. What have you got, Jimmy and Alvin?"

"You take my goods and you don't pay for them and then you go to work for Breslau? And you want me to be happy, you want me to shrug my shoulders and walk away? You know what that makes me look like?"

I did not see him give a sign, but Jimmy smashed Mike on the side of the head and knocked him down. Alvin kicked him in the stomach. I heard Mike groan. They turned to me.

"Leave him alone," Mike struggled out. "I'm warning you, you fucking sons of bitches. You touch him once, I'll cut your fucking balls off." Alvin kicked him again. Somewhere Mike grabbed a handful of small stones and flung it up at Alvin, and quickly another handful at Jimmy. Alvin kicked him again. Mike rolled over and managed to push up onto his hands and knees. It was dark now but not fully so, just in the split between the last of light and the full night, the pause in the swing of sidereal time that charted the turning of a globe, so even now—*even now!*—I could not forget that I knew everything. Alvin took a step toward Mike, and as he drew back his foot to kick him again, I dove at him, taking him low and bringing him down.

"Run, Nicky," Mike wheezed out. But this was my chance, and not for anything in this world was I going to lose it.

"Bastard," Alvin said as he rolled me off of him and socked me. I got to my knees and he socked me again and I went down. Blood ran out of my nose into my mouth. I felt a tooth loosen. Like a Masai youth become a warrior, a true member of his tribe, I thought, exalting even in my terror.

Bang, I heard.

"Guns," I said to Mike. "*Guns.*"

"Naw," he grunted back. "Don't worry Nicky. These punks, they don't have guns."

"Sure we got guns," Alvin said. "You have a gun, Jimmy?"

"Yeah," Jimmy said, "sure I got a gun."

"Bullshit," Mike wheezed. "They don't have guns. Don't worry, Nick. If they had guns, they might shoot themselves. They couldn't figure out which end was which." Jimmy kicked Mike again.

Bang, I heard again, louder. Pop, sputter, growl. Bang. Was this going on in my head, after the blast of light and the ringing, inside of that these other noises? But they were not in my head. A car was coming down the road, its headlights flickering. Bucking down the road came Albert McGuire's car in trouble.

Either the car stopped or Al stopped it on the shoulder next to us, this odd vignette, three men standing over the two of us down. He got out of the car quickly and in a continuous motion bodychecked Alvin and then Jimmy and then the man who had done all the talking. Before the three of them could move he had mauled them again. A deep shoulder jerked upward, a smashing forearm. He dropped them hard. Nothing wasted. So this was a master's strength and knowledge, all-American power. A Hall of Famer. Violence precise and beautiful. A professional. Not like inepts Jimmy and Alvin.

"Gun?" Mike croaked.

Al McGuire twisted the groaning men up and searched them.

"Nothing," he said. "Let's go." We pulled Mike up to his feet. "Can you walk? You'll have to. That car is dead." Mike and I started down the road, Mike leaning on me, but getting his strength back, though maybe not his balance. Al went back to the pile of men and then caught up with us.

"I told them," he said. But what he had told them we did not ask, and did not need to ask. In a few minutes the car with Jimmy and Alvin and their boss passed us on the road back to Cobbton, driving away more quickly now than it had come.

"Bastards," Mike shouted after it. "Fucking stupid bastards. Some people," he said, shaking his head. "But what are you going to do?"

Al McGuire had been working out, running windsprints and then around the football field, doing some blocking drills, getting some massaging from the trainer on his season-bruised body, keeping his edge for the bowl game. Driving back, the car began to falter. Then he saw us.

"But you acted so quickly," I said. "How did you know what was happening? How did you know it was us?" We walked along, Mike fairly steadily now. Thumper didn't reply at first. Then he said, "I didn't know it was you right away, except you get a sense of people, you know? They have a certain shape to them, or something like that. But then I could see who it was quick. But what was happening, I figured that right away. It wasn't like I thought it. I looked and there it was. It's what I'm used to, sort of. It's what I'm trained to do, knock people down."

"You didn't say anything. You didn't ask any questions."

"What was there to ask? Or say? I look at people, how they move, and . . . and I just *know* the answer."

Just like me, I thought.

"See, Nicky? See? Mike shouted. He was elated. Euphoric. "What did I tell you, huh? What's life about? *Luck!* You figure it all out six different ways, and what it comes down to is having the luck or not. So we have got it, Nicky. *We have got it.*"

But not enough of it.

As we entered the dorm Sam Pelton motioned us over to him. He was sitting in the reception office, the great plate glass window now replaced.

"Not you, Thumper," he said.

"That's O.K. I'll wait."

"You guys look a little roughed up," he said.

"Is that it? Is that what you want to tell us?" Mike said.

"No. What I want to tell you is that two gentlemen stopped by an hour ago looking for the two of you. When you came in, I was to tell you to wait for them, and I was to call them. So I'm telling you to wait while I call."

"Alvin and Jimmy," Mike said to me, laughing, and then to Sam Pelton. "Well tell them fuck you for me and Nick. We've just had our little meeting with them. And fuck you too, Sam." He turned to leave.

"I don't think so," Sam Pelton said. "This wasn't a Jimmy or an Alvin. It was Lieutenant Stanley and Sergeant Kransdorf. The state police.

▸35▸
=

They came and got us and took us to the state police substation
out on route 27. They even took Al McGuire. As a material witness, but a witness to what they did not say. But at that point they
did not have to say anything. They expected us to do the talking.

"What about a lawyer?" Mike said. "Don't we get a chance to get
a lawyer?"

Lieutenant Stanley was very patient, kindly even. "You don't
get a lawyer unless you're arrested for something. Then we read
you your rights and then you get a chance to remain silent and to
get a lawyer. But right now we are only having a conversation."
And he began. But it didn't take him long. He spelled out distinctly
Mike's operation, how the cocaine was delivered in the posters to
Joe Casper.

"We know this because Joe Casper told us," Lieutenant Stanley
said. "Plea bargain? You've heard of it?"

"You mean you're going to believe a creep like that?" Mike said.
But the lieutenant did not answer.

"I'm going to ask you a question, and depending what you answer will decide a lot of what is about to happen," Lieutenant Stanley said. "So listen carefully. Where did you get the cocaine from?
The cocaine that you put in the poster tubes that you delivered to
Joe Casper."

"I think we better not answer that, lieutenant. I think we had
better get a lawyer after all," Mike said.

296

"Yes," the lieutenant said. "I think you better had." And we were arrested. Even Al McGuire.

It was, of course, not the easiest phone call I had ever made to my mother.

"You're what?"

"Arrested," I said. "For pushing dope. Someone's got to come to bail me out."

"Again," she said. "How many times have I told you, don't push dope." Sally Burden knew her boy, the wise guy. You can't kid an old mom.

"Mom. Listen. I didn't push dope. But that's not the point. I really have been charged. I really have been arrested. I really do need to get bailed out."

"What? How? What are you talking about? Nick? Nick?" Some sort of nightmare was coming true for her. Nothing she had done had protected me after all. Her life had been a Maginot Line.

"Where are you?" my father's voice cut in. I told him. "Sit tight," he said. "I'm on my way."

At ten o'clock in the morning there were a lot of people inside and outside of Dean Roskov's office, including President Turner and Provost Smith. Lieutenant Stanley and Sergeant Kransdorf. No newspaper people. Not yet.

Meeting followed meetings, but what it came down to mainly was this: Cobbton College wanted to save Al McGuire and Nicholas Burden. From what the police had told them, the overwhelming suspicion was that only Michael Tremain was specifically guilty. Burden was apparently an innocent dupe, and he was only sixteen. McGuire in all probability had nothing to do with it, nothing at all.

All Nick had to do was tell the police what he knew, which was what the police believed anyway. That is what Dean Roskov, alone with me and my parents, told us at five minutes to twelve, everyone else gone now, everything on the verge of being settled.

"And if I do, then what happens?"

"Nothing," the dean said. "You complete the semester, you start another one. Your life goes on. The incident is over, closed. Completely."

"I mean what happens to Mike Tremain?"

"I thought that was clear, Nick," the dean said, but he was willing to repeat it, as much, I think, for my parents' sake as for me. More for them. A kind of emphasis that he was still strongly committed to protecting Nick Burden. "He'll have to be prosecuted. But if he reveals his source, and because he's a first offender of any kind, and with some gentle pressure that the college can use—but maybe above all with your cooperation—he would probably get off with a suspended sentence."

"Probably?" I said, "only probably?"

"It's hard to guarantee this sort of thing. And certainly I can't. I'm not the court. But sure. I'm talking about probabilities. Life *is* probabilities, Nick," he said with more than a little passion, which I was glad to hear.

"And he'd be thrown out of Cobbton," I said.

"He would be expelled. Yes," the dean said.

"But not me."

"No."

"And if I don't cooperate?" I said. But of course the dean did not need to answer that. "I'd like to talk with my parents, please," I said.

"Sure. Stay here. Take what time you need." He rose from behind his wonderful desk.

"It won't take long," I said.

In the dean's office, under the gaze of the anonymous patron on the wall, I asked my father what he thought I should do. If I told them what they wanted to hear, Mike was gone, from Cobbton for sure, but maybe from life. Maybe to jail. At the least he would have a serious police record. If I didn't tell them, then it could be hard on all of us. Even if I was an innocent accomplice, a mere dupe, I did *now* know the actual situation. If I didn't tell them— become their only actual witness—then I could be guilty of withholding evidence. And then I would be gone from Cobbton—or Princeton. And might end up with a police record of my own.

"So what do you think?" I said. "What should I do?"

"Lie," my father said. "He's your friend."

And so I did.

But in less than a week the police turned away from us. Dropped charges. All they would finally have had was Joe Casper's word against mine and a few dozen posters of fabulous women in provocative attitudes. Maybe a few grains of cocaine, but that could have come from anywhere in this day and age, out of the very air we all breathe. And perhaps Cobbton College had gone quietly to work on our behalf as well, or for me, at least. Al McGuire was left untouched.

Out of it all, nothing much was left of the conflagration. The soreness in my jaw was gone, my tooth had firmed up. With the exception of the *National Inquirer*, which finally had a chance to pluck me, ripe at last, hardly anyone would have known anything. SUPERBOY GENIUS IMPLICATED IN DRUG RING SCANDAL the headline ran. There was even a picture of me on the front page, one that Sara had taken as I had flown through the air toward her. Ah, Sara, Sara. But there was only one week left of classes and then finals, the dirty dancing contest, the excitement in the students about the long vacation, the going away. So even the notoriety was blunted. Too many students were scurrying to write the papers they had neglected all semester, to cram for the exams they had not studied for earlier, for them to be deflected for very long.

Mike would not stay for finals.

"What's the point?" he said. We were in our room, the windows opened even though December had toughened up and gotten into winter. "I couldn't make it through four years of this. I need more action." He turned to me. "What I liked was the business and economic theory and economic history. So I can take courses somewhere, you know? Just read." He smiled. "Well, maybe not read." He looked up at his ceiling. "But I got to get out of here. It's not the place for me. And I still got to come up with five thousand dollars plus seven hundred."

"Seven hundred dollars?" I said.

"Sure. Time goes on. Interest goes on. What did you think? Anyway, my father's going to put it up for me. After this, I couldn't keep it from him, right? I'll pay him back. I've got something lined up already. In Florida. In February. A job. It's a start, but I've got ideas. I've been thinking about what Florida needs."

I was almost about to say something about not forgetting the lesson he had learned from this adventure, but I might have meant that he shouldn't play around so close to the edge, but that is not what Mike Tremain had learned. What he had learned only was to be more cautious. Not to fly so close to the sun.

And as for me, what had I learned?

Dean Roskov wanted me to have a meeting with my committee – Lambert, Schwartz, and Culver, but I fended him off. What could we talk about?

Bundled against the weather, I took long walks. I missed my cross-country running. Twice I walked the course I used to run in September and October, so long ago that was. Working out in the gym had no appeal. I had had too much of interiors. I left off any contact with my two classes or, of course, with Culver or Appleton. Or Sara. For what was occurring in me now was not disillusionment or despair or even the darkening of cynicism. Against all the odds, I felt the elation of expectation as if something important was about to happen because I was at that point in any life when important things occur. "After great pain, a formal feeling comes./ The nerves sit ceremonious like tombs." Instead of anger or fury or even sorrow at them, rather I felt poised. Ready for flight. All I had to do now was be at the right place at the right time to find the fulcrum upon which the rest of my life would pivot. If I had been in Steffansville I would have gone up Steuben's Knob and waited. Maybe that is why I walked about and around Cobbton and the campus, in the fields and through the woods like a man trying to be *there* when the angel appeared.

On Thursday evening I called my parents as I always did to assure them that I was fine. In excellent spirits. And I would be home in a week. Next Thursday I would be sitting down to supper with them.

After the call, perhaps from curiousity, I wandered over to Culver's lab. I hadn't been there for nearly a month. Everything was how I had left it. Even the papers in my drawer that Culver had stolen from were there. I took them out and glanced through them and then at what was on the pads, and from there I began to think about all that I had already implied.

If the speed of light was *the* constant in the universe, then *why* was it so? And if it was, then had that always been so, would it always be so? Was there validity at all to the term, to the concept, of always? Did infinity have meaning, or was it only a catchall, a kind of glib etcetera?

I began to work. Einstein, Planck, Heisenberg, Kreutzer, superstring theory, chaos, I swept them all, and all that they had generated into my mind, in what was for me an effortless gesture. Like Al McGuire, of some things I saw enough to know the rest. Soon, nearly as quickly as I could write down an idea, I did, using my colors, discovering ramifications, codifications, implications. More and more quickly I was looking straight down the bore of my ideas, moving and moving in a dance of colors and lines of mathematical thought, answers begetting answers or the possibilities of answers, the assurances that, pursued far enough, what I was spewing out would result in some sort of, some degree of eventual certification. Negative or positive, gates on or off, open or shut, the absolute binary certainty of Boolean logic. In a year or ten or a hundred, of such matters as I was writing out, what could be known, *would* inevitably be known.

The night wore on. Never could there have been such a night as this in the history of physics. Pad after pad, until at the fortieth pad I stopped. One more pad to fill. And then what? Simply remove the papers and start over, go back to pad one and continue? Around and around, heaping concepts upon concepts until all of scientific space was used up?

And then my angel appeared. This is not what I wanted to do. The space I was charting, restructuring forever, was fixed and certain. All I was doing was what would someday be done by someone else, or many others. What I had done would itself have to be worked out in details, be supported by experimental evidence, accepted, rejected, fitted into the enlarging knowledge. But what I was doing was only about a space that was ultimately predictable. It was all about the universe that Einstein's god would imagine, a universe that would be perfect and simple and constant.

But there could be no moral space in such a universe. No secrets. No possibility for failure. No possibility for the endeavors whose failures make us human. Or can make us human. So the universe that I imagined my god would imagine (and that way create, only possible in imagination) would be one of inconstancy, unpredictable, full of the doubt and uncertainty from which my powerful mathematics, my power itself, separated me.

I stripped the pads of all I had written, but I did not destroy them. I made a pile and placed it on the desk. I left them for Culver and science to ponder and pursue. It would take days, months.

Years, in some instances. Let others do that work. I had something else to do.

I returned to the pads with my magic markers and began to draw and strum and pluck the colors and lines into relationships that had no relationship to numbers or the ideas of the physical universe that such numbers meant to probe and describe. But I was after something else. I was after the poetry of the life that pursued the inexplicability of the sublime, the ineffable mystery of humanness. The secrets that would always remain secrets.

I wanted to know what could never be known. Never. I wanted to know why Bruegel could paint a man pissing on the moon and that way make us feel the glory, jest, and riddle of what we were. Mad Meg stalking us all with her sword drawn. I wanted to comprehend directly how Bruegel could see so exactly what we were but yet rise above an easy travesty of life into tragedy and glory. Not the infinitude of mathematical speculation for me, but the infinitude of the space in which the aging Rembrandt floated or the younger de Kooning raged.

On and on where in the earlier hours I had spun out my numbers, now I spun out and in the colors and lines themselves. In wonder I saw things relate and disappear, come together for a moment in an explosion of energy and then dissipate as quickly. Matter and antimatter colliding and annihilating, but a different matter now, far more marvelous than mere protons and neutrons, electrons, quarks. None of this time could begin or end. Whatever god there could be would have to be an artist.

At last, nearly dawn, spent and exhausted (and yet not), I stood in the middle of the white cube and turned and turned to see what I had wrought. Nothing of what I had made coalesced into anything coherent. It was all a muddle of strings and blocks of colors. I knew so little of what I was trying to do. Nothing. But in it all was a defiance. And an assertion. All that color. All that light. But above all there was the leap itself, my leaping. The beginningness.

At last, having failed significantly, now I could begin.

→ 36 →
=

Miss Grant stood beside me looking at my large pad upon which
I had drawn a grouping of circles. The project was to draw some
of the circles according to strict rules of perspective but at the
same time to draw other and overlapping circles that distorted
perspective.

"O.K." she said. "You've got the idea. Not bad. But see here?"
She took my carbon pencil and went over some of my lines. "See
what lovely possibilities you've missed." She handed me back my
pencil. "You're not seeing enough in the overlaps. Use the lines of
perspective as tangents. But that's all. Don't get lost in them."

This was the afternoon class. I was in Kensington Community
College taking the full slate of its summer art program, art classes
every day and all day and homework assignments at night.

"And Nick, I've gone over your color exercises. Nicely done, except maybe you're thinking more about the colors than you're feeling them. It's hard to explain exactly what I mean, but pushing
warm against cool . . . well, sometimes it's the cool that makes
the warm cool. Raw sienna can be quite cool next to something as
warmly blue as ultramarine. It's relational. You get it?"

"Yes," I said, "yes. I think so. Maybe."

"And your life drawing is coming along nicely. You still have a
heavy hand, though. Lighten up. Loosen up. Be more gestural.
Look at the model more than at your paper."

"Yes."

"You're doing fine, Nick. Don't be discouraged."

"Oh, I'm not. I'm not."

"It can take years," Miss Grant said.

"Right," I said, "years and years. And even then you might not get it right," I said.

"You're never really ever through with learning about what you're trying to do. It's as if you don't know what it is until you try it. There's always something you didn't know. You can't predict anything. Once you can predict, you're doing formula. Every painting, no matter how good you are, can fail. There's never any certainty at all."

"Wonderful," I said, "terrific. That's the life for me."

EPILOGUE

Now I have lived long enough to become who I am likely to be, doing what I am likely to do on into whatever of the future I can imagine, which is, after all, no more nor less than can be expected of any human being. And I have come, as well, to aspire only within those dimensions; dimensions, not limits, exactly, but rather measurements, the appraisal of the territory or tract within which any of us constructs a life. Perhaps I mean boundaries, but a boundary does not mean a restraint. In any event, I am feeling very good about the where and what of me.

In my years since Cobbton, and after what turned into my happy, three-year fling with painting (and with delicious failure), I let myself loose into a world that did not need to notice me. A moving target is hard to hit, and there were still plenty of sharpshooters out there trying to get me in the cross-hairs of their own necessities. I had made a bonfire of a lot of contemporary science; there were torching questions my work had asked, incendiary assertions it had made, so where was I now to answer and define? And I had become in the supermarket checkout counter tabloids a kind of Bobby Fisher, a genius who, at the height of his career, inexplicably refused his geniushood: so the popular press would provide the explanation(s), the more lurid the better. For a year or more I think they must have kept three reporters on my case alone.

But at twenty I had no career, so I strapped on a backpack and lit out for the territories to see if I could find one. I traveled across America, into Canada and Mexico. And then to Europe. My easy ability to learn a language was a great advantage. I could already read perfectly any language I encountered, but in no time at all I could function in it, too. I feasted on the art. All I had learned about, I found. The Vermeers in Amsterdam, Bruegel in Brussels and Antwerp. The Titians in the Prado. Botticelli in Florence. Turner and Reubens and Ucello, Van Eyk and Giotto. Whistler and Vuillard. Chartres and Notre Dame and the cathedral at Ulm. Oh what a glutton I was. And what a mockery these artists made of the beautiful but little ideas of time and space that possessed the physicists. Here in the inspirited canvases of Goya or the walls of Fra Angelico were magnitudes of timelessness and space that mathematics could not describe. Different universes to be sure—the collisions of subatomic particles and the collisions of human passions—except at the end of the day, there is only one universe after all, the one that we live in, triumph and fail and triumph in, and die in. All stories, all telling, all that is told come at last to this forever after.

And everywhere I went I was nobody. Nobody special or extraordinary. Or at least special or extraordinary by someone else's definition. I ceased being a target because I ceased to be someone upon whom expectations could be put. I ceased to be the star, like Polaris, from which the heavens could be charted. But I was becoming very special and extraordinary to myself.

And I came to know what I might have known earlier, that what my father said I would have to do—to teach myself to be one person—was what we all have to do. My enormous gifts made it harder but not different. All of us, I am now convinced, must learn to reconcile ourselves with ourselves, and only then to reconcile that self with the self that others think we are. Or want us to be. And in that reconciliation there emerges a wonderful sense of mercy for our humanness, a compassion that enjoins us—entreats us—to make of our mystery in this universe only love. It is what I believe I hear in the last great plays of Shakespeare, in the last music of Beethoven, in the purity and humbling simplicity of Michelangelo's final rough crucifixion.

For I see now that what I have written is a love story. That the career I eventually came to was the search for the metaphors by which I could give shape and utterance to what I heard those years ago working with my father in his garden. I remember clearly, I have the words before me, what I wrote in my journal, the journal I began in my homage to him back in my Cobbton days.

I have been thinking recently of the namelessness of emotional states and how limited the language of emotion is. I have this idea that the location of the feeling of a garden or of *Yarps* in a fog bank or of a father making his breakfast alone in the early morning kitchen is where our truest language is, but not all of us can speak it.I know or can know every language on earth, and the language of all the sciences, and mathematical languages. But I do not know this other language, what I heard in the scrape of your shovel in your garden, the click of the rake through the unlimited stones that rose up through the soil through the winter.

That is what I have come to do – find this other language, give form to this lingua franca of love.

My parents are still very much alive, healthy and vigorous as they slide into and through the middle of middle age, but what are years to them. The printing business has prospered, at least enough so that they can take off for longer pieces of time. Flex time enables my mother to get out of the library for more extended periods. And they have suddenly become ardent bird-watchers, or birders (the currently preferred term). They were always interested in the natural world. We always kept bird feeders full through the winter and noted what we saw. But this birding they have embarked upon is a more serious business. They do the Christmas bird census with the local group (the Steffanville Naturalists Club. Eighty years old. Whoever thought it?) and take trips to Cape May, New Jersey, and Point Pelee in Ontario and Hawk Mountain in Pennsylvania for the important migrations.

Recently I told my mother how good I felt about them doing this, doing it with such a happy urgency. I told her how I thought that only now, after all the years of bearing me, they were truly free.

"You're wrong," she said, "we were always free. We were never trapped. You were a great kid." She was Sally Burden still, still making leaps across logical connections.

"What does what I was have to do with . . . . I mean you did spend a lot of time and energy defending me. Protecting me. Now you don't have to."

She took off her glasses and put down the pencil with which she had been writing and turned fully toward me.

"It was terrific," she said. "Great. Exciting. You. We never regretted a minute of it. Besides," she put her glasses back and started again to write, "what makes you think we've stopped? Protecting you?"

I do not live in Steffanville any longer, have not lived there in any full sense for years. The assignments I give myself to write about frequently take me anywhere in the country or even the world. And there is a young lady in Annapolis, Maryland, who has a marvelous boat. We sail together. A lot.

But when I do return to Steffanville as I always try to do at Thanksgiving, I hike north of the village to Steuben's Rock and climb it, waiting again, as I used to, to know all that I would ever know.

From time to time I hear about Thomas Culver. Not because of news from the world of science but because Cobbton College sends me copies of the alumni newsletter as well as requests for contributions. Apparently Cobbton considers anyone who attended the school, whether they graduated or not, to be alumni. I suspect they make a lot of money through such an expanded definition. I even find myself at times considering sending a few bucks. After all, Cobbton was very good to me. And even from this distance, there are more than a few names that I recognize as still being around. Dean Roskov has become the president. Guzman has published yet another book about yet another twist in topological space. Even Sam Pelton. He went away and got some degrees and came back and is now an assistant dean for Academic Affairs.

About Culver I catch only small snippets of things. The announcement of papers he has delivered, his chairmanship of a committee looking into the creation of a new honors program. His pushing of the administration to give the graduate students and adjunct faculty better pay, at the least medical coverage. All in all, he seems to have become more involved in campus affairs. Sometimes there is a picture of him in the newsletter. He looks the same, or nearly so, but then you can never tell how old the picture is. I still think he looks pale, exceedingly white, like his lab after he changed it for me, and yet with the hint of a dark shadow. I do not try to read his character. He strikes me now, looking at a photograph of him, as transparent, a vehicle through which other energy passes much like the ether that nineteenth century physics believed to exist in the space between the stars.

I do not think he has ever come to play the part in big league physics that he hoped for; at least, his is not a name that appears in the newspaper and magazine articles that occasionally flare up when the next dazzler of a speculation about the cosmos or the atom bursts into public view. What I remember best about Culver, or rather what I liked best in him of what I remember, is the objects he and his wife collected, the objects for which there were no explanation—the untraceable coin, the cloth without a weave. There seems to me now to be more substance to him in what he did not know than in what he was trying to find out.

William Appleton is a different case, if for no other reason than that he eventually wrote a book-length essay in which I, or someone based on me, played a central role, or had a central position. He disguised me and all that, and the book was, in fact, more about prodigy than about just me. But about prodigy all he knew was what he had garnered from what others had written about prodigy, about John Stuart Mill and Norbert Weiner and the tragic William James Siddis and various others. So when it came to details and examples, to the specifics, all he had was me. Or the me he had turned me into. The book had brief notoriety because the publisher pushed the connection of the disguised me to the actual me. But it didn't have so much notoriety as all that, and soon enough it was forgotten.

At first I was angry. I saw the book as an extension of his dishonesty with me, one more betrayal. But in time I came to rather value William Appleton, and also to pity him, but to pity him without condescension. There was intensity and passion in him and a genuine caring about whatever he was doing. For a few months I think I benefitted from that because, as my subsequent life has shown me, that kind of intensity and brilliance is not generally found in people; it's not an experience that is easy to get, though it is an experience worth having. The heat and light given off from such a person helps to melt some of the rough edges of the young, or to temper them. But I pity him because I think that his amazing apartment will all its paraphernalia was an epitome of his life. All clutter and bang. A poetry of sorts, yes, but a cave, too. He lived within the images that all that equipment could bring into him. The closest he could come to more life than that was when, each semester, the curtain went up and he began to perform, perhaps with a new leading lady every now and again.

And about my own leading lady, Sara Logan? About her I can report as much as the world can report. That she married Evan Abbott, the real estate tycoon, and has become the cynosure of New York society. The Hamptons in the summer, Aspen in the winter. Or St. Mortiz or Portofino. Or wherever it is that the Sara Logan Abbotts alight from season to season.

There is this precious irony. She has herself become a figure much found in the vulgar tabloids to which, at last, she sold me. But the real irony is this: I do not think that Sara Logan Abbott minds it. I think that she rather enjoys the absurdity of the attention. The drug addiction, the husband who beats her, the kinky sex, the mysterious disease that is threatening her life. The young lover with whom she is trysting. I can imagine Sara laughing it off, or, more likely, feeling a kind of satisfaction. No one who matters to her would believe any of it, while those who do not matter pay with their attention and curiously, pay with the coin of Sara's realm. Fame indeed. But of course I am imagining a Sara Logan who probably no longer exists, and what she expected from life when she encountered me and what her life has become may bear no resemblance or even connection to each other. Only this: the life she projected when, after lovemaking, we would lie abed and talk, sounded like a life that she would live within terms of her own making. She sounded to me then like someone who would be both the mold and the material that would be poured into it. Adventure was her game, she had said. And so it seems adventures she has had. But these are not the adventures that I think she meant. Now, from the little I can garner (from profiles of Evan Abbott in *The New Yorker* and *New York* magazine and *People*, and *not* that from the distortions of the tabs), she seems to me to be an artifact, an object rather than a subject. An adventuress and not an adventurer. The difference is not sexual.

Is there anything at all left of the love I had for her? Yes, I am happy to say. Nothing we have ever loved so well should ever be entirely lost. And maybe it can't be lost but lingers on like the radiation that continues to permate the universe that resulted from the big bang that we used to think began our space and time. Such love, such first love, is so much a part of whomever we become that to lose it is to lose some critical part of ourselves, for who we ever are is always the sum of who we have ever been.

Al Thumper McGuire did become the all-American and the all-Pro of his destiny, but he did not play as long as he thought he would have to. In his fifth year as a pro (for Tampa Bay. Near all those bonefish flats. He must have been ecstatic.) his knee was mangled beyond repair. They did major surgery over the winter, and he managed to limp through one more year, and then he retired, rich enough to fish every day for the rest of his life. For a week the loss of such a great player provided columns for the nation's sportswriters. Woe, lamentation, and grief. The what-might-have-been tone of such elegies. Thumper, of course, must have been delighted. His injury only got him out of football, it didn't curtail anything important, certainly not fishing.

At last his magnificent body had failed him significantly.

We did not stay in touch with each other, although after his retirement I was tempted to write, or at least send a telegram. But I didn't because our friendship was frozen in the amber of our discovery of ourselves in each other. For that brief moment both of us were a little less lonely inside our gifts because of each other. We wouldn't have had a lot more to go on over the years. To have insisted would have dulled the specialness of that flash from our Cobbton days.

With Mike Tremain I have stayed in contact through the years, or rather he has stayed in contact with me. What I mean is that though I think I would have kept in touch with him, he never gave me the chance to find out. Letters, phone calls, wherever I was, he would find me. Not that that was so difficult to do; still, it was an effort that he always made before I could ever think about it. And I was delighted.

Each time he called (five or six times a year) it was like another chapter in his saga, for indeed that is exactly what it was, a saga, an epic narrative, a chronicle of the heroic deeds of this Odysseus of commerce. And as with any great tale of this sort, it was the engagements themselves that mattered, not the conclusions. He knew this as truly in our Cobbton days as he did in the years following. I remember his unabashed admiration for his father, who never had a stable franchise to sell from, but who never doubted himself just as Mike never did. He was what Mike wanted to be, and that is what he became. And remains. And always will be.

He went to Florida and sold swimming pools until Florida began to run out of water. But even then he was taking the measure of things, in his inimitable way, which was to run in ever widening circles until he bumped into something that he could sell. If crime was up in the Palm Beach enclaves of the very rich, but especially in the Fort Lauderdale havens of the much-less-than rich, there he would sell alarm systems. But very special alarm systems: these were alarm systems that alerted your neighbors.

"Who else will look out for you quicker than your neighbors? The cops, they're busy downtown. They're busy hassling in Liberty City. But the guy across the street, he sits around all day *waiting* for something to happen. The guy around the corner. The lady on the second floor. All around. Somebody tries to break into your house, you're away . . . you're doing your neighbors a *favor* giving them this chance. The alarm goes off, first the cops get called, sure. But then everyone is *around*. You know what I mean? I mean they don't have to go get the robber themselves, nothing like that. They don't have to get involved that way. All they have to do is turn on their lights, start their car, start playing their TVs real loud. You get it? The robber, he knows something is up. So anything UP for a robber is too much. He's out of there. So Nicky, I'm telling you, this is a great idea. This system, it cuts down on crime and builds community relations at the same time."

And that, of course, was Mike. It wasn't the simple product or service he sold, or sold in a simple or direct way. It was always the oblique angle that he sought, the startle and jazz of it. The chance he took, the risk. But in the center of his most outrageous ideas was the tough core of reasonableness. His ideas were *not* the notions of a crazed salesman. It was more that we weren't quite ready for them, or ready for them in the form he gave them. A problem not unfamiliar to many of our greatest artists.

I don't know how well he did financially, though he always claimed everything was terrific, just terrific, and getting better. Why just yesterday he. . . .

He got married and now has two children, girls. "Girls," he told me, were "potentially the best salespeople for some things." Already he had plans for them.

And plans for me. He never relinquished the idea that I was a fabulous resource, that eventually this mother lode of possibility that I was would make itself available to him, to the world, that I would become part of the saga, enter into legend.

That once again there would be a T&B Enterprises, Inc.

How could I tell him that there still was?